The Norsunder War, Book 1

Ship Without Sails

SARTORIAS-DELES BOOKS

HISTORICAL ARC
"Lily and Crown"
Inda
The Fox
King's Shield
Treason's Shore
Time of Daughters (two volumes)
Banner of the Damned

THE YOUNG ALLIES AS KIDS SERIES
The CJ Notebooks
Senrid
Spy Princess
Sartor
Fleeing Peace

A Stranger to Command
Crown Duel
The Trouble with Kings

THE RISE OF THE ALLIANCE SERIES
A Sword Named Truth
The Blood Mage Texts
The Hunters and the Hunted
Nightside of the Sun

Sasharia En Garde
The Wicked Skill

The Norsunder War 1

Ship Without Sails

SHERWOOD SMITH

BOOK VIEW CAFE

BOOK VIEW CAFE

Published by Book View Café
304 S. Jones Blvd., Suite #2906
Las Vegas, NV 89107
www.bookviewcafe.com

ISBN: 978-1-63632-076-2

DRAMATIS PERSONAE

NOTE: This list is building off the Rise of the Alliance List. Norsundrians, Ex-Norsundrians, and Detlev's boys at the end.

Name most frequently used comes first, so sometimes first name, sometimes last, sometimes nickname.

LIGHT MAGIC MAGES AIDING THE ALLIANCE

Erai-Yanya Vithyavadnais: One of a long line of mages dwelling in the ruined city of Roth Drael. Trained partly by the northern Mage School at Bereth Ferian, and partly by Tsauderei, she works independently, her specialty magical wards. She has one son, ARTHUR (see BERETH FERIAN). Erai-Yanya's student mage is the Marloven exile Hibern Askan.

Evend: One-time colleague of Tsauderei, King of Bereth Ferian (a courtesy title only) and head of the mage school there, he surrendered his life to bind rift magic from being used in Sartoriasdeles by Norsunder. His place as titular king was taken by ARTHUR.

Igkai: Hermit mage living on the peninsula on the Sartoran Sea. An oddball all his life, he is a friend to birds and animals — and tolerates humans who do well by animals.

Lilith the Guardian: A lower ranking mage and what might be called an officer of rites and rituals in Ancient Sartor, which was as close to a government as they got. She had one daughter, Erdrael, who was killed along with most of the rest of the population when Norsunder tried to wrest control of the world, for reasons explored in a volume to come. Her name is a modern adaptation, and she found herself trying to combat Norsunder on this and other worlds around the sun Erhal; she comes out of hiding beyond time whenever she finds evidence that Detlev has been in the world, acting for Norsunder's Host of Lords.

Mondros "Rosey": Big, bluff, and bearded, he began life as an exiled son of the disgraced Glenereth family, warlords of Ralanor Veleth. He studied magic, aided by Gwasan Sonscarna, Princess of the Chwahir, whom he married and had a son, REL (see SARTOR). When Mondros made it his life's goal to defeat Wan-Edhe of Chwahirsland, he stashed Rel with a trusted friend, where Rel grew up a part of the family, until the urge to travel caused him to take to the road. Father and son found one another relatively recently.

Murial of Mearsies Heili: Recluse mage, living hidden in the western wilds of Mearsies Heili. Born a princess, she supported the transfer of the throne to her niece CLAIR (see MEARSIES HEILI) on the death of her sister. Protecting the kingdom from a distance, she has seen to it that Clair got magical training.

Oalthoreh: Head of the northern mage school in Bereth Ferian

Tsauderei: Oldest of the senior mages, independent of the two leading mage schools, living in a historic mage retreat located in the mountains bordering Sarendan and Sartor in the Valley of Delfina.

THE YOUNG ALLIES AND OTHERS (LISTED BY KINGDOM)

BERETH FERIAN

Arthur (Yrtur) Vithyavadnais: He adopted the nickname Arthur after his rescue by young world-gate crossing friends. Son of mage Erai-Yanya, he early showed great ability in learning and magic, but he was unhappy living in isolation. He was adopted as heir by Evend, the former head mage of the Bereth Ferian Mage School, and presiding King of the loose federation headquartered at Bereth Ferian. After Evend's death, Arthur shared this courtesy title with Liere Fer Eider in her persona as Sartora, the Girl Who Saved the World.

Evend: (see Light Mages)

Liere Fer Eider: Also known as the Girl Who Saved the World, she was the first of her generation to be born with *Dena Yeresbeth*. At ten years old she left her small town to escape being captured by Siamis, who had extended an enchantment over the world, which Liere later broke. The enchantment is generally known as The Lost Year, as most lived in a dream world while it lasted. She was lauded by all, and given the courtesy title of Queen in Bereth Ferian, a title with no powers or responsibilities whatsoever — but which still chafed her unbearably. Liere was the poster child for Imposter Syndrome until she went to Geth-deles for five years to study magic, and returned recently.

CHWAHIRSLAND (AKA LAND OF THE CHWAHIR)

Jilo: Son of a lowly sergeant, heir to elderly *Prince Kwenz Sonscarna,* he finds himself acting king of Chwahirsland, after Norsunder's removal of the previous king, who had ruled for more than a century. What that means is, he is slowly poisoning himself in trying to remove the toxic accretion of dark magic enchantments over Chwahirsland, and especially its capital.

Prince Kessler Sonscarna: (SEE also Ex-Norsundrians) The single living descendant of the ruling Sonscarnas, who were systematically killed off by Wan-Edhe, blood relations notwithstanding. Prince Kessler escaped at a young age, made his way to a martial arts group where he mastered military arts. He allied with a Norsundrian mage, Dejain, and began to assemble followers for his plan to remove all the hereditary rulers of the world, and replace them with his followers, chosen solely on merit. When defeated, he was forced into Norsunder by Dejain, who betrayed him.

Wan-Edhe (born Shnit Sonscarna), King of the Chwahir: Descendant of the ruling Sonscarna family, has ruled for close to a century. A powerful dark magic mage, he has managed to create a powerful citadel in the heart of his kingdom, where time itself is distorted in his effort to ensure that he will live, and rule, forever. He killed off his family and descendants, including his brilliant heir, Princess Gwasan; only his grandson Kessler escaped, but years of abuse told on Kessler's emotional landscape.

COLEND

"Bee" (Aural) Keperi: Chief scribe to Shontande Lirendi. Being blind, he does all his work by memorization.

King Carlael Lirendi: Regarded generally as Mad King Carlael before he was assassinated by Efael of Norsunder. He was as beautiful as he was strange. He mostly existed in a world of dreams imposed by magic, from which he emerged now and then, very alert and very aware. There was a regency council made up of the chief nobles who oversaw the kingdom when he was unable to respond to the world around him, and they ruled until very recently, refusing to relinquish power, though Carlael's son Shontande had come of age.

Prince Shontande Lirendi: Son of Carlael, King of Colend, and new king.

Karhin Keperi: She was a teenage scribe student in a small town in the west of Colend, who volunteered to function as the center of the young allies' communication network. An indefatigable letter writer, she first met Puddlenose of the Mearsieans, and gradually got drawn into the Alliance; she was murdered by one of Detlev's boys, and she is still missed.

Lisbet Keperi: Younger sister of Thad and Karhin.

Thad Keperi: Red-haired brother of Karhin, also a scribe student, but much less passionate about the scribe life. Very social, and friend to all the Alliance; he and his brother Bee are very close to Shontande Lirendi.

ENAERAN

Adon Marsael: Distantly related to the royal Elsarion family, tried to take throne. Allied with Norsunder in order to keep the throne.

Andri Elsarion: Inherited his throne very recently, after years of civil war.

Gared Inmael: Close friend and adoptive brother of Andri Elsarion: it was Gared's father, the Elsarion Master of Horse, who took in Andri when he was disinherited. The boys grew up together.

Marten (Martande) Eldias: Lifelong friend to Andri Elsarion.

Baras Parael Otobris: the new king's Commander of the King's Guard.

Thadara Otobris, Duchas of Merith: The new king's Chief Minister and treasurer, who has her eye on marrying Andri and sharing his throne.

EVERON

King Berthold and Queen Mersedes Carinna Delieth: Former king and queen, survivors of rough earlier years. Mersedes, daughter of a con man, became one of the Knights of Dei, dedicated to protecting the kingdom. They were both killed (at different times) by Henerek of Norsunder, who had come from Everon, and had been booted out of the elite Knights of Dei for countless crimes.

Prince Glenn Delieth: Heir to the throne of Everon, and convinced that a strong army solves all questions, especially the threat of Norsunder attacking; he died in a duel with David, one of Detlev's boys, after forcing the fight on him.

Hatahra Delieth (Tahra), Queen of Everon: Younger sister of Glenn, passionate about numbers, and in her unrelenting hatred of Detlev and his boys. When the war begins, has two children, Jessan and "Carl", and two infants.

Roderic Dei: Commander of the Knights of Dei, once defenders and protectors of the realm. The Knights were decimated in the war Henerek brought, and Kessler Sonscarna finished. Roderic Dei survived to serve as regent for Tahra Delieth until she reached the age of majority.

MARLOVEN HESS

Crystal Ingrid Montredaun-An: Daughter and heir to Senrid, the king. Five years old. Her chief passion is dogs.

Forthan, Retren: A young man from a farm background, Forthan is the best of the leaders to come out of the military academy. He became Harskiald, a resurrected title that means trusted commander in chief of Marloven Hess's standing army; before then, commanders in chief were appointed per mission.

Hibern Askan: Light magic student, tutored by Erai-Yanya of Roth Drael, who learned in the northern mage school. Hibern was disinherited by her family.

Keriam, Janec: Career military man, Commander of the Marloven military academy, also titular head of the Palace Guard. Acted as guardian and foster-father to Senrid, protecting him from the regent as much as possible.

Senelac, Fenis: Wife to Retren Forthan, and head of horse training for the military academy, equal rank to the Master of Horse in the city guard.

Senrid Montredaun-An: Young king of Marloven Hess, a mage studying both dark and light magic. First friend to Liere Fer Eider, and second to make his unity in *Dena Yeresbeth*. The Marloven army is one of the most formidable in the world.

Stad, Indevan (Van): Second in command, Marloven army

MEARSIES HEILI

Clair of Mearsies Heili: Young queen of Mearsies Heili, a small agrarian polity on the northeast corner of the continent Toar. Niece of the hermit-mage *Murial*, and cousin to the wandering boy known only as *Puddlenose*, she has adopted a group of girls, most of them runaways. Her right-hand and designated 'heir' is *C.J.*

C.J. (Cherenneh Jenet): Found by Clair, who traveled through the World-gate, C.J. is from Earth, adopted into Clair's gang of runaways and rejects. She learns magic fitfully, and is generally regarded as the leader of Clair's gang of girls.

CJ's Gang of Girls: Falinneh and Dhana currently wear human form but are not actually human; Seshe has a mysterious past, suspected of being a runaway princess (which is actually correct); Irenne thought the world was a stage and she was the heroine of the play, which got her killed by accident by one of Detlev's boys, but she is still very much a presence among the girls; Diana is a martial artist and forester; Sherry and Gwen are followers. They are a very tight found family.

Mearsieanne: Once Queen of Mearsies Heili after she walked in and took an empty throne and renamed herself. She was taken by Norsunder, and existed beyond time for nearly a century, while her son, then her granddaughter, ruled. On her return to the present time, she stepped in and in the nicest way possible, shouldered aside Clair, her great-granddaughter and the girl queen, in order to show her how ruling ought to be done.

Murial: *(see LIGHT MAGES)*

Puddlenose of Mearsies Heili: Bereft of family at a very young age, thus no one knows what his actual name was. He was abducted and used by The King of the Chwahir in his complicated plots, he was rescued several times by Rosey (Mondros, see LIGHT MAGES). He wanders the world, determined to have fun. His chief companion is a world-gate wanderer from Earth named Christoph, but sometimes he's joined by Rel (see SARTOR). Gradually he traveled on land less and on the sea more, until he was made second in command by Captain Heraford of the *Tzasilia*, former privateer.

REMALNA

Bran (Branaric) Astiar, Count of Tlanth: brother to Meliara, wife NEE

Meliara Astiar, Queen of Remalna: children Alaraec and Elestra

Nadav Savona: Vidanric's oldest friend and chief aid, son Nadav

Vidanric Renselaeus, King of Remalna: children Alaraec and Elestra

RALANOR VELETH

Flian Elandersi, Queen of Ralanor Veleth: was a princess from Lygiera, distant cousin to Garian Herlester of Drath.

Jaim Szinzar: Brother to the king, and nominal leader of the army, though Jason commands in action.

Jaimas Szinzar: Younger child of king and queen

Jason Szinzar, King of Ralanor Veleth: military background, inherited the throne, and the care of his siblings, at a young age. His chief rival is PRINCE GARIAN HERLESTER OF DRATH

Jewel Szinzar: married to the King of Lygiera, MAXL ELANDERSI, has several children

Liara Viana Szinzar: Eldest child of king and queen

Markham Glenereth: disinherited, technically denied the Glenereth name, though the king intended that to be temporary. Liege to the king, a martial artist of superlative skill.

Lexan Glenereth: son of Markham Glenereth

SARENDAN

Darian Irad: After his defeat in a vicious civil war, Darian Irad stepped down from the throne and ended up as a military consultant on the sister-world Geth-deles. On his nephew Peitar's assassination, Darian Irad insisted that he was a regent for Peitar's son Darian, and not a king: he had gone to Geth, where he married and had a family.

Darian Selenna: son of Peitar Selenna, and heir to the throne. Has Dena Yeresbeth.

Derek Diamagan: Charismatic leader of the revolution, a commoner who wished to overthrow all the nobles, and institute common rule. He was a far better speech maker than he was an organizer; his revolution was a disaster. Close friend of Peitar Selenna until his assassination by Siamis, at that time nominally of Norsunder.

Lilah Selenna, Princess of Sarendan: Younger Sister to Peitar. She, with friends *Bren* (artist), *Innon* (a noble-born accountant at heart) and *Deon* were deeply involved in the revolution.

Peitar Selenna, King of Sarendan: Reluctant king who would rather study magic, he came to the throne after an especially vicious civil war. He, nephew to the former king, Darian Irad, was one of the leaders of the revolution, but advocated non-violent means. His accession was a compromise between the commoners, who adore him, and the nobles, who recognized that at least he is nominally one of their own; on his assassination, he was, at his own order, replaced by his uncle.

SARTOR

Atan, (Queen Yustnesveas Landis V): New young queen of Sartor, after the oldest kingdom in the world was removed from time by nearly a century. She was found as an infant on the border by Tsauderei the mage, and raised by him before the enchantment was broken. She began her queenship as a mage student, with little training in statecraft, but well-read in history.

Gehlei: Former guard in the days before Sartor was enchanted for a century, escaped with the infant Atan. Raised Atan to age fifteen along with Tsauderei the mage.

Hinder and Sinder: Morvende (cave dwellers), friends of Atan.

Julian Landis: born Julian Dei, she is Atan's cousin who wore the Child Spell for a considerable time. She relinquished it on Atan's promise that she would not be considered an heir, nor a princess. She is a wanderer by nature, and was happiest when staying with Dtheldevor of Wnelder Vee's gang.

Mistress Veltos Jhaer: Head of the prestigious Sartoran mage guild, until the enchantment the foremost mage school in the world. Now a century behind. She was further burdened by guilt for having lost the kingdom to enchantment. Assassinated by Efael of Norsunder, she was replaced for a time by Tsauderei the mage.

Rel: Known as Rel the shepherd's son, and more widely as Rel the Traveler, he was happily raised by a guardian in Tser Mearsies until wanderlust caused him to leave home. Met Puddlenose of the Mearsians, and consequently became tangled in some of the Mearsians' adventures. Friends with Atan, and one of the Rescuers. He was the only outsider ever invited to join the Knights of Dei in Everon; in the previous volume he discovered his parentage (SEE Mondros the mage), which he is still trying to process.

Rescuers: The name given to a band of children who had lived in a magic-protected forest during the enchantment. They sheltered Atan before the enchantment was broken. Ostensibly highly regarded as heroes by the Sartorans, there are the aristocratic Rescuers, and the non-aristocratic, Rel among them.

SLES ADRAN

Bartal na Shagal, King of Sles Adran: Allied with Adon Marsael of Enaeran, and Norsunder.

Navor Mandracar: army commander and close friend of the king.

VASANDE LEROR

Kyale Marlonen: Adoptive sister to Leander, relishes being a princess, and is jealous of Leander's attention.

Leander Tlennen-Hess: Like Senrid, a young king, though of a tiny polity that historically belonged to the Marlovens, then broke away four centuries previous. Leander and Senrid have a lot in common, and would be friends, except for Leander's jealous stepsister:

Llhei: Sarendan-trained nanny (sister to Lizana, nurse to the royal children of *Sarendan*), governess to Kyale, remained after evil Queen Mara Jinia defeated.

Alaxandar: Captain of royal guard, quit under evil queen Mara Jinia, protected Leander.

WNELDER VEE

Dtheldevor: Daughter of a privateer (some say pirate) who was killed when Dtheldevor was small, but not before she was taught martial arts. She became the champion for the young prince Murgeh Troiad, sailing against pirates infesting the shores, and helping to fight off an enterprising Norsundrian.

She has a hideout called Dthel Rendm, on one of the hundreds of islands off Wnelder Vee's coast. She did the Child Spell decades ago; in lived time she is in her late seventies. She accepts kids on the Wander on her ship and her island, but her most loyal shipmates are: Sarmonwilda, born a dawnsinger; Sharly, a centaur from the northern reaches, and Sidres, another centaur; Gloriel and Peridot Warren (twins, from Earth, born with mundane names) and Joey and Ellen Warren.

Her most frequent visitor who doesn't live with the privateers is Julian Dei Landis of Sartor.

Murgeh Troiad: erstwhile king in Wnelder Vee. Though kingship is little more than a title — the guilds do what little governing is required in small, very rural Wnelder Vee — he resisted even that much, preferring to wander the world and master music. He is actually considerably skilled as a bard.

NORSUNDER

Aldon: Military leader with a thirst for warfare, the bloodier the better

Alsaes: First came to notice as Kessler Sonscarna's companion in Kessler's plan to take over the world. Given a mortal wound, surrendered self in exchange for bloodknife spell to preserve his life. Extremely vain. Dyes hair blond to hide Chwahir origins.

Benin: Ambitious mage, his specialty the soul-bound (people caught at the point of death, their wills bound to the command of whoever holds the soul-bound magic). Benin tends to not wait until potential soul-bound are dead in order to experiment.

Bergan: one of Imry Llyenthur's staff.

Bostian: Ambitious Norsundrian military captain, obsessed with making himself king of Sartor.

Dejain: Mage specializing in dark magic, one of a succession of Norsunder Base commanders, who tended to be summarily replaced by violence. Now deceased

Duin, Fassler: Imry Llyenthur's chief aide-de-camp. Born in Chwahirsland.

Efael: Considers himself one of the Host of Lords, the authors of Norsunder. Has a penchant for cruelty. He is the Host of Lords' chief assassin, bloodhound, interrogator; he and his sister Yeres consider Detlev their rival for a seat among the Host of Lords.

Elzhier: One of Connanre of the Host's best spies. She joined Norsunder as a young, angry teen.

Henerek: Ambitious low-ranking young Norsunder military captain, originated in Everon. Wanted to be one of the Knights of Dei, but was cashiered due to excess cruelty, drunkenness, and inability to follow orders. Led a brutal war in Everon, now deceased.

Host of Lords: Authors of Norsunder, existing beyond time, readying for a second try at taking the world. Or worlds. Why, and who they are, will become clearer in the succeeding volumes.

Hyath: Very young, ambitious, and cruel mage studying under Yeres.

Imry Llyenthur: Shares field command of invasion with Efael of the Host. A mage and a martial artist, he has Dena Yeresbeth. He's essentially a strategist.

Lesca: Apparently lazy steward in charge of Norsunder Base. Overlook her at your peril.

Yeres: She and Efael, her brother, were born off-world, and so thoroughly and spectacularly corrupted that they caught the attention of Svirle of Yssel, one of the authors of Norsunder. Yeres is a powerful mage. She and Efael gladly execute the errands that the Host of Lords, steeped in evil, consider too distasteful.

Ex-Norsundrians

Detlev Reverael ne Hindraeldrei: Chief visible mage and sometime military leader, answerable to Norsunder's Host of Lords. Born four thousand years ago, has lived in and outside time ever since. Like his nephew Siamis, has Dena Yeresbeth. Left Norsunder in 4753: much speculation on both sides as to why.

Kessler Sonscarna: Renegade Chwahir prince with considerable military abilities, forced into Norsunder as a result of treachery by the mage Dejain. Hates Norsunder. (See *Chwahirsland* below)

Siamis Reverael: Nephew to Detlev. Formidable mage, and like Detlev, has Dena Yeresbeth. Left Norsunder previous to Detlev, after furnishing the means to free the Venn from an eight-century-old binding of their magic. Adopted Yanli, the last descendant of someone Siamis was close to on his first visit to Sartorias-deles. He has reason to believe that the woman, Isa Cassadas, was pregnant with his child before he was forced to return to Norsunder. They were both teenagers.

Sveneric Reverael Hindraeldrei: Detlev's son, trained with the boys.

Detlev's Boys

Adam: Artist, formidable talents in Dena Yeresbeth, artist until his hands were ruined by Efael

Alaki (Ferret): Acutely observant, aware of overlapping worlds, spy

Curtas: Strongly responsive to line and harmony, especially in building

David: Captain of the group, best in most areas

Edde (Noser): Taken from another world, at best a mascot

Laban: Volatile and longing for what he cannot have, a Dei descendant

Leefan: Quiet, strong martial artist, cousin to Rolfin

Mal Venn (MV): Martial artist, studying magic, excellent sailor

Rolfin: Cousin to Leefan, superlative martial artist

Roy: Strong Dena Yeresbeth, mage and scholar

Silvanas: Martial artist and horse master

FOR MORE INFORMATION

Visit the Sartorias-deles wiki at http://reqfd.net/s-d/

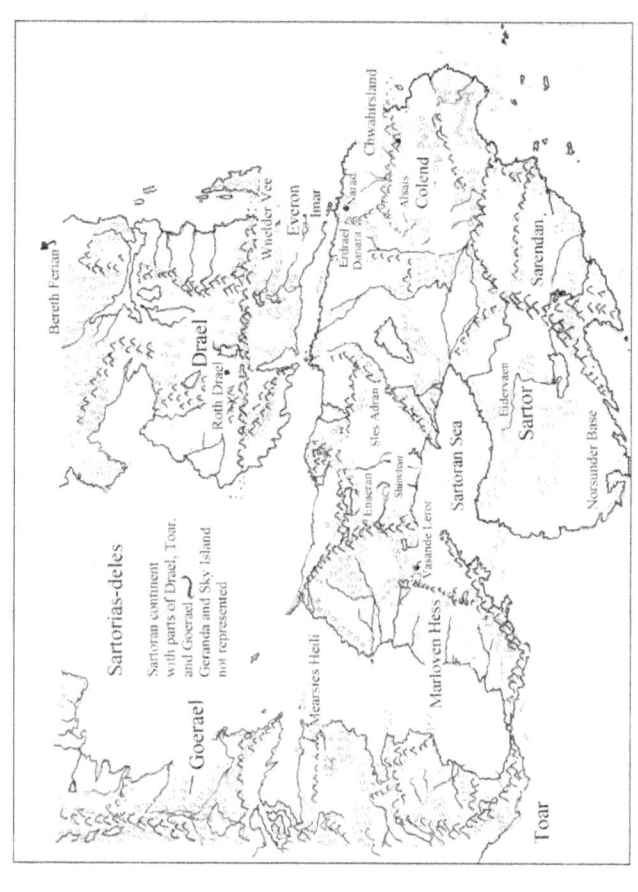

Sartorias-deles

Sartoran continent
with parts of Drael, Toar,
and Goerael
Geranda and Sky Island
not represented

Goerael

Bereth Ferian

Drael

Roth Drael

Wheðler Vee

Everon

Imar

Erdrael
Danara Sarad
Alsais
Colend

Chwahirsland

Sarendan

Sartor

Eidervaen

Norsunder Base

Sartoran Sea

Sles Adran

Enneran

Shendoro

Vasande Leror

Marloven Hess

Mearsies Heili

Toar

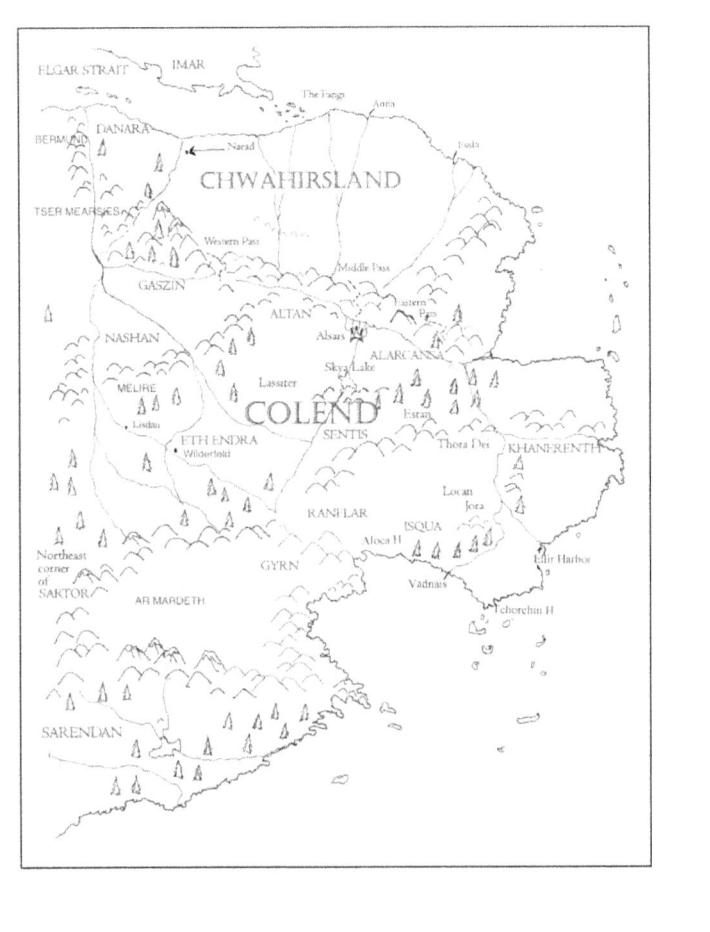

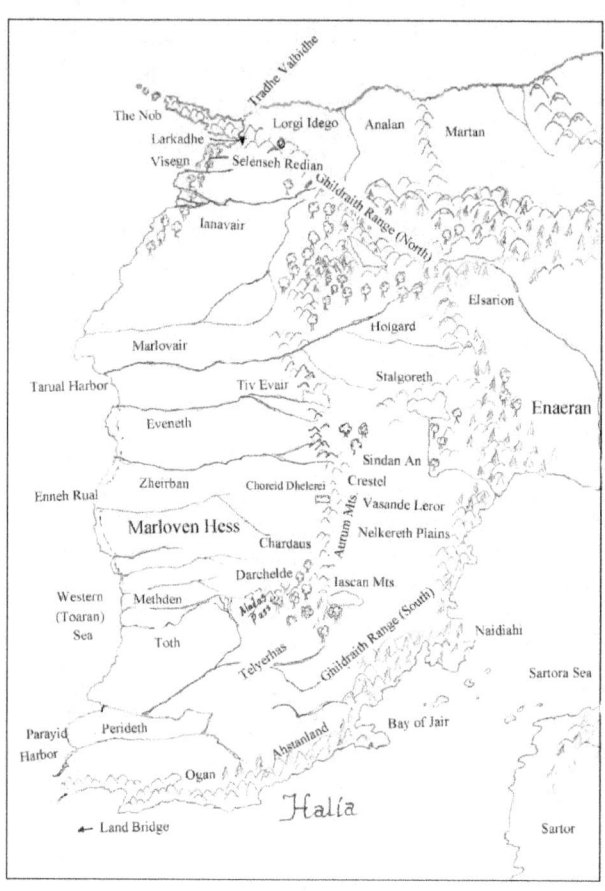

The Nob

Tradhe Valbdhe

Larkadhe
Lorgi Idego
Analan
Martan

Visegn
Selenseh Redian

Ghildraith Range (North)

Ianavair

Elsarion

Hoigard

Marlovair

Stalgoreth

Tarual Harbor
Tiv Evair
Enaeran

Eveneth

Sindan An

Enneh Rual
Zheirban
Choreid Dhelerei
Crestel

Vasande Leror

Marloven Hess
Nelkereth Plains

Chardaus

Darchelde
Iascan Mts

Western
(Toaran)
Sea
Methden
Alsais
Pass
Naidiahi

Toth
Sartora Sea

Telyerhas
Ghildraith Range (South)

Parayid
Harbor
Perideth
Bay of Jair

Ahstanland
Sartor

Ogan
Halia

← Land Bridge

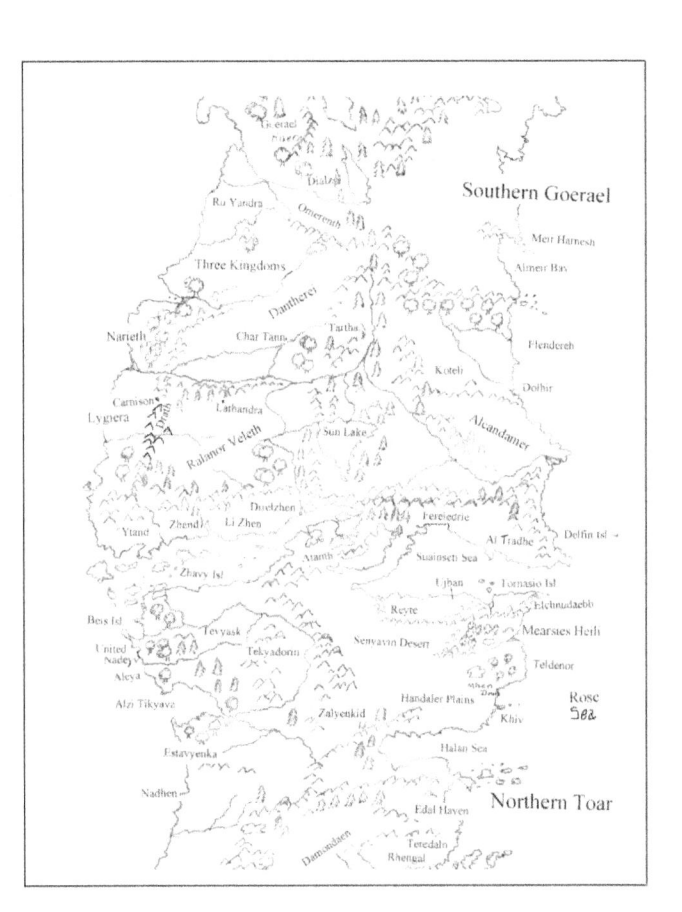

Southern Goerael

Northern Toar

Part One

One

I STATED AT THE beginning of these chronicles that most people believe Norsunder to exist as a vast army with a single motivation, an oversimplification that borders on outright lie.

This much was true: Those in command of Norsunder withdrew from the temporal realm after the Fall of Ancient Sartor nearly wiped out magic as well as humanity from the world early 4800 years ago. With the dwindling of magic, magic-related talents vanished forever—or so humans thought.

But magic slowly manifested in the world again before Norsunder was aware or ready, this being the disadvantage of existing outside of time.

My record commences the day the world of Sartorias-deles became aware that Norsunder was back for a second try, beginning the Norsunder War.

I will begin in Choreid Dhelerei, capital of Marloven Hess, which appeared to be unchanged to the two newly-arrived figures staring upward.

Choreid Dhelerei, to Liere Fer Eider, appeared to be the embodiment not just of power, but of order. Stability. Her gaze moved over the sun-warmed, peachy stone walls of the fortified city as she breathed in the combined smells of sage and plains grass and faint, oh so faint, the distant sea, until her daughter Lyren-Sartora twitched impatiently by her side.

"Why did you do the magic transfer to the outer Destination?" Lyren-Sartora asked, elbowing Liere impatiently in the ribs. "You couldn't have forgotten the inside one! It's only been a couple of years since you were here last—"

"Five," Liere said.

"Fine, five, but that's not fifty!"

Liere had not forgotten. She was one of the half-dozen people who Marloven Hess's wary king had trusted enough to transfer straight inside his fortress.

"Now we have to walk all the way!" Lyren-Sartora hissed a loud sigh.

"It's a perfect afternoon for a walk," Liere replied. "And I wanted to see if anything's changed."

"Does anything ever change in Marloven Hess?" Lyren-Sartora snarked; at thirteen she was already an expert at the teenage eye roll.

"No," Liere said, but maybe its king had. She looked up at the massive city gates and wondered if any enemy (other than Marlovens themselves) had ever tried to breach them.

The sight, the scents, overwhelmed her with how much she'd missed this place. No, how much she'd missed Senrid, the only person she'd been able to tell everything as soon as she thought it. And yet here she was, mentally rehearsing what she ought to say, and what would be best left unsaid.

Lyren-Sartora was also intent on personal concerns, though of a very different sort. She was annoyed with Liere, who had never seemed like a mother, but more like a devoted, darling, exasperating, very, very different older sister. Lyren-Sartora did try to hide her exasperation. Liere had vanished for nearly *five years*. When Lyren-Sartora finally got her back again, instead of being like a sister, Liere had acted like a typical grownup and became besotted with that yellow-haired Elsarion king in Enaeran. So now, even though Lyren-Sartora had Liere back again, it was only for a month, before she'd go off to bury herself in backward Enaeran to live with *him*.

Someone should *do* something. Maybe Senrid would know what to do, what to say, how to bring back the old Liere.

They passed inside the gates and headed toward the royal castle that, like the city, was an artifact of Marloven history. But now these same buildings, even the afternoon slant of sunlight, all seemed to have Senrid's personal mark in some way Liere could not quite explain. Widely as she had traveled, Choreid

Dhelerei had never seemed just another city. It was Senrid's city.

Shafts of afternoon sunlight warmed the western facades of the heavy stone buildings Senrid had fought so hard to hold. Some of those massive relics of the bad old days revealed small alterations after all; here and there windows and handsome carving broke up the martial expanses. Windows high up, of course. After all, the inhabitants were still Marlovens, and one did not overcome a millennium of militant acculturation in a few years.

Had their leader entirely overcome his?

Liere and Lyren-Sartora dodged wagons, riders, carts, and even foot traffic. No coaches. Things obviously hadn't changed that much—Marlovens obviously still rode horseback, drove carts, or walked.

Along the street, banners folded or shutters pulled to as shopkeepers closed for the day. Laden horses and empty carts wound their slow way back toward the city gates. The air carried—besides dust and the ubiquitous smell of horse—the familiar aromas of herb-laced rice, cabbage, chicken or fish cooking in various shops and inns along the way. Rye bread baking. All so familiar.

Liere tipped her head up, breathing in the blend of summer sage and wild onion and garlic and mustard that sent her back to herself as a child, sitting cross-legged opposite Senrid in his rooms up in that castle, eating from dishes they set on the floor so they could look at maps or books all spread about them, and argue about history, and how they would change the world. How curious that a mere memory, and a happy one at that time, would cause her eyes to sting. It had to be this unsettling sense that she'd lost something precious, or that she'd arrived a little too late.

A strange sensation. She'd lost nothing. And she was about to mend that misunderstanding that she had caused, however unconsciously.

As they reached the top of the street on which the royal castle was built, Liere spied something new: a theatre. Music, plays—how Senrid's vile uncle would have hated it all!

Between the steep roofs of two tall townhouses rose a sentry tower. Half a street more, and there were the black and gold screaming eagle banners snapping in the high breeze. They reached the castle walls—as high as the city walls, if not higher—just as the shadows began to meld and the sand-colored stone took on mellow, muted sunset tones.

The main gate stood wide, and a sentry on top scanned them for weapons. Inside the main courtyard, little traffic impeded Liere's view of the broad flagged expanse.

"I'll meet you inside," Lyren-Sartora declared, and took off, ducking through a doorway into the residence portion of the royal castle, leaving Liere alone.

A runner clad in gray approached, and courteously inquired her name and her business. She watched him assess her: young, slender, long wheat-colored hair like so many from this area of the world; plainly dressed in a dusty summer robe over riding clothes much like anything found along the entire continent; a single jewel—set in a ring—on one thumb. She waited calmly for his gaze to travel back up from her sandals to her eyes, and his expression altered to speculation.

"Is the king here?" she asked, sidestepping his questions.

"Are you expected?" he countered.

"Ah. He's here, then. No, I am not expected. I'm a personal friend, back from a long journey."

"Name?" the stable runner repeated.

"Liere Fer Eider."

"Oh." That was as involuntary as the widening of his eyes. This time he visibly restrained himself from giving her another toe-to-topknot once-over. Instead he hailed a castle runner and passed her along, with a formal "Take this person to the king, please," followed by a surreptitious violent gesture and a breathed *Sartora* just behind her shoulder that Liere's pleasant expression gave no hint she'd overheard.

Sartora. It seemed she would never be rid of it. But she supposed they would no longer call her the Little Girl.

They trod up the stone stairs to the residence level. Once Senrid had put back some of the tapestries his mother brought from the south before the bad days of Uncle Tdanerend, it seemed Senrid hadn't made any further alteration.

"Wait." Liere stopped the runner from knocking at the closed door of Senrid's study. "I'd like to surprise him."

The runner faded back, palm to heart.

Liere opened the door. Senrid sat at his desk, head bent. The nearly horizontal beam of ochre light slanting through the four tall windows outlined his short, wavy blond hair, but the rest of him blended into the gathering shadows.

He did not look up. "That you, brat?" he asked, and her breath caught at the timbre of his voice — so familiar, and yet unfamiliar. Tenor, a young man's voice.

Liere looked down at his desk, then exclaimed, "I've never seen so many gems and jewels in my life. Have you turned to thievery?"

Senrid's head lifted. Instead of the round face so vivid in memory, this face was square, the bones that had been hinted at before now defined in young manhood. But there were the same steady, observant gray-blue eyes.

"Liere," he exclaimed, dropping a diamond-glittering necklace on the desk and standing up. "Come in!" When they were ten and fifteen, he had been half a hand taller than she. And that was still true. "I'd heard you were back," he observed.

She approached the desk, gazing on the glory spread over the desk; that was easier than meeting his eyes. Guilt. Time to get it out. "Before I say anything else, I want to apologize for my *stupid* advice. Before I left. About — children."

He flattened one hand in the old, familiar gesture and flicked it to the side, as though pushing something away. "Not stupid. I knew how much those two brats were running you. I saw later how wrong my timing was. And in thinking your answer was aimed at me. When your target was you yourself, as usual. I was a rock skull not to recognize it. But I did think it was a great idea to go off to Geth-deles. Get away from all the old expectations, yes?"

"Yes." Liere breathed a sigh of relief. They were right back where they had been. Of course they were. "That was it exactly."

"From the surface your jaunt seems to have gone well," he observed.

She looked down at herself, and blushed, for the first time — ever. Then she laughed. "You, too." She turned to the desk, relieved to leave a suddenly awkward subject behind. "What's all this wealth?"

"Family stuff. What Leander calls, when he's being sarcastic, crown jewels. I was looking for something else when I came across this stash that I suspect my mother had put away. Decided to sort it all out. See what I want to keep."

Still marveling at the glittering gems and bracelets and brooches and tiaras and rings that she would have thought utterly foreign to Marlovens, she said, "We must have both released the Child Spell around the same time."

"I did it before you left, actually." Senrid lifted a shoulder. "Seemed ridiculous to hide from Detlev when he was no longer a threat."

"As far as I can tell, Detlev has been living unmolested on the coast of Sartor ever since I left. Surely Norsunder has to be angry at him for leaving them."

Senrid smiled. "Oh, I think they're angry enough. As for retribution, who knows if they've tried? I'm sure Detlev's house being located in an otherwise unsettled area is no coincidence."

Liere shuddered. The air had cleared, yet she still wasn't as comfortable as she'd been in the old days. She felt odd, a little as if she had tried to put on a pair of shoes that she'd worn at ten, expecting them to fit the same.

She wandered to one of the tall windows, and looked out over the rooftops of the Marloven military training school as she resisted the impulse to listen in the mental realm. She couldn't hear Senrid's thoughts anyway. His mind-shield was if anything stronger than ever.

As she stood there gazing out, Senrid gazed at her, trying to find something to say. This sense that his skull had emptied between his ears had to be the surprise of her sudden reappearance. The changes in Marloven Hess — Detlev — Norsunder — his long friendship with Liere, as natural as air, until she abruptly left the world without telling him; it was hard to concentrate on any one of these things. Leaving him staring as if his life depended on finding traces of his skinny little friend wearing her brother's cast-off clothes, her hair cut by a knife, in this straight-backed, slender young woman wearing a simple summer robe over linen riding clothes, her hair, which he had never seen longer than her collarbones, now falling past her hips. Her face was an oval, dominated by her light brown eyes that looked golden in the vanishing sunlight.

She turned. "Lyren-Sartora said something or other before we transferred. Something concerning Leander, you, and a deal?"

"Oh, that." He could think again. "You know Leander's been hot on all our historical connections, and he's known since I got rid of my uncle that I'm not going to sic my vast army on tiny Vasande Leror. Which he hates being king of. To him, the logical conclusion is to reunite under one banner. The way we once were."

To Liere, Senrid no longer looked distracted in that odd, staring way. For the first time, she wondered if her surprise visit might be a serious interruption.

"We help each other with ruling matters. He's been here dutifully, though he doesn't do much beside read in the archive, and I go over there, where I've tended to as much as I can without Kyale finding out, while he buries himself in studies. Not that there's much beyond an hour or two of tasks over there to tend to on any given day. He's impatient to make it permanent because he hates ruling, and if war does come, he wants our protection."

"What would he do if he hands off Vasande Leror to you?"

"He wants to go north to study magic more deeply and work with Arthur, perhaps as a herald-mage."

"Does Kyale agree?"

"Of course not." Senrid's lip curled, his tone sardonic—at least one thing seemed unchanged. "She likes being a princess. To her that's all that matters. Though they both released the Child Spell when I did, Kyale," Senrid said, "is the same as she ever was."

"I take it you still don't keep a court."

"Marlovens have never been courtiers," he responded with a brief, wry smile. "You ought to remember that much."

"I do. I also remember that you once wanted to become less of an army masquerading as a kingdom. Seems to me a court—separating your powerful families from their own private armies—might be a way to do that?"

"The jarls still report to me at Convocation, and those with sons and daughters at the Summer Games. Even if I could get the jarls to stay here longer, what would I offer them? Worse, would I have to entertain them? Ruling—learning—are enough."

"They can make their own entertainment. That's what courtiers do," Liere said.

"I've considered that." Senrid turned his gaze to the desk littered with stones, rings, necklaces, orders, brooches—how many generations of Montredaun-An jewelry? Liere wondered if Senrid even knew. They looked hard and cold in the gathering gloom.

He snapped his fingers and glowglobes in all four corners of the room lit. The jewels seemed to come alive, glittering and sparkling gloriously. "One of the reasons why I had this stuff dragged out. To see what there is, though I can't imagine using any of it. Or, maybe I should shut it away for my descendants to deal with in another couple hundred years."

He bent and picked up a large gold-carved brooch, heavily encrusted with diamonds and opals. "Sent all the way from Colend to a long-ago queen," he commented. "Did you know that the Lirendis crossed my barbarian forebears? Ugly, isn't it? There was some sort of insult implied in the design. Typical of Colend, an insult buried in a gaudy compliment." Impulse, so rare, prompted him to offer in a mocking voice, "Want any?"

Liere laughed, and joined him at the desk so she could better examine the variety of jewels there. "No, thanks. Not yet, anyway."

Not yet. "You're moving out of Bereth Ferian?"

Surprised at his perception—she'd forgotten how fast he was—Liere glanced up from the jewels to his face. "Yes I am," she said slowly. "It's Arthur's city. The old federation against the Venn is long gone. The mage school is expanding, and with it, Arthur's beloved library. My courtesy rank there was at best symbolic, and is now even more meaningless. There's plenty of space, but no place for me. But, well, maybe I've found somewhere I do belong." Her chin came up at that, her tone firm, as if she expected challenge, and she flicked open her hand, almost forgetting the ring on her thumb. She clutched it before it could fly off.

Senrid reached forward and took her hand, examining the ring. A man's ring, a signet. A king's ring, meant for sealing edicts. Such things were seldom handed off to friends, or even to occasional favorites.

Again, his mind seemed blank—too many things to think about seemed to mean he couldn't think at all. He stared down at the old ring on her thumb, trying to define his reaction. He couldn't. He was too distracted by the cool silken feel of her fingers lying so lightly in his, the warmth beneath, the subtle beat of her pulse, by the ephemeral scent of roses that was not any perfume, but that seemed to emanate from her skin, and by how her hands had changed, from the thin, nail-bitten fingers of the child Sartora to the slender, graceful hand of a young woman—graceful but strong, with the calluses of hard work across the palm.

Liere glanced down, wondering what had caught his attention. Her ring—of course. Heat seared down deep inside her at the reminder of Andri Malcolin Elsarion's proximity.

She frowned down at the ring, trying to see it the way Senrid would see it. Obviously old. On either side of the stone a crest cut into the setting, surrounded by diamond chips. He would have seen that crest before; it had once, if Andri was right, been connected to his own family centuries previous.

Senrid gave her a wry smile. "I'll admit I don't know much about it, but I thought rings that don't fit were worn on chains. You don't lose 'em that way." He picked up a thin, strong chain from the table, strung the ring through it, and fastened the catch. Then he rounded his desk and handed Liere the chain.

She put it over her head, pulled her hair through, and dropped the ring inside her under-tunic, where it thumped against her skin. "Thanks," she said. "I didn't think of that."

"Whose is it?"

"That's a rather long story—"

"So tell me in three sentences, rather than one."

"It belongs to Andri Malcolin Elsarion. One of the crests you saw on the ring is his family's, the other his kingdom's. Enaeran. Three sentences."

Enaeran. Yes, he'd been right.

He picked up a simple silver clasp with a sapphire stone. "Ah. I like this one." He dropped it on the table. She looked down, wondering for the first time if Senrid had ever considered marriage. The subject seemed somehow a trespass, though she had never in their long friendship thought in such a way—but then in all their years and conversations, they had never once broached that path.

Senrid's eyes narrowed: farsense. "The Girl in My Life is approaching right now, dragging your venture into family life."

Liere laughed as a fair-haired child of not quite five ran in, with Lyren-Sartora right behind her.

"Hoola-loola-loo," Lyren-Sartora breathed, her gaze going immediately to the table. "Whom did you rob?" She moved to the gems, her fingers touching, then picking up, then donning. She'd put on about six rings and two necklaces before a new voice spoke from behind Liere.

"Please, Monta, may I?"

Liere watched with interest as the child moved to Senrid's chair and put her hands on his arm. Crystal Ingrid had Senrid's features in a rounded, childish form. Light blond curls dangled in a messy tangle down her back, and her eyes were the same gray-blue shade as her father's. The child's smock and loose trousers were grubby, and she whiffed of wet dog.

"Please?" Her voice was soft, her diction marked by the clear precision peculiar to children with Dena Yeresbeth. It was obvious from Crystal Ingrid's manner that father and daughter had an easy relationship.

Senrid heaved a loud sigh and waved a hand.

Crystal Ingrid pounced on the jewels and began bedecking herself with a speed that would match her with Lyren-Sartora's glitter in moments.

"Monta?" Liere asked.

"She's called me that since she was two," Senrid said, as he watched the daughters posturing. "I'm not sure, but I think it's the result of Kyale's having tried to teach her to say Mountain-Grown Bonehead."

Liere nodded, remembering this insult Kyale had made of Senrid's family name. It sounded likely.

"Mirror. We must see what we look like," Lyren-Sartora pronounced. She whirled around, a blaze of rainbow lights sparkling at her waist, neck, ears, forehead, and fingers.

"Two more," Crystal Ingrid protested, struggling to pin a fourth brooch to the sagging front of her dog hair-covered smock. Lyren-Sartora swooped to help as a steward appeared at the door to announce dinner.

"You brats dejewel," Senrid said. "I don't want that stuff dropping into the soup. Bad for the teeth. And wash up! You two may as well stay, since they've probably laid places for you," he added, turning his thumb from Lyren-Sartora to Liere.

"All right," Lyren-Sartora said with the ease of long familiarity, as Liere thought, laid places? As in a dining room, rather than a tray here in the study? That was new, too. But of course he'd want to set a good example for the child.

Lyren-Sartora said carelessly, as one who had the right, "Liere and me will eat here, but then we're going on to see what the Mearsieans are up to. Maybe even get a second dessert, if we time it right."

Crystal Ingrid clapped her hands. "Then you come back," she said. "So we can play."

Senrid bent down to help his daughter get rid of her jewels. Liere watched his fingers, patient and gentle, and the way the child smiled back at him. She listened to the tenderness in his voice, a new note, something she'd never heard before, though she would have said that all his moods, and tones, were familiar as daylight.

Lyren-Sartora watched Liere watching, struggling with jealousy. She couldn't help thinking that Liere had never looked that way at her when she was four, though she'd been much smarter than Crystal Ingrid.

Then she hated herself for the thought. She knew the truth. She hadn't been smarter, she'd just showed off more. But she was aware of a kernel of anger in her heart. She'd been a show-off at four because she'd had to be, their lives had been so weird, traveling all over the world, Liere lost in depression as often as not. Crystal Ingrid never had to do anything to get attention, she just always had it. She always had order.

But that wasn't her fault.

Lyren-Sartora took Crystal Ingrid's hand as they raced off to wash up, leaving the other two to chat about the academy, and the just-finished Summer Games until the four were together again, and Crystal Ingrid wanted to know if Liere had a dog

Two

WHEN LEANDER TLENNEN-HESS walked into Senrid's study, the first thing he saw was the neat arrangement of the jewels in various piles.

"It's about time," he said by way of greeting, and gestured at the piles. "I recognize most of those pieces. Want to know which ones are actually genuine Montredaun-An heirlooms and which is loot?"

Senrid laughed. "Knowing my ancestors, I figured most of it was loot, outside of this gaudy Colendi brooch. Did we rob any of your ancestors?"

"Nope." Leander sat down at the table, running his gaze over the collection of jewels and gems before him. "Many of these are legitimately inherited. Brought by brides from outside the kingdom, or sent to them, like your brooch. Now that ring there—" He touched a fine platinum band set with a pale yellow stone. "That's old. I believe it belonged to the Cassadas, before the Marlovans rode in and booted the Iascans out of their castles. Could that possibly be the ghost queen's ring? Naw. On the other hand, who better to unload a supposedly haunted ring onto than your conquerors?"

When Senrid didn't react, Leander looked up.

Senrid shook his head. "Sorry. I thought I..." He tapped his head, then shook it again. "No sign of attack yet."

Leander let out his breath in a long sigh. "I don't know what's worse, dreading the inevitable or —"

He stopped, and Senrid finished, "Oh, war will be worse. Never fear. If it's short, it will be only because we fell fast."

That dispassionate assurance made Leander's insides cramp. He and Senrid had both changed since the days when, as boys, they'd struggled against adult opportunists who wanted the thrones they'd inherited far too young. They'd become friends, they shared goals, and discoveries, and insights into magic-learning, but every so often something would point up the differences. Senrid's acceptance of the inevitability of bloodshed was typically Marloven, and Leander knew he would never get used to it—even if his own name testified to his ancestors' Marloven roots.

"A cheery view," he said, trying for a lighter tone. Waving a hand at the jewel piles, he said, "What are these divisions, anyway? Inherited from ancestors and gifts from outside? Which could cover loot."

"Neither. Ones I like and ones I don't want to see again."

Leander nodded, unsurprised. Here was another difference; Vasande Leror had largely gone back to its Iascan roots, while Marloven Hess was emphatically Marloven Hess. The black-and-tan Marloven uniform still outnumbered other kinds of clothing on the streets of Choreid Dhelerei. Senrid still moved with the trained economy of one who regularly drilled with hand-to-hand fighting and shot arrows several times a week just for fun. And he thought like a warrior-king. There were long wargames out on the plains every summer, and competitions in weapons forms. Jewelry meant nothing to Marlovens, but their tiny, easily overlooked medals meant everything. "Well, why not? No need to display some ancestor's terrible taste. Throw 'em back into a box for Crystal Ingrid to sort out some day."

"There's that," Senrid said, not ready to admit to anyone he'd taken the stuff out in an attempt to distract himself from the urge to pester Tsauderei, Atan, and everyone else for news. If he'd been a dog, all his hackles would be up. But instinct wasn't always to be trusted—he'd learned that over and over.

Leander said, "You didn't ask about my trip."

"And now I will ask about your trip," Senrid retorted promptly.

Leander flashed a wry smile. "I found stuff written in Early Iascan. Did you know there never was an alphabet for Marlovan? When they settled into the Iascan castles, they adopted the Iascan alphabet along with their furniture, and then all the vocabulary that had to do with castle life, sometimes forcing it into Marlovan verb forms, though for a few generations they kept the languages separate."

Senrid shrugged slightly. "I always thought your Crestellian was an old Iascan dialect."

"You were right. Iascan and Crestellian are much the same. The name was changed for political reasons, not linguistic. But the change in alphabets—the Marlo*van* of those days—was deliberately switched from Venn runes. I thought it had evolved."

"There's a difference?"

"Yes." Leander was usually the mildest of persons, but this sort of talk excited him, his startling green eyes wide. Leander had always been taller, ever since they were boys of fifteen, but now he was a hand taller instead of head and shoulders. His face had lengthened into fine, sculpted bones that caused heads to turn.

For a time, Leander launched into a passionate, detailed linguistic explanation, but he halted mid-sentence when he saw that he had lost his audience. "What is it? You look disturbed." Then he spotted Senrid's golden notecase among the jewelry and gems. Leander couldn't remember Senrid ever taking much interest in writing letters, except as a duty. "You're not having trouble with those strategy sessions again, are you?"

"Again?" Senrid repeated. "Never recovered from the first accusations about how much I relished war, and was this a pretense to find out their defensive secrets."

"The king of Perideth," Leander stated. "That idiot is always going to see you as a villain. It's a convenience, and everyone knows it."

"I wish that was true. But it isn't. He was annoying, yes, but the biggest hypocrite was that bleater from Ianavair going on about how much I love the glory of war, as if his history, one shared with us, isn't exactly as bloody. 'Glory'." Senrid spat the word. "I lost that illusion the first time I met Detlev. But they don't believe that Norsunder is coming."

"They don't want to believe it," Leander said. "Who does? I think what's worse than not knowing when it will come is not knowing why. Anyway, I brought the book if you'd like to look at it sometime."

"Lend me the book," Senrid said. "It might be something Crystal Ingrid will take an interest in a couple years down the road. Oh. Guess who joined us for dinner tonight?"

"Uncle Tdanerend." Leander cackled.

"Liere fer Eider."

"Really! I heard from Arthur that she was back. Did she say where she'd been? Or what she'd been up to?"

Senrid flicked his fingers outward. "There was not much opportunity for serious talk..." His voice drifted.

Leander joked, "What's the matter? I just grow another head?"

Senrid gave him a puzzled frown. "Didn't you feel that?"

"I guess not."

"Listen!"

Leander listened, but heard nothing unusual. Then he realized Senrid meant in an inner sense. Leander could not listen on that level, but he was sensitive enough to feel differences in atmospherics, and this he tried to do now.

No, everything still seemed the same, except for an undercurrent of coldness—but that could be his imagination supplying what he was looking for. Senrid's expression made it clear the change could not be anything but bad.

"What was it like?" Leander asked.

Senrid closed his eyes, trying to evaluate that inner impression. Something had happened somewhere; some powerful mind with powerful intent had crossed from there to here.

It was beginning. He didn't know where, or how, but the "when" had happened.

Leander waited, and Senrid sat back in his chair. "Felt like a knife-blade tickling down my back. Invisible knife—"

"Invisible back," Leander finished the ancient joke. "Maybe I'd best get home and check our border protections."

"And get some sleep," Senrid said, smiling grimly. "While you still can."

⸻

Hibern, disinherited daughter of the mage Latvian Askan, transferred by magic from Roth Drael back to where she'd been born: Marloven Hess.

While she no longer regarded Senrid's kingdom as home, her first thought on receiving bad news through the mage guild scribes was that she ought to warn Senrid. Her mage tutor Erai-Yanya, busy writing letters, nodded an absent permission, and Hibern transferred directly to the castle in Choreid Dhelerei, glad that Senrid's protective magic still permitted her a pass-through.

She bustled straight to Senrid's study, knowing that he had magic tracers in place, and snapped the glow globe into light. Sure enough, within a very short time Senrid appeared, looking awake and alert despite a half-buttoned shirt and bare feet.

"Trouble," he said as soon as he saw her. It wasn't even a question — not midway through the night.

"Family items?" she said by way of greeting, pointing at the jewels.

"Yes. Everyone but Leander thinks it's loot. What's going on?"

"Norsunder."

He didn't react with horror, the way Erai-Yanya had. He perched on the edge of the desk and waited expectantly, though she saw the tic of a vein in his neck.

She said: "Last night the advisor to the King of Halarialgre — Arman, or something — threw the king in the dungeon and his newly trained body of border guards stepped into the key cities and border castles. Two hours later the king of Kerga recognized Halarialgre's change in government and declared an alliance."

Senrid's gaze diffused in what Hibern recognized as internal map review. "What about the scribe guild communication?"

"The scribe desks are fine," she said reassuringly — all the mages had insisted there were wards and spells aplenty protecting the oldest webwork of spells in the world. "How do you think we found out so fast? The scribes are doing exactly what they are trained to do: sharing messages with the 'urgent' sigil before passing on anything else. Anyway, the Kergan army is now marching on Mearne. A well-trained army, I'm told. Fast moving. By tonight, the capital of Mearne will have fallen, if —"

Senrid was half-listening. "Halarialgre. Kerga. Mearne. I know my maps well, but these are the countries that usually edge maps. Honas, Atan calls them—handy word, if you overlook the Sartoran superiority, because Sartor would never be honas. But—" He frowned. "Hibern. All they need is Hanbria, and the little one—yeah, Fils Flor—and this half of the continent we are now standing on is entirely cut off from the east."

Hibern sighed. "I see you've jumped ahead of me. You won't be surprised to hear that Arman is a Norsundrian. His name is actually Kifellian—he seems to have originated in Colend—Alsaes."

Senrid moved to his map stand, pulled out a rolled map, and threw it on the table. Then he swept aside his jewels with one hand, and with the other snapped the map open, dumping jewels at each corner to keep it flat. "Let's take a look."

Hibern moved to the table, admiring Senrid's neatly drawn and labeled map as they oriented on the Elgar Strait. Just south of it, tucked against the Fal Mountains, were Hanbria and Fils Flor. And south of them, forming a line from strait to ocean, Halarialgre, Kerga (or Old Faleth, as it was still known by some of the inhabitants; in a land where governments seldom lasted a generation, of course there would be factions that could not even agree on what to call themselves, the two names duly noted in Senrid's precise script), Mearne. "An effective land barrier," he said, tapping the map. "What are your lighter mages doing?"

"Don't know about either the Sartoran guild or the northern. Tsauderei is so frail he never leaves his valley, and Erai-Yanya said that Lilith the Guardian is off-world. Nobody can find Detlev, not that anyone I know thinks of him as an ally. An informer, maybe. She thinks we should gather some magic workers and go down there to start setting up defenses—"

"Obviously Detlev's gone. He wouldn't agree with anything that stupid," Senrid interrupted. "What's with these other highland countries on the other side of the Fals? Dritian, and all these?" His fingers swept the map.

"Don't know. But what's so stupid about magical defenses—"

"Because they'd be setting up old-fashioned wards, Hibern," he cut in. "Detlev's on our side now!"

"Um, so he says?" she said blankly, thoroughly confused.

Senrid grinned. "All I'm saying is, look at this like a Marloven, not like a lighter mage. We're facing a strategic change. Rushing down there to set up lighter magic defenses is what we used to do against Detlev when he messed around with various types of border wards and enchantments. We're up against someone totally different now. Someones, maybe. Who will not only have known what Detlev did, but will count on us following our old patterns."

"I think you'd better tell Erai-Yanya," Hibern said.

"Right. A couple of things first. Those armies will be marching outward..." Senrid threw himself into his desk chair, and yanked a piece of paper over. "If they are really cutting the continent in half by taking the smaller kingdoms first, then it's time to warn the others."

"How many of those rulers would pay any attention to an evil Marloven?" Hibern asked, leaning against the desk, her black eyes narrowed with irony. "Didn't you try to get them to discuss a defensive alliance?"

"That," he said, "was theoretical. Maybe they won't hold their noses against my Marloven stench when they learn that Norsunder is here. Now. Ah, though it might be faster if you do it."

Hibern looked down at the map, trying to see things as a Marloven. Cutting the continent in half? "What bothers me is, where are they coming from? Why didn't anyone know?"

He said, "Because we were looking for armies. Norsunder Base. Rift magic. We weren't looking for what sounds like systematic infiltration in all these little polities."

Hibern's mouth tightened. "I'll do it. Warning it is." She transferred out, knowing that Erai-Yanya had the highest priority marker for the scribe network, shared with the two mage guilds' leaders, and with Tsauderei. The scribes — without making it obvious — rated mages' urgent affairs above kings'.

Senrid walked to the door and looked out at the duty runner. "Summon Forthan. Orders to commanders, defense alert. No drill."

The runner, a fifteen-year-old academy student, thrilled in every nerve at the sudden responsibility in the middle of what was supposed to be a boring punishment night duty for what really hadn't been all that much of a prank. War? She smacked her fist against her tunic, whirled and ran.

Senrid had already retreated back to his desk, and whispered another spell, an alert he and Leander had long ago set up. Three breaths later Leander appeared, looking tousled and rumpled in last night's clothes, a red line down one cheek, revealing that Leander still fell asleep over his studies.

"Trouble," Senrid said. "I'm raising the kingdom to defense alert. See what you can find out through the lighter mages? They seem to be commandeering the scribe desks, and they'll tell you more than they'll tell me. I'll return shortly."

Senrid scrambled into socks and boots then transferred to Erai-Yanya's ruined building in Roth Drael, and leaned against a wall to recover from the sickening jolt. Here it was early morning. Sun streamed through the arched windows, bisecting the old work table in three stripes of brightness, lighting up books, old and new.

Erai-Yanya was not alone. Liere Fer Eider had also arrived, and both were bent over the huge map that Senrid had made for Erai-Yanya at Hibern's request.

Liere glanced up, surprised to see Senrid there. Then she turned back to Erai-Yanya, who as always was barefoot, her hair half coming down over an old, rumpled robe, her face superficially calm. But Roth Drael's early morning sunlight revealed the deepened lines around eyes and mouth, and streaks of gray in her hair. She winced when she turned her head, as if she had a canyon-sized headache. Erai-Yanya, who had seemed ageless, had somehow gotten old. Liere's heart squeezed.

Erai-Yanya cast a quick look at Hibern, raising her brows in question when she saw Senrid.

"He can explain better than I did," Hibern said. "I agree with him."

Senrid came forward, distracted by Liere tracing a finger along the line of small kingdoms where Norsunder had just emerged, her shining hair a long ruffled fall over her arm to curl on the table at her hip.

She glanced up, her disconcerting golden gaze meeting his. "You weren't planning to go to Hanbria to helpfully set up magic wards, were you?"

"That's exactly what I came to warn you people about." He waved at Erai-Yanya, and hitched a leg over the edge of the table. "You also smelled a fart."

The crudity made Erai-Yanya frown, but Liere only shrugged. "Norsunder. Worse," she said, and sighed. "You wouldn't happen to know where Detlev is right now?"

Senrid turned up his palms. "David would know, or one of his boys."

"Arthur says he can't seem to locate any of them. Roy has not returned to Bereth Ferian. It's as if they've all disappeared," Liere said, a faint crease between her brows.

"I don't like that at all," Erai-Yanya stated.

Senrid looked up. "If you mean they've pulled a triple switch and are on Norsunder's side again, save your worry for something else. If they can't be found, then Detlev's already given them orders."

Erai-Yanya's mouth tightened.

Hibern backed away, sitting quietly in the window seat, to give the others space. The room was not all that small, but somehow the three before her made it seem crowded.

Erai-Yanya said, "I never studied war, so what 'orders' Detlev might see fit to hand out is confusing as well as disturbing. What I do understand is that we are wasting time while another kingdom might be falling to Norsunder. And we are doing nothing. I want to know why we shouldn't go to help?"

Senrid lifted one shoulder. "Run off and set up your useless defense if it makes you feel better —"

"Button it," Liere said calmly. "Sarcasm never helps."

Senrid looked vaguely surprised. Hibern wondered if anyone — besides Kyale Marlonen, and Senrid was inured to her constant abuse — had dared to tell him to button it in the last few years.

He flashed his toothy, challenging smile, and Liere said, "What do you suggest we do?"

Senrid gazed down the length of the table at Liere, who stared right back, composed and assured, unlike the old days when she gnawed her nails to the quick with anxious dithering.

Senrid snorted a laugh. "I don't have any good ideas — I don't know enough yet. The last time we had Norsundrians running through countries I thought it was all-out war, but it turned out only to be Prince Kessler trashing Everon to show his Norsundrian rival Henerek how it's done. Then he got yanked —"

"By Detlev," Liere said. "That was the second time Siamis tried his enchantment." Her eyes narrowed, and her tone changed. "Senrid, do you think —"

"The whole thing was a feint after all?"

"Prince Kessler's terrible slaughter in Everon was no feint," Liere said quickly.

"But Detlev muzzled him, didn't he? Wasn't that right before he jumped the fence?"

Liere blinked, gaze going diffuse. "I remember the talk while I was a prisoner at Geth-deles —"

Erai-Yanya rapped her knuckles on the desk, breaking the spell of the quick exchange. "It seems to me that you are wasting time, going over events of years ago, while we have an emergency here."

Senrid was going to retort that understanding Siamis's real motivation then might very well apply to what was unfolding now, but Liere caught his eye and gave a tiny shake of her head. She said apologetically to Erai-Yanya, "I'm still very much a learner, but it seems to me that going to Hanbria to lay down wards might put us a couple steps behind the Norsundrians, if they are expecting that."

"What do we do, then? Don't tell me 'nothing'." Erai-Yanya turned to Hibern. "What do you think? Why do you agree with them?"

As Hibern chose her words, she was distracted by the strengthening sunlight haloing Liere's face, striking glints of fiery gold in her hair as she studied the map. Hibern's gaze leaped from Liere to Senrid, who had gone so still that Hibern could see the slight rise and fall of the linen fabric of his shirt as he breathed. His profile was in shadow, but she could see tension in every line of his body.

"Senrid's right that that was our response in the old days. The way this attack has been framed makes me think they know it. Planned for it," Hibern said, to break that silence.

Erai-Yanya was going to speak, when her golden notecase gave an audible chime. She grabbed it and flicked open the note inside. "The Sartoran mage guild is calling for mages."

Liere looked up at Senrid, and both said at the same time, "The scribe desks?" Liere waved a hand. "I don't know what's going on in Sartor, but if this is more widespread than we thought, Senrid, won't everyone in Halia start looking to Marloven Hess to defend them against Norsunder?"

Senrid's gaze dropped to the map. "I've given the alert. Nothing else for me to do at this moment. It's still the middle of the night at home."

"I have a regular transfer spell set up for the Queen of

Sartor," Erai-Yanya said to Liere. "Sartor three times." She stepped onto her Destination square, whispered, and vanished.

Liere traced a finger down that line of little countries on the east side of Sles Adran, her other hand pressing the fabric of her robe over the ring bumping between her ribs. She fought, and won, the instinct to transfer to Andri. Enaeran lay west of Sles Adran, was far from the site of the trouble, and even had it been near, he had been dealing with civil war most of his life. There was nothing she could do except dither were she to go to Enaeran, whereas she would be of use to the mages.

She moved to the Destination and transferred to Sartor.

Hibern knew she ought to follow, but, aware that the Sartoran Mage Guild did not trust Senrid, she was trying to think of something diplomatic to say when Senrid reached down and brushed his fingers over the Western countries on his neatly lettered map, a slow, thoughtful gesture totally unlike his usual nervy quickness.

Hibern said, "I really hope we can avoid catastrophe."

"Too late," Senrid said, and transferred home.

Three

Eidervaen, capital of Sartor

ATAN, QUEEN OF SARTOR had already been having a vile week. It began when Adam, one of Detlev's gang, walked into Eidervaen and requested an interview. In himself, Adam was about as harmless in appearance as a baby bird or a bunny, his manner friendly, even kindly. She was briefly distracted by the fact that despite the warm, summery day, he wore gloves.

"What is it?" she said, with the thinnest veil of civility.

Adam said, "I was sent to convey a couple of warnings, as a courtesy—"

"You mean, sent by Detlev," she interrupted.

"If you like," Adam replied evenly. "The first warning is that Norsunder appears to have found a way around the rift magic up in Fhleria, and they appear to be heading north toward Land of the Venn. Secondly, what had appeared to be random—the Norsundrian Yeres snatching young men, some of them kings, seems to have become a pattern. It is thought that she is keeping them prisoner to impose some kind of mind control spell, then sending them home again so she, or someone, can rule through them."

"'Appears to have'... 'appears to be'... 'appears'. Tchah! 'It is thought' by Detlev, you mean."

"Yes, but he's not alone in that," Adam said, his voice gentle.

"Is something expected in return?"

"Nothing." Adam hesitated—it was his idea to offer to trade information—but it did not take Dena Yeresbeth to feel her distrust and resentment.

He seemed about to add something, then gave his head a little shake and transferred.

"Rude," Atan said to the air where he had stood. And, "I don't believe it."

She didn't want to believe it.

She didn't want it to be true for the Venn's sake, as well as the Fhlerians, though their government sounded terrible. She didn't want it to be true because she didn't trust Detlev. He might be telling the truth. Some truth. He was famous— infamous—for telling exactly as much truth as he wanted you to know for his own convenience, leaving you more confused than ever.

The next day began with one message, then a flurry of them, about the little kingdoms directly north of Sartor, on the other side of the Sartoran Sea. Within a few hours, the chief of the Sartoran Mage Guild demanded an emergency meeting to report that the scribe desks were...flickering.

"Flickering?" Atan repeated. "I didn't think that was possible."

The woman was more than twice Atan's age. Anxiety stiffened her hands as she said, "I've never seen the like. Ever. It might only be the unprecedented number of messages, all marked urgent, except that the northern school reported experiencing the same."

"You are reinforcing the wards?"

"We began straightaway. But we need help. May we call in the mages?"

"Do."

Atan returned to her schedule, which never let up, ever. The moment she could break free, she crossed the palace grounds to the scribes' wing, where she discovered Liere Fer Eider along with Erai-Yanya and Hibern. They were so busy with magic books that Atan backed away again.

She went to bed late, and slept badly.

She woke early, waved off breakfast, and decided to walk

to the guardhouse, where she knew Rel was staying for his three-day watch. She dressed for walking and started out—and nearly ran headlong into Rel.

"Aren't you on duty one more day?" she asked as he put out his hands to steady her, and though it suited her very well to be tall and big, she secretly enjoyed the fact that Rel could catch her mid-stride and not stagger. "Bad news," she added.

At the same time he said, "Bad news."

They stared at the other.

"You first," she said.

"No, you first," he said. "Want to get it out?"

She very much wanted to get it out. She had initially decided she was not going to dignify Detlev's "courtesy" news by repeating it, but what came out first was a comprehensive slander of Adam, Detlev, and his minions. Then she went on to the scribes—what were they doing over there? This heated and totally unfair diatribe ended with a sweeping condemnation of the entire scribe guild.

As always, Rel listened. He had never offered an unasked opinion, especially on the subject of magic, though he was now an adept at the rare and mysterious form called "vagabond magic."

Feeling somewhat lighter for having unburdened herself, without the vestige of an effort in fairness, Atan said, "I got it out—and now my sympathies are completely with them. The fact that they put Erai-Yanya and Liere to work is disturbing. Usually no one is allowed near the chief scribe desk who hasn't been with the heralds and scribes ten years at the least. Your news?"

He put his hands on her shoulders, and said softly, "Norsunder Base is on the march."

Her breath whooshed out as if she'd been punched in the gut.

"You know I've been rotating the city watch out on the south road, as far as we dare go. Late yesterday my scout saw an enormous dust cloud, the kind that only rises from large numbers. He stayed the night to make sure it wasn't a dust storm down there. The dust was still in the air when the sun came up. He used the transfer token I gave him. Reported just now."

"How long do we have before they get here?"

"I'd say a week at the outside. Call it five days if they run."

All Atan's petty resentments vanished like smoke. Five days, and a week's worth of urgent tasks. A month's.

And she had to be the last to leave. So get started, she scolded herself. "Rel, it's time to put your plans into action. I'll summon all the runners to warn the city," she said heavily. "And the council."

She went to Gehlei, her steward, who had first trained as a guard. It was ridiculous to be reluctant to tell her the grim news, as if speaking the words made it more real. Rel wouldn't have said anything if it wasn't already inescapably real.

Gehlei's expression didn't change as she began dictating orders to her own staff. While pages sped through the palace and the streets, Atan forced herself to go straight to chief scribe desk, which ordinarily no one was permitted near except the queen. The place was crowded with mages pulled in from all over Sartor.

As Atan paused in the door, looking at tense shoulders, flickering fingers and bent heads, she imagined the same occurring all over the world—wherever there were scribe desks. Not all kingdoms had them. Having been raised by a mage, she had been astonished to learn that the scribe guild, the largest guild in the world, not only had numerous branches— intersecting with mages and heralds and the wood guild for example—but subsidiary branches that, depending on where you lived, might take precedence.

In Colend, she'd learned, the most elite branch served custom that required beautiful lettering on fine, perfumed paper, which was folded into exquisite shapes before delivery. This branch, she discovered after she met Senrid, was missing altogether in Marloven Hess, where the scribe guild was quite small, confined to writing letters for those who couldn't, and to bringing letters from other places, sorting them, and seeing that they got to their recipients.

The most vital was this room, the scribe desk. The "desk" was actually scry stones, in which a letter—appended with the proper sigils—appeared at the recipient's designated scribe desk. A scribe copied it out for its recipient, or read it to same. This method was used by business people and scribes, as the scribes could send as many copies as they had sigils for, without having to fatigue themselves recopying the same message.

Messages went out all over the world this way. In Sartor,

the scribe and mage guild shared responsibility for tending the scribe desk.

Someone noticed her, and nearly dropped his stack of books. "Your majesty."

The others rose and bowed, but she waved them back to sit before she said, "Norsunder is coming. We might have five days. Get that news out. And all of you, when you are not on duty, discuss with your families what you want to do. We've rehearsed for this for weeks. It has become real." She spoke as evenly as she could, hoping to forestall an outbreak of exclamations and questions that she could not answer.

When the day shift bent over their desks, she looked past them. "Liere? When did you come?"

"Yesterday afternoon, your time. You were busy, and they needed us, so we volunteered and they put us straight to work. I just finished my stint," Liere said, her eyes marked with tiredness. It was clear she had labored through the night. "I was going to fetch something to eat." *And then go to*...where? She ought to go to Bereth Ferian, though she knew Lyren-Sartora would resent being checked on. She wanted to go to Enaeran...

"Come upstairs." When Liere fell in step beside her. Atan said, "I thought it was a small matter. Making a rush of messages into a large matter. I realized this morning that I just wanted it to be a small matter, and I tried to shove the blame onto them."

Liere said, "It's frightening, something we've always thought was indestructible, if not quite inviolable, coming apart before our eyes almost as fast as we worked to repair it."

"Tell me exactly what's going on. Not the mechanics of the scrying—I know the basics and I still can't make sense out of it. Though I know that the scribe desk has occasionally been misused, I thought it was indestructible."

Liere thumbed her temples, and Atan wondered when she'd slept last. But none of them were going to be getting much rest. Liere said, "Misused. I think they began by suspecting that someone was illegally copying or corrupting or suppressing messages."

Atan said grimly, "It happens. Occasionally. I haven't had any cases in my lifetime, I'm glad to say."

Both reflected on the fact that the scribe guild, which was mostly filled with scholarly types, was fairly easygoing until someone tried to use the system for their own ends. The chiefs invariably made those people disappear — exiled and forbidden to take any guild position, Atan knew, for she had to sign the edicts, but the young scribes all whispered that miscreants vanished...forever.

Liere rubbed her arms against a sudden chill. "The messages are not stable. The guild chief thinks they might be bespelled to send copies... somewhere. Others say it's impossible, it's too many messages at once." Liere faced Atan. "Then there are some who think there is tampering deep within the fundamental spells. Someone," she said quietly, "on the inside, might be trying to bring the entire system down."

"But they don't know for certain? No traces?"

"No, which is why no one has said anything to you. The evidence seems to lie more with the absence of traces."

The breakfast arrived then, and over it Atan found herself talking about the mountain of messages she had been dealing with over the past day or so.

"From what I can gather, some are ignoring the news. I understand that. They regard those countries as too far away, too small to think about. Some even seem to think that the people there are imagining things, or are making up stories to get mages to come and donate spells that they won't have to pay for. Or, those little countries are always squabbling, what's one more enemy." Atan's expression soured. "I wonder what they will say when Norsunder attacks Eidervaen?"

Liere had no chance to respond as shrill women's voices rose from outside the open windows.

The royal residence was three stories up, beyond the high wall bordering a long alleyway. It was supposed to be kept clear for palace traffic, but city people used it as a shortcut from time to time.

Atan and Liere went to the window and looked down at one of the small passenger carts, drawn by pretty little goats. This one had no passenger. It was piled high with baskets and sacks, as a woman tried to put another sack atop the pile. Two small children and a whimpering toddler stood close to their mother as the driver tried to block her. "No you can't. It's already too much for my goats. They are not oxen. They can't pull loads like this!"

"How else am I to get our things to the caravan?" a red-faced woman yelled. "I'm going to have to carry the baby. As for your goats, you should have thought of how much they're going to pull when you charged me three sixes—that's more than double the going rate!"

Atan tsked and went to summon a steward to settle the altercation. While she was gone, Liere stared at the crumbs on her plate, remnants of a meal she was not even aware of having eaten. Tiredness was no longer an annoyance to fight off with strength of will and deep breathing—if she persisted she would do something stupid.

When Atan returned, Liere said, "I believe I ought to return to Bereth Ferian."

Atan accepted that, aware that Liere was the first to be leaving to check on homes and relations, and probably wouldn't return. And there was nothing she could say beyond encouragement: "I'm sure that Lyren-Sartora will insist that she's just fine, but I'm glad you are going to make sure."

Liere sensed that unspoken regret, to which there was no answer. She walked to the Destination, though she was tired enough to wish she could transfer right from there. But courtesy was the more important when chaos howled around the corners of civil life. She stepped into the Destination when it was her turn, did the magic to return to Bereth Ferian—and nothing happened.

Was the fog of exhaustion already making her stupid? Mindful—exaggeratedly careful—she repeated the words and sign. Nothing.

Alarm burned through her nerves. Though people were waiting, she shut her eyes and reached mentally for Lyren-Sartora: nothing. That meant a firm mind-shield. That was good practice, but not welcome now; Liere could fix an image of her and transfer directly to her, but that was extremely dangerous to do if it turned out the target person was somewhere without space for a second person.

She reached for Arthur—and recoiled from intense relief and horror and anger. She braced and transferred into a blast of icy air; Arthur stood in the entryway to the Bereth Ferian mage academy.

As reaction wrung through her, she stared witlessly at Arthur, who was besplattered with blood. "Arthur—"

"Oalthoreh. Dead. Shot through the heart. Crossbow. She must have been dead before she fell." He looked down at himself. "It's her blood."

Oalthoreh? The head of the northern magic school was a

grim, tough old woman. Liere had found her difficult to deal with, but respected her. Thought of her as an ancient tree, weathering time and storms.

"The scribe desk chief and one other, all shot by crossbow," Arthur husked.

"The Destination—"

"Destroyed. Many of the advanced students who could transfer left. I don't know who. They all panicked. Those left are the young ones, who don't know transfer magic. I've got them hidden."

"Lyren-Sartora? Yanli?"

"I sent them to my mother's in Roth Drael," Arthur said. "There, I know they will be safe enough. The wards are centuries old. Norsunder can't do magic there."

"But..." *Siamis did*, Liere began to say, and choked it off. She remembered very well how Siamis had chased her and Senrid there, and then remained after she left. He'd done plenty of magic.

That was another bit of possible support for her theory that Siamis had broken with Detlev earlier than anyone could have suspected. Except if that was true, why was he so cruel to Senrid? She had never had the courage to ask Siamis directly. Maybe that time had come...

"Liere?" Arthur peered into her face.

"Sorry. Tired. I was up all night, reinforcing wards on the scribe desk. Kept dissolving..."

Arthur waved that away—he knew. "Help me go through the school. Find students who might be hiding. Transfer them home. Whoever shot Oalthoreh might still be around. We have to send them all home."

"What about Roy? Siamis? Mac, even?"

Arthur shrugged. "Gone. No word."

"Let's get to work."

Four

Shiovhan, capital of Enaeran

ENAERAN WAS ONE OF those kingdoms whose scribe guild merely distributed letters and wrote for people who couldn't. Enaeran was too impoverished, and its kings too suspicious of magic, for messages to go any way but by hand.

That meant messages traveled as fast as a horse could gallop.

That same day in Brydon, Enaeran's royal palace, Gared Inmael, oldest friend to Andri Malcolin Elsarion, opened the door to the informal interview chamber and waved a mud-splashed courier in. The courier handed Andri a dispatch.

Andri hid a spurt of laughter. Bowing. Hah! Six months before he'd been an outlaw, now he *was* the law.

And so went Enaeraneth history.

He slid his boot knife under the seal, and began to read the dispatch.

Gared silently offered the courier some coffee and a roll. The young man accepted gratefully as Andri said, "It's from Porganal."

"Never a good sign," Gared observed, waving the courier to one of the empty chairs.

"He's always done right by us," Andri said, reading the note again. "I'm glad he finally got promoted. I hope the ambassador did, too, after enduring us for twenty-some years."

Gared nodded soberly. "Porganal's gabby. Good heart. But he's an Adrani. If he's writing to you officially, won't be with good news. It'll be whatever Bartal told him to say."

"Right about that. Heh! Here's a surprise. Bartal has received word that several of the kings over the mountains to their east have fallen to Norsundrian infiltrators."

Each reacted characteristically, Andri barking a laugh and Gared shaking his head at the reminder of how very close they had come to being the news themselves when they discovered that Adon Marsael, Andri's distant cousin who tried hard to kill Andri and make himself king, was allied with Norsunder.

Andri snapped the backs of his fingers against the paper. "Further, Adrani border patrols report raiders sneaking along the Adrani mountains to the north. They are dealing with most of them, but a band was sighted heading this way. As per our recent treaty, King Bartal is breaking off a company to send to our aid."

Thadara Otobris, having just entered after seeing the messenger from a window, bowed silently to Andri, scowled at the messenger for daring to sit in the presence of the king, and ignored Gared, who in her eyes was a servant. He ought not to speak until spoken to. He never had anything worthwhile to say. She maintained a pointed silence, waiting for Andri to acknowledge her.

Andri closed his eyes, trying to think, but his thoughts kept scattering. No rest for the wicked, it seemed. Two weeks a king—still recovering from severe wounds—and here he was, facing possible attack. "Raiders," he repeated. He knew city fighting. But he knew nothing about running a battle over land.

He sensed the intensity of Thadara's focus, something he'd warded for several years now. He looked up. There she was, a skinny, somewhat sallow person whose supercilious expression hid a loyal and a brilliant mind when it came to the complexities of trade and treasury. "Thadara, I really need your father," he said apologetically.

Her chin lifted. Anyone else who made any attempt to send her on an errand, even one of state, would be verbally annihilated, but Andri was the exception. "As your Commander of the King's Guard, he ought to be apprised at once," she said. "I will bring him directly." Thereby implying that whatever state discussion was to occur, she planned to be there.

Andri sank into the chair beside the messenger, one hand pressing absently to his side, where the worst of his wounds had barely formed new skin. The healers had nagged him diligently about having risen far too soon, but he'd ignored them out of necessity.

He shut his eyes, thinking, as he often did, of Liere Fer Eider, the Worldsaver. Sometimes, particularly at night when fever would come back, he wondered if she had been a dream. She was exactly as amazing as the legends. More. But she wasn't a dream—his most trusted followers all talked about her. She had gone away with his father's ring, promising to return.

He wanted her to return, especially now, and yet he wondered if life in Enaeran would confine her like an eagle in a cage...

He nodded off, and Gared motioned everyone out. From the color along Andri's cheekbones, he might be feverish again. Sleep, the healers had said, would be best, but there never seemed to be time.

It seemed two breaths later when Andri woke with a start. Gared silently handed him some listerblossom mixed with willow bark. "Baron Otobris is back," he murmured.

Andri had barely enough time to drink it and marshal his soggy wits before Baras Otobris marched in, wearing full court garb plus his sword, his daughter with him. A stiff-necked, rigid individual who tolerated few people and liked fewer, he was the only one person of the elder generation still alive after years of civil war who had had actual military training.

He bowed decorously, and Andri held out the note from the former ambassador's aide. "This is all we know, Commander."

"You trust this missive, your majesty?" Otobris barked.

Andri hid a wince at how loud the man always spoke, as if he was already on the field giving orders to an army. "It came under the royal seal."

"First we must send scouts to ascertain numbers and direction," Otobris stated.

Andri turned to Gared, who tipped his head toward the empty chair next to Andri and said, "Already sent."

Otobris did not like Gared having assumed responsibility, but he acknowledged the necessity for speed. "Then, your majesty, permit me to muster the Guard, so that we may ride out the moment we receive the scouts' report."

"Maybe set out as soon as you muster?" Andri suggested. "This report says they are in the north. Bartal is sending a force to our aid, but I don't want Adrani aid if we can avoid it. I want to take care of the problem on our own."

The baras jerked his chin down in a tiny nod of approval. "My own thought as well, your majesty: we'd do well to intercept these raiders before they touch our border. How will depend on numbers and location."

"Talk to me," Andri said. "What can we do?" *When we have so few in the King's Guard*, was the unspoken addition.

"Ideally we have a fixed force, a maneuverable force, and reserves," the baras said, holding up three fingers. "In reality we have no reserve. Due to the depredations caused by the traitor Adon Marsael, we don't have a fixed force, except our city patrol. But if I may observe, in the two weeks I have had the honor to command the King's Guard—whose numbers are beginning to increase—I believe that our maneuverability and our front line is not discreditable."

"That's good. I know we should choose the field if we can. Isn't that a basic lesson? It sure is in city fighting. What kind of field?"

"We want to draw them into terrain from which we can flank them, terrain that will make the most of our numbers. A flat field is neutral. If we can get them into a valley or chasm, then the steep sides serve to reinforce us, especially with trees to shield us."

"Right, so it's not that different from city fighting. We used the rooftops. Go on. I see you have something else to say."

"It is this, your majesty. I do not believe that you ought to ride with us."

"Of course I will," Andri said. "Won't I look like a rabbit not to be there with you?"

"Most kings," Thadara stated, "do not ride to war. They command from headquarters."

"Enaeraneth kings ride to war," Andri countered. "I haven't read much history since I was ten or so, but I do remember that."

The baras said woodenly, "Which is one reason why we have had so many kings."

Several looked at the ceiling, out the window, or at the floor, except for Gared, who turned a laugh into a cough.

"I thought you were on my side," Andri said, side-eyeing him without turning his body.

And Gared saw it—Otobris's sober gaze lingered pointedly on the bandages Andri still wore. Then he slowly shook his head.

Thadara, irritated that Gared—who ought not even to be there—would be permitted to offer an opinion, said, "*Your majesty*, you have been ill."

Andri locked his jaw; Thadara was the only person who could make a rebuke of that stupid honorific that he still wasn't used to. In the ringing tone of one who knows she has the moral high ground, Thadara could not resist driving her point home. "Warriors we have. We only have one king."

"But I can't lurk here, waiting around," Andri protested.

Thadara then surprised him by saying, "I agree with that. What you ought to do is leave for Sartor. Only you can get to the Queen of Sartor, who professed alliance when she sent that envoy. We need the magical aid that would bring us..."

"Out of backwardness."

"I was going to say, that would enable communications and perhaps something that would ward enemies who use magic." Thadara was reluctant to mention Liere's name, lest it somehow bring her back.

"My Sartoran is terrible," Andri stated. "My princely tutoring ended when I was ten."

"None of us speak correct court Sartoran," Thadara was driven to admit, though she loathed appearing unsophisticated. But she had a point to make. "At least you're a king. If the envoy does not return with magical aid, you are the only one who can ask for it. None of us would get past the first gate."

Gared said, "It'll take a few days to get there, but you can always get them to send you back by one of those magical spells."

Andri sighed. When Gared and Thadara were in agreement, it was usually a bad idea to dismiss them out of hand. He looked at the window, then back. "Commander Otobris, summon the King's Guard and start for the north, with outriders watching for the scouts."

Baras Otobris bowed and strode out, baldric swinging, sword clattering.

Andri faced his new ministers and trusted friends. "I can

see the need to ask for help. We're used to civil war, but this Norsunder threat—magic—is way beyond us. If he had an army coming, I would stay and fight. But I trust Otobris will know better than I how to turf out raiders. And if worse comes to worse, the Adranis will be there to serve as the reinforcement he mentioned. I don't like Bartal, but I'm sure he's as worried about Norsunder as I am. Maybe more so as they are right on his eastern border. Which is surely why he's actually heeding the treaty, the slimy worm."

The others agreed, and Andri declared the meeting over, but waved at Gared to stay.

Thadara was the last to leave, lingering with a disapproving glare back at Gared. But Andri merely waited until the door closed behind her.

"You're not going to sneak up north?" Gared said, appalled.

'No. I know when I'm beaten. But. You aren't going, either."

Gared crossed his arms. "What is this, 'if I can't go you can't go either'?"

"Sure." Andri grinned unrepentantly, then the smile vanished. "Otobris is just like—ah, his forebears," he said, sidestepping Thadara's name. "If you go, he'll put you in charge of the horses. You won't be anywhere near any action."

Gared shrugged. "If your da hadn't died, and mine, I'd be tending horses now."

"Gared, I need someone to watch the city. Thadara is Chief Minister, and she's been excellent with the treasury. But..." Andri stopped. The man he'd respected most while growing up had been Gared's father, the Master of Horse. Who had once said to Andri that people were like horses, made up of good traits and bad. If you worked with the good traits, sometimes that solved the bad. And when it didn't, you looked past them.

So it was with Thadara. She had been superlative while wresting the treasury from those who'd stolen it, and she'd produced what looked to Andri like a miracle of a budget that would get the kingdom out of trouble in the shortest time — she had probably worked on it secretly for a year.

The problem was, she wanted to be queen. And kept stepping on everyone's toes, including Andri's, because the same quality that made her chase down and account for every six-sided coin also made her unswervingly convinced that Andri ought to crown her and let her rule.

Andri said, "I need you here, in charge of the city. The court, the nobles, will be fine. But if Thadara tries running the city, you know she'll offend everyone and there'll be trouble."

Gared could not argue with that. He went off to tend to household patrol matters, and Andri used the time to do as much as he could while lying down. His ministers were all new, his court informal — much to Thadara's disgust — which at least meant they accepted the fact that the king himself had to ride so Sartor for aid. Fighting, they all understood. Magic was beyond them.

Late that afternoon, the King's Guard lined up in the vast courtyard before the king's balcony. Each had weapons and a pack of stores. Andri was also there, ready to ride south.

Unseen by them, Baras Parael Otobris, Commander of the King's Guard personally accompanied Andri to the end of the broad promenade along the ridge above the rest of the city; he would have sent an honor guard, but Andri said privately, "I'm used to running alone, and you need everyone you have. I'll be fine. No one is looking for me, and few outside the capital know my face."

All true. The commander accepted that with a bow. They parted there, Andri riding down a side path, his hat pulled low over his head.

Otobris rode back to the parade square before Brydon's main wing, where his Guard was assembling in their rows, everyone talking. Otobris was deep in thought; he had despised Andri Elsarion, who had been what had seemed at a distance a spoiled, drunken excuse for a prince — but Andri had managed to survive, and Adon Marsael's turning out to be allied with Norsunder made it clear he'd been lying about Andri, exactly as he'd lied to Otobris, promising he would become a minister. A minister. Never a commander.

Andri had come to him the very day he became king, saying, "I understand you trained in Khanerenth."

"Your father sent me," Otobris said. "Seven years, I spent at that military school."

Seven very hard years, where his accent had guaranteed extra rough treatment. But he'd endured it, and even began to excel, leading larger and larger groups as his tactical knowledge widened to strategic thinking.

But when he'd come home at last, full of medals earned, he hadn't seen Alored's enthusiasm turn to distrust until it was too late.

But Alored was gone, and his son had said, "Will you take command of the King's Guard," as if of course he was worthy of trust.

Commander Otobris took a few proud moments to inspect his ranks in their lines. They desperately needed more training; as well their first action would be against mere bush slinkers.

"About face," he roared. "At a walk till we clear the city."

They set out at a clatter, everyone excited at the prospect of whipping a rabble of brigands, and impressing those Adranis in spite of their fancy uniforms and fine weapons. Everyone, from Otobris riding at the front with a plumed helm down to the new stable girl, was eager to get to the enemy first.

By nightfall the King's Guard camped in a field alongside the river. They'd ridden hard. The next day, they left the great river road and headed north toward the contested territory of Ovaish, which belonged to Enaeran, but the Adranis coveted for its rich land and skilled artisans.

Two days later they met up with the tired, mud-splattered scouts, who exclaimed, "They're coming! About half a day off, straight east."

"Number?"

"About the same," the scout said, waving at the King's Guard.

Otobris looked stern at this unmilitary behavior and the imprecision of the report. This was likely one of Gared Inmael's apprentice bakers or shoemakers playing at being a warrior. "Very well. Return to Shiovhan."

The scout was dismissed with a careless wave. Mindful of his orders from Gared, the scout did not argue. He asked to trade mounts, which was granted, got something to eat, and then rode out of sight—and circled back to watch. *Otobris won't tell us anything*, Gared had said. *Andri will want us to know how it goes.*

Commander Otobris had been surveying the terrain as they rode. Now that he had an approximate number, direction, and time of arrival, uncertain as it was, it was enough to work with. He'd already picked his ground when they halted to water the animals.

As a brief thunderstorm rumbled overhead, charging the air with the heavy scent of drenched wild mustard, the Adrani reinforcements appeared out of the slanting gray curtain, muffled in matching cloaks, their hats dripping as they rode in disciplined twos on the other side of the river. That road was far better kept, an Adrani trade town in the distance.

Navor Mandracar rode at the head, remembered from when he had been a brash young patrol captain when Adon Marsael had invited the Adranis into Enaeran years before, triggering riots in Shiovhan.

As well Andri Elsarion did not want Adrani aid. Otobris had not liked to arrogant Mandracar then; even wily old Count Nalwy, the Adrani Commander in Chief, would be preferable. But he didn't want either of their disparaging pairs of eyes on his patched, half-trained force, until he could get a year or two of drill into them.

Otobris forded the stream to meet him, saying, "Take them south, would you? There's far too many — I'm afraid that the attackers will catch sight of your dust and hedge off."

Mandracar, a big, brawny man with glossy black hair, did not argue that the rain had damped any possible dust. He bowed over his horse's withers and held up his hand, winding it in a circle.

His Adranis — this "company" was at least double Otobris's number, maybe more — reversed in perfect order and began to retreat toward the line of cedar in the distance, marking the border of someone's land.

Otobris waved at his chosen bait. Twenty of his best riders trotted east. The rest of the King's Guard slogged through wet grass to hide behind dripping trees, protecting their bowstrings as well as they could. Otobris positioned them along a slope above a stream feeding the little river that formed the eastern border of Ovaish. On the flat side, he put his strongest, hiding under cover until they should be given the signal. Nothing lay behind them except those distant cedars.

West lay the river, a natural border. Otobris sent three scouts east, so that he would have warning well ahead of the bait coming in lathered.

As it happened, they did not need the scouts. The summer storm had long moved in a tumbled blue line to the east. The rumble of horse hooves vibrated underfoot, causing tiny stones to leap and tinkle. The King's Guards felt the chase before the scouts galloped belly flat into the trap shouting, "Here they come!"

Otobris waved them off to the remounts held by the young stable hands at a distance behind a hill; the King's Guards readied themselves, bows now taut, arrows at hand, every pair of eyes turned eastward toward the chase.

The twenty galloped up, then moved to single file, a threat through a long needle. The brigands followed...

Otobris raised his hand. "Shoot!"

Each brigand raised a shield a heartbeat before the arrows hissed through the air.

Bang! Thud! Arrows fell harmlessly on shields as brigands turned with disciplined efficiency, unhooked their own bows from saddles on steaming horses, and then shot back.

The fight was fierce, the brigands very well trained. Too well trained, he saw too late. Otobris rode along the ridge from tree to tree, gazing down—until a horse snorted behind him.

Otobris turned. He froze at the sight of the Adrani reinforcements ranged up close in a half-circle around his trap, four deep. Thirty years between his last wargame and this exercise, and he had forgotten to look behind him.

He found Mandracar by his plumed helm, and raised his hand to wave him off when Mandracar plucked up the bow hooked at his saddle, nocked an arrow, and in a smooth movement, pulled and shot.

Otobris had a single heartbeat to assimilate that the target was not a brigand coming up behind, but himself, before the arrow thunked into his chest. He rocked in the saddle, before pain wrung down him in waves, and his breath stuttered. He tried to blink away the clouds smearing his vision; he barely recognized the shorter, slimmer, swarthy figure behind Mandracar who threw back his shrouding cloak.

"Adan Marsael?" he whispered, and then fell dead, his startled horse shying and then galloping for the river.

It took a few moments longer before the bewildered King's Guard understood that the brigands were actually Adranis, and that they were surrounded. The Adranis sent up a derisive cheer at their easy win; in turn, none of them noticed the scout at a prudent distance wheeling his horse and galloping for home.

Mandracar bowed, and extended a hand to Adon Marsael, who called, "If you lay your weapons down now, we won't have to leave a slaughter here for the local farmers to have to clean up. Shall we?"

Bewildered looks turned to grim realization, fear, sullen anger, sidled glances. They hadn't a hope of winning, and their commander lay dead on the ground. Swords dropped into the mud. Bows clattered on top.

"Good. Good! Now, let's go back home, and restore order, shall we? But first, an unfortunate accident, unavoidable in the rain." Adon Marsael said cheerily as he drew his sword and searched among the faces. "Ah, where is Andri Elsarion?"

Five

TWO DAYS' EASY RIDE from the eastern end of the Sartoran Sea, in the tiny kingdom of Remalna, Meliara Astiar, the queen, said to the king on their way out of morning court, "Danric, hot as it is, I've got to get some ginger steep."

Vidanric cast a puzzled glance at Meliara. Then his brow cleared. He dropped a kiss on her damp forehead, which expression she perfectly understood. She'd told him two days previously what she'd suspected for a couple of weeks, that their third child was on the way.

He was happy—she knew it—but he was also distracted. "I'm going to my desk, then I'll meet you in the nursery."

She watched him run up the stairs for the third time that morning while fighting another, stronger surge of nausea. She leaned her forehead on the marble stair rail, and closed her eyes; she should have eaten breakfast, though it was so very warm already... All she had to do was get up the stairs to the nursery...

She was vaguely aware of footsteps, but shut everything out until she registered a smooth, green scent. Oh! She breathed it in more deeply, drawing it into her lungs, where it dissipated the nastiness that had threatened to claw its way to her throat.

She opened her eyes to discover a maidservant standing there with a fresh pot and a cup already poured. "The king sent me," she said.

Meliara lifted the cup and sipped, ignoring the scald on her tongue. The ginger and whatever other herbs were in the steamed brew banished the nausea like fog before the sun.

A short time later, she sank gratefully onto a cushion in the nursery, where two round, tousled heads were bent over a structure that seemed to be made up of wooden blocks, twigs, and rocks from the garden: her son seemingly frail, his pale hair falling forward over his brow, his friend-like-a-brother sturdier, shoulders already giving signs of strength to come, his glossy black hair hiding his profile.

"Raec? Let's get the water," Nadav Savona said.

"Won't hold," Alaraec replied. Mel hugged herself. Alaraec — not Shevraeth. She hadn't wanted her son called by his title, and though Danric had grown up hearing it when it was his, he'd agreed.

"Sure it will hold," Nadav asserted with the certainty of near seven years.

Raec didn't argue. He never argued — unlike his mother, Meliara sometimes thought, in secret relief. He was more like his father, or maybe his Uncle Bran. He smiled sunnily, turned his head, and spotted his small sister Elestra, who lay on her stomach directly under the window, apparently oblivious to the strong sun shining in as she pored intently over a book of drawings.

"Les," Raec said, his tone so exactly like that used by Meliara's brother Branaric when he'd called her "Mel" at the same age, her heart constricted at the memory. "Fetch us a cup? We have to hold this lake together."

Elestra jumped up and trotted to the pitcher, lank brown braids swinging. Just as Meliara had done when she was small.

Nadav took the cup from her unsteady hands, poured it into the middle of the mess, then gave a cry of dismay. "It's leaking!"

"I think we have to put a bowl under." Raec's gray gaze was serious as he considered. "And put the rocks around the outside. Then we don't have to see the bowl."

Elestra pointed. "Your water messed."

Meliara loved the way her kids spoke, loved every error,

every tumbled set of ideas. They would get correction soon enough when the tutors got at them.

Three heads turned her way. She'd thought they were oblivious to her presence. No, they'd noticed, she was just unimportant compared to the work going on. "Mama?" Raec asked.

Since she'd already disrupted them, she supposed she ought to be a proper mother and get them to prepare for the noon meal. "Time to clean up."

"Do we have to do it *now*?"

Vidanric's voice came from behind. "If this room is tidy before we eat, we might make a surprise trip afterward."

Meliara turned her head, ready for a smile, a kiss, but her questioning gaze met a strained glance from Vidanric.

The three yelled in delight, and began dismantling their project; Elestra tottered off for a rag.

"What is it?" Mel asked, whispering, though the children paid no heed. Or seemed to, she amended mentally.

"A note from my contact in Sles Adran," Danric said, and led her outside the door. He gave a nod to the minder on duty, who slipped inside to supervise the children.

"Another note? Isn't that the second one today?"

"Third. Meliara, I told you a few days ago about that row of small countries north of us."

"I remember. Norsunder, allies with each other, hoped most of it was rumor. Trouble with the scribe desks, not just ours, but at the guild hall and even in Sartor." Meliara had been studying magic, but scrying still was difficult—and the scribe desk was really nothing but scrying. As well they didn't really use the scribe desk within the palace; the one at the guild hall was far more popular with merchants conducting trade outside the country.

"The scribe desks are dead," Vidanric said. "No letters via magic transfer, except through the golden notecases, which do not rely on the scribe magic. Second, Enaeran has fallen."

"Enaeran," she repeated. "Wait, didn't they just end a civil war?"

"There is worse news. Bartal na Shagal is allied with Norsunder, backing Adon Marsael, who marched into Enaeran yesterday with an Adrani army to retake it. My contact says it was the last message reported before the scribe desks went dead."

Meliara scowled. "You were right about Bartal of Sles Adran."

"I'd hoped to be wrong," Vidanric murmured.

"What does that mean for us?"

"What it seems to mean right now is that Sles Adran is offering itself as a staging base for Norsunder. No doubt supplies as well. What they get out of it, I suspect, is being left alone, at least while Norsunder invades everywhere else."

"Everywhere else like...here?" Meliara asked, looking wildly at the windows in fearful expectation of armed warriors smashing in. "An army is going to overrun *us?*" Horror chilled her, then she said loyally, "We have a wonderful army. And you've been doing those strategy meetings with Senrid of Marloven Hess. You've been *hosting* them! That means we know how to fight Norsunder off, right?"

He said gently, "We have a small number of good-hearted and fairly well-trained people willing to rise as a militia to protect our borders from roaming parties of brigands, but we wouldn't be able to resist if Lamanca sent a force over the border, much less Sles Adran."

He held out his hand, and she gripped it. "You mean, we just surrender? Let them rule us without a fight?"

"Not without a fight," Danric said. "But that might have to come later. Meliara, the truth is that if any of our larger neighbors invaded, our army would not last a day."

Mel gazed back at him, sick with helpless anger. "Then what was the use of all those meetings with the Queen of Sartor, and Senrid, and the rest of them?"

"To plan for how to deal with disaster," he said heavily.

Her eyes stung. Just this morning everyone was joking in court, teasing Branaric about his absent-mindedness. *Next year's Name Day?* Trisha had resurrected the old joke when Bran had forgotten a date. *Next year for sure*, Bran had said. He never minded being teased.

She'd hoped with all her being that they were done with war. They'd earned the right to peaceful lives. Remalna was not only peaceful but prosperous again, children being born to families nearly wiped out by the horrible Galdran Merindar.

But Norsunder didn't care about fairness.

She wanted to stamp and rant. And she knew that Danric would listen, but what effect would a rant have now? Nothing beyond her own satisfaction. Certainly not Danric's.

She drew a deep breath. "All right. It sounds like we have to go straight to the contingency plans. When do we start?"

Danric kissed her, wordless acknowledgement of her own private battle fought and won. She sensed his own battle fought and won in the quick tumble of words that followed, "I just now sent pages to spread the news through court, and to the guild hall to get word out to the people. Some will insist on fighting. Others will want to head for the hills, as our ancestors did."

"What about us," Meliara asked.

His smile thinned. "I've a different task."

She sucked in a breath of pleasure. "To save the kingdom?"

"We can't defend against invading armies," he said gently. "My Adrani merchant said that the last report he had from Enaeran is a massive manhunt for their new king. Which matches the pattern established in the fallen countries so far: the capture and holding of rulers—killing the ones who can lead armies—and occupation."

"Capturing rulers? As hostages?"

"That, but, according to a message from Atan yesterday, she admitted she is forced to give credence to a rumor that Norsunder is going to bespell these people somehow. Then put them back in to rule, but following directives from someone else."

"Who?"

"Norsunder." Vidanric threw his hands wide. "I realize that can actually mean different things, but at this moment all I see is evil intent. I wrote to the others in our alliance, suggesting we attempt to free these people, and hide them up in our hills. Norsunder has avoided the Colorwoods in the past. I don't see that changing now."

"Hostage rescue," she repeated. "How..." She saw the tension in his face, and decided discussion could wait. She had never been good at planning. Her strengths lay elsewhere. "What shall I do?"

"Take the children up into Tlanth, and hole up in your old hideout. It could be that some of the other court children will be sent with you. Whatever happens, I want to prevent the enemy from using our children against us."

Six

REL KNEW NOTHING OF strategy and didn't particularly want to learn. He hated war, and sometimes had found his mind wandering during those strategy sessions. But when Senrid made specific suggestions, he'd listened.

One of those suggestions had been: when you have a very small force, you augment it with everything available. Including your knowledge of the home ground. The land. The water. The trees.

For weeks, Rel's teams had boobytrapped the road Norsunder Base's force would have to take. Every bridge was carefully tampered with so that it would collapse. Streams were dammed to brimming pools, ready to swamp camps and wash out roads. Mage students volunteered to tramp over the rough terrain for days, along with Rel's city guard. As a result, illusions not only replaced the old direction plinths, but they obscured landmarks, hiding ditches and swampy pools, and making good road look treacherous, so that nothing could be trusted.

There was no stopping the Norsunder invasion. Rel and his guard knew that. But their hard work paid off by slowing them down. Rel, hiding under cover with a handful of his best fighters — everyone else firmly sent away — watched with fierce pleasure as two bridges collapsed while marching warriors were in the middle. After that, the Norsundrians had to find ways around all bridges, which took even longer than pulling themselves out of the water amid splinters and rocks.

Each precious day won enabled Atan, working feverishly in the city, to strengthen old wards, and to shift her government's records to the Tower of Knowledge. It had been protected for centuries during times of troubles, a gift of non-human peoples to her earliest ancestors in trade for their promise to protect the land and all life, not just the humans building on the land.

As Atan raced about, she wondered what Shendoral would do about the invasion. There was no knowing. Shendoral was...strange. In that woodland, time could not be trusted, but one law was inescapable: take a life, lose a life.

But Norsunder knew that. They would give that woodland wide berth.

The scribe desk scry stones had gone blank, but Atan still had her golden notecase. At first, she carried it with her, but the steady progression of grim news made it so that every time the internal alert pinged her, she jumped, then had to suppress the instinct to throw the thing, as if she could reject whatever terrible thing had happened now. She began leaving it in her room, and forcing herself to deal with it all at once.

Because each day's news seemed worse than the previous.

She hadn't thought it was possible to get worse than the first night when Rel appeared in her suite, hair dripping rain. "We've finished the bridges," he said. "News?"

"The scribe desks have blanked," she reported, laying her hand on her golden notecase. "Erai-Yanya and Arthur both report that Oalthoreh was assassinated. Bereth Ferian's Destination is down. Arthur also says that the young king in Land of the Venn is not answering letters — Arthur was going to offer him sanctuary in Roth Drael."

Rel shook his head, hoping that Karendal of the Venn was merely hiding. "Always thought Oalthoreh was too tough to die."

"Even the toughest can't withstand a crossbow bolt," Atan retorted dryly. "We will not be seeing the northern mages back to help. Arthur has sent them to their homes to hide, until we know more."

Rel looked at the golden notecase. "You should probably keep that on you, not just near you."

Atan whispered, "I can't bear it."

Rel didn't argue.

He was gone before morning, back to his boobytrapping. He reappeared two days later, to find her sitting at the window, staring down at the Purrad in a sightless way that shot alarm through him, tired as he was.

"Atan?"

Her expression was strange. "Sles Adran has marched on the little countries bordering the sea. Including Remalna. At least Vidanric and Meliara are safe. After that, the news..." She took a shuddering breath. "My ambassador in Colend reported that the entire regency council—the former regency council—is dead. Shontande Lirendi is a prisoner, no one knows where."

Rel knelt down beside her. "Colend has been invaded?"

That was when the tears began to gather in her eyes and fall. "That was the last message. My ambassador has not written back."

He put her arms around her, neither speaking. He left that night, for what he knew was the last set of obstructions. They had won nearly ten days. The city seemed like it was empty, with no one on the streets. The rare window lit golden.

When he returned midday the next day, she was gone, but lying on the desk was her golden notecase, with a much-folded letter lying open beside it.

Next to it, a thin paper in a shaky hand that Rel realized with a shock was Tsauderei's. Giving a report on Sarendan, over the mountains east of Sartor.

Four days ago ten boats landed off the shore and marched on Miraleste during the night. The fighting was fierce over the following days, until they cornered and killed Darian Irad today. He took a horde of them with him. They killed Lilah first.

The only good news I can report is that little Prince Darian could not be found; I'm told that Lilah's last words were to beg him to run while she charged the enemy. Mirah saw her fall, and swears her death was so quick that she had not time to suffer. I have to remind myself that sometimes the most violent deaths are the best in that they are quick. And yet, in all my long life, the ending of young lives has never gotten any easier to accept. And Lilah's is so much worse because she was never a threat to anyone.

At least Darian Irad heeded your warning and sent his wife, daughter, and the little son off to Geth- deles. But I don't know who will tell them. I don't want it to be me.

Rel threw the paper down, walking about the room without seeing anything. Darian Irad had begun life as a military prince, then a king, constantly prepared for war. Apparently he ended as one, though strictly speaking he had insisted he was a regent.

But Lilah? Happy, friendly Lilah, who knew nothing of weapons? Killing her was just cruel.

Rel sank down into a chair, his appetite gone. There Atan found him much later, sitting in the dark.

She lit a lamp and came to him. "I've booted the rest of the servants out. Told them to go hide. Those who insisted on staying at least know what they're facing. More or less," she said, taking his hands. Hers were trembling. "I saw Tsauderei's handwriting, so shaky, and I couldn't read it. Then I couldn't not read it. Oh, Rel, I walked out and tried to stay busy, but memory kept striking my heart. Everywhere I go, no matter what I do, I see the shapes and shadows of Lilah and even Peitar, though he's been gone, what, five years? Six? It seems like yesterday."

Her voice softened to a low murmur. "It was that day when we first regained the kingdom. I walked into my parents' room, and though it had been a century, that room looked as if they had just walked out. My mother's nightdress flung across the bed. Though we had regained the kingdom, it still hurt—and Lilah understood. Young as she was, she had lost both parents to tragedy. She understood."

A small silence, then Atan sniffed and wiped her eyes. "All right. I'm ready. Let's hear it. I can feel it, you've got more bad news, We might as well share it since we cannot prevent it."

"They'll be here tomorrow," he said.

"I know." She drew an unsteady breath. "Rel, they're still grabbing leaders. Let's stick to our plan."

"I don't like it," he said.

"I know," she said again, low and tender. "But we'll do it, just the same. I have to be here, or they will kill everyone they see. You do not have to be here. If our plan fails—if I die but they let the people live—it's the last gift I can give Sartor."

He drew her wordlessly into his arms.

The next day she dressed for riding. She and Rel went down to the Destination together, and though he still looked unhappy, she said, "All you are to them is a target. We have our plan."

And he was gone.

Linet appeared, somewhat human if one overlooked the blue skin. "Take it out of the world," Atan said.

Linet nodded, and the Destination glowed pearlescent, then...there was just an empty space.

"Put a chair in it," Atan said to Gehlei, her steward, and Gehlei's wife, who had insisted on staying, though she was an artisan, not a palace servant. "An ugly one. Then hide."

The two went away, Atan walked alone to the tower to fetch her father's sword. It lay on a pillow, a heavy weapon passed down through generations of Landises. He had from time to time come to look it, never touching it, knowing that father's hand had gripped it last, loosening only in death. Her father, a visionary and poet, who had loathed strife, but had died after seeing the greatness of his kingdom torn apart in the useless destruction of war.

She hefted it, and turned it over, then made an experimental pass. She could tell from its weight that it had been made for a sizable figure; her father had been a short, slim man, but she took after older ancestors in size.

She held the sword as she led the defenders out through the old gates to the road. There she stopped, gazing at the broad fields beyond the city, brown from the late summer sun. She turned her head to both sides, details preternaturally sharp: the wind in the grasses, an early leaf fluttering from a twisted oak. The determination, the desperation in the faces around her as her untrained, undisciplined, formless army cleaved together in a mass before the gates.

Images. Cruel as shards of glass, the high, fear-edged voices as people exchanged words— "Make them face the sun if you can," and "Why don't you sit down? I know how bad your knee is" —a pair of duchases determined to face the enemy trembling, knuckles white on the grips of jewel-hilted, inherited weapons; a pair of brown eyes in a young face, watching, the young hands gripping a scythe. A woman with an old-style halberd, a vein beating in her high temple.

From the rear of the group voices rose in an old marching song. As people joined, the sound swelled, gathering strength, sung by high, tight voices, the timing ragged, as some rode, some walked, forward, forward, to meet that line now visible.

The Norsundrians halted, waiting motionless in the formation she had read about in old accounts. The outer shape of war had changed little; it was individual actions that decided it. She recognized the heavily cavalry at the back, skirmishers on the wings. At the front, lances, armor. Crossbows interspersed among the foot, and the faster bowmen. And ranks of foot-soldiers, at least five to every one of her haphazardly armed subjects, all lined and ready to advance. A ridiculous number, considering that they had to know that the only military Sartor had was Rel's small city guard.

The Sartorans had lost before they began, and she knew her people knew it. She saw it in the pale faces, the nervous hands, the anguish under the brave voices as the wind whipped away the brave melody. But still the singers persisted, as old Duchas Chechye's mare sidled and snorted, her ears slanting back.

She met Chechye's eyes, old, discerning. "It's our choice to be here," he said, his voice hoarse, and not pitched to carry. "We die quick and clean and with honor, or else at their leisure." He jerked his head contemptuously toward the dark line. His helm glinted in the sun.

Not if I can prevent it, she did not say aloud. My last act as queen. Atan's sword hilt was slippery in her cold, sweaty palm.

Her people milled about, some pushing forward to see, others arguing for space. Silence had fallen in the front; in the rear, she still heard the song.

An old woman brandishing an iron frying pan. Near them, two boys the age she had been when she first walked into Eidervaen in a dress she had made herself—fifteen—laughing boisterously, one's neck so, so skinny.

Then, from the one of the Norsundrian cavalry wings, a

Norsundrian kicked his horse into a gallop right off the line. Not one of the heavy cavalry — this one wore only mail and a coat. A messenger?

The song wavered, and died.

The messenger rode directly to Atan, and reined in hard. Atan looked at that face. A youngish man, pale, his brown hair — same color as her own — neatly cut, his demeanor contemptuous.

"Yustnesveas Landis," he said, his voice carrying. "My commander Bostian offers you the chance of surrendering your person immediately, or we slaughter this band of idiots before moving on and torching your city. If you surrender, your people will submit to martial rule, but we will not loot or burn."

"Refused," Chechye said.

"Return to your commander and tell him I agree."

The young man wheeled his horse, and he rode away again at the gallop.

"Why didn't you tell him no?" Chechye said, as the growing ring of people crowded about to listen. "Better death than dishonor. Better Eidervaen be rubble than house that filth."

"Filth washes away, Albar," she said, and did the magic to return her father's sword to its pillow in the tower. She raised her voice. "The way he worded it, people would be dying for me. Not for honor. Not for Sartor."

The enemy was on the move. People turned to face them.

Atan walked forward, braced for humiliation, but they were taking no chances. A big man emerged out of the orderly ranks. "What are you waiting for?" he said, waving a hand. "Make it happen."

That same young man from before slapped a transfer coin against her shoulder, and magic wrenched her away, flinging her back into the world amid a nostril-singing whiff of burnt metal. Her first dark magic transfer.

Seven

Sartoran Sea to Sartor's Border

WHILE HIS NEW KING'S Guard rode north, Andri Elsarion rode south to Ghend, where he bought passage on a trade ship fighting contrary winds to Ela Harbor in Mardgar, the eastmost point of the Sartoran Sea.

He slept through the first two days of the ship journey, which helped him beat the fever at last. The following days he tried to contain his impatience with the slowness of sea travel. He'd never seen the ocean before, which changed color not just every day, but several times a day, depending on sun and clouds. He occupied himself watching the mysterious manipulation of ropes and sails and helm that kept them tacking against the winds.

The sailors liked to scare the more demanding passengers with graphic descriptions of land people being snatched by mer folk, ships smashed beneath the water at a strike by huge undersea creatures, and the like. Andri listened unmoved; he figured no creature, whether with tentacles or fins, could be any worse than someone like Adon Marsael, or Yeres of Norsunder.

They smelled land before they saw it, a heavy scent of growing things. It reminded Andri of the way fields smelled after a spring rain.

Eventually they saw the uneven juts of land on either side, stretching out like ruffled wings to enfold them and pull them to the harbor in the center. But as soon as the little trade vessel spotted the forest of masts blocking their view of Ela, the captain scowled and spat over the side. "Not good," he said. "Not good at all."

"What?" a merchant harrumphed, elbowing up next to the captain. "What do you mean, not good?"

Andri leaned on the rail at the captain's other side. "What is it you see?"

"Usually there's ten, twenty ship waiting in them roads for the tide to turn, for to carry 'em out. I never in sixty year seen so many. They must be a hundred there, waitin'. Well, we won't be huntin' a berth, methinks."

"What does that mean?" another merchant asked, her expression worried. "I have an entire year's worth of yeath down in the hold."

"You can always sell yeath," the big merchant said, scowling. "The wool market, now..."

The captain ignored the bickering about prices, commodities, and who had it worse when a market might be uncertain, saying to Andri, "We'll speak one or two, soon's we're in earshot. Then we'll know what's what."

The trader drifted closer to the waiting mass of ships. The crew focused on trickly navigation, weaving between waiting ships on the last of the tide.

As they passed within shouting distance, occasionally one of the sailors up on the foremast called, "What news?"

The first one who answered roared, "Don't you know nothin'? They say Sartor's under siege!"

"Who is besieging them?"

"Nightlanders, that's the rumor. Might be anyone," came the answer as the two ships drew farther apart. "Market is a wreck unless you got travel goods."

The following ship said, "Harbor's a mess. Prices sky high, no food to be had. We're moving on."

The next shouted, "Don't know nothin' about Sartor, but word is, the Adranis are going a-conquering. And they're right there." A thick finger pointed along the northern shore. "All I know is, war kills trade."

Several ships were packed with worried faces, loaded so

much they rode low in the water.

The closer they drew to the harbor, the wilder the rumors got. When Andri overheard that all of Sartor was on fire, every head turned toward the south, where the sky was clear and summer-bright. After that, he paid no attention to anything beginning with the words *they say*, or *rumor has it*.

The captain was wrong about berths along the piers. These were all filled with ships loading people aboard, mostly merchants by the looks of them.

The trader anchored far out, and lowered a longboat. Andri joined those who wanted to go ashore. The last he heard of the trader was the captain leaning over the rail and arguing hoarsely with a man in a little boat flying a bright red flag; a harbor boat, someone said. The shouting match over what sounded like swingeing prices for anchorage faded behind them.

Andri had thought the sea was crowded, but that was nothing compared to the land. He elbowed his way through thick crowds of people seeking passage on any vessel going. Wild prices got quoted, cursed, and shouted on all sides — five, ten times higher than he'd paid to travel from Ghend to Mardgar.

He gave up the idea of finding an inn or hiring a horse, though the sun was nearly touching the waters westward by then. It was summer, the sky clear. He could sleep outside if he had to. And he had saved the biscuits they'd passed out for the morning meal; they'd be stale by nightfall but he'd eaten stale biscuits before. If anything, they were more filling because it took so long to gnaw them.

He found the southern road, with a stone plinth saying SARTOR in three different alphabets. This was the right direction. Maybe the crowds would begin to thin.

They did not. He began walking on the verge after a solid hour, from distant bell clang to bell clang, of trying to make headway through the flow of riders, carters, and people trudging toward Ela Harbor. Here and there fancy carriages, with teams of horses — once he saw a highly decorated coach and six — were stuck, unable to get past the rest, in spite of the outriders bawling, "Make way!"

When dark began to fall, he peered in both directions until he spotted the type of greenery that grew alongside streams. He followed one up until he got a hill between him and the refugees — by now he knew they were not traders but refugees—and camped, after eating one of his biscuits.

Glad he'd brought a cloak in spite of the weather, he wrapped up, lay on sweet grass, and slept until the darkness began to lift. Working at the rock-hard last biscuit, he started toward the road still jammed with refugees, many of whom had clearly camped right where they sat down in the road.

What now? Turning right around and going home seemed impossible, and might even be stupid unless he found out what was going on. So far, all he had were rumors.

He tried asking people who looked like they knew what they were doing, but the language barrier kept him from understanding the answer outside of a few common words. Even so, he recognized "Norsunder" and "They say."

Push on, he decided. He'd come this far. Unless he saw actual fighting, he'd go until he found definite news.

By midmorning, as he toiled along the verge of the road, which meant surmounting hills and ditches, he began to realize that he was not the only traveler going south. At first his attention was idle when he spotted a slight figure with brown braids ahead. When he caught sight of that same figure a couple of times, he realized it was not searching among the refugees, as he'd surmised.

He increased his stride when he spotted the angles of rooftops on a distant hill. The sky had begun to cloud when he reached the town. It was as crowded as the harbor had been. He heard a mix of languages, some familiar enough for him to understand snatches of talk: "It'll be over in a week," and "I can't believe what they are asking for bread!" and "I'll stay here as long as my goods hold out. Where would I go?"

Word of an inn donating soup spread; he found himself in a press of people, and ended up in a line. Patience was rewarded—everyone got a ladle of bean soup. He drank his in three swallows, put the cup in the cleaning bucket as ordered, and wondered if he ought to rejoin the line again or not. Three sips of soup on top of one small biscuit was not enough to ward hunger.

But in the time he stood uncertainly, the groans and angry shouts as word spread that the donated soup was gone, made the decision for him.

He sheltered under an awning as the storm passed overhead, then set out again into a dripping world. The town gave way to road again, on both sides nothing but fields of long brown grass, punctuated by old oak, as the sun crawled toward the sea in the west. Clouds sailed overhead, casting the world in shadow, light, shadow.

Atop the road, he saw that figure again. A girl, he was fairly certain. Curious, he lengthened his strides. The hills began to get steeper; as he topped each he saw he was getting closer, until he finally caught up with her as the late afternoon sun smoldered above a distant hill.

"Going to Sartor too?" he asked, having dredged up his old Sartoran lessons.

She turned, then stared in surprise. Was she familiar? He was fairly certain she was familiar; he had definitely seen that scar down one side of her face.

"Andri Elsarion?" she asked, speaking his own language.

"You know me?"

"I saw you once or twice," she said. "How's Jaydi?"

"He hates morning school," Andri said. "How do you know him? How do you know me?"

"My name is Julian," the girl said. She was an ordinary teenage girl, sturdily made, her only distinctive feature a pair of protuberant eyes with heavy lower lids. "I'm the one who sicced Liere Fer Eider on you."

"What?"

"I traveled through there, stopped for a meal, and saw a boy and a girl being chased by a mob of blue uniforms."

"Talipin," Andri sighed.

"I saw a sack of peas. Kicked it over. The pursuit tripped and fell. The boy came back around. Introduced himself as Jaydi. They were trying to get food. I helped them, and Jaydi asked me if I knew anything about Norsunder—he was worried about his leader, you, and said he thought he over-heard something about Norsunder."

"Jaydi always had good instincts. That, and he's incurably nosy." Andri laughed. "You speak my language really well for someone there such a short time."

"My cousin put the Universal Language Spell on me," Julian said. "Anyway, I told my cousin, and she told Liere."

Andri accepted that, assuming the cousin was one of the underlings working for the Queen of Sartor. He was more interested in the Universal Language Spell—which he could ask about later. "So my reputation has preceded me? I wonder if that will be a help or a hindrance with yon queen." He jerked his chin southwards toward Sartor.

"If you mean my cousin," Julian said, "she listens to what others say about a person, but she reserves judgment for what the person himself says or does. Or herself. Here, let's talk while we go."

"Your cousin?" Andri repeated. "Who is..."

"Yustnesveas Landis. I call her Atan."

"Oh." Atan—Liere had mentioned an Atan, Andri remembered. He'd thought she was one of the queen's staff. Trying to assimilate the fact that this girl without princess trappings or outriders was cousin to the Queen of Sartor, he said, "I wondered why you're going south. We seem to be the only ones heading that way."

"Got a warning." Julian shook her head. "A bird. Sent by this old hermit mage named Igkai I met once. Heard of him?"

"I don't know any mages, young or old," Andri began, then he remembered that Liere knew magic.

"Mostly takes care of animals. I happened to help once, when, oh, it's a long story. The thing is, if he sends a messenger, it's never a good idea to ignore them. 'Trouble, trouble, trouble,' the bird said, right in my face. It knew me. I don't know how. I didn't remember it, but Aronis, a friend, thinks some animals have a kind of Dena Yeresbeth—oh, never mind what that is. I left the ship I was on. I've been hurrying back to Eidervaen."

"Trouble that a mage warned you about? A mage who talks to animals?" He was thinking: mysterious mages, Universal Language Spell, talking birds...he was entering Liere's world.

He said, "I'm on my way to ask for magical help. Figured if I pointed south and said *Sartor?* people would wave me along, and your queen would take pity on me. How far to the Sartoran border?" Andri peered down the road. He was tired, but restless. The mention of Liere Fer Eider intensified his hunger to be home.

Julian squinted against the sinking sun at the distant mountains. "Few days. There's a huge inn ahead, at the crossroads. I was hoping to make it by nightfall. Hire a horse, but I suspect those are not to be found."

Andri lifted his shoulder in an assenting shrug. "I've noticed herds of them here and there in the distant hills. Abandoned, I suspect, by people heading for the sea."

"I've seen them. But I can't run fast enough to catch one," Julian said.

"Ah, there's a trick to catching horses."

"Magic?"

"I don't know any magic. You make them curious."

"Teach me that trick! Town's over to the right," Julian said. "If we hurry we might make it before it goes completely dark."

They skirted the road altogether, which was still filled with refugees. Not a good sign, but Andri reserved judgment; he'd come this far, at least he ought to get solid news. And this girl spoke both languages. All languages?

Presently they spotted the crossroads town. Fewer traveled the east-west road. Most were heading north,

Julian pointed at a long, low building. Yellow light shone through windows, highlighting old curtains. They passed under the sign written in vertical characters, and Julian said knowledgeably that the sign had to date back at the least to the reign of Yustnesveas's father, a century ago—before enchantment had frozen them all in time.

"What's it say?" Andri asked.

"Post of the Autumn City," Julian translated. She snorted. "Down here, just about every place lays claims to the days of Old Sartor."

"Eidervaen was one of the Ancient Sartoran cities, right?" Andri asked as they entered the crowded.

"Autumn City—Ildervaen." Julian said.

Her attitude was casual, as if the weight of all that history was as everyday as the weight of stone, of ageless trees and mountains. For the first time since his headlong flight from home, Andri felt the excitement of actually being in Sartor, most ancient kingdom in the world.

A stable hand came out of the barn, a lantern swinging in her hand, and Julian addressed her. "Filled up?"

"Rooms are gone, but you can swing a hammock here in the stable."

Julian translated for Andri, who said, "Grab it."

"If they let us get a hammock, that ought to mean they have food," Julian said. "My stomach is so empty it's stuck to my spine."

They entered a massive common room. Julian watched Andri assess the people in the huge common room made of timber so old it had turned the color of stone. He chose a spot between two exits, with his back to a wall. She also watched the other patrons' appraisals of Andri: the cat-like walk despite scruffy riding boots, the sword at his side that he wore so comfortably, the hilts visible in his boot tops and at his belt. But he nodded, smiled, made no threatening gestures, and so the other people turned back to their conversations.

Julian had debated what to say and do. She still didn't know what had happened after Liere left for Enaeran. She said to Andri, "If you'll order two of whatever they're offering, even if it's leftover leek soup, I'll see if I can find someone who knows what's happening in Eidervaen."

She took off, walking among the tired travelers, until she vanished behind a pillar. A harried woman appeared, and said in a rush, "All that's left is fish and potato soup."

"We'll take it," Andri said quickly.

The woman went away, Julian came back, her eyes gleaming with unshed tears, her face a white line. "I have to leave *now*."

"First tell me what's wrong."

"Norsunder took Eidervaen," she said tightly, ignoring the hot tears blinding her. "My cousin sent the people out herself, before they got her. There's bad news everywhere. The king on the north side of the Sartoran Sea came out as a Norsundrian ally. Sles Adran. The woman, a scribe, said the scribe desks are no more, but the last she heard is, Norsunder is taking leaders prisoner for some evil spell or other. Rel's guard is only a few people. I have to go help her..."

Andri looked away, his mind reeling with anger, remorse, worry. It didn't take Dena Yeresbeth to perceive Julian's agonizing over what she could do to fight Norsunder.

"Who else in this country knows magic?" Andri asked.

Julian choked on a sob of fury. "If Sartor fell you can be sure Enaeran was overrun days ago. Nobody will be able to help you. Now get out of my way, I've got to go—"

Andri said, "Look here, Julian. That news has to be a few days old, this far from your capital. That means you're too late to do anything for your cousin. If Norsunder is here, and you ride into Eidervaen as the queen's cousin, you're asking to be grabbed and used as a hostage against whoever's left. You're free right now. Use it to Sartor's advantage."

"How?" She sniffed and scrubbed her nose defiantly on her damp tunic.

"By finding out the current news, and an ally who can help us."

"Us?" She sniffed and snorted.

Andri smiled grimly. "If it's true that Enaeran is overrun—and I mean to find out—then I need to avoid being added to their collection of kings. Is this Rel any kind of aid?"

"Rel? He's the best—"

"Great. Let's find him. Where does he live?"

"Wait, wait, wait. There was this plan, Atan told me before I went sailing. She said if Norsunder attacked, that the alliance was to meet up in this very small town in a small kingdom, to plan how to fight back. Rel even bought a house there, as a contingency."

"Are there mages in this alliance?"

"It's full of them!"

"How long does it take to get there from here?"

"Three or four weeks, if the weather permits and the mounts are fast..."

Andri paused as the innkeeper thumped down two half-full plates with more potato than fish, but at least there was bread.

Andri leaned toward Julian. "Assuming Enaeran's lost, what say we team up. You handle the language, I'll find horses. How about we try to make it in two?" he invited.

Eight

Zranf - Halarialgre

WHILE ANDRI AND JULIAN began their ride inland, Bostian, the conqueror of Sartor, began to consider where he could stash his new prisoner Queen Yustnesveas, last of the long Landis line. The problem was, though he styled himself King of Sartor now, he was not in command of the invasion by any sense. And both commanders of the invasion wanted that precious prisoner for themselves. But the action was far too complicated to take the time to lay on the needed wards and spells quite yet.

Then there was the question of a suitable prison for so important a prisoner. It required a formidable keep—which Eidervaen did not have. That had been offered by Bartal na Shagal of Sles Adran. And that was the problem. Bostian had perforce sent her on, but he intended that to be temporary. He needed Yustnesveas Landis in a formidable keep commanded by someone who was too stupid to turn around and use this vitally important prisoner against him while he went on to more interesting pursuits than guard duty.

And he knew just the person.

The royal city of Tsranf, carved into a spectacularly steep granite escarpment, had been built centuries ago as a fortress.

Though traders and civilians had moved in when one of its kings made it his capital four hundred fifty years ago, it had never succeeded in being rendered less martial in appearance — not that any subsequent rulers could agree on what to do long enough to actually put plans in motion.

In an area famed for sudden changes of government, constant factional squabbling, rotten roads, and the rise and fall of robber chieftains like wildflowers in summer, one thing could be trusted: the sturdiness of their buildings — once the people actually agreed on what to put up. Living so close to mountains, where storms were guaranteed to boil up with far more power than the same weather patterns generated over the lowlands, notions such as government might be ephemeral, but since everyone agreed buildings had to be sturdy, that meant they had to last, and that meant the design should please the most.

The southeastern portion of the city, being closest (and even right on the banks of) the river Fal, belonged to trade. Those merchants took no interest in the ornamental corbels and window boxes preferred by those higher up in the city; they wanted raised bridges and pillars to accommodate the spring floods.

The city had never been popular with the court during peacetime because the sun vanished behind the mountain early in spring and summer, and very early during fall and winter, leaving the city in shadow. Tsranf was gloomy, always considerably colder than the weather elsewhere, and the rocky ground grew little beyond the most stubborn scrubby trees and shrubs.

Various rulers or councils of rulers of Halarialgre, balked of redesign, had done their best to ornament the expanses of gray stone. The result was a strange combination of five or six architectural embellishments, showing the history of its growth: one level featured widened and arched windows, another carvings of figures and arabesques along roofs and at corners; a third was half-hidden by exceedingly scrubby vines and long, droopy trees planted directly next the walls.

It had never been conquered until now — and, as usual with formidable fortresses, that had been from within.

Bostian looked up at the fortress, assessing its defenses. He surveyed the positioning and demeanor of the guards, most of whom sported new gray coats.

Yes, this would do.

When the pair atop the open gate saw his Norsunder gray, they waved him through the open gate. Inside, an armed guard opened a door onto a corridor as dark as midnight despite a row of torches.

One door stood open, letting in the morning sun. Bostian took in a chamber cluttered with delicately made furnishings of white and gold, all shoved out of the way. Only a finely carved table remained in the center of the room, its surface littered with papers, maps, and the remnants of a recent meal.

Sitting in a big, comfortable wing-back chair clearly brought from somewhere else was a man of medium height and build, his booted feet on the table, his attention on dispatches. His hair was dyed blond, which did not at all hide his Chwahir origins to a discerning eye, and his gray uniform was perfectly tailored, cuffs edged with gold.

Bostian regarded him with amusement, knowing that Alsaes loved being a commander. As a boy running from the law, he'd teamed up with a renegade prince from Chwahirsland, Kessler Sonscarna, until a knife thrown by an enemy had caused Alsaes to promise anything if the Norsundrian mage Dejain would save him.

Bostian despised Alsaes as a weasel who didn't even know he was a mere flunky; Alsaes, in his view, thought of himself as a commander because he currently had control over a civilian population, just the sort of work he loved the most. Battle held no real attraction for weasels. This particular weasel liked issuing orders and seeing them carried out. He liked marching, and parades, and well-fitting uniforms, and swords flashing in unison. And even better than sex, he loved ritual executions and punishments, with the victim made fast. In short, he liked order, and fear, and the sight of someone else's pain.

"Bostian! Settling in as the King of Sartor now?"

"Not quite yet."

"You've been replaced? Already?" Alsaes's insinuating tone irritated Bostian, who squashed down the reaction.

"No. The city is mostly empty, until my flock of sheep find their way home again. Asiarch is seeing to that, while he finds me ships for my boys. Easy here?"

"Superficially," Alsaes said, adding with typical self-importance, "Our hands are somewhat tied by the orders not to raze any cities. A day of slaughter would be salutary."

Bostian grinned. "There's room for experimentation."

Alsaes said, "Was Sartor tough?"

Irritation flashed through Bostian, but he knew that you didn't get information without giving it. "Tough? No. It was a slog." And he did like bragging, even to weasels. Weasels, he'd found, usually knew more than they realized they did; the new commander in chief was nearly as touchy as Efael, and neither liked sharing information unless they had decided to pass it along. You found a lot out by asking what orders they handed out to the weasels.

Bostian added, "My timetable was thrown off by the Queen of Sartor's boytoy. Rel the Traveler, or Farmboy. Whatever he calls himself. Ruined the road in and then smoked. But I'll catch up with him. That type, he won't be able to resist coming back. We'll have a fine welcome waiting."

Bostian made a spitting motion, then said, "We saw three days of fairly hot work in Miraleste before we brought down Darian Irad, and after that his command fell apart. That's when I hopped over to Sartor, and left Ririn in charge of the mopping up."

"Isn't Ririn a mage?"

"The trouble was all magic wards, traps, and illusions after we took down Darian Irad. I needed a mage to clean out that mess."

"Darian Irad," Alsaes repeated, and memory provided vivid images: he and Kessler watching, unseen, as Darian Irad trained his army, what, twenty, twenty-five years before? "I remember him. One of the few kings Kessler wanted to take the field against himself."

Bostian nodded, willing to acknowledge excellence — in defeat. Made him look better. "Knew how to train, and what to do with 'em when they were trained. Too bad he hadn't another five, six years. Could have put something worthwhile up against us."

"Couldn't be a lighter mage," Alsaes commented, looking askance. Everyone knew light magic was useless, or nearly so, for warfare.

"Whoever it is knows something about our magic. Lost people — permanently — to some fairly clever traps. Irad, now, I made sure when we had him we'd use a bloodknife and stash him for later — he's too good to lose. Oversaw that myself. But damned if someone didn't somehow dissolve the spell. Then there was Darian Selenna. Efael himself wanted the brat, and I made sure we had our insider put a tracer on him, but as soon as I got to Miraleste the tracer was blocked. We think it was either Detlev or one of his boys."

"Couldn't be. They're all idiots," Alsaes repeated, with distaste. "And so is Detlev."

"Idiot or not, I'd like to be the one to catch up with him," Bostian commented.

"That would be a coup," Alsaes said complacently, as if such a contest was beneath him. "Of course everyone else thinks so, too. But nobody as assiduously as our new commander. Llyenthur. Isn't that an old pirate port? What kind of a name is that?"

Says the weasel who named himself after the Colendi capital, only changing one vowel, Bostian thought with hidden amusement. "Llyenthur and Ghanthur," he said. "Old, even ancient, Brotherhood of Blood lairs, at least twice that I know of. I'm sure we have many volunteers from that end of Drael."

Alsaes lifted a shoulder. "My point is, nobody hates Detlev more than he, excepting maybe Efael. Second to how much they loathe each other." He sniggered, almost a giggle, and Bostian remembered why he disliked spending any time around this weasel. But he was here to a purpose.

Alsaes went on disparagingly, "Everyone is blaming Detlev for their blunders. Never knew he could be in twenty-five places at once."

Bostian bit down on a pungent comment about those who needed their "commands" handed to them after someone else did the work. "What I hear is, someone's been raiding Yeres's stash of rulers before she can empty their brains," he said.

Alsaes waved a languid hand; *he* hadn't lost any prisoners, which was all that mattered. The mages had only recently finished warding each of the cells up in the main tower, and layering a Destination in each. He already had two prisoners — but the orders on them were strictly hands off. Aldon wanted the pleasure of taking traitors apart, piece by piece, when he got the leisure. "If you ask me, there wouldn't be a problem if Yeres would stop hiding in the Beyond, only coming out an hour or two a week to deal with the prisoners."

Bostian agreed heartily. Once he had Yustnesveas Landis safely stashed, he had no interest whatsoever in the occupation plans — except for Sartor, which was *his*. Occupation was the next wave's problem, once the Host was able to somehow get them over from the Beyond. He was not averse to some judicious bootlicking if it would get him what he wanted without having to promise a favor. Always dangerous. "We lose a prize like the Landis queen of Sartor before Yeres can mind-rip her, I hate to think of the fatigue of tracking her down again. Bartal has her now, but I don't know how trustworthy he really is."

Bait dangled—and Alsaes, being a weasel, snatched at it. "Bartal," he said, "is only to be trusted with lesser tasks. Why don't you leave her to me? Nobody gets in or out of this fortress without my permission. Nobody."

Brag, brag, brag. Bostian gave him a little show of being impressed. "You do seem to have the best defense of them all. Ah, it's too much trouble."

Alsaes waved that negligent hand again, and Bostian indulged himself with imagining how Alsaes would look after one stroke from his sword took that hand off. "You'll be doing me a favor," Alsaes said. "It's boring here, with nothing but relays and logistics to monitor while I wait for more prisoners. I could torture her with daily sitreps, who's captured and who's dead, before Yeres comes to get her."

"If you're sure..."

"I'll issue an order to Bartal na Shagal," Alsaes said, relishing the fact that he could give orders to a long-established king. He picked up a pen, dipped it, wrote with a flourish, and slammed the paper into the dispatch tray. It vanished. "There! Done."

Bostian said obsequiously, "I like your style—make a decision, problem solved." Now to make it look like that had not been his purpose. He glanced down at the map—and was surprised to discover that it appeared to be current. "*You* get sitreps?"

"Didn't you hear what I said?" Alsaes smirked. "I was first in. Besides Aldon, of course. But he was behind a ward. There had to be a relay desk somewhere, until Duin gets Llyenthur's command center set up."

While Alsaes settled in to blather on about what could plainly be seen on the map, Bostian was thinking, Duin. There was the connection. Imry Llyenthur's aide was a Chwahir, as was Alsaes.

Lisdan - Melire

In a straight line to the east, a group of people assembled on a riverbank, water chuckling over stones nearby. It was morning in Halarialgre, but the sun had reached its zenith here in Melire.

Rel the Traveler gestured them in close. "Thank you for coming, fellow vagabonds. I'm sure you are all aware that Norsunder knows about this magic, but as yet they seem to consider it harmless, useful only for illusion. They don't even seem to know that it is untraceable, because it's mostly only used for illusion which is by nature ephemeral."

The vagabonds, all trained by Autumn of Bermund, smiled at one another.

"What you might not be aware of is if we all work together as a group at sunrise, noon, sunset, or midnight, alongside running water, and we share a specific goal, we can weave stronger magic—such as transfers."

This was indeed new to more than half of them, all people trained after Rel's initial group. Rel didn't know them, but the half-dawnsinger Aronis Harper did. It was he who had brought them all together.

Attention sharpened as Rel went on, "I am asking you to help me make strong magic. I warn you now, if we act, we risk Norsunder possibly discovering that vagabond magic is a lot stronger than mere illusion."

No one spoke.

Rel nodded, put his hands together in the peace, and bowed his thanks.

"I want to rescue Atan, perhaps better known to you as Yustnesveas Landis—but we will use her private name. Norsunder once laid spells over her full name, and we can assume they will again. Atan surrendered herself four days ago, to prevent wholesale slaughter. With the sun directly overhead, the magic currents are strongest. Let us join together and I will navigate."

Aronis Harper said, "Join hands."

And while the vagabonds pleached sun and the magic currents coruscating in the air, in Sles Adran, Atan sat, bound and gagged, on the balcony outside her prison room.

She had come out of the transfer to discover that she was the prisoner of a fellow monarch, the suave, polished Bartal na Shagal. He had been apologetic at the necessity, but (he shrugged, elegant in velvet and winking gems) the times decreed that one ally oneself with the strongest power. The alternative...

With an elegant, smiling gesture he indicated herself and she had to suppress the nearly overwhelming urge to kick that hand and spit in his eye. But her part was to project a passive, harmless front. So she merely smiled back.

The first day had not been that bad, if one overlooked being a prisoner. The royal castle belonging to the Shagals was quite old, built into mountains. She had been given a tower room with a magnificent view, if she ignored the fully armed guards, mail gleaming coldly beneath their gray-lavender battle tunics. They were awake and alert, posted along turrets, walls, and patrolling ceaselessly below the castle.

Leaving her time to reflect on the madness of the past days. And to wonder how the Norsundrians had felt when they marched into her royal palace to discover that every candlestick, every tapestry, every plate and spoon and picture had been taken away. The place had been empty, except for the heaviest and ugliest pieces of furniture. And the dirt on the floors left from so many feet going in and out. Left unswept as silent protest by the servants.

But the real blow would be the ward over the Destination, the oldest in the world, made by Linet of the Loi once Atan had sent Rel off. No human would be able to use it.

The second day, Bartal had not come himself, but sent a couple of burly guards, both women, to stand over her while she ate, and then they bound and blindfolded her. This was new. She wondered who, where, might have escaped or been rescued, and tried to rejoice for their sake. Every small win was a victory for them all

She lost track of time after that, but struggled to resign herself to whatever would happen. This plan was hers. She knew Rel would do his best to wrangle his mysterious magic; if it didn't work, she had left specific instructions that Rel was to be regarded as king...

Footsteps—early. Wasn't it morning? Or had she completely lost her place in time?

Someone entered the room. "You're going to Zranf," someone said shortly, and smacked a transfer token against her arm.

Once again magic ripped her out of the world and flung her violently back in again. This new space was winter-cold, and smelled of dank stone. Why this new transfer? She hoped it was because the enemy were fighting among themselves...

On the riverbank, the ambient magic in the air glowed and swirled around Rel as the transfer shifted him through space, and then dissolved in scintillate glitters at the edges of his vision. He saw Atan, and put his arms around her, the vagabond magic absorbing the knots and twists of dark magic distorted into the transfer spell.

Atan stiffened, but there was his familiar scent. She braced for yet another transfer wrench, but all she felt was a gentle whoosh, as if they danced on air. A soft breeze touched her skin, and then she heard the sound of a stream.

She leaned against Rel's solid form as unknown voices chattered briefly around her in the high, happy tones of congratulation. Rel was working at her bonds; when her hands and eyes were free, she found herself facing Rel and a short, golden-haired young man—a dawnsinger?

"It works. It works. That means we can try to find others," Aronis exclaimed.

Atan opened her mouth to object, that it was too dangerous, but then she remembered she and Rel had an agreement: he would not fight Bostian's invaders, which—at fifty-six city guards against several thousand could only have one end. But he was going to use what abilities he had elsewhere. And she had no authority over Aronis whatsoever.

Atan found a grassy spot beside the stream, and dropped with a thump. She was aware of gratitude and relief, or aware that she ought to be feeling them, but her emotions as yet were stilled, stunned, like a bird that has owned the skies—until it hits the glass.

Atan had earned her way, step by step, to being one of the most powerful and influential persons in the world. In this plan—her plan—she had surrendered all that power. All of it. She could not even tell Rel what do to anymore; he had this vagabond skill, and a company of others who shared it, and they were going to act as they saw fit. Not as she directed.

She turned her head as Rel and his group drew together, murmuring plans. Atan did not try to listen in. Though Tsauderei had seen to it that she had a thorough grounding in light magic, she did not understand vagabond magic. Rel had explained and explained about the currents of magic in the air, but she just could not perceive them. She'd tried. She believed they were there—or that he believed they were there.

Something had to be there, because here she was. This magic was more than mere illusion, or Rel never could have breached that cell that had smelled of thick stone untouched by sunlight.

She caught a few more words—Remalna, and Color-woods—and knew that Rel, or maybe this Aronis, had to be in contact with Vidanric Renselaeus. Good. A place to send anyone else they rescued.

The vagabonds broke up, and Rel dropped down beside her, smiling. It was the first real smile she'd seen in weeks.

"We'll stop at my house so you'll know where it is, but then we'll go straight to the tailor. She's waiting for you. The sooner we establish our personas here, the better."

"Very well."

A short time later, Atan found herself before a small shop. A weather-battered sign in the midlands alphabet stated, *Embeth Tailors*. Rel knocked on the door.

An older woman answered, looking from one to the other. "Here is your new tailor, Ma," Rel said.

Startled, Atan glanced up at him—to see an illusory beard shadowing half his face.

"Come in, come in," Ma Embeth said to Atan. "I'm in desperate need—things are so unsettled—you won't mind if I start you on stitchwork first, to evaluate your skills?"

Atan blinked, and Ma Embeth wondered if this tall, imposing young woman with the frog eyes might be a bit slow, as Atan finally understood that she had come full circle, from Queen of Sartor back to a semblance of the girl in the hut high on Sartor's border, who made her own clothes as she dreamed of what it might be like to be queen.

She remembered her manners from those days, and bowed. "Whatever you say, Honor Embeth."

Zranf - Halarialgre

Bostian shut out Alsaes's streams of numbers, as if all that could possibly impress anyone. How had this man spent time next to that mad genius Prince Kessler Sonscarna and not learned anything about strategy?

Bostian knew the commanders did not want anyone encroaching, and the easiest way to prevent it was to control who had access to what information. And yet it was all here! He studied the map intently. Even if Imry Llyenthur looked like a shopkeeper's flunky, he had recovered first, while Efael was still ranting and cursing and threatening, when the scribe desk takeover failed from within, denying both sides that aid to swift and universal comms.

Another glance at the map, as Alsaes blathered on with his predictions about what the head snakes would do next. Heh. Llyenthur was making the most of what he had, until reinforcements could be brought over. Once he'd effectively divided the Sartoran continent in half, he was targeting the toughest countries on each continent first, which of course would keep them from coming to anyone else's aid. He was also deploying locals as much as possible. The Fhlerians first, with Aldon at their head—Fhleria being a ridiculous name when everybody knew that all those people along the west coast of Drael were Venn right down to the bone. Nothing tougher than Venn on Venn. Ah, that ought to keep Aldon busy.

Below Drael, on the Sartoran mainland, the most trouble-some militaries were the Chwahir—but Efael had control there, the Chwahir ships and army deployed not only over Colend and its neighbors, but from the markers on the map, shiploads of them on their way to Toar. Then there were the Adranis. Who had been wooed and seduced, their considerable army now filling in the gaps where the Chwahir and Bostian's own force had yet to go.

His gaze followed the ship markers over to Toar, whose most formidable military was midlands in Damondaen.

"... and straight north, in Goerael, by far the toughest military is Ralanor Veleth. Llyenthur has it slated next. He's arrogant enough to see to it himself, but for occupation, he's putting in a mix of Aldon's own plus leftover Fhlerians, while other forces are in transit. Fhlerians and Aldon's own companies. I predict that'll go badly unless they—" Alsaes, indignant that Bostian wasn't listening, broke off his predictions to say somewhat peevishly, "You mentioned Asiarch. New orders?"

"No, no, I put him to the task of closing down the harbors and finding me transport," Bostian said, and ladled on more treacle, "I'm sure you understand the intent there. Once he throws enough of these idiots into the sea, and fires a ship or two as an object lesson, the sheep will troop back home again. He can oversee that and settle them while I'm gone."

"To?"

"Seems young Llyenthur wants to run this one himself, once he's done in Ralanor Veleth. But there ought to be enough fun for us all." Bostian tapped the subcontinent of Halia.

"Ah," Alsaes said, nodding knowledgeably. "Marloven Hess."

Nine

Lathandra – Ralanor Veleth

EMPIRES AND KINGDOMS RISE and fall, as everyone knows. Still, reputations persist, one of these being that the most formidable military kingdoms in the world are the Venn, the Chwahir, the Velethi of Ralanor Veleth, the Fhlerians, and the Marlovens of Marloven Hess. All of whom, except for the Chwahir — who predate the others — are in some wise related to the Venn.

The Fhlerians and the Venn had fallen to Norsunder, both from within, one by treachery and the second by magic. We have seen the Chwahirs' situation.

The only time of year one often woke to clear skies in Ralanor Veleth's weather-worn, war-battered royal castle, sitting on its hill in the center of the capital city Lathandra, was early spring.

It began as an ordinary, uneventful morning.

Princess Liara Viana — generally known as Viana — loved dawn practice in the salle, the sounds of clashing steel and Uncle Jaim's laugh as he and Papa practiced with some of the castle guard. She also loved breakfast afterward, especially the rare times they all were together.

This particular morning it was just the royal family. Mama had a letter that kept folding back into its crinkly fan-shape beside her plate. There was Jaimas's small blond head—the same color of hair as Mama—bent over the book in his lap.

Lexy wasn't there, and Uncle Markham never ate with them, she didn't know why, even though ever since she was small she'd heard Mama say, if Markham Glenereth came in, *Won't you sit down and join us?* and his *I have already eaten, thank you.* Though sometimes he'd accept a cup of coffee if Papa wanted to talk to him about this or that. He'd stand against the wall, chatting, then go when the conversation was done.

It had become a kind of ritual, grave, polite, friendly on either side, but other than that the adult emotions (as usual) completely undecipherable. As undecipherable as Mama insisting that Viana call him Uncle Markham, though they were not blood relations, and his insisting on living at the army barracks, though Mama seemed to like Lexy staying with Viana and her brother in the nursery wing.

Then Markham came in to say that a courier from the north had just arrived, and Papa rose immediately to leave. Two steps, almost to the door, then he turned around again, and hugged Mama as he bent to kiss her.

After that he said to Markham, "I'll handle this. Have something to drink."

Mama smiled as Papa went out, Viana looked at Mama's disarranged long hair remembering Aunt Jewel's scolding voice on her last visit, *Really, Flian, you are thirty-five years old, and to be wearing your hair down like a girl not yet old enough to be presented makes you ridiculous,* to which Mama had said only, *Jason likes it, and no one else here cares.* Aunt Jewel had sighed, rolling her eyes, and Aledra had rolled her eyes as well, fussing with her golden curls.

Jaimas looked up from his book. He noticed the light slanting in through the south window. The scattering of crumbs on the plates, Mama pouring more steep, and sighing as she turned back to her letter. No need to ask who it was from: those long, closely written letters were always from Aunt Jewel.

And there was Viana scowling at her plate. Mind-touch: Viana thinking about Aunt Jewel and Aledra.

Papa's mood, sensed from across the castle: wariness, and a wish to talk to Mama. And on this side of the castle, Mama wishing the letter were a lot shorter, so she could follow Papa and find out what the courier said.

Jaimas had learned — they all had learned — that listening to others' thoughts was trespass. Not that Viana was very good at it, but Jaimas kept hearing them, especially in dreams, and so did Lexy, though Lexy, being the oldest of the three, had mastered the inner door.

Jaimas hadn't. But distance "hearing" was hard, it could make him dizzy, which made it easier to do right: He resolutely turned his attention away from Papa, even though he wanted to know what the footman downstairs had said to make Papa wary. Instead, he returned to his book, sinking slowly back into the past, until the sudden sounds of shouting.

For Lexan Glenereth, the morning had not been one of unalloyed happiness. Ambivalence had shadowed him for at least a year, sometimes more, sometimes less. He still slept in the nursery because it seemed to please the queen, who was unfailingly kind.

Having invented a task so he wouldn't have to breakfast with the royal family, he emerged from the stables with Racer and Salty, his and Liara Viana's mounts, in time to see the king exit through the residence door, trailing an increasing number of runners.

The unexpected flurry of people caused Lexan to halt, reins in his hands. Salty nuzzled his shoulder to get him moving again, but his gaze caught on the light brown hair of the slim man on the roof. He should know anyone stationed on rooftops. Alarm, uncertainty — should he say anything? He drew a breath to say he did not know what when shock rang through him at the twang of a crossbow.

Then the thud of impact, and the sight of the king falling, his hands flinging wide.

Falling, falling, and the others springing to catch him, though the looseness of those hands made it clear to even those who didn't feel, on the mental plane, the lightning-flight of spirit sundered from flesh that meant King Jason Szinzar was dead before he hit the ground.

And then memory stops for a merciful time.

But if you live, then memory has to begin again, and you feel pain afresh. For Lexan that rebirth of memory came with his father's dark gaze, and the pressure of strong fingers on his jaw. *Do you hear me? See the queen and the children to the border hideout. Now.*

The next memory was the queen's face, distorted by the wildness of grief and anger, but there was her familiar blue-and-silver gown, and her long pale hair, and her hands clutching tightly to Viana and Jaimas, their faces wet with tears.

"Lexan. Get them to safety," Lexan's father ordered, sharp-voiced.

Memory: The queen—who Lexan couldn't call Aunt Flian, even though he knew it puzzled and hurt her—saying tersely, "Markham, he's just a boy."

"I will." Was that someone else using Lexan's voice?

His father stilled, then whirled and ran to join Jaim as they began mobilizing the guard.

The fugue broke briefly during the silent ride west, stopping only to change horses. Shocked faces as the news was spoken, though not by Lexan. He couldn't get the foul words past his lips, as if not speaking would make them not true: *The king is dead.*

Viana's sudden, stormy crying.

Jaimas pale as paper. Silent. No sound, no speech.

Then fugue again, until suddenly they were in Drath. Did no one really speak all that time? Lexan's mind blurred that part. Instead, his memory offered his sensory vigilance—sight, sound, smells—and his awareness of the six guards equally watchful, as they rode up into Drath, enemy territory. He had something to do, though the world had changed forever. He was under orders. He was to keep the queen and the royal children safe.

Lexan had been to Drath with his father and Jaim as they sneaked across the dense wooded mountainsides up to the old caves where Jaim Szinzar had long ago hidden out, when the adults were all young. Since those olden days, Prince Garian Herlester had occasionally played a nasty game of *Tag, you're mine* off and on with people trying to cross Drath's mountains to get to Lygiera, or from Lygiera to Ralanor Veleth. It had been costly to spring them—especially stinging as Drath did not need the gold. Lexan had gone on training missions through Drath, the mission being to get couriers—and self—alive west and then east again.

They rode into a little clearing, the sound of running water beyond thick fir trees, as suddenly they were surrounded by twenty or more Drath border riders, all armed, dressed in the purple surcoats that had always meant danger.

But next thing he saw was the queen sliding off her horse, and running toward a tall man with red hair, her fingers spread as if to strike. The man caught her by the wrists, as she cried, "Was it you, Garian? If you killed him, just gut me now!"

The man with the red hair signed to the guards to lower their weapons as he said, "It's war, Flian. Norsunder is marching over the border right this moment." And when the queen stared at him, gulping and sobbing, and wiping her face on her wrist like any child, he added with a sort of sardonic mildness, "If Jason is dead, then so is the game. Come along, let's get you somewhere safe, you and the brats. Then I need to get back to planning some traps for our Norsundrian friends. They can come up here, but they are not going to find it easy."

The fugue ended at last as they entered cool caves smelling of fresh water. Servants moved about, lugging baskets of quilts and cushions and lap-desks, books and paper and clothing, as they attempted to turn a cave into a civilized dwelling.

Through their midst, arrogantly unheeding, strode Garian Herlester, at his side a slim youth with red hair and a hard, sardonic hazel gaze mirror to his father's. Prince Garian ignored Lexan and addressed Viana, who was standing next to him, "Here's my son, Garian-Rafael Herlester. You can call him Rafael, to make life easier for us all. Get to know one other. We will, no doubt, all be mired up here together for a very long time."

As Rafael's insolent, slack-lidded gaze widened to take in Viana's wary blue stare, Lexan's heartbeat drummed, a warning that he faced more problems than a war.

———⁘———

Word spread among the Norsundrians that Llyenthur himself had got past the guards in Lathandra to take out Jason Szinzar, the best military commander in all of Goerael, perhaps in that half of the world.

Alsaes triumphantly put a marker on the map, smirking as if he had personally cranked the crossbow, then decided that after a day and a night alone, the new prisoner ought to be in a properly humble spirit. She could probably have a little water, and maybe a bite of bread if she begged nicely. And he could have some fun gloating. Tell her how thoroughly the lighters were losing.

But when he got up to the prison tower with his keys, it was to find an empty room.

"Where's the prisoner?" he bellowed.

The place was so impregnable it had seemed unnecessary to post guards up here in the eternal darkness. No lighter spells could broach the wards.

"Where is she?"

The watch captain said, "Sir, we did not unlock the door, according to orders."

"She should be here," Alsaes retorted, pointing.

There was no possible answer to be made to that, as they looked at the empty room.

"Each of these cells has its own Destination." Alsaes stated — and again there was no answer to be made. They all knew that. They had all tested the transfers.

Disaster! Alsaes wanted to have them all flogged, but that would take time, and he knew who would pay unless he either found her or found an excuse. Llyenthur was far too busy at the moment to care about Yeres's prisoners, but Yeres would be in a fury. And either of them was very nasty when crossed.

How to shift the blame? Bostian was long gone. Bartal na Shagal! He'd had the Landis woman first!

Alsaes wrote to demand the transfer of Yustnesveas Landis. Bartal wrote back:

> *All my guards witnessed the transfer promptly on receipt of your missive yesterday. Is there a problem?*

Is there a problem? Yes! Now, a new problem, damn it all. Bartal would be blabbing, or nosing, and he'd certainly be gloating. Alsaes brooded. His only hope of survival was if it could be proved the problem was with transfers — ah.

The vital question was, who would be the perfect tool?

He sat there, unconsciously stroking the numb skin over the bloodknife scar that Dejain had left when she'd saved him from bleeding to death. Nobody liked bloodknives except to use against others, but he didn't mind his now that Dejain was safely dead. As long as no one knew about it, he couldn't be tortured by mind, or commanded...

Then he had it: who better than Hyath, one of Yeres's pet mages? The first time Alsaes saw her, she stood in a circle of men, coyly twirling a ringlet around her finger as she chirped, "I'm only sixteen, but I'm very mature for my age." And to prove it, she snatched a dagger from one of them, ran out, and cut the throat of a random passerby.

That had caused an enormous uproar, just when they were supposed to be undercover, but Yeres had cooed and petted Hyath, who showed her devotion to her master by dressing in that same odd style, draped with fabric held together by cords at breast and waist, her hair bound up by cords as well.

Hyath was ambitious, determined to be Yeres's right hand—more confident than smart.

All messages were supposed to be copied to Duin, but as yet there wasn't the magic in place to assure that—all the relay mages were neck-deep in sabotaging and reproducing the lighter notecase magic. Still, it was only prudent to assume every message might be seen by other eyes than the recipient. He had to word it so that it sounded routine.

> *Hyath: On a routine check of the prison*
> *Destinations, we encountered a problem with the*
> *spells.*

Strictly true—but no mention of Yustnesveas Landis.

Hyath turned up a short time later, pouting. "We're *done* with that! I *personally* watched flunkies test every cell." She slammed a grubby book down on Alsaes's desk. "Right now we're warding every lighter Destination in this book. You better have something important, or I'll tell Yeres you're wasting our time. She *hates* that."

Alsaes said, "Your transfer wards to the prison tower failed."

"That's *impossible!* There is *nothing* wrong with my spells," she fluted. "You stupid old people fumbled the transfer."

"No, we didn't," Alsaes said grimly, hiding how very much he resented the "old people" at not quite forty. "I sent the order, Bartal in Sles Adran obeyed—and no prisoner turned up."

"Impossible."

"See for yourself," Alsaes invited.

"You should have told me at once. Traces dissipate over time," she retorted, but darted upstairs as fast as Alsaes had come down.

At first impatiently, then more slowly and uncertainly, she

paced the room, her silver-painted toenails in their sandals gleaming like steel in the torchlight.

Finally she said fretfully, "I don't understand it. There was no lighter spell interference, that much I can tell. There's no trace at all, other than the fragments of the test transfer." She touched the walls. "We'll have to assume the prisoner is dead. Yeres will be annoyed...oh, you soul-sucking shits! We're going to have to do all the transfer Destinations for every single cell again!"

Alsaes assumed a serious expression as Hyath stamped and screamed. As he'd hoped, the blame had thoroughly transferred to Hyath.

Ten

Mearsies Heili

THERE WAS ONLY ONE person who knew that Mearsies Heili, a small and unfamed rural polity near the northeastern end of the Toaran continent, was soon to become one of the most important places in the world.

There was no overt sign of that as CJ, a twelve-year-old with long black hair and tear-blotchy eyes, transferred up to the gleaming white palace atop Mount Marcus, overlooking the tiny capital city terraced below the peak.

CJ slunk in, looking for Clair, who was once a girl queen, demoted to heir again on the reappearance of her great-grandmother Mearsieanne, after a century of imprisonment by Norsunder. Clair had sneaked into the kitchen to eat something while reading, though Mearsieanne wanted everyone using the formal dining room, dressed formally and using manners suited to their rank.

CJ and Clair gave one another quick glances, saw that they were alone, and recognized in the other a mirror to their guilty relief. They were still trying to come to terms with the horrible news sent by Lyren-Sartora, who had been hiding in Roth Drael: Norsunder was conquering left, right, and center, with what sounded like cruel and relentless ease.

One of the first put to the sword was their old friend Lilah Selenna of Sarendan.

CJ had stormed and cried in the safety of their underground hideout as she wished terrible retribution on the Norsundrians. Clair had found herself running hard through the peaceful forest, running until her muscles turned to jelly. The next day she got up and ran again. And again.

CJ had kept her foul temper and crying jags confined to the underground, until she was too exhausted to weep anymore. Now here she was, forcing herself back into the world again.

"Is there some kind of plan?" she asked, though there had been no messages on the MC, which was the scribe desk Clair had made when she was ten years old. As the desk (the scrying spell had been worked into a blotter) only carried messages between two places — the magic to connect to the greater scribe world had been beyond her — it was still functioning.

Clair shook her head. "No one has written to me since Senrid's last a day or two ago, saying that he thinks the notecases are somehow being copied by Norsunder. Since he was right about the scribe guild desks all along, I locked mine in a trunk."

"I'm not sorry," CJ mumbled, her heart swamped anew by this reminder of how horrible it was to receive the message about Lilah. "Yes I am. Kind of. Oh, I wish there was a way to only get good news, and not have to have the rotten news."

Clair didn't answer, since they both knew it was impossible. Instead, she asked, "Feel any better?"

"No. Where are the rest of the girls?"

"All over. Falinneh and Gwen and Seshe went to Aunt Murial. Dhana went to the water people when everyone dispersed. You know her. She will reappear when the rest do, probably at dinner time. Seshe and Diana are up in the towers." Clair pointed over her head. "Seshe finds it peaceful. I think Diana is looking at the sea, watching for enemies, but hoping Captain Heraford or a ship we know shows up."

CJ tipped back her head, though she could not see the towers from inside the kitchen, of course. But she'd been in them countless times, and though she and the girls had never caught the rooms at it, she was convinced they popped in and out of time somehow.

A guilty thought slithered in: maybe she ought to try to lose herself in one, and come out when Norsudner was defeated. Except what about everybody else? No, better to stay and try to find a way to help defeat them. Somehow.

Clair added, with an attempt to lighten the mood, "Falinneh said she was going to be working on her book on villains."

"Inspired by Norsunder's attack?" CJ said. "Or is it a story about how she would like to crunch them good?"

Clair flashed a reluctant grin, and shoved back a lock of her white hair. "Who knows, with Falinneh? She complained over breakfast that she was stuck on a sentence with a comma in it. That's when I offered to send them to Aunt Murial, who said there's a new litter of pups. I'm...on watch," Clair admitted.

Cold dread gripped the back of CJ's neck. But she shook it off. Instead she looked down at Clair's four-year-old daughter Aurora, who sat on the floor teaching two battered dolls to swordfight.

It still seemed strange to her that the Birth Spell had worked for Clair, but then they weren't really kids anymore, and yet they were. They looked like kids, free of that disgusting mess called "puberty". CJ loathed the very idea of adulthood. As long as the girls all kept the Child Spell, they could *feel* like kids, and that was good enough for her.

Maybe when Aurora got to their age, she'd do the spell, too, and feel like a sister, but never a replacement for Irenne, never never never...

CJ glanced toward the door for Mearsieanne, Clair's great-grandmother, another who had done the Child Spell long ago. Mearsieanne was...strange. She'd been born in another era altogether, but everybody worked hard to get along. However, she had her limits, and one of those was that the name Detlev— or any variation—was not to be spoken in her presence. To her it was worse than profanity.

"What about Detsie-poopsie-potsie?" CJ whispered. "Any chance, now that he's on our side, he'll wipe out Norsunder for us?"

Clair smiled briefly at the old nickname for Detlev from his villain days. It was CJ and the girls who had seized on the silly pejorative "poopsies" for Detlev's boys—a name they were supposed to find insulting, but which, to CJ's initial dismay, appeared to have had the opposite effect.

Clair shook her head, thinking briefly of those strange, tense days she'd been forced to live with Detlev and his boys on the fifth world. She'd learned a lot about Norsunder, about those who sought power on any terms—and about group loyalty.

"Detlev will be a target, too," Clair said. "Maybe he'll help, maybe he'll hide out. Nobody's mentioned him, so maybe he's already gone. But we learned during the days when Siamis was a villain that we can't just expect the senior mages to solve our problems."

"Then what use is his being on our side?" CJ mumbled not-quite under her breath, her blue eyes narrowed and her chin up. When Clair didn't answer, she added, "Where's Mearsieanne?"

"Still working on her magic project. No, I don't know what it is. But I'm sure she'll tell us when she's ready to." Clair looked calm, sitting there at the table, her glistening white hair framing her square face, her light green eyes steady.

She sounded calm, too, but CJ instinctively knew how hard it was for Clair to deal with an ancestor—a beloved ancestor—returned unexpectedly to modern times. Clair's style of ruling small, rural Mearsies Heili had been what CJ thought of as hands-off, certainly informal. Mearsieanne was the opposite, slowly returning power to her firm hands, her goal to create a court again so she could preside and keep her benevolent eye on nobles.

"She said we shouldn't worry," Clair added, smiling slightly.

Aurora was still busy maneuvering the dolls back and forth, whispering insults in squeaky voices. She was a sturdy, compact child, with the typical square face of Clair's family.

CJ sighed, flopping onto a chair. She dug the ends of her straight black hair from under her, then examined the ends as she said, "I can't help worrying. Wish I could show those creeps just what I think of their rotten, cabbage-brained plans!"

Aurora looked up in interest when she heard the beginnings of the Mearsieans' invented form of cursing, but when CJ ended it, she gave a small sigh of disappointment and returned to her game.

CJ noticed. "Hey, Aurora, what do you think of the Norsundrians?"

Aurora's head lifted again, and she narrowed her Clair-green eyes. In her piping voice she let out a stream of insults she'd been taught, expecting—and getting—approval from the big girls.

Clair laughed. "She's fierce enough as it is, CJ."

Aurora looked from one to the other and said, "Next year I get to learn bow and arrows. You promised." She added in a tentative voice, "Crystal Ingrid already gets lessons with a bow."

Clair hesitated, not wanting to point out that Crystal Ingrid Montredaun-An of Marloven Hess, though an excellent playmate and a wonderful, bright child, was also stubborn as steel. Clair didn't disapprove—it was probably best for a Marloven princess. "They do those things earlier in Marloven Hess," Clair finally said, seeing that Aurora was waiting for an answer.

Then she remembered the news, and wondered if there would be a next year. "Yes," she said firmly. "Yes, you can."

Aurora clapped, and returned to her game. Clair watched, grateful that the Birth Spell had worked for her, though she had not relinquished the Child Spell.

Deep within her, a voice whispered *Yet*.

But she quickly smothered that thought, casting a guilty look at CJ. Better to think about the Birth Spell. Who knew why it worked for anyone? Much more reassuring was the notion that Aurora had a place in the world. And, looking at her daughter's white-striped brown hair, she wondered where in her family's past the morvende entered, and why. Each year Aurora's hair whitened more; the brown would probably be gone before the child turned six.

Aurora went on with her game, making noises to imitate swords clashing.

Clair watched Aurora's small fingers as she considered Aurora's favorite playmate, Crystal Ingrid. The two girls were a lot alike, in that they both loved animals, though Crystal Ingrid didn't seem to have the Mearsiean taste for silliness. How much of what shaped children was the habits of those raising them, and how much inherited?

As CJ crouched down onto the floor, Aurora's dolls abandoned their swords. Under CJ's guidance, Aurora watching with shivering glee, the dolls began a pie fight as CJ said in a squeaky whisper, "And here's a prune-cheese-rotten-pineapple nightmare, just for you!" CJ's fingers worked illusion magic, and the dolls got splattered with brightly-colored glop as Aurora gusted with laughter.

Her laughter brought back Lilah for a heartbreaking moment. Lilah had laughed like that, gusty and merry and free.

Clair tried to breathe against the rock of grief in the middle of her chest, and dropped down beside them to join in the game.

While they could still play.

Watching unseen from the hallway was Mearsieanne. She saw in Clair's face all the love and care that Mearsieanne wished she could have seen in the girls' faces for her, instead of the careful politeness and determined good will they'd shown these past few years. Mearsieanne knew that both were grieving hard at the news of the death of their friend Lilah from halfway around the world. They were still grieving for Irenne, one of Clair's gang, years later. Grieving more for them than they probably would when—

Ah, self-pity never did anyone any good.

It was all Detlev's fault, Mearsieanne thought for the hundred-thousandth time, a *useless* thought. An ally! She couldn't express the depth of her scorn at the mere idea. But she didn't argue with Clair about it, or even with CJ who had managed, for some reason, to make a kind of truce with some of Detlev's filthy criminal boys despite their having murdered Irenne.

No use in trying to convince Clair and CJ that Detlev would surely betray them. Mearsieanne would simply look after her own.

―――――――――――

Aunt Murial sent the three girls back at nightfall.

Mearsieanne, Clair, CJ, Aurora and Clair's collection of runaway and orphaned girls sat at the dinner table on the terrace, overlooking the forest and the setting sun, eating, drinking, laughing. The dinner lasted a long time; soon branches of candles were lit, and Mearsieanne studied each face. Diana's dark eyes, her scruffy clothes and sweet smile. Diana had been spending more and more time with Dtheldevor's gang of privateer youths, whose island base was clear on the other side of the world.

Mearsieanne disapproved of Dtheldevor, though she was another who had never removed the Child Spell. Dtheldevor lived a wild, free life, attacking pirates on the sea, and collecting orphans and restless wanderers. Mearsieanne was quite aware that both CJ and Clair dreaded Diana moving away for good, though neither said anything. Clair had always insisted that people were free to come and go.

Except, was anyone ever truly free of a family?

For so they were. Clair recognized that, as well as Seshe, the eldest before she did the Child Spell. Seshe was tall, her long hair bound in locks, her eyes kind and patient and perceptive — more perceptive, perhaps, than most of the other girls knew. Mearsieanne suspected Seshe would be the first to relinquish the Child Spell. She did not want to see that.

Her mind shied to Sherry, her large blue eyes and bouncy curls making her look younger than her twelve years. Sherry lived for laughter, as did Falinneh of the million freckles and bright red braids. A shapechanger, Falinneh could be anything with human shape, but she was most comfortable in this form.

Gwen was their willing third, often adding to the laughter with her talent for imitating voices. Dhana, thin, graceful, her face changeable as the weather, not quite human, but who had taken — for a time — human form.

Irenne's chair empty — for no one would ever forget the one who had died.

Clair and CJ sat side by side, CJ black-haired, short, and skinny, moody and funny and passionate about hates as well as loves. She was a perfect foil for Clair, whitehaired and square, who never express emotions easily, even though Mearsieanne knew she felt them.

Who better to know than her own relation, back in their lives? They had accepted her, though Mearsieanne had to admit it had not been easy despite everyone's good will. Well, Mearsieanne had a gift to give them, a gift so great it could not be hinted at until it was given.

Until that time came she watched them all, enjoying every moment, no longer impatient at the lack of manners, the bare feet and silly clothes. They were inventing the future, one she felt she could only watch, as one watched a play — from the audience, and not participating on the stage.

They were inventing the future, and she was going to make certain they were around to live in it.

A sudden burst of clapping interrupted her thoughts.

"A fine song," Seshe declared.

"If only Wan-Edhe of the Chwahir would be so obliging as to play his part right," Mearsieanne proclaimed, for she'd just caught a questioning glance from Clair. She smiled all around, and was glad when Falinneh—of course—picked up on her comment.

"Yes! Especially the part about his being surprised by his shadow and crashes into a wall—"

Snickering, Gwen stuttered, "And h-his n-n-n-ose swells, b-b-blocks his v-vision—"

"—and he mixes his beard into his soup, and eats it—" Falinneh waggled her fork under her chin.

"And poisons himself!" Diana ended by grabbing her throat and making a long series of gagging noises that sent Gwen, Falinneh, and Aurora into fresh paroxysms.

"I think you should send a copy of the song to him," Clair said. "He'd appreciate it so much."

They went on about the hated villain, whose penchant for cruelty had shadowed their lives for so long, until the second dessert was served.

When that was done, Aurora was banished to bed and storytelling started; Mearsieanne initiated it by a question about one of the less harrowing adventures with the Chwahir, knowing that it would open up the talk to reminiscence.

And so it did, until voices got tired and there were yawns all around. Some of the girls still preferred to transfer down to their rooms in the underground hideout rather than sleep in the beautiful palace—except for Falinneh, who declared she was too full from double helpings of both desserts, and so she dozed off right on the patio. Mearsieanne was aware of covert looks sent her way—they were expecting her to scold—but she said nothing, just swallowed in her aching throat, and forced a smile. CJ got blankets for Falinneh, and left.

Eleven

MORNING DAWNED CLOUDY BUT warm. The clouds broke up almost immediately, but Falinneh slept on, unbothered by the sun, which was still at a mellow angle. Not until Diana appeared and shook her awake did she snort and look about.

"Falinneh." Diana was not smiling. "Clair wants us all together." She whirled around and ran inside.

Falinneh ripped free of her blankets and also ran inside, but Diana had vanished. Falinneh slid down the banister and burst into the throne room, yelling, "Hey! Diana said—" She slid to a stop when she realized the room was empty. "Where are you!"

"Here!" came CJ's voice.

"Which here!"

"Library!"

Falinneh groaned, toiled back up the stairs, and slammed into the library, where she saw all the girls gathered—that is, all except Mearsieanne. And Diana.

"Huh?" Falinneh looked around. "Diana said—"

"She went downstairs." CJ pointed at the floor. "Downstairs" in that tone meant down to ground level. "Wants to protect the forest."

Clair fingered the medallion around her own neck, a match for the ones the girls all wore. "I have a temporary transfer-ward on her. If the Norsundrians appear, I'll transfer her up. But she doesn't know it."

Falinneh collapsed onto a pillow on the ground. "Norsunder? *Here?*"

"It's actually Chwahir, but we know that Wan-Edhe is under Norsunder's control. Yesterday Ben saw a contingent of Chwahir, with Norsundrians in gray leading, when he was flying the borders. They marched through Reyte and Ujban yesterday. More of them came in ships in the middle of the night, and they broke my border protections just before dawn. They're marching inland through the old No One's Land."

"Just like the bad old days," Falinneh said in a small voice.

Mearsies Heili had no army. Some of the towns had raised and trained militias ten years before, but those were not even remotely an effective fighting force, as enthusiasm for constant drilling had tapered off in recent years. It had become no more than an excuse to gather, work through a couple of basic sword forms—after which came the real point of the day, a picnic of good eats with old friends.

"Did you let the governors know?" Falinneh asked.

Clair nodded. "Sent all six a message. Whatever remains of our old militia, the bells are now ringing to summon them."

CJ pointed to the magic books lying about. "We're trying to stop them from here. At least they won't reach any people before they show up below." She pointed down the mountain.

"Mearsieanne?" Falinneh asked.

CJ and Clair both shook their heads. Clair said quietly, "I can't trace her. But I sent Ben to find her, and help if he can."

Ben would take an animal or bird shape—and if anyone could find Mearsieanne, it would be he.

Falinneh nodded, serious for once. "And us?"

CJ's brow glowered, but the paleness of her face, her hunched shoulders and trembling fingers revealed her anxiety. "We do magic to defend our home as long as we can."

No one said anything about what would happen when they failed, but the sudden silence made it clear everyone was contemplating it.

Unknown to them, Mearsieanne stood at the lip of a cave low on the western foot of Mount Marcus. She wore a green velvet gown, trimmed with ribbons, that had been in the back of her closet for years—the gown she'd worn when she was first crowned. She'd been wearing it when she was taken prisoner;

she'd almost burned it when she became free again, then she decided that, no, she would wear it again on a day of triumph. She'd always hoped that that would be the day she stood over Detlev's bloody corpse.

The corpse today would not be his, but she still intended a triumph.

She carefully laid a knife across her lap, humming the melody of CJ's song.

Nothing was visible on the horizon.

She looked up behind her at the crags and cliffs of Mount Marcus, and the young pine and aspen. Trees, living symbols of life, of peace. Mearsieanne gazed beyond the trees, upward at the summit, and the glistening white towers beyond, their strange, iridescent not-quite-stone gleaming in a bright aura. The gleam gradually blurred, and she blinked. Tears? No! She refused to weep.

So she closed her eyes, listening to the peculiar resonance of the jewel-cave deep within the mountain behind her — the Selenseh Redian. Strange, usually she couldn't bear the way the caves had made her head feel. But at this moment that resonance, almost beyond hearing, was quite distinct, very much like the echo of a great chord just after the singers have stopped.

She opened her eyes, and looked southward. A dark line had become visible; the advancing warriors from Chwahirsland and Norsunder.

She drew a deep breath — and heard the screech of an eagle.

She looked up. The bird circled, then dove down, shimmered, and there was Ben.

"Clair's discovered my block on her tracers, hasn't she?"

Ben nodded, his expression anxious, his eyes watchful.

"And she sent you?"

"In case you needed company now — or help," Ben said.

"Dear Clair," Mearsieanne whispered. "Company indeed." She studied Ben's pleasant face, his sun-streaked hair, and sensed eyes besides Ben's. "Tell me. Is she seeing through you somehow, with that Dena Yeresbeth stuff?"

Ben shook his head. "You know she doesn't like mind-touch." He folded up his skinny knees under his chin, his hands tense.

Neither of them thought to look behind them, into the entrance to the cave.

"You needn't stay," Mearsieanne said.

"It's them't bother me." He jerked a bony shoulder eastward. "You gonna use that knife on 'em somehow?"

"Hardly." She laughed. It was a sound empty of joy, and she shivered. "You love it here, don't you, Ben?"

"Yes." His brows canted at a wistful angle. "For Mearsies Heili, then?"

"A crude way of putting it. I am for Mearsies Heili, not this stupid weapon. It represents nothing good. I'm your opposite, Ben. I originated here, yet it's no longer my home — only my love. There we share something —" Her voice suspended, and she waited.

Ben waited.

She said, after sniffing, "This is a very difficult enchantment. I've worked on it for four years, with help from mages who kept my secret, without knowing how I would bind the enchantment." Mearsieanne didn't mention the slightly disturbing fact that occasionally exactly the book she needed would appear on the shelves in the library, as if it had been there for generations. Or the fact that occasionally she had gone to bed on a knotty problem, to find the figure of an indistinct mage, so blurred she could never make out the gender, who would tell her how to unravel the knot. And on waking, she invariably discovered that the solution wasn't silly dream logic, but real.

Ben understood from the tremor in her voice that it was important to listen, and not to interrupt.

"This enchantment," she said, "will keep the Norsundrians from crossing our border, unless Clair invites them in. It's a reverse of that idiot Siamis's enchantment spell, only this one is far, *far* more powerful. Do you know what an enchantment is, Ben?"

He knew — Clair had explained years ago when discovering why he could transform into animals — but he cooperatively shook his head.

"A magic spell is simple. That is, specific. An enchantment is only achieved through more than one spell bound together by what we call a key. Wards are hundreds of spells, and I have fashioned a very powerful ward indeed, years of work. And I am the key."

She paused, and he nodded, his gaze steady and sympathetic.

"The key is me, Ben, but I will be beyond life, where Norsunder cannot reach me. It's an impossible spell in light magic unless one has lived beyond one's lifetime, and I know I have." She frowned at the knife. "I wish there was an easier way, but I don't have Dena Yeresbeth—"

Not true, thought Siamis, the hidden watcher.

"—so if these caves won't do it, the knife will have to."

She stood up, still not looking behind her as she walked determinedly deeper into the Selenseh Redian, Ben following uncertainly.

She faltered when her nascent Dena Yeresbeth, warded from discovery by Norsunder for over a century, sensed the otherness of the inner cave.

Her intent had been to slit her own throat, and finish the enchantment with her last breath. But the deeper she walked into the cave, the lighter she felt, not dizzy, no, but as if her mind had cut free of the limitations of her own skull, and drifted above the clouds.

"Oh, I don't feel bad..." She exhaled, then turned her face skyward, laughing and crying both. "Do you know, I wanted to use this knife in anger, right before the Chwahirs' faces, but the bitterness is gone, and it no longer matters." She stooped and brushed the back of her hand against Ben's cheek.

Ben staggered, overwhelmed. He found he could not go on, though he had promised to stay with her, and he was worried about that knife. He closed his eyes for a moment, or for what he'd meant to be a moment as within the cave, Siamis guided Mearsieanne's willing spirit to the Selenseh Redian's dimension beyond the physical world and time.

With her last breath, she finished her spell.

Ben's eyes were shut so he did not see the sudden flash of light, nor hear the abyssal *voom* and the outward ringing wind that was not a wind that laid down magic from border to border as Mearsieanne's enchantment warded the entire kingdom.

He did not, at first, see that the invaders were gone—caught in a fog between time and place.

Ben opened his eyes to find himself alone, the knife lying unstained at his feet where it had fallen.

"Mearsieanne?" he called.

Silence.

Puzzled, a little upset, he went to tell Clair as he had been bidden, as Siamis emerged from hiding. Time to get to work sorting the befogged invaders; the easiest to push beyond the ward would be those with Norsunder's magic clinging to them. The tougher ones would be those not quite sure which side they would fall on. These he'd have to consider one by one, but that was the price he would pay to protect one of the most powerful, and sacred, spots in the world to the eyes and minds who perceived the world in other than political paradigms.

As for the Chwahir invaders, the lost or wavering would find themselves wandering along the uninhabited shore somewhere to the north. Maybe they'd even make a run for freedom.

Ben carried the news, and the knife, back up to the white castle, where Clair and CJ listened, at first mystified, then Clair's expression shuttered. "Thanks, Ben," she said. "Could you fly high enough so no enemy will see you, and scout where they are now?"

Ben ran toward the open window. He flung himself out, skinny arms sweeping back as they became wings, his body shimmering into bird form. CJ watched, longing to be able to do just that.

Clair said to CJ, "I think you and I should check on Mearsieanne's...things, before the others come around."

CJ gripped her hands tight, as Clair led the way to Mearsieanne's suite, paused before the door — and then opened it slowly, without knocking. It was then that CJ began to suspect what Clair already knew.

The two walked into a clean room, empty of all personal items. Only the furnishings remained. Even the bedding was gone, though Clair suspected she would discover it all put through the cleaning frame, folded, and stashed among the linens downstairs.

She walked to the closet. All those pretty dresses: gone.

"Where are her clothes?" CJ whispered — as if Mearsieanne could hear her.

"I suspect she sent them off as donations somewhere. A place she earmarked during these last four years. She's been planning this a long time. But couldn't tell us." To CJ's horror, Clair's chest heaved on a sob. Tears slipped down her cheeks, but then she drew a hard, shuddering breath. "It's what she wanted. And if Ben is right about what she said..." She faced CJ. "Let's go wait for Ben."

It was not a long wait. "Gone," he said. "No sign of them."

"Out on the water, too?"

"Oh, the ships are out there. I don't know about up north. I can scout, but it'll take some time to get there and back. But there are none here." He pointed out toward the base of the mountain.

"Please do," Clair asked. "It's important."

The rest of the day passed as if in a dream. CJ stayed with Clair, who seemed to want her company, though neither said anything. Even when they found a neat stack of papers on Mearsieanne's desk in the library, notes in her careful, old-fashioned hand detailing her thoughts about kingdom matters.

Clair read through every one, and made two piles. CJ occupied herself as best she could, understanding that her part was to be company. She finally grabbed a book, though later she couldn't say what she'd read.

Finally Clair looked up, tapping the smaller pile. "These things I will finish the way she wanted. I think they are good for everybody." She tapped the larger pile. "These, I won't, because I don't think we need to become a little Colend. What I remember of Colend. Nothing wrong with Colend," she added a little desperately, as if CJ had argued. No, as if she herself argued with Mearsieanne's ghost. "Colend is exactly right for Colend. But it isn't for us."

She carried the papers to the archive, wrote the date and the contents down, and added them to the trunk of kingdom records, which every few decades were bound into books by industrious scribes with not much else to do.

Then the girls gathered in the kitchen for dinner, an old, comfortable habit. Of them only Clair and thoughtful Seshe noticed the abandonment of the etiquette Mearsieanne had tried so hard to impose, and both felt pulses of guilt. But not strong enough to say anything.

Ben returned before they finished dessert. "The Chwahir and their Norsunder leaders — they are the ones wearing gray — are still in Reyte and Ujban but they can't get over the hills into our land. I did a little listening. A patrol tried, got lost in a fog, and found themselves far away — still on that side."

Clair nodded slowly. "So, what we have is a haven inside a ward, that Norsunder can't cross. But it sounds like nobody else has one, at least last we heard. It seems unfair for only us to have it."

CJ considered that. "Should we tell the alliance? But how? Mearsieanne didn't leave anything with instructions on How To Ward A Kingdom Against Norsunder."

"She didn't," Clair repeated, wondering why not. She'd thought Mearsieanne favored some of her fellow rulers. She'd even been friends with Tahra of Everon. She had often consulted Clair's Aunt Murial, and Erai-Yanya of Roth Drael. But Mearsieanne had left no note, even. And now she was beyond asking.

It never occurred to either of them that the home so everyday to them was unique in the world—the only kingdom built around a Selenseh Redian, directly above a pool of the indigenous beings whose magic was the most powerful in the world. And directly above the Selenseh Redian, their white palace, which had its own secrets.

In short, this was the only place in the world that could sustain such a ward.

CJ scowled. "You said we can't write notes. And the Destinations don't work."

"Oh, they work, but the enemy has been warding all the Destinations in the book to force transfers straight to the Norsundrians," Clair said. "That's what Arthur's last message warned of, and I believe him."

"Using a person as a destination to transfer to is dangerous," CJ said.

"Very. But maybe it's the thing to do? Only who?"

CJ was thinking rapidly. Clair was queen again. Yay! But maybe she ought not to yell about how much better things would be now. It wouldn't be right. As queen, Clair would have to get back to queening, after a suitable memorial. That meant CJ was a princess again, and *that* meant she ought to be helping, instead of staying out of Mearsieanne's way—her one job, before.

"I'll go," she said. "Maybe, if I go, the alliance will finally believe I'm not a villain."

"CJ, they never thought you were."

"Yes they did. Well, I think most stopped, but Atan still thought so. But if I went to someone like Rel—Rel! Hey, didn't he have some plan for if Norsunder attacked, people were supposed to sneak into some podunky town?"

Clair did not ask what podunky meant — it had to be one of CJ's leftover Earth terms.

CJ went on, "Rel's almost always outside. Do you think I ought to transfer to him?"

"We don't know where he is," Clair said doubtfully. While transferring to someone underage didn't bother her, transferring to adults did. "It would be very bad manners to transfer to him if he's in the bath or asleep in bed."

"My little bit of DY isn't good enough to reach him."

Clair was going to claim the same, except that she knew that if she concentrated hard on someone she knew fairly well, she sometimes got glimpses from their surface thoughts — all she would allow herself. She tried now, then said, "It's morning where he is. He's on a street."

"All right," CJ said. "I'm going."

"I'll go with you," Falinneh said promptly.

"Me, too," Dhana said.

"I will, as well," Seshe said, and saw Clair's forehead tension ease; nothing had to be said, but Seshe understood Clair's worry that the farther the alliance moved into adulthood, the more left out, in numerous ways, CJ was going to feel. Seshe was expert at being a buffer.

"If Norsunder is doing evil wards," Clair said, "then I'm going to fix your medallions so that you'll transfer back directly to the Selenseh Redian."

"Ugh," CJ said — but she didn't argue; she was full of virtuous determination to do everything right so They would stop looking at her as if she'd barfed on their shoes.

Twelve

Royal Castle at Choreid Dhelerei, Capital of Marloven Hess

LEANDER TLENNEN-HESS TOILED up the stairs, past guards at every landing. He felt their gazes on him as he passed. Was all this tension his or theirs?

Outside Senrid's study a jumble of Marloven black-and-tan resolved into two armed guards and a row of runners ready to be sent on errands. They parted when they saw Leander, but did not salute. Respect, Leander noted with some irony, rested here not with birth as in some places (including his own home, his adopted sister's fretful fallback when she felt ignored), or with looks and style as in many royal courts, or even with scholarly attainments as in the scribe guilds, heralds, archives, and of course in the mage schools. So many human hierarchies, sometimes clashing terribly: their friend Rel had been respected as long as Leander had known him simply because he was huge.

But here, only military rank gained respect. The best Leander could hope for was tolerance.

He passed into Senrid's study and stopped short. In the few days he'd been gone, the room, which hadn't changed for years, had been transformed into what he'd always imagined a war command center would look like. All that was missing was the tent around them.

Senrid's desk had been pushed into the center of the room, up against another big table of roughly the same size. Spread over it lay the biggest map Leander had ever seen. It was astonishingly detailed, the hills bisecting Vasande Leror molded out of clay. Leander recognized the passes, detailed enough that for a moment a peculiar sensation passed through him, as if he flew overhead.

He shut his eyes and it was a map again. Rivers had been painted in blue. All the Marloven cities outside the capital were blocks. On another table off to one side some aides were in the process of building a wooden simulacrum of Choreid Dhelerei. Readying for possible invasion of the city? Leander flinched inwardly.

Senrid and a couple of his captains stood around the kingdom map. Leander recognized Retren Forthan among them, a big, husky man half a head taller than Senrid, with regular features and hair beginning to thin at his temples, young as he was. Forthan alone wore the plain gold shoulder flashes of a commander in chief, whereas Senrid still wore no rank markers on his uniform.

Senrid was talking. "We have to consider that King Halmaer Nothalin is once again supplying Norsunder, as he did at the end of my uncle's reign."

"Perideth," one of the assembled captains muttered, and made a spitting motion to the side.

Senrid glanced up. "Leander. You're back. Vasande Leror ready?"

"All those who wanted to evacuate are gone. I spent the day riding around to inspect. If Norsunder tries crossing the southern pass to come across Vasande Leror, they won't find an oat or a piece of hay, much less food. Oh, I saw a huge dust cloud in the south—I suspect that was your academy horses. It'll take an army to find them now."

"Good." Senrid's lack of reaction meant he already knew it. Leander realized then that he was interrupting a strategy session, but before he could leave, Senrid said, "Stay a moment? Forthan, the rest of you captains, we'll wait on the first sighting."

Fists struck chests, and everyone except Commander Keriam walked out. He remained at the map, years and years of experience helping him calculate with fair accuracy how far a scout could travel in a day. He was replacing the scout pins in the map one by one, so they could monitor approximate positions.

Senrid followed the exiting captains to the door, stuck his head out, and said, "Runners dismissed except for the duty runner."

Senrid turned back into the study, making a mental check on his daughter: still napping. She'd rouse soon, and then they'd have dinner. He meant to keep life as normal as possible as long as possible.

"I sent Kyale to put her stuff in the guest chamber," Leander said, his thoughts running parallel. "She's off to your theater, as usual, but she did volunteer to play with Crystal Ingrid if it becomes necessary to keep her busy. And Llhei is with us," he added.

Senrid interpreted that successfully: Kyale's old nanny had consented to come with them, to act as both Kyale's servant, but also, to help with Crystal Ingrid if Kyale ran off to watch plays. Crystal Ingrid had met Llhei a few times, and had liked her, especially as Llhei always offered the sorts of treats seldom found in Marloven Hess; Senrid himself couldn't stand treacle-cakes and honey-candies, but he remembered his cousin had loved such sweets.

"They're both welcome." Senrid turned up his hand; Kyale's feud with him had become more habit than not in the last couple of years. As Kyale had never extended her dislike of him to Crystal Ingrid, he could put up with Kyale's craving for attention and drama. "You can stay there if you want, though I'd rather you take the room across here. So you're in reach if I need backup with the magic."

Leander held up the worn old carryall that Kyale had never succeeded in getting him to throw away, as not suitable for a king. "That's why I brought this along, in case." He went to the room across from Senrid's study, tossed the carryall in, then came back. "What am I looking at?" he asked, studying the map as Commander Keriam replaced another pin a finger's breadth from the northern border of Marloven Hess.

"Readiness, merely," Senrid said. "It'll get a lot more specific once they invade."

"I take it you don't know how many of them there are."

"Not until our scouts can get back across the border. All we know is that the enemy has overrun Halia from both ends, closing in on us."

"You don't seem to have anyone much over by Vasande Leror," Leander commented, doing his best to hide how sickened the news about Halia being overrun made him feel: he'd known it was all real, and yet each dawn filled with light exactly the same as always, birds sang, the wind rustled in trees. Signs of peace. Once.

"That's because I doubt they will come at us from the east, so most of East Army is backing up Stad in the North, and Forthan in the south. Summers are just as dry in the mountain passes as they are in the Nelkereth, as you know. And if your people have cleaned out all storage, than any scouts of theirs who slip by my roaming patrols will not find forage for a sizable force. As for the west, if we get ship sightings, the four western cities will reinforce West Army. The Rualese are cooperating with us, I'm relieved to say."

Leander, the historian, reflected that the people of the coast—a mixture of Iascan and Toaran from directly across the sea—had stubbornly resisted total integration with the Marlovens for centuries. Mostly because their faces were always toward the sea. When the last treaty, forced on Senrid's grandfather, gave them a long, narrow country of their own, Enneh Rual, things had pretty much continued exactly as they always had. Political boundaries meant little to them.

Senrid went on, " The last report I had from the Delfin Islands was a fleet of Chwahir, but they were sticking to the coast of Toar."

"Nothing since?"

"Nothing since."

Leander thought of his golden notecase left behind on his desk, Senrid having warned him that they were useless now. He said bleakly, "I don't know what to think. After so long. Centuries. The scribe desks went down in a matter of a few days."

"My guess is," Senrid said, "that was Siamis."

"What?" Leander's voice cracked. "He's an enemy after all?"

"No. I have no proof, but I think he's been working on it for years, without telling anyone. The lighters wouldn't listen— they were all confident that the magic couldn't be breached. Tsauderei is the most reasonable of them, but even he waved off the possibility as impossible. So—again, just a guess—Siamis took the system down before Norsunder could compromise it, and duplicate all urgent letters, thereby tracing every one of their capital list targets without having to stir off their stools."

"Oh." Leander looked blank.

"Leander, I told you years ago that first year academy students learn that command is another word for management of communication, and control of resources—"

"—which means your fighters, supplies, and what you called terrain. I remember that much, though little else. I thought 'communication' meant your tower beacons and runners and codes and passwords."

Senrid smiled grimly. "Civ communication is a part of that. Especially when they are targets."

Leander frowned the little markers on the map. "When I consider that each of these represents a number of living, breathing people, all with families they love, I feel sick."

"Take your complaint to the enemy," Senrid said, but without any heat. "We all hate it. They didn't give us a choice."

Leander said, his gaze on the map. "A lot of places are surrendering. Nothing bad has happened to them."

"First of all, that's as of now. Do you really believe Norsunder would go to all this trouble to become benign overlords?"

"No, I don't," Leander said, flinching. "Never mind."

But Senrid went on, because he had a purpose, one that had given him uncounted sleepless nights—and Leander had in a sense brought it up first. Best to get it out now. "Secondly, Norsunder is leaving the conquered kingdoms more or less alone right now because most civilians are too shocked and frightened to give them much trouble. But that's the first stage." Senrid leaned against his desk, arms crossed. "What do you think will happen to us if I surrender? Are the Norsundrians going to let us go back to our usual lives, when so much of my population is armed?"

"No. Right."

"And then there's me. I've had a target on my back as long as I can remember."

"The threat of capturing leaders and putting spells on them. We've always talked about it. But it's been theory more than practice, right? Has it happened? Successfully? I remember your uncle trying various spells on you to control you."

"I warded those," Senrid said, as though it had been easy, as if he hadn't been ten or eleven when he had to begin defending his life against his uncle. "My cousin Ndand bore the brunt of his experiments, until I figured it out and put protective wards on her, too." Senrid frowned and dismissed the subject with a quick, flat-handed wave. "That's the past. And it's not my incompetent uncle behind mind control spells, it's Yeres, who, I'm told, has been trying for ages to reproduce Dena Yeresbeth by magic. Or what she thinks is Dena Yeresbeth—mainly an ability to invade and control others' minds."

Leander listened to the quick flow of words, sensing an undercurrent of desperation.

"If they did that to you, your people would be sent to fight their wars, is that what you fear?"

"Oh, if it were only that easy. I think they have enough people who want to fight wars. For the strike troops, killing is their sport. What would be far worse is me, under compulsion, sending my people to root out and destroy any sign of resistance. Because we'd know how to spot it."

An image struck Leander: a blank-eyed Senrid sending people like Ret Forthan and Janred Senelac, his top commanders who were decent, even pleasant individuals aside from all their training and practice in military matters, to spy out and slaughter civilians who tried to resist Norsunder's mail fist.

Senrid went on, "No, we won't be surrendering at the outset, the way Sartor did. If we have to fight, we'd much rather be fighting against Norsunder than for them."

Leander sighed, suppressing the observation that if you trained for war, somebody was going to want to put that to use. Senrid knew that. He wanted to change it. But changing centuries of training and thinking was akin to changing the course of a river by digging with a spoon. You could do it, but not overnight. "Have they actually succeeded in mind-controlling anyone?"

"The last I heard, Norsunder had successfully subverted the Venn through their own protectors. Using blood magic. They intended to use it on the young king, but he slit his own throat first."

Leander turned away, as if he could get physical distance from the horror. "I wish I hadn't asked."

Senrid said, soberly, "But you wondered. And you need to hear the answer. *I* need you to hear the answer, because I want you to promise me: if they do get hold of me, and magically rip my brains out and replace them with some semblance of drooling obedience, I want you to take me out. Promise. Please." He turned out his palm toward Commander Keriam, who was finishing with the pins, his head bent over the map. "Keriam and I promised each other. Forthan and I, too. Jan Senelac and Forthan as well, with each other and us. They're not likely to try it with anyone else."

Leander was not ready for this conversation. But Senrid's steady gaze, the vein beating in his temple, made it clear how much it meant to him. "I'll do it."

Senrid let out a sigh of relief. "Thank you." Then, in a more normal voice, "The pup is awake. Dinner will be soon."

Leander discovered that his hands were sweating and put them behind his back as he followed Senrid out, the two of them watched soberly by the man who'd acted as father to the orphan king since Senrid was five.

Crystal Ingrid had woken, and was busy with her dolls.

She looked up on Senrid coming through the open door. In that moment, less than a heartbeat, Senrid perceived his tension mirrored in the child. So he forced himself to lean in the doorway, and to smile.

Her reaction was quick, inadvertent, relieved. Then she said loudly, "'Ware! Here comes the dragon!"

He responded to the cue and advanced, making a terrible face. The dolls were abandoned and father chased daughter long enough to reassure her, then he set her on his shoulder and said, "Off to dinner. And look, Uncle Leader is here!"

"Is Princess Kitty here, too?"

"She went to the theater, but she promised to play with you later."

"We'll do stories! She does stories with me. Last time, my princess was fighting pirates, and..." Her piping voice outlined a very unlikely plot all the way to the dining room.

The next morning, tiny, silvery-haired Kyale was in the dining room with Leander, gowned in expensive silks and ribbons as if for a garden party. She and Leander sat on either side of

Crystal Ingrid as one of the kitchen runners set down a tray of fresh-baked pastry, and Kyale was in the middle of describing the play she had attended. But she broke off and pointed to the pastries, saying, "Crystal Ingrid! Want a fresh apple tart?"

Crystal Ingrid turned to Senrid, who opened his hand toward her. Again, he sensed her tension: she did not have to ask permission to eat a tart. Her unspoken question—instinctive, still not even formed into words—asked if there was time, if whatever made him tense was too dire for tartlets. It hurt him to see his tension mirrored in her, and he didn't know how to fix that, except to try harder to hide his thoughts.

By supper-time, Crystal Ingrid's unconscious tension had turned into worry. She'd had to stay in her rooms and play. All day. And Monta hadn't played with her. She could check by mind-touch on his whereabouts—and did—but he was always busy, his mind racing much too fast through images and words she didn't comprehend.

She paid scarce heed to words and images that she didn't understand. She was used to that. Something else was wrong, something that he hid from her.

Monta had never hidden anything before, except certain memories he'd said she was not yet old enough to experience. She trusted that, ever since she'd dove into one of his dreams, and saw her father when small hurt very bad by a rage-faced man called *Uncle Tdanerend*, which had haunted her own dreams for many nights.

This was different. It wasn't memories of Norsunder or Uncle Tdanerend. And it wasn't the war. That made him angry. It was something else. She wanted to find it. To fix it, the way he always fixed things when she was troubled in spirit. Lyren-Sartora had told her on her last visit that she was going to be as good at farsense as Liere—

Crystal Ingrid saw a vivid mental image of the person who had come visiting with Lyren-Sartora a few days ago. Long golden hair, peachy-brown skin, golden eyes—she recognized her then, from many, many images in the good memories he'd shared. There was only this one memory of her in her new form; Crystal Ingrid reached to pursue it.

And rammed into mental block.

She felt her unbody-self thump into her body-self so fast that it left her a little dizzy, and she looked up, and blinked. They were still sitting at supper. There was her spoon, and her half-eaten soup, and the row of high windows showed dark outside, and she was still holding a piece of bread. The spicy smell of the fish soup made the air warm.

She looked up. Monta's eyes were serious. "We don't do anything together," she said. "I want to play. I want you to read to me." Was that what was wrong? No, that was a part, but what about that person?

"We're at war. It takes all my time. You know that."

"But just now. You were not talking to Harskiald Forthan or Commander Keriam. we are alone, and you were thinking, and I saw —"

He interrupted. "You know what I said about mind-touch without permission."

He loathed shutting her out. Seeing her unhappy made him feel wretched. But how else to teach her to respect personal boundaries?

She studied him, listening with voice and mind. There was no joy in his voice, no forgiveness. Uncle Leander looked down at his plate, and Princess Kitty scowled at Monta.

Crystal Ingrid slid off her chair and ran out of the room, slamming the door with both hands. Then she ran to her room, which she'd been stuck in all day long, without ever getting to go outside, even though there wasn't any ice.

She flopped onto the floor trying not to cry; her unhappiness washed through her mind and crashed back into him, cold as ice.

A knock at her door.

Monta had made her learn to close doors and knock when she turned four, and she hated that, too. But she liked to slam them when she was mad.

Another knock. "Come in," she said, like a grownup.

The door opened, and Senrid entered. As soon as Crystal Ingrid saw him, her frustration found words. Her voice was small. "I want to understand why you were thinking about —"

"I don't want to talk about my thoughts," he said, sitting on the floor beside her. "You are old enough to recognize boundaries."

"But that other one, that wasn't thoughts, it was memory," she protested, remembering the horror of the Norsunder prison, seen through his eyes. When no one cared what happened to him there. She shivered in reaction, wrestling with too many emotions, and he made no move to hold her, or help her, or even to smile, though he sat right beside her. And his surface thoughts were still shielded away.

A sob escaped her, but then she felt his arms around her, and his thoughts were forgiving and kind. "How did that old memory make you feel?"

"Awful, awful, awful," she sobbed.

"Did it help you in any way? Teach you anything good?"

"Nonononono,"

"That is exactly why we have to learn boundaries," he said quietly. "Not to protect me, but to protect you."

Her breath shuddered, but she was able to stop crying. Oh. He didn't want her feeling whatever it was that bothered him, just as he wanted to protect her from his terrible memories. She relaxed against his arm. Boundaries made sense now. They were important.

He gave her a squeeze, while making the inward decision to evoke the hard mental shield that had been habitual for so long, relaxed when she was born. But she had vocabulary now, and had to learn to express feelings in words.

He knew the terrible isolation of a hard shield. But she was so quick, so unnervingly prescient, her Dena Yeresbeth potentially far stronger than his own. He cuddled her until her breathing eased, as he rebuilt that mental shield.

And though the pressure of time—of need—was almost inexorable, he shoved that aside so that she could see the outward signs of reassurance. She studied his face, and he saw her features relax into the focus of comprehension.

He said, "Come back to the dining room and finish your supper, then we'll play."

Her inward happiness was like sudden sunlight after a winter of rain; he had to see it, not feel it, for to shut his thoughts in, he must shut hers out.

But people almost five are not subtle about masking their feelings. She gobbled down her dinner, then gleefully ran through the palace halls, Senrid roaring villainously and Crystal Ingrid shrieking defiance.

She could feel how much the castle people liked seeing it and hearing it. She buoyed her spirits on their reassurance, then she remembered, boundaries! She shut them out as they kept up the game, which ended, as always, at the arrival of a dust-covered runner.

Thirteen

EARLY ON A BRIGHT, hot morning, a half-circle of scouts and patrol captains stood well back of their commander, who walked along a cliff, peering into Marloven Hess from the extremity of the southern border. The only one facing Imry Llyenthur was the company captain, Ronzic.

Llyenthur studied the Marloven night patrol returning from its rounds, and watched the day patrol ride out. Then he squinted up at the sun roasting them from above, early as it was. "Why didn't I bring a hat? Duin."

"Here."

"Make a note. Hat."

"Done."

The captains and scouts exchanged looks, then froze when Imry Llyenthur turned to regard them. "What makes you think they aren't ready for us?"

He looked so bland, standing there in a half-laced tunic-shirt, no coat, baggy trousers. Mocs instead of boots. Maybe mid-twenties. If that. Some had found it hilarious that Dran Llyenthur, his father, was not only named for a sometimes pirate port, he'd been an actual pirate as well as an assassin, with a taste for luxury living. But Aldon—older and bigger and lethally ambitious—was up north, following orders, and this

Imry Llyenthur was here, the one the Host had picked to hand out the orders.

He turned back to peer into the valley, hazy in the sunshine, as if they were on a picnic, and not poised to attack.

Ronzic realized that the question was not rhetorical when Llyenthur glanced over his shoulder, brows raised. Fassler Duin, who had begun his present posting as Llyenthur's aide-de-camp by stepping over the previous incumbent's corpse, held his breath.

Ronzic said, "Regular patrols, not increased in number, or pushed to a wider perimeter. Same number of sentries on yon walls as last year, when we first posted watches here."

They couldn't step beyond the border without setting off an alert; the standing orders were to observe until the mages could take down Senrid Montredaun-An's wards. That would be the attack signal.

"Yes," Imry Llyenthur said, hands clasped behind him. The fabric of his loose sleeves revealed the outline of wrist knives; word was, when he was annoyed he struck fast, which was good, instead of playing around like Aldon, and especially Efael. Not so good: you didn't get a second chance to lie, finesse, or even explain. Rumor also insisted he had that mind-invasion skill, like Detlev, which meant he'd know if you were lying or finessing before you got the words out.

Emboldened, Ronzic ventured further. "All the reports agree, Senrid Montredaun-An never went through the Marloven academy. He's never run anything but their summer wargames, where no one dares touch him."

"And so you assume he's a strutting blowhard like Prince Valta down there in Perideth? Could be you're right."

Unspoken—but Llyenthur knew quite well—was Ronzic's desire to commence the attack before Bostian, now somewhere in the pass east of Telyerhas, could get here, so he would not have to share command.

Nothing wrong with ambition—within limits. And Bostian was a week late, which no doubt pleased Efael.

Timing was tight, but there were no senior mages free. Llyenthur had gone himself to Tsranf to examine the cell in question; he didn't care one way or another about the Queen of Sartor, or Yeres's cherished plan to play puppet-master. His single purpose had been to check the wards he'd laid himself against Detlev's appearance. The ward was still tight, and there was no corpse waiting to be discovered, which meant Detlev had not been anywhere near. Or any of his boys.

But someone had used a form of magic Llyenthur hadn't thought anyone in this world knew.

He'd corroborated Alsaes's lies, thereby losing Ririn, but the gain was Yeres's mages thrown into redoing every one of the wards and spells over the fortress, thinking that they had somehow erred in the fatiguingly complicated setup. Redoing it from the first layer spells ought to keep them all busy, especially as Efael was pulling them in two directions in his attempt to refashion Wan-Edhe's pocket Norsunder in Chwahirsland. It had been nearly dismantled by that mysterious ghost Jilo, whose motivations were as impossible to guess as his location.

Unfortunately, all these things would not keep Efael busy long enough.

Marloven Hess had better fall fast.

"It seems," Llyenthur said, "I'll have to deal with the wards myself, while you get ready to ride."

Late that night, Senrid felt the internal poke of an alert: someone was attacking his wards. "Leander!"

The door across the hall slammed open, followed by the sound of stumbling footsteps, and Leander appeared, still doing up the buttons of his shirt.

"Attack on the wards," Senrid said. "It means they're coming. I'm trying to reinforce the transfer alert." Senrid pointed to the waiting magic books.

Leander was going to protest that he didn't know dark magic, which was very dangerous to mess with, but Senrid knew that.

Senrid said to the unspoken question, "I can't prevent transfers. That kind of magic is destructive. If you go to Jilo's capital, you'll get a firsthand example of just how much. But the ward that I count on most lets me know exactly where someone transfers within my borders." He brandished a pair of shank buttons. "This one will get me to whoever transferred in, and this one," he touched the second wooden shank, "has a stone spell on it. While they are recovering, all I have to do it toss and touch. Instant statue. So. What I need from you are deflecting wards, whatever you can make in lighter magic. Think of it as papering over my ward, hiding it..."

Leander threw himself into a chair, blinking his eyes into focus, after almost an hour of sleep. They both knew that magic was not going to halt the invasion. But the alerts helped, and the transfer ward kept Norsunder's mages out.

Senrid ran to the door and said to the wide-eyed duty runner, "Go to the tower. Signal: *enemy in sight*. Summon all runners. Put up the priority pennons." Which meant his gallopers would get fresh horses before any commander, even.

Word spread with the speed of the beacon fires lighting across plains and hills.

By the last watch of the night, it had spread from north to south. At the camp inward of the southern border, Retren Forthan listened to the first five squeak-voiced words stuttered out by his teenage duty runner, and waved the boy to silence. "You. Ride back to the royal city, message received."

The boy's hand slapped his chest, but he clearly wanted to stay.

Forthan would never insult an ardent sixteen-year-old by citing his age; he was a father himself. "The king might have a message for you to bring back," he added, in his sternest voice.

The boy gulped and ran out; that should keep him safe for at least a week.

As soon as Forthan heard his footsteps chuffing toward the picket line through the dry, crackling grasses, he left the command tent, which was already being packed up by his efficient personal runners, and went to the tent he shared with his family.

"Time to vanish," he said to Fenis Senelac, his wife. And to his children, "You know the plan." He finished with a hard hug to each. He felt a tension in his eldest's body, and recognized resistance. Of course Mardran wanted to stay and be a hero, because all his favorite ballads were about heroes fighting against all odds. "Mardran. You are under your mother's orders. Got that?"

Mardran Senelac's gaze shifted sideways as he turned up his palm.

"I want to hear your promise."

Foiled, Mardran crossed his arms, his face a scowl. "I promise. Since you think I'm a baby and a coward."

Forthan wished he could laugh, and point out how very

young Mardran sounded, but he knew that would make things so much worse. "When I get back, we'll see how tough you are in the field," he said, coaxing.

Mardran muttered under his breath, but the tightness in his shoulders eased a fraction.

Over the children's heads, Fenis gave Ret Forthan a wry smile; she had grown up with brothers, and he could trust her to be vigilant in case Mardran was tempted to sneak away. He kissed her and walked out, his mind leaving the worries of the father and husband, assuming the emotional armor of a harskiald as he issued orders at every step.

The same kind of leave-taking took place all over the kingdom, especially at the northern and southern borders: everyone expected a two-prong attack.

Which was what they got.

The sun had not quite risen when Ronzic's company stormed the border fortress. Everything went as drilled; the heavy horses first, bearing the pieces of two catapults as the light riders kept up a ceiling of arrows at the Marloven wall sentries. Still, some popped up to shoot at those building the catapults. Two builders fell, two sentries vanished, one with an arrow in an arm not shielded in time, the other shot in the chest, which was exposed for an instant as he pulled his bow.

Teams of three brought big boulders, of which there were plenty. They'd nearly battered the door to pieces when the Norsundrian foot warriors arrived running, spears and swords at the ready, teams carrying ladders.

That was when the doors opened and the Marlovens came out on the attack. Archers popped up on the wall and began shooting, one arrow to a warrior.

Ronzic's company, outnumbering the defenders by two, began pushing the Marlovens back toward the gates when horns rang through the hills, echoing, and Forthan himself, with an entire flight—hidden all this time—galloped up to surround the Norsundrians and cut them to pieces.

Imry Llyenthur, watching through a spyglass from behind a willow, saw Ronzic drop, hacked up by three Marloven youths. "And that," he murmured, "is why I wanted Bostian here first." He counted the Marloven numbers, assessed their fighting ability, and brought Ronzic's second in command, Capnias, forward. Capnias was belligerent, mean as a snake, but too impetuous to be more than adequate as a commander.

As long as he did what he was told, he could hold things until Bostian arrived.

Llyenthur then transferred to the northern border, as he still hadn't managed to break the wards. He found the Norsundrians in judicious retreat, chased by the remains of a vast cavalry charge that, their commander swore shortly after, "seemed to come right up out of the ground."

"You won't be caught short twice," Llyenthur observed.

The commander paled under the mud. "No. We won't." He eyed Llyenthur. "I thought you'd be scouting by magic."

"I can't breach the border until I bring down the wards. That is, I can, but Senrid Montredaun-An will know exactly where I am, just as he knows numbers crossing the border as long as there is anything tainted with magic. But that will change soon. Here's what I want..."

The next day, the attacks were different.

In the north, small bands of skirmishers tried to draw the Marlovens over the border. The rest remained in Dragon Teeth formation, which broke up charges at the outset.

In the south, the Norsundrian reinforcement forayed against Methden in the kingdom's extreme southwest corner, at the opposite end from the previous attack. The Jarl of Methden's defensive force boiled out in a fury, driving the Norsundrians back—but again, the Marlovens could not be lured past the border.

The raids continued through the night, the following day under cover of hard rain, and through the next night, catching and scragging a scout or two and in the south, one patrol. But the Norsundrians also suffered losses, lured into treacherous ground, where they became pincushions.

Reports went both ways.

Five days in, the Norsundrians still had not breached the border, but Llyenthur, having waited while watching and evaluating, received Bostian's outriders: they would arrive in the next day or so. Meanwhile, Capnias had at least caught and shot a few spies. And his company was eager for battle.

Llyenthur, forced to act as his own mage as well as to see to overall command, reviewed the internal map.

In Halia's extreme north, Llyenthur's army, which had finished locking down Visegn, had left a small occupation company to hold Larkadhe, the little kingdom's principle city, and marched south, teaching Ianavair a very hard lesson in the dangers of relying on a centuries-old reputation. His reinforcements were almost here, and he still had those ships full of Chwahir foot-warriors, though he suspected that Efael had tampered with the command structure, as he had pretty much taken over Chwahirsland, ruling through Wan-Edhe.

Llyenthur passed down the commands to attack in force.

Capnias, predictably, was like an arrow shot from a bow.

Forthan's instincts were honed by years of observing the patterns of human violence. He used the precious transfer tokens Senrid had given him—he knew how long it took to make them, and he also knew how long it took to recover—to warn the Jarl of Methden at the other end of the southern border, and Jan Senelac in the north. "They are coming in hard next, I'm sure of it," he said. "I heard about your charge. Sounded like something straight out of a ballad."

Jan Senelac grinned, briefly calling to mind the boys they'd been in the academy, pulling pranks on one another, when the worst punishment was a couple of swats across the shoulder blades with a senior's yew wand.

Jan's smile vanished. "They're using Dragon's Teeth to march."

Forthan wiped his hair out of his eyes, then said, "You're doing what? Sting and run?"

Senelac opened his hand in agreement.

"Good. The river is at its lowest. They'll ford it with ease. If they have the numbers, don't try to hold the plains. Harass the shit out of them. Especially at night. The king is sending half of Zheirban north to back Eveneth—we still have to hold something in reserve in the west. He says that those ships someone reported up north somewhere could be even with us by now."

Senelac said, "My brother is with West Army. If he comes, we'll hit them back together."

Forthan endured one more transfer back to the south, though it felt like a hammer to every joint, especially his skull. When he wiped his nose and saw blood, he shoved the rest of the transfer tokens back into his pocket for the day.

Fourteen

IN CHOREID DHELEREI, TENSION evidenced in quick conversations, knots of people moving about with intent, rather
than strolling, though most did their best to go about daily life.
But the sight of mud-covered gallopers on foam-flecked horses
going in and out of the royal castle rung the tension out faster,
the count of messengers spreading from lips to ears: Senrid
began sending someone down to the castle gate to post what
news they had.

Kyale arrived that night at the theater to find the play
abandoned. Instead—typical Marlovens, she thought, rolling
her eyes—they were singing war ballads, drums rolling and
pounding the galloping rhythms. She turned around and went
back to the castle, where she did her best to entertain Crystal
Ingrid, who never got enough stories about adventuring
princesses. They played and played, but whenever Senrid poke
his head in briefly, Crystal Ingrid forgot what they were doing
and cried out happily, "Monta!"

Kyale tried to keep her annoyance to herself. Who was
working the hardest to keep the child occupied? Not Senrid!
But who gets all the attention when he walks in?

She complained later that night to Llhei, who stroked her
hair as if she were still six and not the equivalent of sixteen,

saying, "He's her father."

Kyale, who never had a father, muttered, "I never felt that way about Mother."

Llhei's wrinkled face softened with patient, affectionate humor; the nanny had been a part of Leander's and Kyale's lives since they were small, providing what little parenting either had had, and she had been past middle age when she came to them. So it was understandable that they didn't see how very old she was now. "Actually, you did. And at that same age. It's just that she never repaid your loyalty with her attention, except when it would gain her something. Let them be. It's good for them both."

Kyale muttered that nothing was good for Senrid, or good enough. Nevertheless, when she poked her head in the study, and saw his blond head and Leander's dark one bent over their books as they muttered incomprehensibly back and forth, she decided that at least studying was fun for Leander.

Which it was—and fraught in a way, as well.

Kyale often insisted that Senrid had no feelings, but Leander was sure that Senrid felt the same emotions as everyone else, though these were hidden behind thick mental scars. When the three of them reached the age of interest, it had seemed inevitable that he'd crush hard on Senrid, who was so smart, so capable. So fascinating in a restless, nervy way. But the heat of possible intimacy had never woken in Senrid's gaze; he smiled at Leander with the same steady friendship of their boyhood, and Leander had suspected that Senrid's attractions swerved firmly toward girls.

He was sure of it two years ago, when—after a long day of study—the subject of small town versus city had come up, Leander mentioning that Crestel only had one small pleasure house, with only two men among the staff.

Senrid had offered to take him to his favorite place not far from his royal castle, promising as many men as women on its staff. Leander found that Senrid was clearly well liked—for himself, not for being a king, as there was nothing obsequious in the cheery greetings. It was also clear from his brief conversation that for him, sex was a recreational sport, but as yet his emotions had not been engaged, and Leander had assumed that fatherhood as well as ruling a vast land like Marloven Hess left him little time for matters of the heart.

Leander's crush had long since cooled to friendship, but

what lingered was an affection that rendered him sensitive to the subtle changes in Senrid's even, precise speech, his quick manner, his observant gaze. They had not spent so much time solely in one another's company since their first meeting as boys, for Keriam—though in the room with them—remained occupied with the map and logistical matters, only addressing Senrid occasionally.

Another day passed, culminating in a dinner tense with dread and expectation, Senrid looking up every time someone passed the dining room's outer door. Kyale went to sleep early, leaving Senrid and Leander to return to the study and the magic books as they fought through the night against the still-unknown Norsundrian mage over the border wards; when she came by the study the next morning, they were still there, the books piled higher.

"Breakfast is ready," she said loudly. "Crystal Ingrid is right here."

Leander said, "Thank you."

Kyale noted no thanks from Senrid—of course not—but he got up, and took Crystal Ingrid's hand as they went down to the dining room.

But they'd scarcely eaten a bite when a runner appeared at the door, and Senrid bolted from his chair like a shot. He charged into the study a short time later, trailed by the little princess. Leander was right behind her.

There were warriors in battle gear, a tall man with a sun-weathered face, sun-streaked dark hair, and large hands. One side of his head was smeared with blood and he had a bandage twisted round one arm in two places. Crystal Ingrid halted when she recognized the Harskiald, Retren Forthan.

"...drove them back to the flatlands along the Faral by shooting from both cliffs in Aladas. They retreated, but we took losses in getting them there," Forthan said as he struck his fist to his chest.

"How many?" Senrid asked, wondering if he should send Crystal Ingrid out of the room. No, maybe it was better for her to hear what she would one day have to command.

Crystal Ingrid knew when Monta used that tone, there would be no playing today, either. But so far, nobody had told her she had to stay inside! She slipped out to see who among her favorite dogs might be in the castle yard to play with.

Kyale glimpsed her on the stairs, remembered that both of

Crystal Ingrid's minders had been reassigned to runner duty, and she remembered her promise. That dirty courtyard! At least Crystal Ingrid would keep herself busy, especially if there were any castle children about. Nevertheless, she heaved a martyred sigh as she turned about and followed the child.

In the study, silence gripped them all, Senrid standing with head bowed. How many names he knew in those companies!

He finally forced his gaze to the map. "You'll need reinforcements."

Then he stopped. Reinforcements from where? He scrutinized the map, as if an unassigned army would suddenly spring into being. "Call up the academy seniors," he said to Keriam, knowing that the seniors would whoop with triumph, and their families would watch them ride off with grim faces.

Keriam's own face was grim as he touched fist to chest, and began writing an order.

"But they are not to act independently," Senrid added. "Put them directly under...Van Stad, who's still there between Methden and Darchelde, yes?"

Senrid glanced at Forthan, who turned up his hand. "I've got Stad west of the Faral, watching all those old horse thief paths. He could use the reinforcement."

As a young runner dashed out, carrying Keriam's written order, Senrid began drumming his fingers on the table, the books, the back of a chair as he paced back and forth. "There's a different command style now. These past few days were testing forays. We won a couple of minor clashes, but now they know exactly what we can put into the field. What worries me is that this commander also knows our strengths. And we don't know theirs."

"What does that mean?" Leander asked.

"Forthan has pulled back to the most defensible ground. It's the right move, but I suspect Norsunder directed the shape of this battle before crossing the border."

Forthan's mouth tightened. But he didn't disagree.

"Forthan, I have to go see for myself. I'll report to you down south."

Forthan saluted, fist to heart, grimaced as he braced for another magic jolt, and transferred out.

Leander turned to Senrid to object, caught Keriam's eye, and remained silent.

Keriam said evenly, "Might not that be predicted as well?"

"I'm sure it is. And I know they'd love laying me by the heels. But Forthan and I between us knew every fold in the ground from countless war games over the years. What looks like flat plain in the north isn't." Senrid's hand rippled through the air, miming subtly undulating ground covered by streams during snowmelt and spring rains, dry the rest of the year — including now. "I've laid in countless Destinations for just this purpose."

Keriam said, "I suggest you go armed."

Senrid held out his right hand, flexed his fingers, and a blade dropped from the wrist sheath.

Keriam flattened his palm. "If they get that close... Take a bow?"

Senrid cocked his head. Grinned. "Great idea."

He ran down to the armory, got his favorite bow and a quiver of arrows, then shifted by magic-transfer to Eveneth in the west.

When the transfer-malaise diminished, he stood on the highest tower, looking down at the double-ringed city and the distant, regular blobs indicating the enemy, barely discernable in the weakening light as clouds moved slowly overhead. The wind off the far-off sea was cold and strong, promising heavy weather soon.

He breathed deeply, trying to clear his head before he ran down the tower steps to confer with Jarl Eveneth, who would have to send more of his backup north.

Senrid spent the rest of the day shifting from city to front to city, overseeing each situation himself. Each transfer took its toll, feeling roughly like falling from a running horse. But he knew how to land and roll; he took note of each captain's reports, and needs, and then, close to midnight, gathered his remaining strength and transferred home.

He dropped the bow on a side table and looked down at his desk, tried to force the blurred map into clarity, and gave up. When had he slept last? He couldn't remember. A short nap would make him think faster. Sleep while he still could.

He checked on Crystal Ingrid, whose dreams were full of play and song, then retreated to his own room and, leaving his lamps lit, lay on top of his bed, closing his eyes —

A sound jolted him awake before he could identify it: footsteps. Outside his room.

He looked down, realizing he hadn't even undressed. He

leaped through his cleaning frame and ran for the study, which was still lit, the night runner there with Leander and Kyale.

Senrid was surprised to see her there, and braced inwardly for her usual attack, but kept his eyes on the runner. "Report?"

The runner said, "Storm hit—both sides bogged now, visibility zero. But they've surrounded Marlovair completely, and are on the way toward Eveneth. I was trying to figure out how to place the markers."

"I'll do it. Thanks." Senrid waved a hand, and the runner went outside.

Senrid stood motionless, looking down at the map, as Kyale groaned inwardly. She'd gone to bed early the past couple of days in protest. Of what, she couldn't really say. Maybe it was her desire to wake up and find life normal again. In any case, no one had noticed.

Anyway, if the enemies had come over the border, wasn't that a bad thing?

She looked at Senrid, who paid no attention to her. She crossed her arms, and said as coldly as she could, "Have I your *permission* to speak?"

Senrid looked up, his eyes narrowed. "No. And you never will, so bite back the drama."

Kyale glared at him, then turned her shoulder to Senrid and said to her brother, "We'll go to Lisdan now?"

Senrid fought to say nothing. He could not—should not—keep Leander here. He desired more than anything to throw Norsunder out of his kingdom, and so far Forthan and his captains were holding in the south. But the north, much harder to hold, was falling. And if Norsunder brought in heavy reinforcements, if they brought in more mages, if, if, if.

He rubbed his eyes. Despite the talk of reuniting the lands, Leander was not a Marloven.

"Go ahead, if you need to," he said to Leander. "If things go bad here, people know what to do. Keriam has so well drilled the academy—his former scrubs now commanding ridings and wings—that even if I'm scragged and Keriam himself is killed, his training will echo right down the ranks to the most distant farmers in their field."

Leander had never found much meaning in military or political power, but he had in the relationships that made up civilization—defined at this moment as trust and loyalty. Trust. Senrid needed help, but he wasn't going to beg. All the implications of trust hovered in the air around them, unspoken; after Crystal Ingrid was born, Senrid had said, *If something happens to me, will you be her regent?*

Trust. Part of that was, loyalty to friends had to be freely chosen.

"What about Crystal Ingrid?" he asked.

Senrid slewed around, looking surprised at the question. "What about her?"

"If we have to go to Lisdan. Should we take her with us?"

Senrid hesitated, his rejection of the idea visceral. He said slowly, trying to separate sense from sentiment, "She's not quite five. She'd see it as me abandoning her. And I'm not sure she wouldn't get someone to send her right back. But more important than that." Senrid drew a deep breath. "I respect Rel. I know he is doing his best. But with all those kingdoms falling around that area, who's to say it's any safer than here?"

"All true," Leander said. "Except that right now, all of Norsunder seems to be coming at you."

"Right." Senrid pinched his fingers between his brow. "How about this. If the enemy breaches the city, then take her, no matter how hard she fights you."

Leander swallowed painfully. "I will." Then he turned to Kyale. "I can send you to Lisdan."

"Not without you," she said. She'd heard about Lisdan. The entire idea was to hide in plain sight—which meant not being a princess. Rel had set himself up as some sort of person finding workers, and Kyale suspected that the jobs he would find would be the ones nobody wanted. That would be bearable if she wasn't all alone. If she had a friend to share it with. But Lilah Selenna was gone.

How that hurt to think of! Kyale's mind shied away. "Besides, I offered to help by playing with Crystal Ingrid, and already three of her castle friends have been sent to stay with grandmothers and uncles."

Senrid looked past Leander to Kyale, her silvery eyes huge. Annoying Kyale might be, but not impossible. She was a lot like her cats, selfish but good-hearted as long as you didn't expect them to do much besides purr and be ornamental. Crystal Ingrid loved her stories, and there was always Llhei. They and the overworked castle staff could between them be his backup.

"I'd appreciate that," Senrid said. "Let's get some rest."

While we can, Leander thought.

Fifteen

EARLY THE NEXT MORNING, Leander crossed the hall to find Senrid hard at work in his study.

Senrid glanced up, pointed at a pile of books, and said, "You're here. Good. Keriam's handling any dispatches that come in. I've got to see what's going on in the north."

"Then let me see if I can think up some magical aid."

Senrid grabbed his bow and quiver, then vanished, but the intensity of his presence remained in the room.

Leander took in Senrid's detailed drawing on the map, covered with various colored markers that he knew denoted the cavalry and foot of both sides. He could translate the markers into numbers, but he didn't know what it all meant.

Magic, though, he knew.

He pulled over the books Senrid had painstakingly copied from Leander's own study-books—pages covered with his characteristic neat hand. Another was copied from Hibern's books on border-wards, protections, and enchantments, and the fourth was something Leander hadn't seen before. After a fast leafing over the old pages, he knew that he was acquainted with most of the aspects of illusory magic illustrated in it. Apparently Senrid was looking for ways to baffle or confuse the enemy.

Leander ran his thumb absently along the edge of the table, following the time-smoothed bumps where some long-ago Marloven prince or princess had sawed with a knife. He shut out the evidence of things Senrid had written, made. Touched. He had to get his focus on the magical dilemma.

Kyale appeared, silken skirts rustling. "Crystal Ingrid is in the bath. Llhei said she'd get her dressed, which frees up the Marloven servants."

"Are there any left? I thought they'd all become runners."

Kyale shrugged. "One or two, but it's mostly Llhei and me. It's boring watching her splash around in the bath. What can I do?"

"Listen to me reason something out?" Leander asked.

Kyale sat down. "The magic in your books has never made sense to me yet, but go ahead."

"Light magic does not destroy."

She knew that much. "That's why it's called light."

"It falls apart if one tries to force destruction. Also because it's deemed as weak against the destructive power of dark magic, which uses a lot more magic."

"Burns it out," Kyale said. "You can smell it. Like a pot left on the boil until it's dry. Go on."

"If we're to make light magic effective against the advancing enemy, we need to come at them...sideways. Unexpected."

She sighed. "If only we could use my pretty magic."

Leander blinked. "To make what pretty?" His smile was too sad for sarcasm.

Kyale lifted a shoulder. "I know it's not really useful, just...pretty. Mostly."

"Mostly?" Leander learned forward. "Talk to me about it. What have you learned lately?"

Kyale was surprised. In her young days, when she'd talked about colors in the air, people had either looked at her as if she was dreaming, or as if she'd made up stories to be interesting. (Which, ah, she had. Though this was *different*.) Nobody had ever believed her, even Leander, because they really didn't see the colors. She'd eventually learned to blink the ribbons of floating color away, finding them distracting.

"As always, I can only describe them as translucent ribbons of light that you can't touch. Iridescent, too, if that means bright as stars that change color as they...eel through the air." Her fingers swooped gracefully. "Or, you can, but it doesn't feel like silk or velvet. It feels more like...like when an ant walks on your arm. Only like hundreds of ants. Thousands."

Leander shut his eyes, needing to go through it step by step. "Then you got sick a few winters back, you were bored, and you said you pulled the ribbons out of the air, and made light balls, and your cats chased the light balls."

"Yes. Which meant *they* could see them. So I pulled the ribbons out to make toys, mostly lights, but then one day when I was on the way back from Crestel, and a sudden rainstorm struck, and I didn't want to ruin my gown—you know."

"Tell me exactly what you did."

"I pulled and stretched the ribbons over my head, like a rain canopy. And it worked."

"That means you can affect water."

"Enough to keep it off my head, I can. I haven't really done much with water. Water being water. Wet. You know I hate being wet."

"You warded water. It may seem like very little to you, but think about it. Water is a very powerful element."

Kyale looked at him as if he'd grown horns. "As CJ of the Mearsieans says, *oh-h-h-h*-kay?"

"Do you think you could draw water as well as ward it? Pull it up, from the ground? To swamp an invading army?"

Her eyes widened. "I—if there are enough ribbons—maybe?"

Leander was scrambling among the papers on the desk set aside for magic purposes. "Here it is." He held up a paper with Destination markings on it. "Right outside Eveneth, which the enemy is marching on. Let me fix that onto these transfer tokens of Senrid's."

They soon stood on a hill, looking out at a vast column approaching a walled city in the middle distance, the morning light golden on the stone walls. The late summer storm that had battered the land through the night had departed, leaving a washed blue sky.

The enemy was too far away to make out individuals, but that long dark line was frightening enough. Kyale stepped behind a wind-twisted juniper. Leander joined her, tall and so handsome, standing close enough that their arms touched, but as usual, he was no more aware of her proximity than he had been when they were both children.

Kyale tried to shake away the prickles of her own awareness. She hated it when that awareness wreathed around the wrong person. A stable groom. A paper-maker. Leander, who was her brother, even if they unrelated by blood. They had lived as brother and sister. And anyway, he liked the boys. So did she, that was the problem, as there weren't any of suitable rank in stupid little Vasande Leror—

"Kitty?" Leander asked, giving her an inquiring look. "Recovered from the transfer?"

"Yes." She flung back her hair. "What exactly should we do?"

"I realize our magic can't halt them, or hurt them, but if we slow them, it might buy the Marlovens time."

Kyale blinked at the sky, her fingers nipping at nothing, and rolling mere air between them. Then she flung her hands out. Leander still saw nothing, but a few breaths later the front lines of that marching army wavered.

"Mud," Kyale said. "I pulled up all the water from the ground."

"Do it again," he said—and got an idea. "Can you throw some of your lights on that hill way out there, to the north?"

"What kind of lights?"

"Like the reflection of sun off steel?"

Kyale made a face, having no inward picture to match. But then she thought of lights winking in sconce mirrors, and sunlight reflecting off water, and began working on that, as Leander cast his mind back to his early days of learning magic, when he was an outlaw in the forest.

He remembered nearly slaying some of the boys with laughter when a messenger's horse farted, and he captured the stink in an illusory bubble, a trick he had spent weeks dreaming up when he was thirteen. Later, he'd figured out how to capture similar stenches from boggy ground.

You never know what will become useful was his fleeting thought as he muttered the spell to multiply his bubble twofold, fourfold, fourfold again, and so on until it was so unwieldy he risked losing it. He then sent the bubble wobbling and quivering toward the column.

He worked magic for a time, until his brain buzzed and he could no longer hold the spells without a break to recoup his strength. "I'm spent," he admitted. "Maybe another try after some breakfast."

"All right," Kyale said. It had been fun, just her and Leander. But they hadn't stopped the army, just slowed them a little. If she were closer, she could have the fun of seeing them slop around and fall down. But then she and Leander might get caught.

They transferred back. Once she recovered, she ran off to see if Crystal Ingrid was done with her bath.

Leander walked more slowly, looking around as he tried to refocus his mind.

It was strange, the differences between the Marloven royal castle and his own. One would think that a warrior-culture like Marloven Hess would run itself on austere lines, but actually the reverse was true. His own place in Crestel had been an old provincial fortress, and the changes were cosmetic at best. He had scarcely half a dozen servants, for he had grown up living as an outlaw where everyone took care of him or herself, or they worked together for the common good. It embarrassed him to have people cleaning up after him, or preparing meals that he was perfectly capable of cooking himself. He was actually a very good cook—good at scouting ingredients and finding a way to make them tasty together, simmered over an open fire. It was an art, and he enjoyed it.

Kyale, having grown up differently, was ashamed of his attitudes; those six servants were mostly there for her benefit. Ironic that Senrid's place almost needed an army just for the domestic chores, for all that accumulated wealth in the form of furnishings and various textile arts needed constant care; the castle's population was probably near the number of people in Leander's entire capital city, which was more of a small crossroads market town anywhere else.

Leander wandered down the long halls, with their large, stylized frescoes of raptors and running horses and long plains with great tumbling clouds. Senrid's castle was enormous, built back when Marloven kings kept huge retinues of personal guards as well as complicated households of clan and hostages.

This place was old, rarely changed, and yet every line, every stone, evoked Senrid. As it should. It had shaped him. Despite his stated wishes to change, the old ways still persisted in warfare being the most honorable vocation for male or female, in particular the arrow-shooting, sabre-swift light cavalry on their fast, mettlesome Nelkereth horses.

"They are needed now," Leander murmured under his

breath as he found his way to the kitchens, and some food.

The kitchen staff was also diminished, more than half loaned out to quartermasters all over the kingdom. While Senrid forced down stale rye biscuits, which he had never liked even when fresh, he used Forthan as a Destination.

Forthan stared at his king while Senrid recovered, not liking what he saw; when Senrid shed the transfer reaction, he was shocked by the gauntness of Forthan's face in the merciless sunlight. Neither had slept or ate well for days, and it showed.

Forthan saluted, then said, "My best scout says that the two Norsunder commanders kept separate from the other. None of us can understand the language, but we know the sounds of griping, and all the scouts agree that the older force, the one we've driven back, resents the newcomers."

"Can we use that?"

"Maybe." Forthan turned up his hands. "Once? Like any other ruse? It's river land, yes, but I know this territory, after chasing horse thieves over and around it for a couple of years. The area between their camps is flat and treeless, but if you know where to go, it's ideal for an ambush. There's one of the Faral streams with steep banks. Overgrown with brambles and other thorny plants. I can put Van Stad and his company to infiltrate the brambles. Stad will curse me for a year to come—he loathes bogs, but..."

The Marlovens had noted that the Old Stench (their name for the Norsundrian commander who'd been trying to breach the border for days) was as impetuous as he was brutal. They counted up every patrol and scout they found savaged.

The new one was far more systematic. For one thing, his perimeters were strictly line of sight, so they hadn't been able to get near enough to obtain a reliable head count, other than "lots."

They also conjectured that Old Stench and New Stench did not get along, for they had not combined their commands. Instead they sent gallopers back and forth, protected by heavily armed patrols, unfortunately.

But, as Forthan said to his disappointed scouts, "Every bit we learn is nearly as good as a kill."

When a cloud-smeared, cold morning dawned, it was Old

Stench's camp that the freshly-arrived academy seniors rode along, taunting the Norsundrians on the other side of the river. High, derisive cackles and shrill fox-yips as they rode back and forth along the banks got the Norsundrians awake and out in the frosty morning.

Capnias (Old Stench to the Marlovens) was a renegade from Sarendan, joined Norsunder after King Darian Irad was defeated by Peitar Selenna. He'd thrived in an atmosphere of violence ever since, but had been balked of the command he'd always dreamed of by Bostian. He could not conceive that it was only desperation that forced Llyenthur to promote him, until Bostian should arrive.

Bostian was here, but as yet there had been no orders demoting him again. Now was the time to demonstrate that he was far better than Bostian. He stood outside his tent and peered across the water. "It's nothing but boys," he exclaimed.

A high, cackling voice heckled — boys, not the least afraid of him.

He turned to his captains. "Go get them. Kill them all, and be back in time for breakfast."

His captains — like-minded all — didn't need a second invitation.

After weeks of mellow weather, that last storm had brought down the winds from the mountains to the east, where the snow never melted; those who knew Halia's weather patterns were aware that summer was over, and the cold east winds would slowly prevail. The day was raw; sleet intermittent. Capnias's warriors had noted that the river was low, at the deepest chest high, and as the Marlovens knew, the Faral was fed from the nearer mountains, without much time in the sun to warm.

By the time they crossed the river, Capnias's warriors were so chilled that they could scarcely hold their weapons. It didn't help that they hadn't eaten yet.

The boys' captain sounded the horn that pulled the academy seniors into a skirmishing line, and as the Norsundrians sloshed to shore, they attacked. Though the Marloven academy seniors were vastly outnumbered, the Norsundrians were hampered by the wet and cold.

They might have all died right there if Bostian (New Stench) hadn't been apprised of the commotion, and discovered that their commander was in the north again. Still no orders from

Llyenthur—which was fine. Excellent, even.

He ordered half his company to go rescue the idiots. Forthan's main wing, watching from the heights rode down to the attack, and Bostian, seeing the ruse, winded the retreat.

That was when Van Stad's company rose from the brambles and attacked Capnias's flank.

Incandescent with rage, Bostian rode to Capnias's camp, where the survivors were straggling in, heading straight to the cook tent.

Bostian marched up to Capnias, drawing his sword. Capnias reached for his, and though he fought like the snake he was, he had never been a match for a huge iron-hided snorter like Bostian.

As Capnias fell dead, Bostian turned to his company. "Join us, or die right here."

By the time Llyenthur turned up, the two camps had become one, the remains of Capnias's command reassigned and dispersed among Bostian's warriors.

Bostian, still angry, gave a report. It was then that Liliveth, one of Capnias's scouts, came forward. "I found something," she said—not saying when.

Llyenthur waved a negligent hand in invitation to speak. Bostian, who had placed her with Capnias, gave no sign of recognition.

"The Marlovens," she said, "can choke us any time they want because there's only one way into Marloven Hess, through the Aladas Pass farther up the Faral River. Eh, and past Methden, but that's in the west."

She pointed at the map, explaining that she'd checked all the old roads. Ever since the Marlovens had lost the south, they had halted trade as well, the roads now overgrown. "Only single file over those, and slow," she explained. "There's one that winds up a back way to the ridge below the highest cliff. That's sheer rock. Nobody can climb that. We wouldn't need to. The ridge is above their line of archers, who get there up the slope inside the pass. The back way is slippery and bramble-choked. I think only goats use it. But we could push through. We'd have the whole pass below us."

Why this revelation now? Ah, because she was Bostian's insider—and she had waited until Llyenthur was back, rather than reporting to Capnias, which bettered her chance of being boosted to head scout.

A lot of lives had been lost, but that could not be directly laid to Capnias's stupidity as well as to Liliveth's ruse in holding back her report. Always a tradeoff. Llyenthur mentally shut out the north, the duel with Efael, the Chwahir ships off the coast, the magic battle with Senrid Montredaun-An, and eyed the map: yes, time to step up the pace.

Past time.

"Right. Bostian, you've got the numbers now. Set up the trap. You yourself will have to be the bait."

Bostian shrugged. "I can send Capnias's leftovers with Liliveth here—they're burning for vengeance."

"Do it under cover of night. I need some time to take down the last of Senrid Montredaun-An's wards, and to land my ships full of Chwahir at Tarual for the march west on Choreid Dhelerei."

Bostian and Liliveth smiled at each other. Now the fun would begin, and afterward a little fun with each other; I'll be Queen of Sartor by next year, she exulted.

Sixteen

THE MARLOVENS DID NOT have long to celebrate the action against Old Stench at the Faral River, for within half a watch Senrid's head jerked back, and he slammed his hand on the table, causing everyone in the room to jump.

"My wards are down," he said, his voice low and flat. "That means their mages can get in and out, and I can't find them."

Leander said, "Is there anything we can do magic-wise?" He snapped his fingers. "I can create illusions of you that linger for a breath or two then vanish."

"That sounds good."

"I'll think of more. Things that slow them up."

"Yes. Make spells they have to check, then dispel. I'm going to try to lay some tracers over places they might go." He transferred out.

He was back sooner than anyone had expected, his face taut with tension. "Twelve ships on the horizon," he said. "We are about to open a third front."

Senrid resisted the almost overwhelming desire to return so that he could hurry Van Senelac in his race to Tarual Harbor to get there before those ships could land the enemy. But Senrid could not be in two places at once. He had to trust his commanders; they had all shared the same training, and they had the same goal. But only Senrid could fight with magic. He desperately needed that transfer ward back in place. He knew the Norsundrian commander was hopping about; he could feel the shift in focus.

He and Leander worked together as the day progressed, and upstairs, Kyale Marlonen kept her promise. Not that it was hard. She loved imagination games, and Senrid's daughter had plenty of imagination. But it was more and more difficult to know what was happening. At home, Kyale could interrupt Leander whenever she wanted, but not here. At the best of times Kyale had always regarded Senrid as knife-tongued, with a heart of stone. All that was so very much worse now.

"Let's play with the jewels," she said to Crystal Ingrid.

"I don't know where they are," the child replied.

"You can ask Monta. He won't bite *your* nose off," Kyale replied.

She followed Crystal Ingrid into the command center, where Crystal Ingrid went directly up to Senrid and leaned against him. He blinked, obviously disturbed from whatever he'd been thinking about, then bent and gave Crystal a quick, hard hug. They conversed in low tones—Crystal Ingrid very proud of remembering to use her words while keeping mental boundaries.

Kyale hovered in the background, unnerved at Senrid's appearance. He was usually fastidiously neat, but now his white shirt looked slept in, and his hair writhed in curly worms on his forehead.

Leander looked tired, too; when he saw Kyale's expression, he distracted her from her growing anxiety by asking if she'd had a chance to eat.

Senrid made an effort that Leander could feel, and said in an even voice, "Crystal Ingrid, we're going to take a break. How about if you read to us from your favorite book?"

The child leaped up. "Can I read CJ's pie fight?"

"We love that pie fight story," Kyale enthused, not being able to resist a delicate reminder that she was the one who had made the little book for Crystal Ingrid.

Twitching her shoulders with nearly five-year-old import-ance, Crystal Ingrid ran out and returned with the book that Kyale had translated and copied out for her, written in simple words. It had proved to be popular because it had her friend Aurora's mom Clair in it, as well as all the others Crystal Ingrid knew. She liked stories best about people she knew.

Crystal Ingrid read slowly, then looked up, expecting praise. She got it from her father and Uncle Leander, as Kyale smirked.

"Kyale, thank you for keeping her happy," Senrid said as Crystal Ingrid scampered toward the door to put the book away. "If she wants those jewels, fine. Have a runner fetch 'em from storage again. They can't be buried too deeply."

Crystal Ingrid paused at the door, then said triumphantly to Senrid, "*Princess Kitty* plays with me."

Senrid's reaction was peculiar, kind of a smile and a wince. Kyale felt a slight twinge of guilt at some of the remarks she might have made that might not have been completely fair — but then, she quickly reassured herself, it didn't really matter since everyone knew Senrid hadn't any feelings to hurt.

She hurried after Crystal Ingrid, hearing Senrid say, "How about a quick bite? Then I'm off to Eveneth and the west."

Nope, no feelings.

While Senrid and Leander got back to work, in the west a race against time brought the last third of West Army plus companies from all the western jarlates at the gallop, to try to get to the Enneh Rual's coast to halt the debarking of the new invaders.

Enneh Rual was a snake-shaped kingdom that strung along the coastline, for centuries home to the old Iascans in their round, cone-roofed houses with east-facing doors.

The Marlovens topped the ancient palisades that formed the border between Marloven Hess and Enneh Rual to discover that they were too late.

At the first sighting of the twelve warships slanting into the small harbor, the Rualese had picked up the things they'd packed up weeks ago, and melted away, leaving their houses bare to wood and stone. This way they had survived the invasion of the Marolo-Venn in ancient days, and it worked now. The Chwahir rowed ashore, floating their great spars, and formed up in columns around those carrying the shoulder slings that distributed the weight of the massive battering rams. A couple of scouting parties systematically scavenged through the houses, then they rejoined the others, who marched in perfect step across the narrow land, toward the palisades.

The Marlovens ranged across the top. They were too late to attack the boats, which they weren't really trained for. They could charge these foot warriors, for only the captains had horses.

Van Marlovair, the West Army captain commanding, exchanged glances with the other captains. Marlovens were trained to charge, but they only had four heavy cavalry riders with them—all the rest were with the border force. They had been picked because they were skirmishers, fast and light, their tearshaped shields used to deflect, not bear the brunt of attacks.

Even at a distance, those tall, rounded Chwahir shields looked heavy.

"Our horses need rest," someone murmured.

"It's either rest and attack on flat ground, or charge and use the momentum of the slope."

Palms turned up: charge it was.

The Chwahir and their two commanders, shifted to the ships by Efael two days previous, saw the long line of Marlovens atop the ridge, lances at the ready, shields out. At a single note from a horn, they readied.

The Norsundrian in command barked, "Halt!"

The Chwahir halted as one.

The Norsundrian shook his head—even the undead warriors some liked to use did not obey with such precision. It was inhuman; though the Chwahir civilians had been ground down for generations, it was all toward one purpose: in support of the massive Chwahir army, trained to act as one body.

"Get in your formation," he began, then cursed, trying to recollect some of the ten or so words of Chwahir he'd bothered to learn.

The quartermaster ran up, puffing. "Listen, "shields' is all you need to say."

"What?"

"Shields, in Chwahir. Then watch."

"Shields!" the Norsundrian commander bawled in Chwahir.

The word was nearly drowned by the horns from the hills, and the high, screeching "Yip-yip-yip!" of the Marlovens riding at a deceptively slow trot down the hill.

Thump! The Chwahir wheeled and stamped, again in perfect precision. And then, before the Norsundrians' astonished eyes, the three spars were laid out and the Chwahir snapped like puzzle pieces into squares thirty-two across and thirty-two deep, the inner three squares lined behind the spars.

Wham! Crash!

Line by line their huge, curving shields, like pieces cut from a cylinder, locked together in front, at the sides, and overhead. Thump! Pikes thrust through the upper gap between the shields in the first row—huge horse-killers. The men in the front, the largest, were braced by the thirty-one behind them.

Efael's captains prudently got behind the squares.

Then the Marlovens were on them.

The Marlovens' four heavies, having practiced with lances for years, recognized the horse-killers at a glance as the trot accelerated to a thundering charge across the last hundred paces. Then the crash of impact.

They struck the horse-killers down, all but the two at the extreme left—but there was no warding the collision of the front-line horses into a shield wall thirty-two deep. The carnage was terrible on both sides, the Chwahir squares as solid as rock. The surviving Marloven horses swerved and galloped alongside the human-smelling squares, ears flat.

The Marlovens tooted the retreat, swarmed around the squares and rode back for the hills, as the squares just held— they had not received command to break and chase.

"Get them! Get them!" the commander bellowed. "You rabbit-gutted platter-faces, go get them!"

The second commander, getting a hint from the quartermaster, yelled in Chwahir, "Pursue!"

The Chwahir, still in square formation, began to march in their version of quickstep—which of course was not going to catch horse riders—their round, pale faces turned toward the commanders, alike in their complete lack of expression.

Llyenthur's quartermaster, said, "There's a reason the Chwahir in foregone days were called iron tortoises. Had nothing to do with courage. Everything to do with what you just saw. Start 'em marching. We'll push the piss-hairs back to their capital, then jam their own spears down their gullets."

"In these squares?" the commander asked doubtfully, supervisory jealousy momentarily forgotten: they knew what Efael would do to them if they failed. Then he shrugged. They could always flog the platter-faces into smaller squares, with orders not to let anyone get between them.

The Chwahir could have told them that they had many different formations, including one for chargers. But they had been trained to never respond unless asked a direct question, a habit strengthened by a deep (unspoken) resentment of the fact that their own commanders had been taken from them—some said killed, others said held by The Hate—and these foreigners put over them who didn't speak a word of their language.

"Form up," he bellowed, as the quartermaster shouted the words in Chwahir. "We're marching straight east to the capital, and you're to kill anything in the way."

Thump! Right feet stepped in unison. Crash! Shields hit the ground, then pulled in tight to left and right sides. The squares metamorphosed into columns in drilled precision, the slings reappeared, the spars lifted, and the Chwahir began to march, right, left, right, left, perfectly in unison.

Up on the hills, under cover of a band of cold rain coming through, the Marlovens wheeled and reformed as the silhouette of a young man blinked into existence.

"It's the king!"

Van Marlovair motioned his officers to surround Senrid protectively, though the Chwahir were at the foot of the hill.

Senrid's breath hissed as he fought transfer reaction, then said hoarsely, "Report?"

With a grim glance down at the motionless forms of the dead left from that charge, Van Marlovair gave a succinct summary, beginning with the Chwahir numbers, which were roughly three times theirs.

Senrid listened, then said, "Marlovair, set aside a party to Disappear the dead properly. The rest of you, pull back until nightfall, and run harassment. I'll try to find you other help." He glanced toward the palisades; the rhythmic thump of the Chwahir walking in lockstep could be felt through the ground, though they had not yet crested the hill. "Go!"

They did—except for those detailed to deal with the dead. They galloped off toward a dip in the terrain. Senrid watched them disperse as he braced himself, then he transferred back to Choreid Dhelerei.

He dropped his bow and blinked rapidly, his fingers trembling as he rubbed his eyes. Then he said to Keriam and Leander, "Eveneth fell."

Keriam looked away sharply. Leander bowed his head.

Senrid drew in a harsh breath. "As for the west, we have

twelve ships of Chwahir on the march." He repeated Marlovair's report, then added, "No word from Forthan at Aladas?"

Leander shook his head as Keriam flattened his hand, palm down, fingers flicking outward in negation.

Senrid ran his hands up his face and through his hair, then said, "Some mage is trying to lay tracers on me. I'm slowing up. How's this? I'll order dinner, transfer around to do the latest check, and return in time for chow."

Leander wanted to ask if he could endure any more transfers—and kept his teeth locked against letting out the words. Senrid was going to do what he thought he must. He sighed, working his head back and forth. When had his neck gotten so stiff? "I think I know a way Kyale can help..." He didn't stop to explain, but ran out, formulating his plan on the way.

He found her in Crystal Ingrid's room, playing some elaborate game with dolls; he heard Kyale's fluting voice instruct Crystal Ingrid, "...and princesses and princes should always marry other princesses and princes."

"I'm going to marry Aurora," Crystal Ingrid announced, as Leander entered the room. "We will have pie fights every day."

She looked up in question at Leander, who forced a smile and an even tone as he said, "Kyale, we need to make mud again. A lot more. I need you to delay an army of Chwahir with that magic."

"Chwahir? How did they get all the way across the continent?"

"Came around by ship," Leander said tiredly. "I'll show you the Destination trail Senrid has laid out. It's easy. All you have to do is keep your chosen image firmly in your mind, and I know you can do that. I've got to stay here and monitor the attempts to trap Senrid by magic." And in a lower voice, in their own home language, he added, "Things are desperate."

Kyale's light gray eyes widened with her delight at being needed. "Llhei!" she called into the next room. "They need me to do magic. I'll be right back," she added to Crystal Ingrid.

"Come with me to see the Destination pattern. Keriam will know how to predict how far they can march in any given time, so you go to the next Destination. I'm going to fix a transfer token for each Destination, to get you there and back, just like always."

"Aren't you going with me?" Kyale asked, surprised.

"I have to stay here and keep sending fake Senrids to random Destinations. The enemy mage keeps getting closer, but Senrid won't stop transferring."

"I hope he enjoys bloody noses and headaches," Kyale muttered, but without much heat. She was too pleased to be needed, and she followed Leander's instructions explicitly.

Commander Keriam had pointed out on the map the likeliest spot the Chwahir might have reached. Kyale braced for the wrench, and found herself wobbling on a slight rise with a line of half-buried stones that must at one time had made a stone wall. Cold wind whipped her skirts and hair.

Keriam's prediction was accurate. With both hands she smeared her hair back, and stared in horror at the advancing warriors. In their black uniforms — unrelieved black, not the black and tan of Marlovens — they looked to her like so many gleaming black ants.

She pulled handfuls of streaming ribbon out of the sky and spread the magic out like a vast sponge, pulling up water from the ground.

The line wavered. They were too far as yet to see detail, but she imagined them knee-deep in brown mud soup, snickered, and reached —

To find the ribbons dissolving like smoke.

That had never happened before.

She wondered if she was losing concentration, and reached farther, to feel the ribbons dissolve in her fingers like sugar in water.

She stamped a foot. Raised her hands —

"That form of magic you're using."

The voice took her by surprise. She whirled around to find a young man with a long face framed by wisps of light brown hair. He was about ten paces away. The lowering afternoon sun shone directly on his face, lighting up eyes that were spring green, nearly as bright as Leander's. His smile was rueful. He'd spoken Marloven with no accent; she lowered her hands, wondering if he was a runner. Except hadn't she seen him before?

He waved at the Chwahir as he approached casually. Step by step. "You were so busy you never noticed me watching your highly entertaining kitchen warfare. Who taught you that?"

He wasn't stopping a polite distance away.

"Nobody," she said, and a heartbeat before he was in arm's reach, she transferred.

Imry Llyenthur studied the spot where she'd been. Who was that girl? Young—not a morvende, though she seemed to have morvende in her background. Definitely not one of Detlev's zoo. Could she possibly be the one responsible for winnowing the Queen of Sartor from the Tsranf cell?

———————

Marlovens knew what siege weapons were. They had taken them now and then through their history, had even built and used them, but the next generation usually abandoned them as unwieldy, cumbering their greatest asset: speed. The Marloven military had at its fundament plains warfare, and nothing substantive had threatened their walled and gated cities since then.

As soon as there was light enough, Norsunder attacked the Aladas Pass with catapults, expertly wielded. Once the stones had succeeded in smashing the Marloven lines off-balance, the enemies charged in a ferocious mass. Forthan had placed the seniors high enough along the slopes at either side so that they were above the battle line, but far enough down that they could make out individual enemies and aim each arrow. He waved the signal pennon himself, and the academy senior class rose as one and sleeted the enemy with a withering blur.

Arrows concentrated on the catapult teams, which kept barrel-sized boulders scything through the air. One, two, five catapultiers dropped, to be replaced: the Norsundrian mass halted, the fighting intensifying.

That was when Liliveth's wing rose from the heights above. She shrilled in gleeful anticipation, and her crossbolt teams picked off the helpless academy seniors—caught between them and the battle below—one by one.

The sun had leaped in the sky when Forthan won free long enough to take a breath. Where were the arrows? He peered up, struck numb. Young bodies lay sprawled over rocks on both sides; not one senior remained alive.

Fury ignited then, and drove him up toward that enemy, slipping in the rubble slick with blood. The air hung thick with battle lust and death and the incoherent roar, terrifying in insensate rage—there were no human beings here, just enemy.

Far away in Choreid Dhelerei, the watch bell clanged, then clanged again.

Senrid slammed down his pen. "Forthan is late reporting on progress."

He vanished, appearing on the highest cliff above the Aladas Pass, one only reachable by humans through magic. He had first been brought there as Detlev's prisoner, the day he became king. They had looked down at a skirmish below, as Detlev uttered what Senrid had taken as dire threats.

He knew now that that had been a warning. And here was what he had warned against.

Senrid took in the carnage, as the last of the Marlovens were cut down by an uncountable mass of Norsundrians, and he understood the lethal weakness in his strategy, and his training: those catapults.

He forced himself to take in details: the seniors midway along both sides of the slopes, every one of them stiffening in death; then his searching gaze found Forthan, bleeding from several wounds, and surrounded by a mound of corpses. Below that ring Norsundrians jostled one another, each wanting to be the one to take him prisoner, as their commander, a man nearly as big as Rel, made his way up toward Forthan. He shouted something, but the wind whipped his words away.

Forthan looked up—and saw at last what he had waited for: the king was here. Forthan's face, little more than a blur, changed. Senrid felt more than saw the grim smile as Forthan formally saluted, fist to heart.

Sick to the soul, Senrid acknowledged what was to come, according Forthan the highest possible honor: his fist laid to his heart.

Forthan, too, had seen too late the weakness in their defense, but right now the world had reduced to agony and chaos and spilled blood, so much blood. The king's salute shot the light of meaning through the madness.

Harskiald Retren Forthan bent and plucked up the screaming eagle banner out of the blood and filth, anchored one end under his foot, and then with three fast slashes, reduced the banner to tatters.

And before the Norsundrian commander could reach to disarm him, he jammed the gory hilt of his cavalry saber against a rock, and drove the blade through his own body, then tumbled past Bostian to the rocks below.

Seventeen

BY THEN SENRID HAD figured out the sequence, the final turning point being those crowing, whooping Norsundrians with the crossbolts along the ridge directly below him had come up along a goat path to take the Marloven seniors by surprise.

Senrid took in those empty eyes staring skyward from eighteen-year-olds whose names he'd known since they were squeak-voiced boys of ten. He drew an arrow and shot the closest strutting Norsundrian, whose high voice screeched above the rest. Liliveth tumbled from boulder to boulder like a tossed ragdoll, followed quickly by the next three scouts. Then Senrid felt the warning tickle of tracer magic — and transferred.

Magic slammed him back into the study.

He staggered against the map table, sending a stack of books tumbling. His bow clattered to the floor study as his anguished face contorted. Alarm shot through Leander, Keriam, and every runner in the room.

"Forthan struck his banner," Senrid whispered.

Keriam's pen dropped to the table. The runners at the door waiting for their turn stilled, stunned.

Leander repeated to himself, *Struck his banner*. The words were at first without meaning, until he recollected the expression from old history and older ballads. Leander hadn't believed that it actually happened. But from the naked grief in Senrid's face, Leander comprehended that it had now: Senrid's harskiald, Retren Forthan, had ripped his sword through the Marlovan banner. Every Marloven, from Forthan down to the youngest runner, had either fought to the death, or if Norsunder had disarmed them by some magical trickery, they had taken their knives to themselves to keep their souls free and their bodies from being harvested into Norsunder.

Keriam rose, gestured to the runners, and they left.

Leander bent to gather up the books scattered on the floor as Senrid's gray-blue gaze wandered sightlessly over the map. Leander's constant cramp of dread tightened into actual pain when Senrid's eyelids gleamed with liquid light that gathered, then dripped unheeded.

Senrid's head snapped back, his face a rictus of pain. But only for a heartbeat. Then he drew a harsh breath, and control shuttered his expression again. "Forthan died with honor. And knew it. And knew we would know it. He—every one of them—will be celebrated one day."

He used the archaic verb form for *it-shall-be*. Leander had never heard Senrid make a vow. He didn't think Marlovens did such things, but remembered that he had never seen any of their most important rituals.

His heartbeat was loud as a drum against his ears, and his hands tingled with fear, but he acknowledged with a nod: Senrid had spoken out loud because he might die. And Leander would be Regent for Crystal Ingrid.

So—if he had to—he would be the one to carry out that vow.

He said, "Yes." Not knowing what else to say.

It was enough. Senrid strove to sound more normal as he said, "Someone at the other end is fast. I wish I knew who it was."

Why? Leander wanted to ask, but he gave up with a mental shrug. Duels of will between military commanders meant nothing to him, he simply hadn't the experience. Of course, translate that into magic terms, and suddenly it was clear: you'd know what kind of spells to prepare against, and which ones might have the best effect, if you knew the mage.

"What I want to know is, where is everyone else?" Leander burst out. Then he raised a hand. "Sorry. Sorry. Now I understand why breaking communication is right up there with attack in the military short list of Must Dos."

"Don't forget logistics," Senrid murmured, his back turned as he gazed sightlessly out the window. "With winter coming on." He glanced over his shoulder. "This year won't be bad — the attack came mostly after harvest. But—"

It was probably necessary to think ahead to next year, but right now Leander could scarcely bear to look ahead to next week. Tomorrow. "I just wish we had Hibern here. She knows so much about wards—though I suppose Erai-Yanya has her fighting magic attacks somewhere else. I guess I thought Liere would turn up, at least. Arthur said she's learned more in her five years than many do in ten."

"She probably would have been, but the last message I received before the notecases became compromised was from Hibern, who said Liere had gone back to Sartor, where Norsunder was running riot," Senrid said, briefly pleased at how detached he sounded.

But he turned his back, unable to fight vivid memory: twice when he'd tried to sleep, his dreams had struck him with jumbled images of her. He had no idea if they were real or fake, and his mental shield was far too tight to test them, especially the one in which Liere was herself asleep, warm and drowsy, her long fall of ruffled hair drifting as she ran her fingers over the scarred contours of the yellow-haired young man in bed beside her.

Senrid had recoiled hard against such trespass; this was the problem with Dena Yeresbeth, as relentless and untamable as the sea. In the second dream, he could feel her exhaustion as viscerally as his own as she said fervently, *They shall not knock us back to the days of savagery*, the jumble of images a five-story stone building with caryatids and corbels, and beyond that a tower of glistening white stone.

"I think she's still there," Senrid said to the window.

Leander sighed. "Of course she is. Where I'd probably be if I wasn't here. Or in Bereth Ferian, or somewhere else being attacked just as hard. But we don't *know*. We can't know, we can't call for help—it's this isolation." The words wrung out of him.

"An effective tactic." Senrid dug the heels of his hands into his eyes, then dropped them, and shook his head. "None of them are an army. What I really need is an army. But even if I had a treaty with my neighbors, the fact that Norsunder came from the north as well as the south means those kingdoms fell before the first foray against my border."

Keriam returned. "I dismissed the third-year academy students serving as runners and auxiliaries. They are to take off their coats, dress civ, and go home, according to the standing order. The city guard, bolstered by next year's seniors, is already putting the city defense plan into readiness." And, quietly, "I intercepted a runner from the signal tower. Van Stad is on his way to reinforce the city guard."

Senrid said, "Marlovair is a week away. No one can find either of the Senelacs, so we'll have to assume that's all the reinforcement we've got, unless they turn up." He stared hard at the map, fighting the sense that his wits had splattered over the landscape. "We are outnumbered. Sieges are seldom successful, but if we're going to lose, let's make them sweat."

"Agreed," Commander Keriam said, though he looked away and wiped his eyes again. Senrid had known those seniors, but mostly by occasional sight. To Keriam, everyone who came through the academy was his child, the son or daughter he'd never had time to have.

Senrid straightened up. "I owe it to Fenis Senelac to be the one to tell her. And she's not far from the border. If Forthan managed to get runners past the enemy, the word is already spreading."

He braced for the wrench and transferred.

The village on the edge of Darchelde was quiet when he arrived. He appeared in the square, and walked to the cottage where Fenis Senelac stayed with Forthan cousins, who were flax farmers.

The family was gathering for a meal, but when Fenis Senelac saw who was coming up the walk, she exclaimed, "It's the king."

"The king?"

"The king is here?"

People ran to and fro, getting cushions and twitching the sparse furnishings straight, but Fenis stood in the middle of the room, her heart thundering: she was afraid she knew what was coming.

A small cousin opened the door. "Senrid-Harvaldar!" she piped.

Senrid uttered a word of greeting, then looked past her to Fenis, who forced her watery knees to carry her forward. "Give it to me straight," she murmured.

Senrid said, so softly only she could hear, "He struck his banner."

She gritted her teeth. Then said, "You heard? Or saw."

"I saw." Senrid put his fist to his chest. "He saw me."

One sob escaped her, shocking the family behind her into silence.

"Let's go outside," Senrid said.

Fenis went out with him, though she would have stayed there for the family to hear. But when a king says "Lets," it isn't quite a suggestion.

"We will go Disappear them properly." Fenis clenched her fists in her effort to keep her voice even. "According to rumor, Norsunder lets the dead lie there to rot. Theirs as well as their kills."

Senrid opened his hand in assent. "A dead warrior is useless to them. And they leave their kills as a warning."

"We can fix that."

"They will be marching on the royal city," Senrid warned. "Take the wood road and then cut to the river. And don't take the children."

Fenis, an old friend, cried angrily, "Shouldn't they know what they're fighting?"

Senrid looked up and away. Then back. "I shot and killed four of them today. Would have killed more, but someone put a tracer on me — never mind what that is. The thing is, I find no regret within me."

"Of course not," she said fiercely. Wiping angrily at her eyes. "Of course not. I wish you'd killed a hundred of them."

He drew an unsteady breath. "Tiredness makes me stupid. I don't have the vocabulary for what I feel when I think of the future. Not remorse, at least, not about fighting Norsunder. We did not start this war. But we did prepare for it, hard. Pridefully."

He paused, and she looked back at him, waiting for his point.

What was his point? He couldn't think, but it was important to try.

He tried again. "Remorse because the kingdom I inherited, I see it floating farther away from my father's vision. He wanted us to honor excellence in other forms of endeavor besides the skills of killing."

"And yet he was knifed in the back by his brother."

"Who was raised by my grandfather to be tough above all things. To believe that every problem can be solved with steel." He glanced at Fenis, saw only grief, anger, and confusion, so he said, "You have never seen any sight like what I saw in that valley. Don't take your children."

"But they should see it. So they know their enemy's works."

And Marloven works, he added silently. "They'll know soon enough. I don't want them growing up thinking that savagery is normal. The sight of that pass would start them on that road." He tapped his forehead. 'You know about Dena Yeresbeth — I've got a tight shield against Crystal Ingrid for that very reason."

Fenis wavered, then struck fist to chest.

"If I can, I will come help you," he added.

She turned her hand down. "You gave Ret what mattered most. Tend to the royal city. The rest of the country. Half of this village is made up of families of those lying in that valley. We'll see to it. And the children will remain behind," she promised.

She kept her word, though the children protested loudly; the young voices, indignant that they were being treated like babies, diminished behind the Disappearance party until they sounded like the cries of birds.

It took a night and a day to get there. The burial teams worked to lay out each Marloven, hands over breast, and at first weapons at sides, as they sang the Hymn to the Fallen over and over until voices gave out. Many of the weapons were harvested, to be hidden in attics and buried in gardens.

Fenis found Ret Forthan at last. She was aware of a pulse of relief that her children were not there after all; she let herself howl, rocking back and forth in her grief. Then she forced her voice to join the song as she tenderly worked his limbs straight, and brushed his thinning hair back from his battered face, his dear face that she had looked upon a thousand and more times as he lay asleep beside her. His expression, relaxed in death, could be called peaceful, but she knew it was merely empty: his spirit had fled into the mystery. All she allowed herself was hope that she would find him when her time came.

Silent, strong in sympathy, her closest friends gathered at either side before Fenis did the spell.

The fallen Norsundrians were Disappeared as they lay.

You've used the time allotted, Svirle's thought invaded Llyenthur's mind.

Then he was gone, having made it clear that at least one of the Host had come out of the Beyond, and had found a place from which to watch. No doubt in Chwahirsland—Llyenthur was certain that Efael had taken over Wan-Edhe's cherished spy eyes, and had wrenched the magic to targets of his own choice, he himself being one of them.

That meant yet another priority demand: warding spy eyes.

In the distance, Bostian and his army laughed and roared in celebration, Bostian trying to overcome the annoyance that the sweetness of a total slaughter was marred by the loss of Liliveth. Ah, there were plenty of scouts, and she'd been starting to get grabby.

He'd relish the good things. One more city and he'd be sailing back to Sartor—by then Asiarch and the rest ought to have burned down that damned weird Shendoral. And broken into that white tower where all the treasure was kept. They'd certainly had enough time.

He raised his cup and laughed.

Llyenthur walked away from the noisy camp to fight the ward that Senrid kept renewing, then halted at the flicker and hot-metal singe of a transfer.

"You're late," Efael sneered. Even in the cold wind, Llyenthur could smell his long, man-leather coat, an atavistically repellent stench.

"I'm partly late because of the blunders in the magic at Tsranf," Llyenthur said—a risk, if Efael had figured out the true cause.

He hadn't; his sneer tightened. "You were supposed to have Marloven Hess kneeling in defeat in a week, and you're about to tie up two continents' strike troops for a siege that could drag through winter. While Senrid Montredaun-An sits in his citadel and picks apart your magic? No doubt capturing spells that will eventually find their way into the hands of our old friend Detlev." Efael's mouth twisted in scorn.

Efael, though a shit, was not completely wrong. He was not completely right, either. It was always going to come down to Choreid Dhelerei at the end—which was why the ancient Marlovans had picked the damn city to be their capital in the first place. And Llyenthur had prepared for that.

But Efael, despite his wish to be perceived as a world-dominating terror, worthy of joining the Host, was not a strategist. He was an assassin, a dungeon-master. And dungeon-masters liked to strut their power before the powerless, and brag. Since he was here, Llyenthur decided, why not let him rant. Perhaps he'd learn something that Efael ought to have kept to himself.

Llyenthur said, to provoke an answer, "Are you pissing your breeches because I waylaid the Chwahir? I won't need them past breaking down the gates. You'll have them back soon enough."

"I should have them back now," Efael retorted. "If you were smart enough to distract Senrid Montredaun-An, you would have been done by now."

"Distract?" Then Llyenthur had it. Efael was angry over some setback—probably losing some of Yeres's puppets—and instead of making her just stay in real time for a few months so she could get her end of things done expeditiously, he was fixating on a victim to take off-world for his games.

Sure enough, Efael's shark-mouth glistened as he whispered, "Why don't I distract him for you? I'm told he has a pretty little daughter."

And there it was, Efael's off-worlder penchants overruling everything else.

Llyenthur shrugged. "I'm reasonably assured you are warded from entering Choreid Dhelerei."

"Ah, but Senrid cannot ward my Black Knives. He does not know them."

Llyenthur waved a hand. "Your Black Knives can do what they want—after I'm done here. Svirle not half an hour ago let me know how much fun he's having watching."

The mention of Svirle halted Efael, whose sharp face turned, as if he could see the Host lurking along the riverside below the ancient Montredaun-An territory of Darchelde. They both sensed that they were being watched. "A week, Imry."

He vanished.

Eighteen

IN CHOREID DHELEREI, RUNNERS went through the city announcing that the gates would close at the first sighting of the enemy on the horizon. The gates stood open for the last time as those who were determined to leave departed — mostly elderly who had been put in charge of others' children. Some of the refugees were sent by Senrid to ready the forges, deep in unmarked caves, that he had set up in case the kingdom did fall.

Each day was marked off on the map by the steady advance of the Chwahir. Senrid watched them from behind a clump of gnarled oak, absorbing the brutal shock of one last charge, with terrible loss on both sides. The Marlovens reformed and then galloped away, Senrid resolving to issue orders to abandon charging the Chwahir squares. They'd fight with other tactics.

Senrid watched the Chwahir march on.

Unlike Norsundrians, the squares reformed around their dead, and when they moved on, there was no sign of anything left behind, not so much as a scrap of fabric or a splinter of a spear. No sign of wounded, either.

Senrid remembered what Jilo had once told him about the Chwahir twi, the all-important group of eight that made up the fundamental order of Chwahir civilization. Families were important, but that was duty, over centuries distorted as women were slowly turned into slaves. But the twi, a group of peers bonded for life, had remained strong until recent years when Wan-Edhe passed laws against that, too, compelling every Chwahir's loyalty solely to himself.

The Chwahir, behind his head, still make twis in secret and called him The Hate.

Senrid wondered if within those squares the wounded were borne up by their twi mates. He would ask Jilo.

He would *not* ask Jilo.

He shook his head, hard. Tiredness was definitely making him stupid. Jilo was somewhere out there, maybe at Lisdan, if Terry of Erdrael Danara was there. Jilo probably knew what was happening to his Chwahir, being used as bludgeon against other lands, by Norsunder. In a way that was a warrior's life, to go where told to go, to fight when told to fight. To die for someone else's quarrel.

But it seemed so hopeless for them to be here. At least Marlovens fought to save their homeland. These Chwahir. Did anyone even know, or care, when they died so far away?

Then Senrid remembered the squares, with no one left behind, and conviction was strong: as long as one Chwahir was left standing, he surely knew the names of those whose components lay at rest beneath the ground.

He had to work harder to halt the killing.

He transferred back to Choreid Dhelerei, as the Chwahir marched steadily east. The night they spotted the towers of Choreid Dhelerei on the horizon, Jan Senelac's skirmishers made a running attack, and when they departed, the two Norsundrian commanders were found among the dead. Neither had been anywhere near the part of the camp that the Marlovens hit, though of course they got the blame.

The following morning the Chwahir said nothing, just stood by motionless as the quartermaster Disappeared the two dead commanders. Llyenthur, exasperated after too many sleepless nights, put the quartermaster back in charge. There was no use in putting one of his own in command of the Chwahir. He knew Efael would be demanding their return as soon as they broke through the gates to Choreid Dhelerei; as yet Efael did not quite dare overt sabotage, not with Svirle watching from afar, but no doubt that would be next.

The magic war continued unabated, Senrid raising the

transfer ward again and again, so that Llyenthur was forced to bring it down every time he wanted to transfer.

Time to act.

———————

Leander looked up blearily from his books when Kyale ran into the tower.

"Senrid, I've laid down three more—oh, Kitty," Leander said blankly, fighting his way out of a magical fog. "Where's Crystal Ingrid?"

"Oh, she's with Llhei."

"Tell you what." He looked around for a glass of water and gulped it down. It got rid of thirst, even if it didn't touch headache, tiredness, or aching body from sitting over the books far too long. "Why don't you stay go up in the harskialdna tower—"

"The what?"

"—the middle tower and use your magic? You can see better up there. I think I'd better go out and take a walk. I was nearly asleep sitting here. Not a good idea when doing magic."

"I'll make a big swamp in the road, how's that?"

"Excellent idea."

Senrid had forced himself on another round of transfers, as he tried to assess the damage and to plant traps in the captured cities. At least Choreid Dhelerei was still holding strong, between military defense and his and Leander's overlapping strategy removing wards as soon as they sensed them.

Leander had added illusory Senrids to every single Destination in as random a pattern as he could manage, until his brains seemed to have gone with the last of the spells. Surely a brief break, no more than a flip (turn of the small sandglass) would help combat the mental fog.

He ran down to the outer court, and through the castle gates. Everyone was armed, with swords, or a variety of knives, or wicked-looking tools. He watched a pair of young people his own age arranging workers into a defensive position before an old inn. They exchanged jokes in desperate-sounding voices.

This cheery yet grim attitude toward city fighting was beyond him, but at least the fresh air did help clear his head somewhat. He jogged back to the castle, where he found Kyale lurking uncertainly in the tower stairs opening into the stable yard. "Leander, I started doing the spells, when one of the sentries said that dark line on the horizon wasn't rain on the way, it's the Chwahir. I came down to find you. Let's get out of here. I'm scared."

"I'll send you if you like, but I promised to stay, and that's what I'm going to do."

"No. I'd only worry."

"Well, then, make yourself useful. Did you happen to see if Senrid is back yet?"

"No—"

The watch bells began to ring a quick double pattern. Leander ran the rest of the way up the stairs and down the hall toward the study. He passed Keriam, who had just stationed runners around the map representing the city, then dashed out to take his place up in the tower for castle defense.

"Kitty, nobody can get at you in a tower," Leander reminded her. "Since the sentries are closing the gates and setting up defenses on the walls now, why not make puddles right before the gates?"

"Of course!" Kyale grinned and flitted off.

Leander turned back to the books, if not exactly fresh, at least not fogged. He jolted as Senrid appeared, close enough that the displaced air knocked him back a little.

Senrid slammed the bow down as Leander said, "They're on the horizon."

"I know. I found Jan Senelac—he's been harrying the Chwahir I was trying to raise some deflections to help them, but then the city ward alerted me. Leander, while we've got the time, I think you'd better transfer to Lisdan. Make sure it's safe. Then let's get Kyale and Crystal Ingrid out of here. Crystal Ingrid will fight us on that, but I'll be the villain. Make it an order."

Leander and the runners at the city map looked at one another in question. "What? Why? The enemy hasn't breached the city yet, have they? I thought they were still a day's march off."

Senrid had gripped his head in his hands, but at this he looked up, his red eyes circled with exhaustion. "Didn't you just catch that? Someone transferred out, not even a turn of the small glass ago. From here. Dark magic."

"Here?" Leander looked around the room, feeling stupid. Unsettled.

"Not in this room. I realize the castle guards have all gone to the armory or the wall, and the line-of-sight order has probably gone out the window, but has anyone seen anyone or anything...not us?"

The runners still looked puzzled, but before he could speak again, he felt a cold, sticky little hand creep into his.

He was about to try to gently disengage that hand, but he realized that never, in her four years, had Crystal Ingrid ever come to him sticky, and he looked down, shock blowing his brain empty as an eggshell when he saw the stark-pale little face, and the bloody smock, with the black-handled knife protruding from her middle.

"Ingrid." Her name came out as a whisper.

He grabbed her up and ran across the hall into the guest room next to Leander's, where he laid her gently down, and fell to his knees beside the bed. "Who?" he asked, holding her gaze, which was frightened and pain-hazed but trusting.

There for a few heartbeats he looked through her eyes into stuttering memory: the hurt cries of a small dog; her proud remembrance of boundaries as she darted out of Llhei's reach.

She stopped when in the courtyard, empty except a tall, smiling young man with eyes the color of Uncle Leander's. "Who are you? Why are you hurting a puppy?" she demanded as the man dropped the little dog, which sped away, tail between its legs.

"Imry Llyenthur," the man said as he dropped a knife from his sleeve. "To get you." He stabbed Crystal Ingrid, the blade deliberately a hair off-center.

She was in such deep shock there was no pain, only cold, cold, as instinct drove her to find Monta, who would make everything right.

Senrid shoved aside anger, and the bloodlust that threatened to detonate mind and heart.

Boundaries? I did it right, did I? Did I? The thought was small, and weak, and very far away.

No, it was desperately, terribly wrong, she should have...

It was too late for should have. He made the greatest effort of his life and forced away regret, guilt, everything but all his love, and reassuring affection.

:*Don't be scared. You can share thoughts now.*

:*I'm not scared. I'm cold. Is the puppy better?*

Yes, it's safe. From that he understood that Imry Llyenthur knew Dena Yeresbeth, and had used her passion for animals to lure her. Senrid wanted to use this knife to jab into his guts. But that would come. That would come. Now he couldn't even withdraw the knife because her lungs would fill with blood and drown her. Her breathing was already shallow — and slowing, her punctured heart laboring less with each beat, as bright blood bubbled at her lips.

He shut his eyes against the sight, enveloping her in as much warmth as he could project: every laugh, joy, happy moment of her short life that they had shared, those memories were what he offered, as she struggled in confusion to stay anchored in the world.

Disassociating from the physical realm, his mind stayed with her as her bewildered consciousness looked outward, then back, and then outward again, until it drifted beyond the ties of the physical world, far into the realm of the spirit. He followed, not caring if the body he left behind lived or died: there was no need greater at that moment than the unconditional love and trust of his young daughter.

But at the last, with a sudden surge her awareness shot like a comet away, flinging him summarily back into the pain of the physical world. Alone. Holding her lifeless body, and rocking back and forth in an agony of grief.

Nineteen

"EEEUW, THERE'S BLOOD ON the floor," Kyale exclaimed, whisking her skirts aside.

"Crystal Ingrid's." Leander was so heartsick he could barely speak.

Kyale's face blanched. "Oh...no." Her eyes rounded. "Llhei? Where is she?"

They found her at the foot of the stairs, leaning against the wall where she'd sat down to catch her breath after chasing fruitlessly around to find where Crystal Ingrid had run off to. Between one breath and the next her ninety years of caring for other people's children had come to a peaceful end.

Leander and Kyale, the two who had loved her longest, Disappeared her together, Kyale sobbing wretchedly for a long time, until he began to wonder if Senrid wanted company or aid, but before either could speak, livid purple lightning bleached the stairwell of all color, followed by a tremendous crack of thunder.

"I hate thunderstorms," Kyale wailed—not that she could be heard.

"There's magic in that," he said, also unheard. Playing with weather could be extremely dangerous as well as destructive.

He never remembered how he got to the study; suddenly

he was there, Keriam's and his eyes meeting. The thunder had scarcely died away when hail hit the four tall windows, which had been standing open. Leander and the runners dashed to fight the outer shutters closed, as hail the size of their fists crashed around, spilling ink, and setting papers into a madly flapping whirlwind.

They cleaned up the mess, no one daring to go find the king. Best to keep busy, all were thinking. Keriam said to Leander, "I'll be in the tower."

"I'll find...something to do," Leander finished after a despairing glance at the water-smeared pile of books and Destination papers and jotted emendations to spells.

He leafed through his books, looking for some spell to negate the absolutely forbidden weather magic, as at the castle and city command centers, watch captains tried to see in the ink-black night.

They knew the enemy was using the storm to get all the way to the gates, but there was no shooting into that wind, except to hurl stones from the walls and hope that they hit something. They could not see where they landed.

Despite the punishing hail, the frigid, ripping winds and the crashing boulders hurled from the walls into blind darkness, the Chwahir moved in unison, fixing the housing for the rams, and building their shield over and around the iron-reinforced spears.

It was near midnight when Leander sensed the tight ward that closed over the city: the unknown mage, free of Senrid's powerful resistance, had been very busy. Leander was helpless to fight the rapid proliferation of spells. Light magic was not made for warfare; it was like using a blanket to beat out a growing wildfire.

Senrid appeared a short time later, his eyes dark-circled. "That," he said in a voice that made Leander's guts clench, "was a diversion."

He pulled one of his books around and flipped pages—but from then on, through that long night, and the day after, measured out by the booming of the rams, they were two steps behind the mage, whose dark magic sped the destruction along: ice in the cracks in the wood of the gates, and a rain of icicles like knives striking all over the city.

Dawn brought only a weak lifting of darkness, revealing tightly packed shields. The Marlovens shot arrows and bolts, which mostly skidding or bounced harmlessly. Out came javelins; a well-thrown one could pierce those shields, but again, the Chwahir merely closed up.

A miasmic cloud floated next, blinding the Marloven defenders. By the time Senrid dissipated that, another attack had replaced it, and one after that, until at noon, after the iron-reinforcing bars on the west gate had been heated up under the touch of magic-imbued metal by Chwahir suicide "volunteers," the first crack appeared.

Llyenthur then transferred waiting boulders into the crack — and the gate exploded under the pressure.

The Chwahir marched in, to find the Marlovens waiting. By now the Marlovens had learned how to deal with the iron tortoises. They'd brought out the old, heavy lances with curved hooks below the blade; the heavy cavalry, those who had been writing their names with lances since they were thirteen, had been feverishly practicing using these on foot, hooking the heavy cylindrical shields and yanking as the second row shot between their shoulders.

The Chwahir suffered, but kept pushing forward, their own spears lunging in unison, like the teeth of a great beast snapping. Arrows and bolts flew both ways, mostly clattering off shields and helms.

The accompanying Norsundrians poured in, striking down anyone in sight, young or old, armed or not; Marlovens from rooftops hurled burning oil at them, and archers at windows filled the air with the hiss and zip of arrows.

The Chwahir reached the first market square — and halted before a mass of Marlovens with their own shield wall.

And so the slaughter began.

Up in Senrid's study, Keriam appeared at the door.

"They've breached the west gate," Keriam said.

"I know."

All three took in the shuttered tightness in Senrid's face as Senrid checked his wrist knives, and slid two more in his boot tops, then a fifth in his belt.

Leander said, "What are you going to do?"

"I lost the magic battle. But I can still fight," Senrid said, then the door snicked shut behind him. Keriam followed; his last duty would be to fight as Senrid's shield arm, whatever happened.

Leander fought down a surge of nausea. If the Marlovens

were going off to get themselves killed because in the military mind, that's what you did, there was nothing he could do to stop it. What could he do? Lay a few illusory traps to slow the enemy, and reinforce Senrid's evacuation orders, designed to preserve as many lives as they could. Because the non-military mind turned first to preserving lives.

It was midnight when nature reacted to the interference of magic in its balance of air and wind, hurling so wild a storm down on the city that no one could see, enemy or defender.

Here and there struggles briefly occurred as Norsunder set up camp inside the gates, the captains in the few houses that their warriors had forcibly cleared. Llyenthur set a protective ward outside the guard perimeter that glowed with weird greenish light, crackling when rain struck it.

A party of Marlovens tried to rush it. They died instantly — and that was the last action of the night.

Late as it was, Leander and Kyale sat in Senrid's study. The castle was silent and unlit — the Residence floor empty, but through the cracks in the shutters, between bouts of hail and thunder, drifted voices rising and falling in an eerie, heart-clawing threnody. This sound seemed to come from everywhere, so uncanny in its controlled anguish that the skin at the back of his neck crept and he gritted his teeth.

Kyale's fists pressed together under her chin, her eyes red and puffy. She whispered, "I didn't think Marlovens sang anything but war ballads."

"I think," Leander whispered back, though they were alone in the room, "we are hearing the Andahi Lament."

"The what? No, don't tell me what year and a bunch of names from history I wouldn't know. What does it mean?"

"What does it sound like it means?"

Kyale's mouth opened, then closed. "Don't tell me," she whispered.

Outside the door slow footsteps. Leander leaped up and in two steps reached the door, peering out. The ruddy torchlight crowned Senrid's fair hair, lying tangled and sweaty on his brow.

"You're still alive," Kyale murmured, her eyes huge.

Senrid cast a bloody knife onto his map table with a contemptuous movement He ignored the clatter, the spattered books, the map that ripped. "Their southern army will be here tomorrow. The city will probably fall by tomorrow night. Let's get you out of here before the search parties come through."

Leander shook his head. "Light magic transfer is warded. I don't want to know where the ward Destination would send us."

Instead of answering, Senrid slapped a pair of transfer tokens—made with dark magic— against them, which wrenched them out of Marloven Hess, and threw them back in Lisdan half the continent away.

Valley of Delfina - Sarendan

Southeast of Melire, in the ancient mage haven called the Valley of Delfina, the old mage Tsauderei sat before his window looking out at a peaceful lake in the center of his high mountain valley, grimly contemplating the immediate horror of war and the prospective barrenness of another Fall.

Communication had been reduced to scrying and transfers, with protections painstakingly worked in: as yet wards against light magic transfer were not world-wide, which would take an immense amount of magic. But more and more kingdoms were warded as the days passed. Erai-Yanya, hiding somewhere in the wilds of the north of Drael, was still able to transport. She had begun coming once a week, bearing any news she had been able to glean.

Tsauderei hated scrying, though he could do it. But those few mages who could also scry were as isolated as he was. Not long after the fall of Sartor, when his not-quite-acknowledged heir showed up, Tsauderei had said, "Wasn't sure I'd ever see your uncharming face again."

MV's grin was brief. "And miss the fun of studying bridge support wards?" He laid down a book.

"Where have you been?"

MV did not miss the change in tone. They got along well— until Tsauderei remembered that MV had been raised by Detlev. Then the doubts crowded back, usually coming out as caustic teasing. Sometimes as straightforward doubt.

Trained in a very hard school, MV had learned not to give any more information than asked for. Sometimes you had to mislead, if the whole truth, within a context that might require days of explaining. would do more harm than good. He pointed at the book. "I was enjoying the summer up in the Elgar Strait, studying yon book."

Which was true—though the entire truth was, he had been watching the coast of Chwahirsland, and when ships full of Chwahir launched, he counted them all, and the direction they sailed in, for Detlev.

He added, "In case you didn't notice, communication went down. While sailing south again, ship patterns were disrupted. At Tchorchin Harbor in Khanerenth I saw Norsundrian gray all over, decided to hide my boat in a cove off Sarendan, and find out what you know."

"Not much." Tsauderei snorted. "You heard anything from your former master?"

MV said—as usual—"If you have questions for Detlev, ask him."

"I would," Tsauderei observed, "if I could reach him."

MV lifted a shoulder. "Clear him within your ward and he might turn up."

Tsauderei did not permit many people direct access to his valley. He wrestled with that question for a few more days, then finally put Detlev's name into that list.

Another week passed—then one morning, the day after Choreid Dhelerei's gates crashed down, not one but two people appeared.

Tsauderei kept his cottage windows wide for as long as possible before closing up for winter. Transfer magic directly outside his west window sent cold air snapping through the little room, mixing the scents of climates separated by continents. Erai-Yanya was expected. Then his old heart began to hammer when he recognized Detlev, who was not expected. Tsauderei still felt deeply ambivalent, but was aware of a very tentative sense of relief.

"MV said you wanted to talk to me," Detlev said wryly, following Erai-Yanya inside the cottage.

Erai-Yanya gave him a dubious look as she crossed to the opposite side, where she could see them both. She didn't quite address Detlev. "Did you know that Oalthoreh is dead? The Bereth Ferian senior mages are all dead. Tarael, our chief contact among the morvende, has vanished, though I hope he is not dead. Igkai has gone silent. And Lilith is also vanished, for she does not answer the summons we had set up years ago." She drew in a shuddering breath. "About the only good news that I can report is that Atan was also taken, but she was rescued. She's alive."

Implication: what, if anything, are you doing about it?

"I believe she is well hidden for now." Tsauderei eyed Detlev, wondering if he ought to point out that while Atan's skills in magery were moderate, and as a commander in war-time she was utterly inexperienced, as a symbol, her power was vast indeed. And that power could be used by either side.

Detlev stood next to Tsauderei's fireplace, dressed plainly in a long tunic over riding trousers, his brown hair tied back. He was just above medium height, on the slender side, but he held himself with the stillness of a master of the lethal arts; he always seemed taller and bigger in memory than he really was in the flesh.

Tsauderei and Erai-Yanya eyed him with the furrowed expressions of question and lingering distrust. Tsauderei remembered that he had — indirectly — asked the man to come, and decided to change his approach. "*All* our protective wards are either down or under attack. Mondros says that Efael of the Host has taken up residence in Chwahirsland. Someone called Aldon, who you warned us about five years ago, is leading Norsunder against Drael's western half, all the way up to the Venn. We know that Bostian, who has always threatened Sartor, conquered it — ".

"Trying to destroy it," Erai-Yanya said, arms tightly crossed.

"Several kings have declared for Norsunder, Sles Adran in particular on this continent, followed by Enaeran's latest king. They appear to change kings as often as Colendi change fashions," he commented dryly. "But we don't know who it was leading Norsunder's attack in Goerael, other than he seems to be a mage as well as a military leader."

Detlev considered swiftly. They wanted answers. They were desperate for answers, and yet the more he answered — the more he knew about enemy movements that they didn't know — the more they would question why, and how, he knew. They did not trust him. And he wanted to maintain the near neutrality he'd won by five years of apparent non-involvement in Sartoran, or world affairs.

"That was Imry Llyenthur. My last encounter with him was more than ten years ago, and I do not know what he has been doing since." Detlev observed his listeners as he answered

Tsauderei's question. Erai-Yanya still looked tense and wary. Tsauderei's reaction was more complex, but one thing was clear: he wanted to ask the questions, and he did not want suggestions.

"There is a purpose, a goal." Tsauderei spoke slowly. "Besides wholesale destruction, as happened four thousand years ago. They have been grabbing rulers and important guild chiefs as well as military leaders."

"So I understand," Detlev said.

Tsauderei went on, still testing, "It seems to me that, if they keep prisoners here and don't shift them to Norsunder, it requires personnel, space, and supplies to hold and maintain them."

Erai-Yanya made a gesture of impatience. "That is military thinking, to which I can contribute nothing. If you need my help for *rescue plans*, scry me."

She vanished.

Detlev said, choosing his words with care, "Yeres's favorite plan has always been to create an empire of mind-controlled puppet rulers whom she can rule from Norsunder."

Tsauderei perceived then that Detlev was, if not testing back, certainly aware of lingering doubts. And yet they needed information! But after a lifetime of profound distrust, turning to Detlev for anything still felt like going out in a lightning storm in order to ignite a candle.

He tried one more time. "Erai-Yanya's perceptions of magic are formidable and subtle, but she sees Norsunder as monolithic evil in both motivation and action. Ever since I began chatting with your boy MV, I have reluctantly come to a differrent conclusion: it's an easy, but ultimately useless assumption. They all have different goals."

He was still wary, so Detlev addressed both his remark and the underlying distrust: "I will return to observing from a distance in hopes of learning more." A quick smile. "You have to remember that they have a grudge against me, and I have been dodging assassins and various attempted attacks."

"Ah," Tsauderei said—and that actually seemed to reassure him. He understood people wanting to kill Detlev.

Who laughed inside as he politely left the cottage before transferring away, after which Tsauderei reached for his scry stone and scryed his favorite debate partner, Mondros.

After explaining everything he could remember of the

encounter, he admitted, "He readily answered, and I believe him, and yet I could not help but wonder if he's in contact with them, in spite of that about assassins and attacks. If pitting us against Norsunder is his long-term goal—after all, everyone has been so sure he had a long-term goal. But his leaving Norsunder five years back still seems mighty sudden to me."

"Without any evidence, let's at least be practical. What would he possibly get out of pitting Norsunder against us?" Mondros scowled, his beard bristling. "He might not be able to do a thing for us in any case, even if he actually wants to. If he's not acting for Norsunder, then they have to be after him. I find the remark about assassins totally convincing."

Tsauderei chuckled. "Yes, I do, too. The one thing I can confidently not only understand, but endorse."

Twenty

Mountains on Sartor-Sarendan border to Marloven Hess

WHILE THEY WERE DISCUSSING Detlev and his possible motivations, he himself transferred to one of his mountaintop Destinations.

He found a portion of his boys waiting, after he'd had Siamis summon them in dreams from the Selenseh Redian in Mearsies Heili. He looked around at the faces, assessing countenance, and mood, both hidden and overt. They were high in the mountains of the north, where spring was just beginning, though that could not be felt in the biting wind.

"Svirle has come out of the Beyond," Detlev said.

The youngest, the boy they all called Noser, flipped his sun-bleached hair back. "Shit-fire!" He glanced around, waiting for the expected laugh. When they'd all been small boys, the laugh might have come, but now he was the only one who had not released the Child Spell, and exclaiming *Shit* or its equivalents had long since lost any vestige of humor.

Roy, who had like the others with Dena Yeresbeth, had sensed that profoundly toxic presence in the mental realm, said softly, "Brief visit or long, do you think?"

"Too early to tell," Detlev replied. "Presently he seemed to be enjoying playing with the spy eyes in Chwahirsland's capital."

David spoke the question in some faces, "Already warded all of you when last I was there. He can't see you, unless you do something stupid to get his attention."

"Or you would have known it by now," Detlev added dryly. "He's watching the fall of Marloven Hess. If he stays long, Ilerian won't be far behind."

"Theronezhe's not here," MV observed. "He's still sitting in the Beyond."

"Is that why Efael started the attack early?" Curtas murmured. "To edge Theronezhe out?"

Detlev gave a short nod. "Probably part of his motivation. Efael wouldn't trust any of Theronezhe's strike troops, even coming over in ones and twos. But I think he and Yeres loosed Alsaes and Bartal in a fit of petulance, the closest he dares to get to objecting to Svirle putting Imry Llyenthur in charge of the invasion."

MV said, "Efael surely likes running the Chwahir, who have been bludgeoned into obedience over centuries."

"Correct," Detlev said. "And I believe that Svirle is prolonging his stay to force Efael to accelerate repair of Wan-Edhe's distortion in Narad, so that they can connect it to Norsunder Beyond. In which case, they will no longer be limited to transferring ones and twos, then finding another Destination. Whole armies would be able to come over, and entire populations forced into the Beyond for Ilerian's gratification." Detlev's gaze rested on his son Sveneric, youngest of them all, whose attention shifted between each speaker.

"Where's that shit Laban?" MV asked, arms crossed. "He go back to Geth to sulk?"

"He's sulking here," David said. "I niffed him at our old rat hole in Wnelder Vee."

Leef snapped his fingers. "Where's Erol? Want me to find him?"

"Erol has orders. Leave him to me," Detlev said. He had been observing those who had yet to speak. He could see that the news about Marloven Hess had disturbed one or two more than the news about Svirle—which they had been warned to expect for most of their lives. But no one had asked the question foremost in their minds, so he addressed it. "There are no specific orders for the rest of you yet. Remember: You have no authority with anyone. You cannot command, and few will listen to any advice you might feel obliged to give."

Silence. Noser muttered curses, but again no one paid him any heed.

"You are to exert yourselves to avoid being captured by any of the Host. Efael and Yeres will be tracking you, not for your brains or ability, but to torture as excruciatingly as possible in order to get my attention. You're worthless to them otherwise."

"We're lazy, incompetent failures," David said appreciatively. "We worked very hard to get that rep."

MV, taking in Noser's flush of resentment, said, "Don't you see the freedom that gives us?"

"Relative freedom," Detlev reminded them. "Avoid using magic, unless you're absolutely certain you're free of tracers or wards."

"Second?" MV asked.

"You are useless as commanders only because as yet no one will follow you. But now is the time to use your brains and skills. Begin with individuals. Build trust with one person at a time. The future is yours to guard and to guide, to the best of your ability. Interpret that how you will."

A reflective silence: Sveneric pensive; David's sardonic gaze turned westward; tall, lean, fire-eyed MV tapping a knife blade against his fingernails as he meditated; Roy rubbing his jaw; Rolfin frowning down at strong brown hands; curly-haired, wild Vana lounging. Competent, pleasant-faced Curtas reflective; Leef, nearly as dark in coloring and powerful in build as his cousin Rolfin, sharing a similar thoughtful expression. Adam looking around, as if contemplating those who were absent, and why. Noser defiant.

Presently, going in singles or twos, they transferred out, until only MV and David were left with Detlev and Sveneric.

Father and son were still, their minds clearly in contact.

David said to MV, "You have a goal?"

"Sure."

"Let me guess. Ships. Or running in the background in Khanerenth?"

MV's expression tightened. "Maybe Jehan could use me and my boat in Khanerenth?"

Before David could answer, Detlev said to him, "Go to Senrid. Do what you can."

"Senrid?" David repeated, and MV's eyes narrowed.

"You know that Siamis has been observing the mental realm, shielding death spirits in case Ilerian comes out to go hunting." He sketched the Ancient Sartoran characters for Dena Yeresbeth. "One of those was Senrid's child."

David whistled; he'd only seen the child once, on a visit to Senrid, but he recollected their bond. "Accident of war, or..."

The dying, in leaving, seldom shielded memories. Detlev silently shared what Siamis had learned, then turned back to MV. "Rel's haven in Lisdan appears to have shifted from fallback to current. I believe no one has thought of outer perimeter scouting."

MV backed away, palms up. "I hear you." He transferred.

David also transferred, to a rooftop overlooking the royal castle in Choreid Dhelerei.

The transfer jolted him into cold night and the stink of death. The outer castle courtyard was empty except for several corpses, mostly but not exclusively Marloven, torchlight flickering over them in a disturbing semblance of movement.

David scanned on the mental plane. Senrid of course was thoroughly blocked, but David located him by the anguished awarenesses in Senrid's company.

David grimaced. It seemed Detlev had not-so-coincidentally sent him at the same time that Senrid was about to Disappear his child.

David moved swiftly along the silent halls of the enormous castle, pausing to scan ahead at every corner. At the garrison end, a work detail of Norsundrians clanked and thumped their way through inventorying the armory, and systematically stripping all war material from the rest of the outbuildings.

David reached the last hall, and peered through the window into a dark courtyard central to the residence wing. David's eyes adjusted to the darkness. He made out figures gathered around an old stone bier on which lay a still little figure, fair curls ordered and smooth, small hands clasped over the childish chest. Senrid—thinner than David had ever seen him—was nearly as still; he was mostly shadow, except for starlight gleaming in his fair hair, the same shade as the child's. Next to Senrid stood an older man. So old Keriam, Senrid's academy headmaster, was still alive.

On the other side of the bier three other people faced Senrid, two women and a young man, all unfamiliar. Senrid lifted his head, as if aware he was being watched, a distant noise — the crash of a door being smashed down — caused all five heads to turn quickly, then back.

From the end of the table Senrid picked up two swords. For a heartbeat David thought he was going to go chasing after whoever was rooting around in the dye outbuilding, but Senrid's movement was too deliberate for that.

David's breath caught when he understood what he was seeing. In complete silence, without the requisite torches, banners, or drums, Senrid laid the swords down, east-west crossed north-south, just beyond the head of the bier where his daughter lay, cold, silent, still. Then, his quick breathing a harsh hiss, he performed the Marloven sword dance. Alone.

Lit only by starlight, he made of the ancient dance a vow of vengeance in the movements sharp as a knife strike, his boot heels and toes tapping out the rhythm counterpoint to a heartbeat.

There was no clashing of the swords — they remained on the ground — but at the end, he picked them up again, and offered one, hilt out, to the young man, a gesture as deliberate as the beginning.

The other sword, Senrid laid at the foot of the bier, Then he moved back to the head and stretched out his hands, muttered a spell, and a tongue of flame appeared above his fingers, a symbol of fire there long enough for him to whisper the words of Disappearance. The light from the little flame glowed in strained, grief-stricken faces, etching cheekbones and taut jaws, then vanished as the child's body also vanished, leaving a stone table where her ancestors had lain for centuries.

A brief silence, then Senrid said, "I'm going back into the city to Disappear as many as I can, then..." He looked up skyward his jaw clenched, his entire body clenched, as if to hold in a howl of rage.

And that was why the city was quiet, David comprehended — the Norsundrians had grabbed up random children. They were no doubt stashed somewhere public, tied up and ready to be executed unless the adults laid down their arms.

"They'll want that formal surrender by daylight," Keriam said. "If I go, they might release the children. I can be a symbol of defeat or a target, if that's what they're looking for, and our people will survive. But not you. Not you."

"I can do it," the young man said tersely.

"No." Senrid's voice was low, but sharp. "Stad, you are now the leader of the resistance."

One of the women spoke up. "Senrid-Harvaldar, you must leave. The people have to hear about your escape. We have to hear about you being quicker than they are, and cleverer than they are. So we know you'll..." Her voice suspended on the words *come back*, and she put her hands over her face.

The other woman, stolid, older, said, "If you are alive, we have hope." She had to be a guild chief.

The five dispersed, and David decided that was his cue.

He ran down the stairs and caught up with Senrid in an archway leading to the east side of the city.

"Senrid," David said.

Senrid's head turned sharply, and recognition brought savage anger and a brief baring of teeth. "What are you doing here? Come to gloat?"

The truth—but not all the truth. Leaving out Detlev and Siamis entirely, David said, "Rolfin and Leef and I just caught up with Jilo, who was making his way, on foot, toward Chwahirsland, after finding out the Chwahir were being used as Efael's hammer."

He saw the words impact Senrid—a reminder of the wider world, and its calamities. "Jilo," Senrid said, barely above a whisper.

"On foot, through a couple of early snowstorms. We would have missed him entirely if he wasn't so physically weak after his last foray into Chwahirsland. As it was, he was maybe half a watch from blundering into a tracer-and-trap ward on the border, which he would have known if he'd actually slept through an entire night since the attack. After we yanked him, he asked after you. Thought I might as well check and give him an answer."

"Where is he?" Senrid asked, in a slightly less flat voice.

"Stashed him with the rest of your allies in Lisdan. Rel promised to keep an eye on him while he recovers."

Senrid looked away, then back at David, his gaze cold with fury as he said, "I am going to kill Imry Llyenthur."

David lifted a shoulder. "Last I heard," he said, "he's back to hunting down royal puppets for Yeres. Some of us have been having fun interfering with that."

Senrid's rage vanished as quickly as it had appeared. His voice was husky with exhaustion and grief, his eyes black pits.

David wondered when he'd slept last. "The Chwahir marched out earlier—after looting the strangest things, according to report," Senrid said. "Not food. It's as if they didn't recognize most of it. Liquor, and things you could only call keepsakes— old two-handed cups with horses painted round the rim, stuff like that, they can't possibly use for fighting. Bostian is still running around outside the city chasing down Jan Senelac, who I hope will scrag as many of them as he can before he goes to ground."

"And you?"

"I am going out to Disappear the dead. It actually seems to matter that it's by my hand, though I lost the kingdom."

Keep him busy. "I can help with that, if you in your turn want to do a little sabotage while you're on your hunt."

Senrid's mouth relaxed incrementally, and David thought, if you need a reason to live, there's nothing like sabotage.

Senrid turned the palms of his hands up in the Marloven gesture of assent.

They slipped through byways, past the cow pasture and through the kitchen garden to the back wall. They vaulted over and ghosted down alleys between storage buildings into the city.

David could see by the wreckage as well as the number of fallen that the fighting had been bitter and fierce, but the Marlovens had lost. It didn't matter that they had been vastly outnumbered, and that that their commander had access to far stronger, and more vicious magic then Senrid knew or would use. The truth being absorbed by every single person in the city, in the kingdom, was that they had lost their kingdom, their capital, for the first time since Marlovans had themselves taken Iasca Leror.

And so their king gave them what he could: Disappearing the bodies of their dead with his own hands. But he could not get to them all. David worked alongside him for an endless length of time that long night, straightening cold, stiff limbs, smoothing clothes and hair, restoring a semblance of dignity before Senrid did his magic. When the clatter and noise of the search, seize, and secure neared, they split up to cover as much area as they could.

Over and over into shocked, grief-twisted, angry faces Senrid said, "I will return," and David said, "Senrid-Harvaldar will return." No one asked who he was, or how he knew that.

They accepted his words, not because he was tall and blond, with a superficial resemblance to most Marlovens. They accepted his words because they were desperate for any sign or symbol of hope no matter how small.

An hour before the dawn watch Norsunder secured the city, and Senrid had to withdraw; the next step, both knew, would be squads sent to hunt him down, and there would be reprisals if Norsunder had any idea that Senrid was being hidden by Marlovens.

"Time to go," David said. "Can you sense the wards? Surely the first one laid down was against your name. You can't transfer out by magic."

Senrid wiped his red-rimmed eyes on his grimy sleeve, his filthy hair hanging down on his forehead. "I have to see it. And if Llyenthur is there, I can shoot him down. Not as good as gutting him with a knife, but it'll suffice."

David said, "He'll have wards up by then. I'll have to send you. At least no one knows I'm here."

Senrid was too weary, too shattered, for any response beyond flicking two fingers in assent.

David transferred them to the roof above the great parade ground, where sure enough all of the city's surviving garrison had been lined up, disarmed, and a number of civilians had been rounded up to watch. The Norsundrian occupation force stood at the perimeter, armed, most smirking, some stone-faced and bored, clearly wanting to get back to looting. David glimpsed Bostian at the head, smothering impatience. He'd be wanting to get back to Sartor, his obsession. Imry Llyenthur wasn't even there.

David hoped Senrid saw, and gained a modicum of satisfaction from, how many of the Norsundrians exhibited signs of wounds.

Keriam was marched out, a sad-looking, sun-faded old Marloven banner excavated from somewhere, and carried in his hands. As all watched, he was required to lay it on the stones at Bostian's feet. The commander gave a sign, and one his minions threw a torch onto the banner, where everyone watched, still and silent, except for the summer breeze stirring hair and clothes, as the banner burned to ash.

What the Norsundrians failed to understand was that they could burn a hundred flags, but the only one that mattered was the one that Forthan had ripped to tappers in defiance, before he denied them his life.

Bostian lifted his voice. "You may go about your business. If you take up arms, this man will be the first to die. For every one of us you attack, we will pick ten of your children — starting with the youngest — and all will perish along with the perpetrators. Disperse."

Under cover of the noise of people moving away, Senrid turned to David. "I have two more things to do."

David complied, and a short time later, they stood in Senrid's wreck of a study. Senrid opened a trunk set underneath the wall map, and took out an old gray coat with long skirts cut for riding.

David knew that at this moment, Senrid didn't care if he lived or died. But he did care about Marloven Hess. And one of his people was going to risk sneaking into that room to check that trunk, and would discover that the battle coat belonging to the former king — not Senrid's peace-loving father, but his infamous, martial grandfather — was missing, and they would know that their own king would return one day with fire and sword.

Senrid slammed the trunk lid down, shut his eyes, and murmured a complicated spell. David sensed magic release deep within the city, and said, "What was that?"

"Something I probably ought to have done long before. Detlev is no longer warded from entering the city."

David answered the unspoken question. "He'd be the first to tell you that he's not an army."

"I never expected it to make any difference," Senrid retorted. "That was mostly to anger whoever Imry Llyenthur puts in here." His teeth showed when he said the name. And before David could respond, "Where next?"

During that long, grim session of Disappearing the dead, David had stayed in contact with MV and Leef. "Right now, in Khanerenth, they are about to shoot a random group of civilians unless the king's military leader, a man only known as Owl, surrenders himself. Want to help mess things up?"

Senrid shrugged into the coat, sashed it, and made sure his wrist knives were still intact. Then he picked up his bow and arrows. "Why not?"

Part Two

One

Tlanth - Remalna

THE NEWS FROM OUTSIDE Remalna's border was grim and getting grimmer.

Meliara and Nee, her sister-by-marriage, had retreated with most of the court children to the rough mountains edging the border. They settled in a complicated cave that had formed the main supply stash nearly ten years before, when Meliara and her brother were leading a revolt against an evil king.

The caves were not comfortable — they were mossy and one end drippy as water trickled down through cracks in the rock and flowed out to tumble down the mountainside — but with the judicious use of firesticks they kept a higher chamber reasonably warm and dry. The court children, usually dressed in embroidered cotton-linen to play in, their silk reserved for on festival days, swiftly adapted to the happy, grubby state of puppies, as long as they were fed and warm.

Julen, Meliara's tough old steward and nanny, kept them firmly on task with lessons, and Captain Nessaren herself, their chief guard, conducted self-defense classes. The children were sufficiently awed by her august presence and worried about distant war to submit willingly to discipline.

For now.

Mel had no illusions about how long children could live in caves and stay civilized; one morning she was sitting at the entrance, staring out into the silvery veil of misting rain that subdued the late summer colors, when she found Nee beside her.

"Those children are so muddy I grabbed what I thought was Kitten, and it turned out to be Tara Savona." Nee shuddered. "What a brat." She cast a glance backward, then sighed. "I know that the morvende are supposed to have this admirable civilization centuries old, and they live in caves, but I have to ask myself, how? Look at us." She glanced down at her moss-streaked riding trousers and sturdy tunic.

Meliara grinned. "You're missing cleaning frames. I never had one until right before I went to court, so for me, it's back to the old ways—" She held up a hand.

Both fell silent. The crack Meliara had heard from down in the valley was followed by another, then the steady thump of equine footfalls. Shortly thereafter Vidanric appeared, leading his horse, followed by a short train of guards and courtiers with rain-washed faces, their clothing indistinguishable greens and browns.

The welcome supplies were unloaded, and those who'd come to see their children sat with them in small groups as a hot meal was prepared.

Vidanric and Mel walked a little ways downstream, and stopped under the relative shelter of a venerable bluewood tree. Her fingertips traced the aqua and cobalt lines in the bark as she said, "Do I want to hear your report?"

"No." His smile was bleak. "But you'll listen, because you love me, and because I have to talk to someone. Sles Adran is back, this time I think to stay."

Regiments of armed warriors from Sles Adran had ridden through Remalna, back and forth on their way to other places, shortly after word had come of western kingdoms falling. Vidanric had insisted that no one get in their way, and so far, there had been a kind of truce, but that felt like the calm before the storm. Some nobles stayed on their land, others sailed away to relatives, and some had joined Meliara up in the caves and woods.

Vidanric shook his head. "This time they came by ship instead of marching over the border. I was in the stable, wearing this." He touched his sturdy brown stable hand's tunic. "Savona was at the dock. I am reasonably sure no one recognized him, as he was dressed for fishing, or he might not have survived." He swallowed, then again, and his hand rose to cover his eyes.

Then he dropped his hand and faced her. "At every stage they chose someone completely at random. First, a strong fellow, one of the anchor gang. Held his arms and a squad shot him with arrows while another with a huge voice shouted, *This is what happens if you resist*. Every stage, Meliara—an old woman at the edge of the city where a crowd had gathered. I think those people were watching one another for signs of what to do, or maybe they were just curious, though I'd given orders for everyone to stay at home. A small boy in the center of Remalna-city. He wasn't doing anything; he'd climbed on that old statue of the Calahanras king on horseback, just to see. They plucked him off and shot him. At the gate to Athanarel, one of the sentries—she'd insisted on staying. Inside, old Nalrin."

"The cook? Why would they..."

"It's random cruelty, don't you see? Everyone is now afraid. When the one shouted for that crowd to scatter back to their homes, they scattered. So did we," he said bitterly. "So did we—I had eight people, only two armed, and there must have been two hundred of them, and more coming. We could have fought, but the result would have been our names added to the list of dead."

"You're alive," Mel said, throwing her arms around him, and hugging him tight; his heartbeat thumped under her ear. "You're alive, and we're up here, so they can't get any of our leaders. That means we've got hope. Since we can't fight and win, we hide in plain sight and endure. And fight covertly."

He was silent.

She lifted her arms, and stepped back to look at him. "There's more?"

Vidanric touched the notecase in his breast pocket. "I've worn this next to my skin ever since the first day, when you and the others left."

She nodded—in the early days, she had written to him each evening, little things the children said, to ease his heart, and to make certain he was alive. Until he sent a note warning her that he'd heard from Senrid the magic was compromised, and not to use the notecase. Even though Meliara was studying magic, she hadn't gained enough expertise even to understand, except vaguely, how the notecase magic worked, much less to fix it. So she'd hidden hers away so she wouldn't be tempted to try it.

"I haven't received any word from Senrid after that first note," Vidanric said, his head bent. "Until yesterday morning. After we'd made it to the outskirts of Lumm. We were holed up in an old barn, and he showed up himself. I thought magic couldn't do that without a Destination. It smelled bad, like a pan that had been left on a fire."

"You can't," Meliara said, then amended, "you shouldn't. It's terribly dangerous."

"He did it, and brought another, a taller fellow I..." Vidanric looked up, his expression odd. Then he said, "Someone Senrid introduced only as David, a mage. Senrid said he'd heard we'd been able to get a number of people to safety."

"Did you explain we hadn't been able to get any more of them after the scribe desks remained blank?"

"I did, and he told me that's why he was here—he said that if we were willing, he, and this David, might send us people to be hidden up in the hills. But we need you to set up a Destination."

"You mean they're coming *here?*"

"Yes."

"Now?"

"If they didn't get lost riding up the path today." Vidanric's smile was brief. "I didn't draw a map, in case. Gave them verbal directions only. Do we have something we could make as a Destination? That is your expertise."

Meliara looked about. She pointed to the rock near the cave entrance, one of the hollowed-out roundels carved out by swirling water eons ago, that they had facetiously named antechambers. While Vidanric waited for the visitors, Meliara laid down a pattern of small stones, then she took him inside to get a meal into him.

Senrid arrived with David a little later. Meliara barely looked at the latter. Her attention was on Senrid, who looked terrible. And it wasn't just the ill-fitting clothes he wore, instead of the black and tan uniform she'd always seen him in. His hands were tense—that she recognized—but his face had planed away the softness of youth, his cheekbones with hollows under them, his eyes bruised-looking.

They dismounted in the misting rain, as voices echoed

down from the cave behind them: no more than the laughter of children, and a girl's shrill squeal of pretend anger.

But Senrid reacted as if someone had struck him across the face. The other one said a little louder than necessary, to claim their attention, "We intend to rescue as many leaders and mages as we can before Norsunder interferes with transfer magic. They will be stepping up the plan to force mind-control spells onto leaders and send them back in as mouthpieces."

Vidanric knew a distraction when he heard one. But all he said was, "That was my understanding. You can send them to us."

David said, "Our first one is a man named Owl. You're ideal here. No one thinks of tiny Remalna, yet you have these mountains protected by those tree people. I expect even Norsunder will be wary of tangling with them."

Vidanric said, "So far, it seems to be true. Send rescues to us." Vidanric turned Meliara's way.

"You can use this Destination," she offered, pointing inside the cave.

David followed her, and after a moment Senrid did as well. Meliara wanted to describe how she'd made it, but her words dried up at the tension in Senrid's face, as if he had the world's worst headache.

The crack of a horse hoof on a fallen branch several paces away brought Senrid's head up, a knife materializing in his hand from his wrist sheath. David's right hand went to the sword he carried. He pulled the blade halfway free, then stilled.

Vidanric's breath hissed. When the other two looked his way, he forced a smile and an easy tone. "Just one of the horses. We have them corralled beyond those trees."

"Got it," Senrid said. "Thanks." Then—quite rudely, Meliara privately thought—he vanished.

The other brought up his hand to make a transfer sign, but Vidanric said quickly, "What happened?"

"Marloven Hess fell. And his little daughter was killed."

Meliara gasped, chill shocking her to the heart. Little Crystal Ingrid had played in Athanarel Castle, stealing tartlets with Elestra, making friends with every dog she met. Dead?

"When?" Vidanric asked.

David glanced upward as if he couldn't remember. "Few days ago." A rueful smile. "We've been on the run a bit." He looked pained. "I expect he'll be running on his own now," he added under his breath.

"Ret Forthan?"

David's smile vanished. "Struck his banner."

Vidanric shook his head slowly. "Jan Senelac? Van Stad?"

"If Van Stad is who I think he is, he'll be running the resistance. Senrid said that Jan Senelac is being pursued, but he expects that company to melt into the hills."

"Thanks," Vidanric said, hollowed by shock.

David lifted a hand in salute. "I'll send Owl along." He, too, vanished.

"Why were you staring at that David? Is he an enemy in disguise?" Meliara hissed the way Vidanric had.

"Didn't you see that sword he held?"

She shrugged. "It was just a sword, though the blade did look kind of rusty."

"That was not rust. Black watered steel," Vidanric said. "Gold handle. It's an exact replica of Adamas Dei of the Black Sword's weapon. I remember reading a description up in Senrid's archive."

"That sounds somewhat pretentious," Mel said, wrinkling her nose. "Who is this fellow, one of Senrid's nobles, or whatever they call nobles in Marloven Hess?"

"Don't know. He wasn't in the academy when I was there. But the sword might not be his idea. Maybe David got it from some pretentious relative." He shook his head again, and said softly, "Five years old."

Meliara's eyes stung. Her throat ached. She wanted to back into the cave to seek warmth, and to check on their children, though she knew they were safe. Each of them grieved for Senrid, Meliara thinking, *What happens to your child happens to my child.*

"Let's get ready for Owl," Vidanric said, lacing his fingers through hers.

Two

Lisdan - Melire

JULIAN LANDIS WAS SITTING alone at a small table in Ale's Haven, the rundown tavern in Lisdan's town center that the alliance was using as a meeting place, when Detlev's son Sveneric sat down across from her. He sniffed the blended aromas of rice boiled with herbs, fish-cakes, and cinnamon, then said, "What's the news?"

Julian jumped, then scowled. She would have sworn she'd checked the room, but suddenly there he was. Nothing much to look at: a slim boy of twelve or thirteen with a quantity of fine brown hair pulled back from a high brow, a roundish face, but his father's hazel eyes gazed out at you with an expression of steady assessment that made a person feel he not only heard every word you said, but would remember it exactly as you said it.

Julian hadn't seen much of Sveneric these past three or four years, though she had been one of his earliest friends since his escape from Norsunder at age eight.

She hated being caught out like that, but decided to pretend it hadn't happened. "I guess someone told you about us meeting here if there was Norsunder trouble."

Sveneric smiled a little. "Is everyone who constitutes your 'us' safely arrived?"

"Only a few. Some are trying to find and bring the rest—"

Cold air whirled through the open door, and Jilo of the Chwahir slouched in, a tall, thin, shambling boy who appeared to be in his late teens, his lank black hair and pasty complexion above old, worn dun travel clothes rendering him nondescript to those unfamiliar with the Chwahir.

"How are you feeling?" Julian asked.

Jilo shrugged one shoulder, and slumped onto a stool, coughing into a besorcelled handkerchief. Judging by the low, crackling sound of that cough, he had to be feeling like someone recently plucked half-dead off the side of a mountain where winter strikes a month or two early. "Fine." His Sartoran accent was peculiar, flattening vowels. "That girl Lyren-Sartora wouldn't leave my room until I drank some concoction that tastes like weeds." He almost smiled. "It was hot. Felt good."

Sveneric asked, "Lyren-Sartora's here? I thought she would be with Liere, wherever she is."

"Nope." Julian tracked the dish of toasted cheese bread that a stocky girl of sixteen or so carried, and licked her lips when it was plunked down in front of her. "Last I heard, she was fighting against the Norsundrian mages trying to break into the Tower of Knowledge."

I want you to go to Lisdan, Detlev had said to Sveneric, after the others had all vanished to various locations over the world. *Your part now is to listen, to stay invisible, and not to act.*

Sveneric considered his ambivalence. He knew without being told that this war was what his father had been training them for all these years. Their toughest, maybe their last run. He could not discern whether the private order stemmed from Detlev requiring him for a crucial part in a plan—or simply a way of stashing him out trouble because he was the youngest. *I'd rather help you,* he'd said to his father.

When I want you, be sure I'll find you. But until then, I want you to be my eyes inside Lisdan.

Sveneric said, "Any plans being made?"

"Not until we have more of us," Julian said, pausing when the waiter appeared again at their table, carrying a pitcher.

Jilo turned up one of the upside-down mugs on the table and nodded at the pitcher. "Rootbrew, please," he said.

"That'll chase away the taste of weeds," Julian said.

The girl poured out the spicy-scented brown liquid, expertly stopping as the foam crested the ceramic mug, and then she went away. Julian continued, "So far, all we've done is agree that the local occupation forces are hands off, or else we'll give ourselves away." She crunched down on her toast, then added, "Because it's harvest time, there's plenty to do. We stay to ourselves. Work for our food and board." Crunch!

"And you've been here…?"

"We got here two weeks ago, me'n Andri Elsarion," Julian said thickly. Julian waved her bread, indicating height. "From Enaeran. You'll like him. He's really good with a sword. And horses. CJ and some of the Mearsieans are also here. They came to tell us that Mearsies Heili is apparently safe from Norsunder, though no one really believes that. Think it's CJ exaggerating, as usual. Dirk Sonscarna is also here, and Hibern, and Leander and Kyale from Vasande, and Dtheldevor and her gang." She looked down. "And the Sarendan gang. What's left of them."

"Senrid?" Sveneric asked, not mentioning that he had been in almost constant contact with Darian Selenna, who was still devastated after losing his aunt and great-uncle. Sveneric knew that everyone missed Lilah—who would have been surprised at her popularity.

Jilo shook his head. "Senrid sent Leander and Kyale, but didn't come himself. Uh, what's Detlev up to, do you know?"

One shoulder lifted slightly. "He'll come when he comes." Sveneric hesitated, then felt a familiar mind-touch—Lyren-Sartora: *You here to help or to nose?*

: *Help.* Sveneric glanced at the windows, but they were fogged. Thinking of his father's words, he added: *If I can.*

: *Then come outside and talk to me.*

He extricated himself with a few words; Jilo wanted to stay and eat, which Julian encouraged him to do with such enthuse-asm that poor Jilo blushed, utterly at sea with social attention.

Sveneric drifted out, and found Lyren-Sartora seated on a wooden fence, her legs swinging.

They gauged one another in silence, pretty much of an age and height. Her once-round face had lengthened to oval, but her large dark-fringed golden eyes were the same.

"Where have you been?" Lyren-Sartora asked.

"I was on Geth, learning their form of magic, until David came to fetch me, when they discovered Yeres hunting boys of certain qualifications. What happened in Bereth Ferian?"

"Magic attack. Whoever it was blasted all of Evend's old protections in scarcely half a day. Arthur was really upset, of course, that they also killed the senior circle of mages. Liere got us organized, and out, leading us cross-country to the woods when they discovered wards messing with light magic transfer. Don't ask me what sort of wards. As soon as someone starts blabbing about magic, I fall asleep. Then she contacted Roy." Lyren-Sartora tapped her forehead. "He used dark magic to transfer us here."

"She's not here with you?"

Lyren-Sartora shook her head, a worried furrow between her brows. "She's in a huge magic fight in Sartor, last I heard. Her mind-shield is better than anyone's." Then she flung her gold-touched dark braids back in what was meant to be a careless gesture. Her dimpled smile was tight. "Liere can take care of herself. I won't worry."

"What about Senrid Montredaun-An?" Sveneric asked.

Lyren-Sartora's pose of unconcern vanished in a spasm of grief. "Kyale says that they killed his little girl." She struggled, her voice going high. "She wasn't even five! What possible threat could she have been?" Her breath hissed in, her arms tight across her middle. "I've cried and cried, and all it does is make me angrier."

Sveneric's innards tightened. "Norsunder probably saw her as a distraction for Senrid."

"That's what Andri said. And it must have worked, because Marloven Hess fell. Senrid hasn't been back, though Leander insisted when he and Kyale showed up that Senrid said he'll come. But he hasn't. Rel told us all that if Senrid does turn up, he would probably really, really hate any fuss."

The wind had turned cold, and gray clouds tumbled unevenly from the northwest. All around Sveneric people bustled along the streets; this was a market-town at the end of harvest-time. He sensed wariness and worry in some of the adults. So far, the war had not touched them except in the occasional patrol riding around — Adranis in purple, Norsundrians in gray — and of course rumor.

His eye was caught by a short figure with long, swinging black hair and vivid blue eyes. A laced bodice and plain woolen skirt similar to what the local girls favored did not at all disguise CJ of the Mearsieans to those who had met her even once.

She spotted them, and Sveneric waited to see what would

transpire. The time was not so very far in the past when the Mearsiean girls, who were as tight-knit a group as Detlev's boys, had regarded Detlev and his boys as deadly enemies—with reason, as MV had killed one of them. He still swore it was an accident. Though they had all been playing with real steel.

"Hey," CJ said, and her gaze transfixed Sveneric. Though she shielded her superficial thoughts, her emotions leaked like sunlight round a flimsy shutter: tentative friendliness and wariness combined. "Somebody said that poopsies were here. I'm glad it's just you, Sveneric."

"Just me for now."

CJ glanced up as a few drops spattered onto them. "Rain!"

"At least it'll dampen this dust," Lyren-Sartora said, with a fastidious glance down at her plain cotton-wool robe over riding trousers.

"Come to our place," CJ said. "It's nearby." She whirled around and led the way between a couple of weather-worn wooden buildings. The three hopped a fence and ran up an alley. They reached a narrow street and a two-story wooden building with the sign Embeth Tailoring on its front just as the downpour started in earnest.

CJ pounded up a worn stone stairway at the side of the building, and thrust open a door. They piled in, chased by a chill blast of wind. CJ used her whole body to slam the door shut, and led them down a short, bare hall as she said, "Atan hired herself on here, and I pretend to be an apprentice. We have to do really boring sewing." CJ made a face. "But it's a place to stay, and the Embeths are nice. And not nosy, as long as the work gets done."

She opened a door onto a room that extended the entire length of the back of the building. Beyond the two mullioned windows slanted gray rain. The hissing roar was barely audible; the building, though utterly unembellished, was sturdy. Warmth emanated from a corner stove—they had their own firestick.

Narrow beds lined the walls, and a wardrobe hulked in the corner opposite the stove. A multi-colored rug covered the plank floor, onto which CJ flung herself. Lyren-Sartora sat cross-legged next to her.

The door opened and Atan walked in. Her face showed only pleasant surprise as she greeted them; when CJ first turned up, she'd taken one look at Rel and said, "You're definitely a grownup now. Well, you were mostly one anyway," she added after twisting a bare foot back and forth, then she ran off to greet the Sarendan refugees.

"That was not a compliment," Atan had observed, struggling not to find that girl really, really annoying.

Then Atan saw that Rel was smiling. And she recalled that even at CJ's worst, he'd always enjoyed her insouciance. Sure enough, he said, "The more trenchant she gets, the more I appreciate her."

"Why?"

"So unlike a courtier — what she says is what she thinks."

"We could do with less of it."

He just shook his head. "I've met plenty of youngsters like her, often with the Child Spell, all with the deep anger of having grown up with violence at home."

"Her father was a monster? Monsters are an easy excuse for hate."

"I think it was more difficult than that, that her father might have been fine, even beloved — except when he was violent. What suffers is trust, especially when your own home is never quite safe. Mondros once said about Puddlenose that when the scars on flesh fade, the ones on the spirit remain. It could be said for her, too."

After that conversation, Atan invited CJ and the Mearsieans to Embeth Tailors, and was surprised when CJ accepted, along with tall, quiet Seshe — and even more surprised when CJ made an effort to behave with manners, do the tedious work, and not ask nosy questions. Atan attributed that to Seshe's influence; it never occurred to Atan that bratty, outspoken CJ was as frightened of her as she was hungry for approval.

"Anyone want some steep?" Atan asked.

"Please," Sveneric said, watching Atan reach for a jug and fill the kettle on the tiny stove.

She then sat on one of the beds, picked up a basket, and began sewing with swift, sure movements, head bent, her brow puckered.

Sveneric had braced for questions — accusations even, because he knew there were many who assumed that Norsunder's attack was Detlev's fault, it was his fault for not preventing it, and it was his fault for not defending the world. Sveneric was very aware that Atan numbered among the many who loathed Detlev and did not trust him at all.

Her posture shut him out. He turned his attention to CJ, who lay on the rug staring up at the rain through the window.

Once again she'd forgotten her mind-shield. *Poopsies.* She knew they were supposed to be allies now, and she hoped that they would turn their nasty skills onto Norsunder, but the truth was, she didn't want any of them around. Especially MV, or David as their leader, though Laban and his sarcasm was fifty times worse, in her view. But she wouldn't mind Adam, and Lilah had said Curtas was as nice as Adam. And she liked Roy.

Sveneric sure didn't act like a poopsie, though she knew he was one. He was so still, and quiet, and his smile was a real smile. And his eyes were like lights—no. CJ frowned, shifting her gaze to the clearing skies outside, lest he see her staring and somehow descry her thoughts. Then she remembered her mind-shield. Lights was stupid. She couldn't read a book by them. Sveneric's eyes were like windows, but yech, that wasn't right either; you couldn't see all the gunk inside his head.

What was it? He seemed to see everything, but when you looked at him, it was almost as if you looked through him, like a clear mountain stream, or a smooth crystal. He wasn't all knots of fire and anger, cruel strength and taunting laughter like some of the poopsies in the old days. Yet he certainly had all the training, for though she had never heard him brag about being Detlev's son (not that anyone in their right mind would consider that a thing to brag about!) or his abilities, she had seen him once, when she'd gone with Clair to Bereth Ferian to visit Arthur, and had found a bunch of poopsies gathered there with Siamis, out in one of the courtyards, playing a game with knives. They threw them back and forth as if they were ropes of silk, laughing the while, and Sveneric had been at least as fast as any of the bigger boys, his skill just as lethal.

She began to hum very faintly, a sound barely audible above the hiss of rain. Lyren-Sartora turned her golden gaze to CJ, and hummed under her in harmony.

Except for the blended voices of the girls, the snap of the fire, and the rain outside, the room was quiet. Sveneric's thoughts drifted as he listened to CJ's clear, melodic soprano, and Lyren-Sartora's ordinary but pitch-perfect counterpoint.

CJ never sang louder. Presently the water boiled, and Atan rose, fetched from the wardrobe a packet of steep, and with the painstaking care that testified to how precious her leaves were, she carefully plucked out three. The air filled with the aroma of summer gardens, of fine herbs and endless clean spaces.

Outside, the wind shifted direction, and the drumming against the windowpanes lessened. Sveneric looked down at CJ's black swath of hair, lying like a shadow against the riotous colors of the rug, before Atan pressed a warm mug into his hands, and he gratefully accepted the unspoken truce as well as the steep.

He sipped the scalding liquid, into which Atan had stirred a dollop of honey with her scissors, and the warmth spread through him. Sveneric's early childhood — spent surrounded by gray stone and steel and among those whose desire for power pervaded every action, night or day — had engendered in him a reverence for such moments. The melodic rise and fall of the girls' voices, the light, the fading summer fragrance, the touch of warmth in his hands: he impressed the memory.

Then drank. By the time he was down to the last light green drops, the rain had abated, and CJ sat up and yawned.

"I'm getting hungry, and the sun'll go soon," she said, looking around at the others. "Seshe offered to do the dinner at Rel's tonight, so it's bound to be good."

Atan gave a nod, her fingers flashing with the needle.

CJ found it odd that the queen of a huge, old country like Sartor didn't mind being a needlewoman, taking orders from fussy people and making their clothes. "When I first got my throne back I had one gown, and my new home was a palace that had been neglected for a century. I learned a lot about how things are made," she'd said, implying that such knowledge was well worth knowing.

CJ cordially hated sewing, but once she settled down to it — if there were people to talk to — it was endurable. She'd much rather be out finding ways to get rid of Norsunder, but for some reason the older ones, like Atan, and Rel, and that yellow-haired one named Andri, felt it better to wait.

CJ waited. Besides, it was fun having so many friends all gathered in one place. They'd had some great games — something Rel had privately praised her for. "You are fortunate in Mearsies Heili," he said. "Mearsieanne was your only loss. Many of these others have faced humiliating defeats, and losses of life, and the rulers all feel to some degree that they abrogated their promises. Don't ask questions, and help keep spirits up. You'll be doing at least as much good as anyone out there swinging swords."

Well, one thing the Mearsieans were good at was games!

"Let's bucket our bones on over," she suggested. "Sveneric needs to meet everybody."

Lyren-Sartora said, "Good idea. Let's go."

Sveneric dunked his cup in the cleaner bucket, and stowed it back on its shelf in the wardrobe with the others.

As they walked up the rain-swept streets toward the end of town. CJ explained the situation, and Sveneric picked the salient facts out of her long, tangled, opinionated ramble: how Rel represented himself as a merchant from the capital, who hired out labor. War or not, the harvest had to be got in.

They soon reached the house, which was undergoing repairs. The ornamental garden before it was neatly kept, and the windows all had curtains hung in them—pulled shut.

As soon as they passed inside, someone bellowed "Dinner!" up the stairs.

The stampede was impressive. To CJ and the younger ones, the gathering was reassuring and fun—always, always, if they could find cause to laugh, then surely disaster would stay at bay?

Sveneric recognized this candle against the darkness of defeat.

Three

THE THICK BANK OF clouds obscuring the setting sun shrouded the farm-dotted Bermundi countryside very quickly in darkness. An old man leading a string of donkeys laden with packs and blankets loudly chivvied his charges up to Upper Arthlatown's newly restored city gate. There, two armed, gray sur-coated Norsundrian gate guards stopped him. Neither bothered to hide their boredom.

"The sun isn't gone yet," the old man said, his voice quavering. "The sun isn't yet gone, and you can't hurry a donkey, much less eight. I can't sleep out here with them —"

The two exchanged words in the flat tone of unending tedium, then one beckoned him forward, speaking in the local dialect of Gran Mearsiean, "Papers, then. Fast. And never come so late again."

"Thank you, thank you." The old man sighed, and he began rustling through a satchel at his side.

One walked up to the first donkey and began a cursory search of the pack. The old man held out his folded, limp papers to the other, who angled them toward the torches above the gate; at the sight of the papers, the pair of armed sentries atop the gate looked away again. Even the mild fun of hassling an old geezer had been denied them: the orders were strict. One of them moved to the winch, and the other peered out into the darkness for the armed resistance they all knew was not going to come—Bermund hadn't resisted in the first place. And when they were told everyone had to have identity papers, or be shot, they'd all lined up to be counted and recorded.

As the gate guards went through the motions of their check, the old man observed from between his lead donkey's twitching ears as a shadow slipped from under the blankets of the sixth donkey and scoot, low to the ground, toward the wall.

The search was soon over. One Norsundrian flung up a gloved hand in signal to the bored, daydreaming lookout above. The huge gate creaked open and the old man clucked to his leader. As soon as the last donkey entered the nearly deserted main street the gate swung shut. The old man wiped his grizzled beard as he took a look around. The shadow was nowhere in sight.

He led his tired animals down the street, then turned up the narrow side alley toward home. Along the way, seemingly from nowhere, a slim young man of medium height emerged from the darkness between two houses. Faint glows from windows shone on light hair and a squarish face.

"Thank you, Jervasi," the newcomer murmured. "I promised you would be in no danger. Now where is the city jail, or anyplace they might keep prisoners?"

Jervasi studied the face before him. A young man, though his face was thinned of flesh so that the bones were sharp-etched in the weak light. Pain bracketed the mouth and creased the youth's forehead. "We never had a jail in Arthlatown," Jervasi said.

"Never?" the whisper was derisive.

"Never. We've had troubles, but never the kind needing a jail. Mostly, the guilds took care of their own, and there was a lot of cleaning and rebuilding, done by troublemakers." Jervasi gestured toward the inner city, which gleamed palely in the darkness. Many of the oldest buildings were half-timbered, the foundations made of white stone.

Jervasi added, "I mark that you need food and rest. Come home with me, at least for this night."

The fellow plainly hesitated, underscoring his need.

"It isn't an invitation, it's advice," Jervasi said. "You gave me good gold just to let you ride under Zoli's blankets, and you kept your word, they didn't see you, so I'm safe, and we're quits, far as I'm concerned. But I see what I see. Beyond your name I won't ask aught of your affairs, and you don't have to give me that if you don't want to."

There was a soft laugh. "Senrid." Foreign accent. Jervasi kept his mind from speculation, as the animals sensed home nearby and quickened their pace.

"Want some help?" Senrid asked when they reached Jervasi's barn.

"No, I'm faster alone. The stairs are just inside that door there, on the other side of the court. You'll find bread, cheese, wine. Blankets in the second room, if you've a need to sleep right away."

It was close to an hour before Jervasi made his way slowly up his narrow stairway, where he found his guest nodding over a half-eaten hunk of stale bread, a lit candle sitting on the small table. Senrid obviously hadn't explored Jervasi's tiny bedroom, for his clothing was still as worn and grimy as before.

"I've a cleaning-frame in the bedroom doorway," Jervasi said.

Senrid's head lifted, and his expression of extreme exhaustion eased a little. Jervasi could see the effort he had to expend just to stand; magic sparkled faintly over the young fellow's body, separating grime from his person and clothing.

"The baths are hard to get to for my old bones," Jervasi said conversationally. "That cleaning frame is my one extravagance."

Senrid opened his hand, a curious gesture. "May I help you with anything?"

Jervasi laughed. His kitchen was scarcely an alcove, just a corner with a tiny fireplace. He wouldn't actually light his firestick until ice formed on the rooftops across the alley. The heat radiating up through the floor from the bakery below usually kept him warm until winter, and if he wanted cooked food, he went downstairs, or to the local inn.

"No need," Jervasi said. So his guest wasn't going to talk. Well, then, on to business. "The new jail is in what used to be the musicians' guild hall, but I've heard that they are also keeping some prisoners in one of the aristo houses near the governor's palace. They promised dire things if anyone tries to free one."

"My family is already dead, and they've taken everything else." Senrid shrugged. "All they can do is shoot me; if there's any hint of trouble for you, I'll be gone in a heartbeat."

Jervasi thought he understood at last, the will to action impelled by grief. He said nothing as he got slowly to his feet and went about fixing two plates of bread-and-cheese. Most like they'd be seeing a lot more like this one before long. With nothing more to lose, he'd likely take any risk. And who knows? Maybe that's what was needed to get the world free again.

A day later, up in the governor's palace. A young woman exclaimed, "Ouch! Blast it!"

Senrid smiled from where he crouched on the roof overhanging this particular bit of garden. He tossed down another pebble, this time into the lap of the thin young woman in the elaborate court robe. She stilled. Her long fingers crushed her aristocratic embroidery briefly, then loosened, but her shoulders stayed tense.

She lifted her head. Senrid saw a narrow face pinched with a kind of aching expectancy. When he leaned up so she could see him, disappointment contracted her expression, then she bent her head, letting wavy dark blond hair swing forward. When she looked up again, two dull spots of red marked her sallow cheeks, but her expression had smoothed, and she gave a nod.

Senrid did not need Dena Yeresbeth to suspect that she'd hoped someone else would be her rescuer—and she was furious with herself for her reaction.

It was just after dark when Senrid got his chance. He'd rigged a rope outside her room, and when the guards below— there were only two for the entire building—changed, he let down his rope-ladder.

The rescue itself was quick but tense, fraught with the young woman's efforts to cooperate without knowing what to do. She got tangled in the rope, and froze, clinging with shaking grip lest she fall. Senrid hauled her up; she crept with trembling limbs onto the roof. He tapped her on the shoulder and motioned.

She forced herself to her hands and knees, then followed him across the roof, catching her knees in her robe's trailing folds. When they reached the ground, they studied one another in the reflected light from the high windows of the palace. He said in Sartoran, "You're from Enaeran?"

She said in a haughtily modulated voice, "I am Thadara Otobris, Duchas of Merith."

Senrid bowed flourishingly, a full Sartoran court-bow as if to a sovereign, and she gasped. A snob she might be, but she was not blind to irony. "Senrid," he said, tapping his chest. "Is Llyenthur by any chance inside?"

"Dropped I. Left," she responded with emphatic distaste, her accent so strong that he decided to switch to Enaeraneth. "If I don't return shortly—if you hear an uproar—horses are tied down that alleyway there."

He vanished then, leaving Thadara to cope with a whirlwind of emotional reactions. Aching all over from that terrifying climb, she stalked toward the place where this Senrid had said the horses were. Her robe, with its embroidered folds and train, suitable for a royal court, was extremely annoying to try to make an escape in. She swept her train over one arm, and kept her arms pressed to her sides so her gold-embroidered sleeves wouldn't catch on quite as many stickers, twigs, and rough places in stones that seemed to positively reach out just to snag her.

She had progressed—stumbling painfully over unseen rocks and ruts in her ballroom slippers—about halfway along the dark lane when horse hooves approached.

There came a familiar whisper, "Mount up."

She opened her eyes. Weak starlight gleamed in blond hair, but not the right hair. This hair was wheat colored rather than lemon, curly instead of straight, peasant-short instead of the long hair of birth and position. Hurt squeezed her heart. This Senrid was obviously not Andri.

"Come! I'm afraid the word is just getting out, and we'd better ride fast."

Thadara smiled into the darkness. There was nothing she would like better. Hacking and smashing and other such sinewy employment was quite beyond her, but fast riding? She'd show this Senrid just what that was.

Her conviction flared into triumph when she swung into the saddle, flinging her train behind her. The horse she sat astride was powerful, and nervous, and beautifully trained— she felt it immediately.

"Ready?"

For answer she whipped the reins either side of the horse's neck, and dug her heels into its sides. The startled animal leaped forward and she fought for control with the practiced exhilaration of one who knows she'll win.

Amazingly enough, Senrid was quick to catch up, and they rode side by side through the dark city, following a circuitous route only known to him. Twice they passed under flaring torches, and she glanced over to see that her companion rode well—though with no real dash—in fact, he was scarcely holding reins.

Her fingers tightened on her own reins, and the horse quivered. She relished the submission of this mighty creature. Soon they slowed, rode slowly down a narrow alley smelling of old hay, and horse, and wet wool, and then into a tiny courtyard next to a jumbled wooden building.

They dismounted, and Thadara followed Senrid into a small stable with only eight stalls. Senrid lit a lamp, and she looked around with interest. She'd only been in her own extensive stables once or twice, and in her father's never.

Senrid had led his horse into the first stall. "If the saddle's too heavy, give a yell," he called.

"Oh!" She stared in surprise. "You don't mean *I'm* to take it off?"

Senrid reappeared, his face sardonic in the lamplight. "I take it you're used to leaving 'em to be put back together by lackeys, eh?"

Stung, she said haughtily, "Where I come from everyone rides hard. I've been riding hard since I was a child, and I don't have to behave like a stable hand to exhibit mastery."

Senrid retorted in an even tone that was somehow worse than anger would have been, "If any academy—anyone rode like that where I come from I'd knock her out of the saddle. That one over there I stole from the Norsundrians. His will has been ruined and his mouth is scarred. You can use that one if we have to ride again. I'm sure he won't notice any more clumsy maltreatment."

Thadara gasped, but Senrid had vanished once again. She was left staring at the unfamiliar buckles and ties of the saddle. She was so angry her fingers shook, but try as she might, she could not lift the saddle.

Senrid reappeared, lifted the loosened saddle off, and put it away. Then he leaned against the wall, arms crossed, and issued step-by-step directions in tending a horse.

She gritted her teeth against retort and carried out his instructions, ignoring her robe dragging in the straw and dust, and the snags in her fine embroidery. When at last he was satisfied, he led the way upstairs, having appeared not to notice her icy silence.

The room upstairs was small, stuffy, and utterly bare except of the wood that made it, saving only a rude table and a couple of awkward chairs. Senrid moved past her and fussed in a tiny closet that seemed to have a bed, a trunk, and a square of carpet that at first she took to be turf.

"Want something to eat?" he asked, speaking her home language.

She shook her head.

Senrid came out and sat in the other chair. "You're from Enaeran, are you not?" he asked. "How'd you end up a prisoner here?"

"The Norsundrians sent Adon Marsael back to our capital. He's a relative to our king. He had thrown in with Norsunder, but he lost the crown anyway. For a short time, until the day came when they marched in..."

She found that he was a good listener, and out it came, the whole story, in emotion-driven detail. How Andri had left to get magic help, then the betrayal by Sles Adran and the death of her father, and how this Norsundrian relation of the royal family had imprisoned the ministers, promising to hold public executions if anyone took any action against Sles Adran's occupiers.

"... And I managed to get us all to wear only mourning white whenever Adon Marsael tried to hold social events, and then this Imry Llyenthur came, and right before my face asked who was the greatest irritant to Adon's court, and Adon looked at me, and that Llyenthur said, 'She will do.' She will do, as if I were not in the room. Then he slapped something against my arm—touched me without permission—and I came here."

She went on to complain about his lack of manners, and added bitterly that there was no point to it, that she had no contact with Andri's old network. That was Martande, and that jumped-up stable hand Gared.

Senrid listened in silence, understanding a lot more than Thadara realized, specifically her yearning to be not just queen, but queen beside Andri Elsarion. And Imry Llyenthur would have discerned that, just as Senrid had.

"You were chosen to be turned by magic into a puppet to keep watch over your own people. Sles Adran's occupiers are all over the middle of the continent by now. He might have them spread thin. They'll want locals doing their work for them. But it takes time to impose mind control spells."

In other words, Senrid had failed once again to catch up with Llyenthur, who'd merely stashed Thadara here as a sop for Yeres.

"Mind control," she repeated in horror, then gave him a haughty look. "Don't I have the right to question you? You said the word academy earlier—you covered it, but I heard it. I read history. Your Halian accent, your name, and your description, matches what I've read about Senrid Montredaun-An of Marloven Hess, over the mountains from us. We are not ignorant, you know: our kingdoms are tied in the past." She sounded affronted.

"That's who I am," Senrid said. "Though that's immaterial now. I take it no one has given you the Universal Language Spell?"

Before she ask what that was, he touched her forehead, said some words, and pain shot through her temples and behind her eyes.

"Sorry about the headache. Dark magic does that." He pulled away his hand. "But you've now got the local tongues— when you hear them spoken, the words will come clear. Tomorrow I'll make a map with a road out."

"Where would I go?" she asked. She was slightly mollified by the discovery that she'd been rescued (and criticized) by a king, not a mere lackey.

"Anywhere in the world. If you want to find Andri Elsarion, I believe he's in Lisdan, central in Melire south and east, on the other side of the Arthla River. Right now, stay here. No noise. This place, rude though you may find it, is someone's home. He is not here—left on his trade route yesterday. I don't want him to return from his route and find it burned by the Norsundrians. If you want to sleep, there's a bed in yon room, and some rather rough blankets, but they are warm. I'll return shortly."

He slipped downstairs and into the night, leaving Thadara to explore the little bedroom, with shuddering disgust, until her feet encountered the carpet. It was so astonishingly soft—very like the beautiful, century-long cultivated lawns she'd thought confined to palaces — that she bent closer, almost burning her own hair with the candle as she inspected the pure green.

Bermund, she thought. Bermund carpet. She'd thought only the wealthy could afford them. Ah, but if they were made here...

She took off her gown, blew out the candle, and lay down in her silken under-dress on the flat hay-stuffed mattress, at first refusing but them pulling the scratchy, mildewed woolen blanket over her. At least it was warm, though she found herself wishing she dared to lie on that carpet instead. What kind of fools would make a carpet a king would covet, yet beds not fit for beasts?

She had barely slid into sleep when she was abruptly woken again by fingers on her arm. She flung off the strange hand and sat up, gasping.

"They're searching," Senrid whispered in the darkness. "The drunken guards who missed your escape."

"Drunken?" she repeated.

"There was sleepweed added to their ale," Senrid said without the least sign of regret. "If they thought they'd have an easy life signing on with Norsunder, they're about to be enlightened. We have an hour at the most. Their numbers are too few for a thorough search. Put these on. They're Jervasi's. I'll get you something better in the morning, but for now it'll have to do. In our favor is the fact that both of you are skinny and much of a size." He thrust something into her arms and withdrew, taking her crimson and gold robe. She heard ripping, and smelled something burning.

But she ignored that and held up the clothing Senrid had handed her, scrutinizing it in the faint light from the other room.

"Done?" Senrid called. His impatience was obvious.

Thadara shrugged out of her under-dress and pulled on the shirt. It was rough, the holes in the front gapping far wider than the exquisitely fitted lacings she was used to; at most there were three holes, and she could see her silken singlet through the gap. She pulled the cord tight, and tied it in a bow, then another bow. The woolen trousers felt repellent against her flesh; they scratched, and smelled musty, and were so voluminous she was forced to use the rope belted through. Below were her bare feet. The final indignity, she thought.

"Hurry."

"I'm done."

Disgust and mortification put her in a rage as she stalked through the door. When the brief snap of the cleaning frame cleared off the mustiness of the clothing, some of the disgust abated, leaving the rage.

She lowered herself on the nearest uncomfortable wooden chair, daring Senrid to make some uncouth remark about her appearance—but Senrid ignored her as he dashed past, then returned with her slippers.

"My clothes—"

"The gown is almost gone, and these go next."

That's why the tiny apartment was so warm; Senrid dashed back into the bedroom and opened a small window she hadn't even seen. Then he opened the kitchen window, and a cold night breeze drifted in, scouring out the heat and the smell of burning fabric.

Senrid stopped in front of her, and said, "The hair, now."

She clapped her hands to her head, staring starkly in horror.

He made a visible effort. "Look. The threat against peoples' lives is real. If they catch you, there will be a public execution, and Jervasi and his family will be next. We have to get you on the road. After this search." He drew a knife she hadn't even realized he was carrying. "Hair grows. But you're leaving here as a stable boy."

She forced her hands into her lap and sat still, tears of disgrace running hot down her cheeks, while Senrid's blade sawed inexorably round her head, and the cool air made her ears and neck feel naked.

Finally he said, "Done. One good thing about a knife, it doesn't make the cut seem recent." He swept up the hair, started into the kitchen, then checked himself. "No. The shoes were bad enough; this stink will raise the street. I've got to do something about the horse anyway. If anyone comes, blow out the light and climb in bed—gah!"

He was staring at the front of her shirt. He frowned, then moved quickly again, and pulled out the bows. She raised her hands in protest, but he was brisk and impersonal, as though dressing a child, as he straightened the lacings so they lay flat. "Caravan boys really don't pucker their shirt fronts and double-bow the ties."

Then he sat in the other chair and pulled up his trousers

legs. To her surprise, she saw that he wore blackweave cavalry boots; they'd been hidden under the long hem of his baggy farm trousers. "No help for it, those feet are a giveaway," he said, and yanked off the boots.

A moment later his long black stockings landed in her lap, still warm, and slightly damp. She shuddered, but at least they didn't smell. He'd been back and forth through the cleaning frame too many times for that. So she pulled them on, and picked up her under-dress, which still lay on the table. The fire was already dying. Feeling as if she had wandered into a dream, she laid the balled-up silk on the fire, and watched it whoosh! into flame.

The flames almost as quickly died away again. She watched, resolutely not touching her head. When she was sure she had control, she felt her hair, which lay jagged-edged over her brow, and curled away from her ears to a square-cut at the back, much like Senrid's.

He returned a few moments later, carrying several daggers, which he tucked in various places out of sight. "Come on," he murmured. "They're at the front of the street." He blew out the candle, but she could still see faintly in light reflected from somewhere; he ripped off his shirt and flung it to the bottom of Jervasi's trunk, and then pulled on an old, worn, patched one. She caught the glint of something golden on a long chain falling against his chest, but she forbore speaking, and it was soon hidden by Jervasi's work shirt. "I buried my boots and your hair in the stable, under the big horse's stall. It'll have to do. Don't give them reason to search more thoroughly. I'm the big brother, so I get the bed, you on the carpet. Now. You're Arnei, I'm Jervasi. You're my cousin..." As he spoke he ran his hands through his hair, tousling it up, and flung himself on the bed.

Thadara lay on the carpet, which was soft on her neck. But between the rest of her and it was the rough, nasty clothing.

"... and you're here from Tser Mearsies to learn the trade— he deals in rugs. I dappled the horse and trimmed his mane. Speak as little as you can. Be stupid, and afraid, but don't be a duchas." He ended on a soft laugh.

Thadara lay flat, her blanket now pulled close about her ears, and counted her heartbeats until the sudden thumping and knocking below indicated that the Norsundrians had arrived.

Bright torchlight flared weirdly as three dark figures

clumped in. Thadara and Senrid sat up. Thadara watched Senrid and tried to mimic his expression, which was utterly unlike his usual. His mouth hung open, his eyes squinted.

"What is it?" He slurred the words. "Dad's not here —"

"Search." The one word was spoken in Gran Mearsiean, as the three proceeded to make a shambles of the tiny rooms.

Thadara was stepped on once before she got up and sat beside Senrid on the bed. A moment later a rough hand pushed them both away, and the mattress was turned off to reveal the empty frame beneath, with some of Jervasi's humble supplies neatly stored below; none of them thought to pull the bed frame away from the wall, where two knives lay within Senrid's reach.

One of the searchers issued a series of questions in a short voice: where was the dad? What were their names? Where were their traveling papers? Thadara nearly panicked until she heard Senrid say, "Dad keeps them with him. Doesn't trust us not to lose 'em and we're not going anywhere."

A fourth then clumped in and said, in Norsundrian, "Two cross-country horses, but neither matches the description."

The four Norsundrians then departed, and Senrid murmured, "I'm off to their headquarters to steal papers for you while they search. Tomorrow, you are on the road."

Four

ONCE THADARA WAS ON her way Senrid checked for wards. Sure enough, one had been placed over the city, preventing dark magic transfer as well as light. That meant someone would soon be coming to make a more thorough search.

Time to go. After a stiff, mortified promise from Thadara to be gentle with the better mount—with any horse—he had kept the maltreated Norsundrian mount, which was bare except for a rope halter, and joined the line at the gate. Outwardly he kept a stolid, vacant demeanor, because he knew the gatekeepers were going to be focusing on people just his age.

When it was his turn, he handed over his papers, to which he'd added some splotches of strong-smelling herbal sauces, and he'd tucked them into his armpit after a long, sweaty run back to Jervasi's.

"Who are you?" the tall, red-haired Norsundrian asked— holding the paper at arm's length.

"Don't it say?" Senrid whined in surprise, pointing at the paper. "Or can't you read neither? They told me it says I'm Thurgan Roth, from Falary, which, you know, I am."

"Do you have any weapons?" the Norsundrian asked with evident impatience.

"Sure!" Senrid gave them a vacuous grin.

The two stepped closer, and he said, "Me pitchfork."

"Your what?"

"M'pitchfork. Don't look fer it. How could I carry a pitchfork into town? It's at home, right where it belongs, on the farm."

The two stepped back, one rolling his eyes, the other scowling. "Your business in town?"

Senrid droned in a nasal whine, "Visitin' me sister. M'dad thought I might work at the dyers, but she says no, I just don't seem to have a turn for the colors, and anyway I miss the farm, and so after a month o'the town sights, I'm ready to go back, then we couldn't, and now we can, but we have to get these-here papers first, so I did, but you know, it's really—"

The one holding his papers thrust them into his hands and gave him a rude shove through the gates, then turned to the next in line.

Senrid mounted his horse and rode away at a gentle walk, humming the old ballad "Yvana Ride Thunder."

Arthlatown to Locan Jora

The long shadows had begun to blend late the next day when he dropped down behind an outcropping of rock on a hillside as a roving patrol of Norsundrians harassed a pair of wagon-driving travelers who'd come from the direction of Hanbria.

Senrid fingered the knife in his sleeve as he eyed the light brown head of one of the Norsundrians. Wrong light brown hair—too short. And too many trees for a clear shot. Too many to attack on his own...

"If you're looking for Llyenthur," a man said softly from directly behind Senrid, "you're wasting time and effort."

Senrid whipped around, fingers gripping his knife hilt—to meet a blank blue stare. He backed up. Black curly hair—height the same as Senrid's own—tight smile with no humor—

"Kessler Sonscarna?" he whispered on an outgoing breath.

The notorious renegade Chwahir prince and ex-Norsundrian dropped down next to Senrid. He wore several weapons, and like Senrid was dressed in black, ready for nighttime action.

Kessler smiled slightly, and tipped his head toward the

patrol. "Want to do something about that?"

Two against that crowd wasn't a whole lot better than one; Senrid discounted the pair of travelers, who did not look as if they'd be any kind of reliable backup. Still...why not? He opened his hand in assent.

Senrid followed Kessler over the hill, bending low to avoid creating a silhouette. Kessler had left a horse near Senrid's own. They mounted; Kessler drew sword and knife, and put his reins in his teeth. Senrid guided his horse with his legs.

The patrol broke formation, the leader began to issue orders, then Kessler cut him down with a slashing backhand blow as his horse plunged past.

Kessler also accounted for most of the rest while Senrid fought with his knives; the last fell heavily, which the two travelers watched in open-mouthed horror, the elder swallowing rapidly before he glance away. Senrid looked away as well. Now that the intensity of danger had receded, he was aware that he had killed yet again. As Kessler slung his blood off his sword, the younger man watched in fascination.

Kessler said to Senrid in Norsundrian, "Nice work, but not for ambushes. I thought you people were supposed to be good with the sword."

Senrid had no desire to explain that his uncle had forbidden him to learn any weapons when he was small, but as knife fighting was quiet, Keriam had been able to teach him on the sly. There would have been no hiding the clang of swords.

But later...he was always so busy, and it seemed easier to continue training with the knives, and shooting, which he enjoyed. Then there was Crystal Ingrid—

He shut down hard on that thought, and angry at the internal ambivalence he was already struggling again, he replied shortly, "I'm not."

Kessler lifted a shoulder, then turned his attention to the travelers. "Where are you going?" he asked in the local language

The two men looked at one another, the younger one revealing his journeyman status in the way he waited for the older one to speak. "Analas."

"Why were they holding you up so long?" Senrid asked. "Did they find out you were carrying mail?"

Both men looked terrified. "How did you know?" The younger one whispered.

"I'll see that the letters get to their recipients, if you'll trust me with them," Kessler said.

The older man rubbed his grizzled head, then jerked his thumb at the restless, confused horses, to which the younger man sprang. The older man gazed uncertainly at Kessler from under bushy brows as he said in a measured tone that revealed deep uneasiness, "We were trying it the once. Never said we'd be permanent couriers. It's too dangerous. Other people's mail is nothing worth losing our lives over." He reached down deep under the goods in one wagon, and located a bag of feed, from which he extracted a packet. "You did for that gang, and I'm grateful, but if they were sent after us, then that means we can't go home. Our livelihood is dead."

"But you aren't. Start over somewhere else," Kessler said, no sympathy evident in his soft, flat, Chwahir-accented words. "By spring all travel will be forbidden." His mouth hardened. "And mark this: the more you compromise, the more you give up, the more they will take." He held out his bloodied hand, and the man silently relinquished the packet. "In turn, you get a good horse." He indicted his, then cast Senrid a questioning look.

Senrid answered the question indirectly by removing the Norsundrian horse's rope halter. He smacked the animal on its flank, and it galloped away, toward the hills. "It's earned its freedom."

Kessler tossed Senrid a transfer token. As soon as Senrid's fingers closed around it, he was wrenched away.

Senrid shook his head free of the sparkle at the edges of his vision, the pang of incipient headache. A village lay in a semi-circle below a ridge of pine and russet cedar, red tile roofs gleaming in the sunlight. Kessler stood nearby, blinking away transfer reaction.

Senrid said, "How are you getting around transfer wards? Won't they trace them?"

"The wards are mostly over cities as yet. And as for that, I'm using something stolen from Norsunder by my ancestors. If I trip a ward, it will point to Wan-Edhe," Kessler said. "Give him some trouble with his so-called allies.
But we are done for now. Come." He gestured toward an outlying house at the edge of a hamlet alongside a river.

"This furniture-maker has already set up a communication network," Kessler said, indicating the house. "He's used to fugitives."

They soon sat in a warm attic room, clean, with mugs of rice-and-vegetable soup in their hands.

Senrid said, "How'd you find me?"

"I've been following your actions."

Kessler's matter-of-fact tone jabbed Senrid's nerves with warning. He laughed inwardly at himself for the reaction.

Kessler went on, "Rescuing Tereneth of Erdrael Danara, I understand because you are friends. But Remalna? No one goes to Remalna. And the scribe from west Colend?"

"Thad Keperi is a very old friend. And he knows how to set up a covert communication system," Senrid said. "I'm tapping his talents to set up a rescue ring. Remalna has those woods."

"Ah," Kessler said. "Yes, more rescues will splinter their attention sufficiently."

"Speaking of Thad. You wouldn't happen to have heard where Shontande Lirendi might be?"

"No idea," Kessler said indifferently.

"Why did you track me?"

"Your friend David is not as careful as he thinks he is." Kessler paused, and Senrid remembered what Kessler had said at the outset of the conversation. He shot a started look at Kessler, whose brows rose.

"Lack of sleep makes anyone stupid. Yes, if I can follow you, so can Llyenthur, who might be laying a trap right now. Though he's divided in enough directions that he might still be a step behind; when you boys shot up the death squad in Khanerenth, it was I who spread the rumor that the responsible party was renegade Norsundrians. Let him spend some time ripping through his own people. That was a nice piece of work, by the way. I liked the added touch of killing the actual killers, but putting all the perimeter guards out of action."

David had explained that that many dead Norsundrians could be turned into an army of soulbound as long as they had a mage on call who knew the spell. Whereas an arrow in the ass, if deep enough to tear muscle, would make it difficult to sit or stand, which would effectively put them out of action. And Imry Llyenthur was very short on numbers, a deliberate move by Efael.

Senrid said, "I can't claim credit for all. I'm a good shot, but Rolfin, one of Detlev's gang, is the best."

Kessler shrugged. "Your other rescues made sense.

Rescuing that Otobris fool doesn't."

"Llyenthur put her there. That means she was slated for whatever soul-sucking spells Yeres is readying."

"He's stashed half-a-dozen much more important prisoners all over the world for Yeres, and you haven't touched any of 'em."

Senrid sipped cautiously at his soup, which was still scalding hot, and regarded Kessler over the brim, testing mentally. He shut down immediately on perceiving a mental landscape unlike any he'd encountered before: fractals. Who thought in fractals?

Yet fractal patterns had a logic of their own. Kessler was reputed to be a brilliant but insane loner who'd managed to extricate himself from Norsunder after learning an amazing amount of their magic in a frighteningly short time. He was also clearly lethal with weaponry.

Senrid said, "Because I had Norsunder's language forced on me when I was a prisoner a long time ago. So I can listen outside camps and headquarters. You ought to know you can't control what desk jockeys gossip about."

"True."

"I chanced to overhear chatter about her being put here, and I haven't heard where these others are. Yet. And I'd hoped to catch up with Llyenthur." He flicked his wrist knife with two fingers. "I'll rescue anyone needing rescuing, but my goal right now is to kill him." Unbidden, the image of Crystal Ingrid swaying with that knife in her chest struck his psyche. "Not fast, either."

"You're one of a long line." Kessler lifted a shoulder. "With Efael at the head of it. Near as I can tell, he rarely spends much time in any one place. They're waiting for you in Lisdan."

"I thought you didn't care what happened to any of us?"

"My boy is there." Kessler drained his mug in one long draught without explaining further, but the fractals flickered through images, one of them Jilo.

Was this episode a result of Senrid having helped Jilo? If so, why hadn't Kessler pulled Jilo off that mountain instead of leaving him to almost perish before Rolfin and David tracked him down? Senrid wanted to ask, but instinct was very strong: if Kessler had any idea his thoughts had shared even that brief and puzzling fragment, he'd vanish altogether.

"I have much awaiting my attention," Kessler said. "The

worst threat right now is not Imry Llyenthur, but in Chwahirsland. Jilo," he added, "ought to visit his old friend Mondros."

He vanished before Senrid could ask why Kessler didn't tell him himself. But anything having to do with Jilo had better be passed on.

All right. One more try at locating Shontande Lirendi for Thad, and then there was no more avoiding Lisdan.

Five

Llyenthur's HQ - Larkadhe

"... AND THE MOST RECENT flag is from Colend. Code Flower," said Duin, Llyenthur's aide-de-camp.

Llyenthur looked from Duin's flat, lugubrious Chwahir face to the dispatch. There, below the word Flower were the words: *Need reinforcements.*

"Everybody needs reinforcements." He tossed the paper into the fire and sorted through the rest of the morning's dispatches. More of Efael's maneuvering behind his back, as expected. "Any sign of when Ilerian is going to bring over the occupation forces?"

"He's in Chwahirsland," Duin said, his flat diction flatter. "Did you want the deployment map? It's updated."

"I know who's where. No matter how pretty you make the map, the truth is, I don't have enough boots on the ground, and Efael—predictably—is hoarding all his Chwahir. Anyway, what I truly need are the administrative desk jockeys. We can bludgeon a populace into stunned quiet, but that won't last. As Efael will no doubt discover. For real control, we need the paper pushers counting heads. Knowing exactly who earns what and spends it where..." Duin wasn't listening. He was merely enduring as he waited for the next order. The perfect aide.

Llyenthur scowled at the map.

At least the war fronts were settled. No. Almost settled. Only the willfully stupid would call Marloven Hess settled, just to name one. Before Llyenthur had booted Bostian back toward Sartor, the idiot had given orders to publicly execute the commanders, but all they had captured was a handful of severely wounded patrol captains. The few surviving comm- anders above that level had smoked. Bostian's gang of looters hadn't even managed to nail down that old man, Keriam, who had raised and trained Senrid. He'd slipped away after Bostian's posturing surrender ceremony that had made no impression whatsoever.

Nor would executions. The dead would become martyrs, the way Forthan had; Llyenthur had changed the orders to putting prisoners (wearing good, heavy chains) to work shoveling stable stalls and the like. The people were to see them cooperatively working. Anyone who didn't work could quietly vanish.

He was going to have to put in time there himself, and also sit on Bostian once he got back to Sartor—he was solid in the field, especially when brute force was needed, but already Sartor was a disaster

The quiet chuff of another paper in the dispatch tray broke the silence. "What now?"

"Urgent request from Ralanor Veleth for reinforcements."

"Another one? I personally took out the king, who was the only capable commander on the entire continent."

Duin looked back, having no opinion to offer—out loud.

Llyenthur paced around the room impatiently. All the reports had stated that the brother was a passable tactician, but couldn't lead anything much bigger than a horse troop, for anything much bigger than a raid. "What did I miss there?"

Duin remained silent.

That had been a fast recon; why spend extra time when all Norsunder talked about wanting to take the field against Jason Szinzar? The solution was obvious—take him out, and they'd fall apart. Except that they hadn't fallen apart, and they were facing some stiff, if disorganized, opposition in the Fhlerians and what was left of Kessler's old strike troops. Whoever it was leading the Velethi was successfully holding a defensive line. How was he going to shift the requisite forces to that continent—and from where? No one was at liberty, not until Ilerian began bringing Theronezhe's people across.

Easy questions first. Like why was it necessary for...what, twenty? twenty-five? Yes, twenty-five well-trained foot to guard one flower-faced aristocratic prince who'd drank and caroused his way through a ten year regency before troubling to plant his royal butt on the throne he'd inherited?

That question would have to be answered in person. Llyenthur glanced out the window of his temporary HQ, mentally calculated the time difference, then shifted to the riverside castle in Colend that he'd designated for holding local prisoners. The commander jolted when he walked in, flushed with annoyance, and started into speech.

Llyenthur cut him off. "Where's Shontande Lirendi?"

Relief lifted the man's brows, quickly suppressed. What was this one hiding? Llyenthur would find out later; he laughed inwardly, enjoying the headlong whitewater of the field. Of course everyone was conspiring right and left. But the real fun was in outrunning 'em all.

"In the old Dazci palace, for now," the man said. "We shifted him two days ago, dead of night. But yesterday there was another rescue run."

"By .. ?"

"I don't know. Some noble, with her personal guard, from the looks of the bodies."

"I take it you killed them all?"

"That was how I understood the orders," the commander hedged, his dark gaze speculative, then he glanced to either side at his listening aides.

Llyenthur waved a hand to clear the room of those aides. When they were alone, he sat down on the table, and leafed through the local reports. "All right, let's hear it." He kept reading, head cocked to listen.

"I can only tell you this: someone in our people has been suborned. I don't know who, or when, or how. But I've had Shontande Lirendi, what, a week? And this is the sixth rescue attempt."

"All women?"

"No. Half, maybe."

Llyenthur tapped the top report, noted that it directly belied one sent to him the day before, but because he knew which was the deceit—not here—he only smiled and said, "Never mind.

I'll take him off your hands."

And transferred to the Dazci palace. Spotted the keep. Found a grizzled Fhlerian vet before the inner door, a pale-haired, hard-faced lifetime warrior.

"Where is he?" Llyenthur asked.

"Off the landing." A thumb jerked upward.

Llyenthur caught the tail end of a brooding stare as he passed. He mounted the stairs quietly, from long habit. The thump and clatter of iron-shod boots were so comforting to the enemy, affording them time to prepare suitable reaction. Llyenthur liked the gift of surprise — when he was the giver. He exerted himself to avoid getting it.

A door closed just as Llyenthur's head cleared the second-floor level. A woman in Norsundrian uniform come out of the room, carrying a tray. She set it down in the window embrasure and with both hands touched the goblet on the tray, running one finger round it, and then, with ritual slowness, she lifted it and drank the remainder of the contents.

Llyenthur permitted his step to be heard at the top. The goblet crashed down on the tray. The woman — had to be thirty, and as hard faced as the Fhlerian captain below — lowered her gaze, picked up her tray, and scurried down the stairs.

Llyenthur watched her go. Her indifference made it clear that she did not recognize him, which was also deliberate on his part. He was merely an interruption to her surreptitious communion with Shontande Lirendi's dirty dishes, which imparted far more information to him than a demanded report would have, had he stomped in wearing command black.

He tested the magic ward on the door, made the pass sign, and entered. The ward was a heavy spell indeed, permeating bones and sinew like a cold fog. He shivered, and shook off the reaction impatiently.

The room was almost bare, except for a narrow cot, neatly made up. Standing at the window, hands behind his back, was a slender male silhouette, dressed in a fine blue robe embroidered with golden dragonflies and reeds.

"I almost killed you, last time we met," Llyenthur said conversationally, and watched Shontande Lirendi swing around, one hand rising in a block, and then dropping again. "In fact, I intended to." Llyenthur spoke not Kifelian, the language of Colend, but Sartoran, which he'd been forced to learn as a youth.

The mellow afternoon light fell across an astoundingly handsome face, making a glory of hair the color of autumn leaves, and side-lighting the dark blue eyes color-dense and light-reflective as rare gems. Llyenthur's tastes in dalliance did not run to men, but he recognized with inward amusement that this Lirendi would make even a statue's cock twitch.

Shontande said, after a protracted pause, "I take it I am to ask why you stayed your hand?" His Sartoran was effortless, and accent-free.

"Don't you want to know?"

Shontande spread his hands. It could have meant anything.

"My personal prisoners," Llyenthur said, "are roughly divided into two types: the hostages, and those of potential use."

"Into which category am I assigned?" The hands were hidden again, behind his back.

"I hadn't yet put you in either," Llyenthur said, watching, and listening on the mental level. "Worthless as a hostage, I thought, for you appear to have contented yourself with squandering the ten years since your father's death wallowing in luxurious pursuit, with no access to power."

Shontande Lirendi could have pointed out that he was a small boy when his father died, but he didn't. "And so?"

Llyenthur thought back to the day he'd come through Colend, surprising Shontande Lirendi at the back end of the fabulous palace in Alsais. He'd been lying on the grass in shades of pale yellow silk, watching a sculptor shape stone around the top of a pillar. Images: the startled wide blue gaze, the realization that he was caught there with no vestige of a weapon at hand. Reaction: unafraid. No, more than that. Ironic. No, mocking, a mockery of self that had intrigued Llyenthur.

"Tell me," he invited, still trying to provoke. "Are you as mad as your father? I could use a figurehead here, but not one who is going to howl at the moon or try to convince others he's a famous name from history."

"I hesitate to point out the obvious," Shontande retorted in his well-bred tenor, "but I am a lapdog, and not a wolf."

Llyenthur laughed, and then impulse prompted him to try his last test. He was fast. He knew that. Relied on it. But still he saw the dark blue eyes—really, they were violet, though hitherto he'd always believed there was no such thing, that it was the claim merely of sickeningly sentimental poetry—shift first to his sleeve, where he wore the wrist sheath that he knew was hidden by his loose shirt.

The outcome was foregone, but still he went through with the motions. Fingered and flung the knife, one movement, to see it blocked.

Shontande was half-a-heartbeat too soon. He deflected the blade, not the hilt, and took a slash, but he didn't regard that either.

Llyenthur paused, waiting to see if he'd dive for the blade and try to fight. One moment Shontande stilled, then—typical Colendi rabbit—he looked away, out the window, his back toward Llyenthur, paying no attention to the blood dripping down his wrist onto the wooden floor.

"Not in the mood for a thrashing, eh?" Llyenthur commented, stooping down to retrieve his knife.

"Is anybody ever?" came the retort.

"There was a time when I liked fights," Llyenthur admitted. "Especially against those who were supposed to be better than me. Speaking of which, did they tell you there have been, to date, six rescue attempts on your behalf? Upwards of fifty dead."

A reaction at last, but too brief to read. Surely that was not self-loathing?

Llyenthur made his decision. "Our time is up. Until the next." He left, making mental note to try once more before leaving this one to Yeres. It would take time to figure out how to turn him, and he didn't have time.

But first, another transfer before Lirendi attracted any more partisans, from either side. Where would he be safe? Ah. Of course.

Llyenthur transferred to the old Larensar castle, carved a thousand years ago into the side of a granite mountaintop in Erdrael Danara, where he currently kept his crucial capital holds. He selected the cell and warded it himself, before transferring Lirendi over.

And then, to the commander, "There's a new one up on the top level. No one is to speak to the prisoner. Don't even open the door. Food to be transferred in—I'll send someone over to set up the spell. Remember, no contact whatsoever. If anyone tries, kill him. Or her," he added wryly. "Or it's your life."

Six

Lisdan – Melire to Chwahir Border

IN SARTOR, REL OFFICIALLY lived in his broom-closet-sized room over the city guard mess hall, but his relationship with Atan was pretty well known. To an ever-increasing number of the common and merchant population, he was the hero who the queen had chosen, and they loved both for it; to many of the nobles, he was the queen's toy, to be endured if he stayed in his place. For of course if she married, it must be to a prince or a king.

They'd decided it would be safer not to live together in Lisdan. There was nothing either could do about their height and builds: they couldn't risk gossip going out among traders about the huge labor merchant and his statuesque partner. Details like that were too likely to catch the ear of a Norsundrian spy.

He'd used vagabond magic to add the beard and mustache, which were now growing out nicely; the silver he added with dye. And in a reversal of his life in Sartor, which they both acknowledged with a sense of irony, When they got together it was she who came to the back door, always with a basket of mending, as her attic room over the tailor shop was shared with

CJ and Seshe.

When the allies began turning up, he found himself increasingly glad that he'd established himself well beforehand. So far, it seemed, the Norsundrians were stretched extremely thin. Once or twice a week a patrol would ride through, seeing what they expected to see, which was ordinary civilians. Lisdan exhibited no sign of the war, except for the scribe house having been turned into storage. This pretense of peace was not going to last—everyone knew that—but he hoped that there would be a plan in place before...what?

That was part of the underlying tension: no one knew.

One dreary, rainy day, the gossip in the wake of a patrol was that Norsundrians were coming through counting households and recording everyone and issuing identity papers that must be carried at all times.

While people exclaimed in outrage—perfect right to go where they wished—never happened before, ever—why couldn't the king defense them? — Rel, Atan, Arthur, and Leander met in Rel's counting office.

"Andri's Sartoran lessons are progressing," Leander said.

"He still won't agree to the Universal Language Spell?" Atan asked.

"He insists that spells can be removed, and he wants to know a language that can get him around the continent," Rel said. "He's not wrong."

Leander put his hands out to the fire. 'If something happens, he said he'll have the spell in a heartbeat. What worries me is, he says that the younger ones are getting restless. Is there a plan?"

"Yes," Atan said, at the same time Rel said, "No."

They looked at one another with semblances of smiles.

Atan said, "The plan so far is to gather and *discuss* plans. But we don't have everyone in the alliance who promised to be here, nor do we have enough information—and it's those missing who are likeliest to know the most."

Arthur looked at his inky fingers as he said slowly, "Andri made a good point when Dtheldevor was complaining about sitting around. What kind of plan can we actually put forward? None of us have armies. Few know magic, and those who do have to be very careful when we try it. Wards are imminent—tighter controls are imminent. Much as I'd love to, I can't smite attackers with a book, or translate them into running away."

The others gave him weak smiles, then Leander said, "We are in a situation we've never been in before. How do we go about planning?"

Atan put down the sewing she'd brought, scowling at the fabric. All those meetings with Senrid had been intended to answer Leander's question. It had all sounded neat. Orderly. Logical. Senrid had warned them that the reality would not be neat, orderly, or logical. She wished he were here so she could tell him he was right, but he was somewhere out there, instead of here, neatly and logically pointing out the next step.

And he had taken the worst blows.

She shook herself mentally, retrieved the subject, then looked up, finding them turned her way. She said, "Which brings us right back to not having enough of the allies here for planning, nor have we enough information—"

Footsteps pounded in the hall outside the room, then the door burst open. CJ appeared, black hair swinging. "Boneribs is here!"

Atan bit back the impulse to say, "Who?" They all had heard her refer to Senrid as Boneribs; while Atan was irritated by CJ's penchant for giving people nicknames whether they wanted them or not, irritation was easy to squelch, unlike outright loathing.

Arthur said quickly as everyone rose, "What will it look like if we all go outside together?"

Leander sat right down again, though he'd been worrying about Senrid since that last terrible night in Choreid Dhelerei. "We don't want to make a new arrival interesting to any gawkers. It should probably be Rel."

Rel had already grabbed his cane, and reached down to stuff cotton in the toe of his shoe to remind him to limp. He left and intercepted Senrid, who had gone out the back end of the alley they'd set as Destination, without realizing that the building next to him was Rel's house.

"Ho there, looking for work?" Rel called in the local language.

Senrid turned sharply, and Rel was glad of the twenty or so paces between them, which gave him time to recover from the shocking change in Senrid. He was thin and tense as wire, the bones of his face pronounced.

Senrid almost didn't recognize Rel. He, too, stared in shock—impressed at how a mustache and short beard, some whitening at the temples, a limp, and a stoop to those powerful shoulders made a very effective disguise. Rel's craggy face looked years older despite the tautness of his skin.

They met, and Senrid glanced at the cane. "I hope that's not real."

Rel understood. "I used to be in masonry, suffered an accident, got into labor exchange."

"Masonry," Senrid repeated appreciatively. It was perfect—what you'd expect of a very big young man, but utterly unrelated to fighting. That unmilitary background and the limp would not get him marked as someone to watch.

Rel decided to let Senrid bring up Marloven Hess, or his daughter, and follow from there. "This is the house, right here. We're still missing several people—no one is really sure what's next."

"Jilo's here, right?"

"He is. Almost recovered, too. Have a message for him, or news?"

"In a way. Kessler Sonscarna warned me, without telling me why."

"Kessler," Rel repeated on an exhale. "No, you wouldn't get a normal warning from him."

Senrid's mouth twisted in what might to some look almost like humor, if mordant. "Had some run-ins with him, have you?"

"You might say that." Rel's deep voice roughened to a near growl, and Senrid uttered a breath of a laugh.

Rel opened the front door, and there were Leander and CJ, Leander's face plainly worried. "I'm glad you're here," Leander said. "What did you find out?"

CJ smacked her hands together and rubbed them. "If you crunched any eleveners, don't stint on the details!"

Farther down a plain hall, Atan stuck her head out a door and called, "Senrid, welcome."

Arthur walked out of that room, saying, "Hungry? The kitchen is right here, and I was about to scald some coffee."

Senrid let out a tense breath he hadn't realized till then that he'd been holding. These were all people he liked. Trusted, even, as much as he trusted anyone besides Keriam and Forthan. Had trusted Forthan. And they were not asking any questions, or worse, saying anything sickening. "Where's Jilo?"

"Here."

Senrid turned, looking up at where Jilo stood at the top of a stairway. "Thought I heard voices," Jilo said. "Come on up."

Senrid ran up the stairs three at a time.

On the second floor a hall ran the length of the house, doors on both sides. Senrid snapped away the illusion blurring the handsome bow he'd lifted from the Norsundrians that morning on another unsuccessful search for Shontande Lirendi. He set the bow inside the door of a room that was nearly bare except for a handsome green rug on the floor, and bedding neatly rolled up and stashed in a corner opposite a trunk with a candle holder on it.

Jilo dropped cross-legged onto the rug in a way so much less awkward than his usual mode of sitting that Senrid guessed floor sitting was common among Chwahir. He sank down onto the rug, which was unexpectedly luxurious. No surprise, given how close to Bermund they were.

Jilo said, "I'm glad to see you at last. Leander wasn't sure if you'd stayed in Marloven Hess."

"I've been here and there," Senrid said. "No success to speak of for my efforts. Including trying to find Shontande Lirendi—I finally got a lead, to discover that he'd been moved again, and I'd just missed him."

Jilo looked down at his tense, nail-bitten hands, his mouth unhappy.

"I did have a strange encounter with Prince Kessler."

Jilo looked up at that. "Every encounter with him is strange." His tone was even, but the way his pupils dilated in his light brown eyes gave away his anxiety.

Senrid outlined the gist of his encounter, after which Jilo said, "I've been thinking about Mondros. No communication, you know. I haven't been sure I could survive a transfer," he admitted.

"Will it help if you have a transfer token so you don't have to hold the transfer spell? All I need is Mondros's Destination."

Jilo blinked. "There are wards going up all the time."

"True. They aren't very good. Yet. The Norsundrian mages are constantly on the hop, and I for one mean to keep it that way. I've gotten practiced at taking them down—I can build that into the token. I make half a dozen at a time, whenever I have to take a break from multiple transfers. I use them when I have to leave very fast." Senrid flashed his toothy grin.

"A token would be great," Jilo said, and turned his earnest

gaze to Senrid. "Will you come with me?"

Senrid hesitated. He wanted more than anything to continue his hunt for Imry Llyenthur, but he recollected Kessler's *Join the line*, which had been the equivalent of a dousing of icy water in the face. Of course there was a long list of people who wanted to kill Llyenthur, behind Efael of Norsunder. Senrid knew little about Efael, other than that he was the assassin who had killed the King of Colend and a lot of Sartoran mages. "Over to you, Efael," Senrid muttered under his breath, and unslung his pack. Looked like he'd be here for a while.

He was still working on the tokens when Rel appeared at the door, carrying a laden tray. "Dinner's ready. You both look like you'd be the better for a meal in you."

Senrid glanced up, the words of denial on his lips. He'd gotten used to ignoring hunger. But he knew that was not going to keep him alert, and fast, if it became habit—and Rel had brought it right to them, a generous gesture. "Thanks. Let me finish the spells on these tokens."

As Rel brought the tray in and set it down on the edge of the rug, Jilo said, "We're going to see Mondros."

Rel's brows lifted, then he gave a short nod. "Will you give him my best? And return with a report?"

Jilo lifted a hand in promise.

They ate in silence, both too tired for much conversation. Senrid took the tray down, relieved that no one was around, dunked the dishes, then ran back up. He'd worked the green rug in as a Destination for their return.

Jilo stood nearby, the two braced themselves, then Jilo vanished, followed by Senrid, who came out of the transfer wrench to find himself on a cliff before a stone cottage. Dry grass crackled beneath his feet.

Jilo had fallen to one knee, arms crossed over his midsection as he breathed harshly against transfer reaction.

Senrid blinked away his own reaction, ignoring the throbbing wrench in his joints as he gazed southward. Below lay gently rolling hills divided by swooping ribbons of blue water reflecting the cold sky overhead.

"Jilo." The voice was low and rough with relief.

Senrid turned as a bearded man wearing a mage robe stepped out of the cottage. He was massive as a tree. Jilo gazed back, red to the ears at that glad tone.

The man shifted his deep-set, dark eyes to Senrid. "And you are..."

"This is Senrid," Jilo said, rising slowly. "He made transfer tokens. I've been..." He waved a hand in a circle.

"I can see what you've been," Mondros said. "Come inside. Let's get some food into you."

"Rel just made us dinner," Jilo mumbled.

"Eat more. I'm afraid a breeze might sweep you right off the cliff and halfway into Colend." A thumb the size of a pinecone jerked toward the gentle hills in the hazy distance.

Jilo said with mild alarm, "If I eat any more, my eyes will pop out. Do you know anything about Shontande?"

Mondros's smile vanished. "No. I've tried a couple of times, though my focus has been increasingly north in Chwahirsland. I think they've moved him. At least once. The only good news I can report is that Erai-Yanya managed to get the Everoneth royal family to Mearsies Heili, with the aid of her mage friend there. But in the process was nearly trapped by a very nasty ward, so she is remaining there. We scry occasionally. I scry with Tsauderei as well," he added. "Come, come, at least drink something. The both of you. I don't know you, young Marloven. You might be as thin as a twig by nature, but those circles under your eyes belie that." He held out a hand toward the cottage.

Senrid followed Jilo inside. He glanced around at the plain furniture, the high bookshelves. The place smelled of baking bread.

Jilo seemed comfortable there, a rarity. Senrid found himself relaxing somewhat at the sense that he could trust this place.

"Senrid got corralled by Kessler," Jilo said. "Who said I ought to come to you. I wanted...I wish...that is, things in Narad must be worse than I feared."

Montrose turned, fists on hips. "Where were you, boy? I tried to find you, but you were lost."

Jilo mumbled something in which the words "woods" and "border" could be made out. His voice strengthened slightly as he finished, "I knew there had to be any number of wards lying in wait. I figured the only way was to walk over the border myself. If I didn't use magic, they couldn't get me."

"Except if there was a ward on your name. I warned you

about that."

Jilo sighed. "I didn't think Wan-Edhe would be able to put a ward over the entire border, just against me. That's such difficult magic."

"Jilo, you know how vindictive that old snake is! He'll stop at nothing to get hold of you," Mondros exclaimed. "Well, I see you were rescued before you blundered into the border, and I trust you will not try that again, until I finish the talisman I promised you. Which is almost done. The reason it's not finished is probably related to what Prince Kessler was alluding to. Could you tell me exactly what he said?"

Senrid outlined his encounter with Kessler, then finished, "If he's concerned, then why isn't he here right now? Why all the ambiguity?"

"No one knows what his plan is, other than that he's at war with Norsunder. What you perhaps need to know is that he has an obsession about trust. He might offer you something, for reasons no one can comprehend. It's always a choice, but if you turn him down you'll never see him again." Mondros poured out hot pressed cider, adding, "In general I don't trust him, but in specific, I absolutely trust him to do what he can against Norsunder. What you say actually heartens me a little. Badly needed."

Mondros sat down at the table across from Jilo and Senrid. "Jilo, the reason I haven't finished your talisman is that there are now two Norsundrians in Narad. The new arrival is far more dangerous than the first one."

"I've been so afraid of what they might do," Jilo said. "I keep having nightmares—all the people lying dead, bleeding from the eyes and ears—"

Mondros held up a hand. "I don't know if that's your worry or you are somehow following events there—which you ought not to do." He tapped his head.

Senrid's scalp crawled. "If it's any of the Host, they can strike at you on the mental plane easier than swatting a gnat."

"I know," Jilo said. "I've kept as hard a mind-shield as I can. It's why David couldn't find me. But what is going on? Has Wan-Edhe undone all my work so soon?"

Mondros's mouth pressed tight, then he said, "*He* hasn't— his progress at repairing that vortex of evil hadn't advanced much beyond the point at which you and I spoke earlier in summer. But whoever it is who joined them in the last week or so has been plucking out, one by one, those wards and traps we worked so hard to make."

"That's bad," Jilo said, his arms crossed over his midsection again.

"It gets worse," Mondros said. "From the few spy eyes of ours that are left, it appears that he's laying down interlocked lattices in order to bridge that vortex to somewhere else, probably Norsunder Beyond, and he's preparing to spend hundreds, thousands, of lives to do it."

"Interlocking lattices," Senrid repeated, and turned to Jilo. "How much farther did you get in studying those since we last tried?"

Jilo remembered that they'd had to abandon the study not long after Crystal Ingrid was born, as Senrid had refused to leave the babe entirely to minders. Something had to give, and the study of lattice wards, especially in dark magic, was so intricate, and so dangerous, that it required much uninterrupted concentration.

"Not much farther," Jilo said. "Though I had more time than you, I still had too many interruptions for concentrating on such volatile magic. Especially as I had to pretty much begin again each time I commenced study."

"Right." Senrid snapped his fingers. "I'd grasp a concept—barely—and next thing I knew, it had fallen out of my head." He turned to Mondros. "I'll help, of course, if you tell me exactly what to do. But I'm a beginner in that type of magic."

"I'm probably not much farther," Mondros admitted. "Jilo is aware of my history—I didn't know the simplest spell when I was your age. Started studying magic rather late. I suspect understanding the fundamentals of lattice wards not only requires a certain kind of mind, but a young one." He looked bleakly at them and smacked his hand on the table, making the dishes jump. "But if it's just us fighting this thing, then it's just us."

Senrid raised his hand. "There's one other. Two, actually. Leander began the study of wards, though he, like Erai-Yanya, who was teaching him, only approach it through light magic. But there's someone who, like us, understands both. Her name is Hibern."

Seven

Eidervaen - Sartor

ILLUSION MAGIC IS SO flimsy that it's barely magic at all; a concentrated stare can break the spell. However, Liere had learned that casting overlapping illusions to hide someone, and another illusion drawing attention to something else nearby — specifically a few brightly colored drifting leaves added to a maple — had so far been effective at hiding Hibern while she worked.

Liere crouched on a roof, shifting her attention between Hibern crouched between a well and a wagon full of fish-smelly barrels that the two of them had pushed there during the night, and a furtive group of Norsundrians muscling a cart full of loot from one alley to the next.

She longed to leap down there and do a little sabotage to the wheels, but she could not risk any attention Hibern's way. They should have left two days ago, when Bostian returned, but Hibern was determined to finish this last ward around the Tower of Knowledge.

Besides, she'd already caused at least ten wagons to come apart and dump their contents, but that was not even a bump in the road of the greedy thieves who had been busy stripping the city of centuries of art while their commander was off rampaging somewhere else.

"S-s-s-t!"

The sound was almost too soft to hear. Liere sensed focus along with the sound, and twisted to peek over the edge of the roof to the jumble of boxes below. She recognized Ielios, the young mage from the Sartoran Guild who had been left in charge of the last of the magical resistance. He, like Liere, wore a knitted cap of dull brown to cover bright hair — in his case, maple-leaf red.

Liere pointed down at Hibern and flattened her hand: wait.

"Search coming," Ielios whispered.

"Go hide," Liere whispered back, and mentally poked Hibern: *Danger coming.*

"I can watch for you from here," Ielios returned.

Liere hated the risk — Ielios was a scholar, his primary area of study preservation, both of materials and of captured images. But he, like those few left fighting the sack of the city, had been learning fast not only practical spells but covert movement. He was responsible for seeing the last mages out of the city, and he took the task seriously.

:Done.

The clatter of horse hooves and the clash of steel echoed down the northward alley, followed by a harsh, booming voice, "What is this? More looting? You soul-sucking shits, get that loot back to my palace, and then it's fifty apiece!"

"But we didn't take it from the —"

"You're arguing with me?"

"No, Commander Bostian!"

"It's *King* Bostian! King! King! King! That'll be a hundred apiece! You! See that they don't slither off!"

"Sire!"

Liere waved violently at Ielios to go.

Ielios gave her a worried glance, then darted off. Liere watched him anxiously until he vanished into the shadows between two buildings, not a heartbeat before Bostian and an armed and mounted host rode into the street, scanning in all directions. She spotted the lift of chin presaging a roof sweep, and ducked flat. She twisted her head, to see that Hibern had crouched behind the cart with the fish barrels.

Bostian and his search party rode on past and up the avenue, paying no attention to the trees, specifically one that seemed to have a lot of drifting leaves that never made it to the flagstones.

As soon as they were out of sight, Liere hooked her arm through the handle of the basket she'd crouched beside then swung from the rain pipe beneath her, and dropped lightly onto the top box. From there a hop to the street as Hibern crossed with heavy, exhausted tread.

"Bostian is out," Liere whispered. "I think he's riding on inspection. Or something."

Hibern dipped her chin in a nod, all she had the strength for. Liere pulled Hibern's arm around her, fitted her shoulder under Hibern's armpit and supported her, speeding their steps.

Tired as she was, Hibern relished the satisfaction of an excellent ward. She clenched her teeth and forced her legs to move faster, though it felt as if each had taken on the heaviness of boulders.

A frantic zigzag between buildings, pausing three times to duck and hide, as a thin, dreary cold rain began to fall, then at last they carefully descended the narrow, steep steps to the basement below a hairdresser's abandoned shop. No Norsundrian would bother to loot here. The stone still maintained some of the heat of summer, though it had lessened noticeably over the past few days.

They moved to the back room, shut the door, then Liere clapped the glow globe to light.

Hibern sank onto a cushion. "That ward," she said, "will send anyone crossing it without the proper sign straight to Shendoral. I made it especially for Bostian."

Liere smiled, but her gaze was steady as she said, "Siamis was very certain that they cannot break the ancient magic over that tower. He said it's inherent in the stone."

"Siamis says," Hibern repeated. "Do you believe him?"

"You still don't?" Liere countered. "He hasn't done anything terrible since he left Norsunder. And he was so good with Lyren-Sartora and Mac before I left. Far better than I was. Arthur liked him."

"Arthur likes any very pretty boy," Hibern retorted.

"And...you don't?"

"Let's say I mistrust Siamis because he's so pretty, and charming, and nice. He was that way when he enchanted the world, if you remember. And yes, I know he's done nothing wrong since he officially left Norsunder. I think it's more that

I'm neutral on the subject of Siamis. He might be right about the tower. But I wanted one last ward to protect it, just because the Sartoran Mage Guild wouldn't let me anywhere near it," Hibern said.

"Ah." Liere's tone was sympathetic.

"When the day comes we are rid of the invaders, I want the senior mages—whoever is left of the senior mages—to recognize my protection there," Hibern added. "And it ought to last. It's a lattice ward." She glanced at the covered basket that Liere had set down. "I'm famished after all that work. What did you scavenge?"

Eidervaen's ancient buildings currently were either empty—the humbler districts—or occupied by terrified inhabitants who either had not evacuated the city for whatever reason, or had been harried back after trying to leave. Those places were identifiable by the shutters pulled tight, with the faintest sliver of light shining in cracks at night. Sometimes no light at all.

Then there were the places that the Norsundrians had taken over, many with broken windows and shattered furnishings and statuary scattered out front. Most of these were the fine mansions on the Parleas Terrace where the nobles once lived. Once they'd dirtied one mansion they moved to the next, rioting and looting while the interim commander was transferring in and out on Bostian's increasing demands from far away.

The best scrounging, Liere had discovered, was early morning when the drunks were snoring. She could strip an entire kitchen without them stirring a hair. But the meals she collected were often odd.

"At the rate they're drinking there won't be a drop of anything fermented or distilled left by snowfall," Hibern commented while Liere signed the firestick she'd lifted.

As usual, she'd found a strange assortment of food that the Norsundrians had either taken at swordpoint from someone else, or forced some local to prepare. Only occasionally had Liere come across actual ingredients like eggs or flour. There was a small, precious jug of oil near the stove that she had found underneath kicked-over tables in a bakery.

Today she had a quarter of a heavy lemon-cake, three biscuits, part of a pepper-fish dish, and the prize, a third of a crock of hearty vegetable soup.

They made a substantial meal. Hibern ate several bites of her lemon cake then fell asleep between one bite and another. Liere settled cross-legged on her cushion, shut her eyes, and sent a tendril out. First, always, to check on Lyren-Sartora, still safe in Lisdan. Then she began to scan her immediate environment.

Liere's scanning had begun very cautiously in the early days, after a pack of Norsundrian mages began hunting and killing the Sartoran Mage Guild. These past few days, after she sensed an extremely powerful mind moving inexorably over the mental realm like the darkest and vastest of clouds covering the entire night sky, she had become cautious again.

That mind was awake: she withdrew instantly. It was enough. There was no immediate danger around them.

She glanced at Hibern, who had curled up, her black hair spilling near the half-eaten cake. Liere carefully withdrew the plate, and poured a cup of water from the jug she'd fetched the night before, knowing that Hibern would waken with a desperate thirst. She set it where Hibern wouldn't knock it over, then she pulled on the rain-proof black cloak she had stolen from another drunken bash a few days previous, and slipped out to do some spying.

She returned a little before midnight, to find Hibern awake and groggy. She'd finished off the entire water jug. She greeted Liere with a wan smile and said, "I'll fetch the water this time." Her speech was slurred with exhaustion.

"No need," Liere said. "Ielios wants to go. We're the last two. Your ward is done, so I think we ought to leave."

"Leave?" Hibern blinked rapidly.

"Ielios says that Bostian's new orders are to crack down on his own people, and register the inhabitants to establish better control over everyone. That is nothing we can effectively fight right now. Ielios is going to retire to Shendoral with the surviving guild mages."

Hibern regarded her in the dim light of the glowglobe. "Do you want to go to Shendoral?"

Liere shook her head. "It's their kingdom. Ielios said we'd be welcome, but I think..." Her gaze diffused for a few heartbeats, then she said, "There's something very bad out there. Far too powerful—I dare not explore on the mental plane. I think we ought to try Lisdan—didn't Arthur say something about meeting there?"

"Yes," Hibern said. "Rel's house. I know the Destination. We can go there. Hear any news. Then I'll go find Erai-Yanya."

It was a relief to contemplate leaving at last. Liere gathered their hoard of supplies into the basket, then slipped out to set the basket outside the door of the nearest family, lost in fearful slumber in the street behind them.

When she returned, Hibern said that she'd finished scanning for traps or wards against the Lisdan Destination, and had worked the Destination into a pair of tokens.

They magic ripped them out of the world and flung them back into a milder night. The visible stars had jerked slantwise in the sky.

"What's the time here? Ought we to go in?"

"Melire, west of Colend." Hibern frowned at the stone pattern in the narrow alley, mentally calculating. "It has to be midway between midnight and dawn here."

Liere was already scanning. "Arthur is awake."

Hibern had gotten used to Liere's ability to "see" through walls; she knew that Liere's eyes were like anyone else's, but her mind did not perceive obstructions such as stone and wood and even the curve of the world. Strange, this Dena Yeresbeth, how some were born with it, and some came to it at a later age, like Arthur. She sometimes idly wondered if it was anything like her weird dreamscapes, when she seemed to be floating up in the clouds, looking down at lights below—probably just candle flames, distorted in typical dream fashion. She fought her third yawn as she followed Liere along the wall and to the front door, which was open.

Arthur met them, lamp in hand. "I thought I sensed you. Welcome back. Come," he added, leading them down a short hall to the back, which opened onto a spacious kitchen. "We always have hot water on the simmer, if you want steep, or some scalded coffee." He pointed to everything, then went to the door.

"I promised Rel that if either of you turned up, I was to let him know."

He vanished on that word, leaving the two alone in the kitchen.

Hibern yawned again, longing for sleep. That nap earlier seemed to have done nothing for her, other than giving her a cramp in her neck.

Arthur reappeared. "Come on up," he whispered. "Atan's

here, too. They both are anxious to hear about Sartor."

Liere obediently followed. After a hesitation, Hibern also followed. She didn't want food, or drink. She badly wanted to lie down. She'd ask Rel where that could happen.

But when she reached the top of the stairs, she was in time to see Liere follow Arthur to a room, vanish inside, and the door shut.

Hibern stood there. What now? Arthur came out again, and was about to speak when a door to Hibern's left opened.

"Hibern?"

"Senrid!"

Eight

Lisdan - Melire

"AM I GLAD TO see you," Senrid said on an exhaled breath.
"Come in. Jilo is here—he's asleep," he added unnecessarily. In
the flickering light of the candle he held, Hibern saw a lump
wrapped in a quilt, from which the sound of deep-sleep
breathing issued, almost a snore.

Senrid whispered in Marlovan, "Where have you been?"

"Sartor." The bedding, she saw, was no more than a quilt
spread on the floor with another on top as a coverlet. They sat
down on his side of the room as she said, "Erai-Yanya
recommended to the Sartoran mage guild." She fought back yet
another yawn. The sooner she got this over, the sooner she
could sleep. "It was just like the last time we went to Sartor to
help with magic protection. Or almost, because I'm no longer
an apprentice. She told them I'm advanced in ward knowledge,
familiar with how dark magic wards are constructed, then she
had to go—she was getting messages from other mages. You
know Tsauderei can't get around anymore. She does his
footwork for him."

"Don't tell me," Senrid said, mouth wry in the flickering
light. "As soon as she was gone, they looked at you as if you cut

a horse-sized fart, and booted you straight out."

"Oh, not *straight* out. They assigned me to patrol the border of Shendoral Wood. Which, in their defense, they genuinely believed needed protection. The Norsundrian invader Bostian hates that place. Apparently issued orders for it to be burned down. But it can't be burned down. The Loi, who are magic beings—"

"I've met them. One, anyway."

"Then you'd know they are very powerful. They can protect that woodland against the likes of Bostian."

"Did he try?"

"His minions did, warriors and mages both. They even sent in a company of their hoarded soul-bound warriors, carrying torches. The idea being that the warriors could immolate themselves while setting fire to the forest. But their fires went out, and the blood-magic on them binding their bodies to that horrible pretense of life went out like snuffed candles. They Disappeared. I merely watched. The wood takes care of itself."

"How did you end up with Liere?"

"She asked for me." Hibern sighed, lowering her voice. "Look, I've always liked her. And I respect the hard work she put in for those years she was gone. But the truth is, she's behind me in all areas of study. Far behind in wards. Yet the Sartoran mages hailed her as the rescuer of the world, and put her right to work with the group protecting that Tower of Knowledge."

Hibern looked over her shoulder, saw the door safely shut, then checked on Jilo, who was still sound asleep. She murmured, "Though the Sartoran mages were powerful and subtle in their own realm—Erai-Yanya has, had, great respect for them—in those first horrible days, several of them vanished. A few to vicious traps. Traps I know I could have found. That's what I study! But a lot of them died by the steel of roaming assassins, until they started implementing a guard system—and Liere began scanning for danger by Dena Yeresbeth. That's when Liere was at her best. Indispensable. The oldest two mages, everyone insisted ought to go hide in Shendoral. That left very few, and Liere insisted they bring me at least to consult."

Senrid opened a hand. "You know it's not you they condemn. It's Marlovens. Our history. Supposedly our evil even corrupted the famous Emras, she who wrote the book on wards, once she left Colend and came to live among us."

"About that," Hibern began, then frowned, eyeing Senrid. "Wait. Wait. You're here. What does that mean, Norsunder hasn't reached that far west yet?"

"No, they're there. We got hit by three continents' worth of strike troops. Leander and I fought the magic battle. Lost there, too."

"Why didn't you—but you couldn't call for me," Hibern said bitterly. "Notecases dead. Scribe desk dead. My family?"

"I don't know," Senrid was forced to admit.

"*Your* family?" Hibern's black eyes met Senrid's bleak gaze, and her breath huffed out as if she'd been punched in the gut. "No."

"That's how I lost the magic battle." Senrid got up and prowled the perimeter of the room, his stockinged feet soundless, hands restless. "I would have pulled you in if I could have contacted you, Hibern. I did need you—but you were shielded,"

He tapped his head, and she opened her hand. Of course she was shielded, as hard and tight as possible. And she could see he understood. There was no hint of blame for her not being in two places at once. But she knew him. If there was anyone to blame, he would always blame himself.

"Even if you had come, I expect the outcome would have been the same. Just...protracted."

She watched, stunned—but not witless. Now she saw what she had missed: the circles around his eyes, his thinness. Even his hair, curling on his neck and over his ears, a neglect she would have thought utterly alien to him. Which it was, under normal circumstances. As if to underscore the changes, he was dressed for the first time in memory in something other than the Marloven uniform.

He sat down again, close enough that she could see the marks of grief in his tired face. If he still wept, she thought, he wept alone. "Listen, we need you now. Jilo and I were with Mondros. Do you know him?"

"Yes, we've met, several times, at Tsauderei's."

"Then you know that he's been watching Chwahirsland..."

She listened to Senrid swiftly outline what she already knew about Mondros's self-appointed task as guardian over Jilo and Chwahirsland, but she was thinking, you don't want to talk about Crystal Ingrid. Maybe you can't bear to. The way I can't bear to talk about the family that disowned me.

Hibern understood — who better?

When Senrid got to the lattice wards, she flogged her tired brain into concentrating on his words, as at the end of the hall, Liere sat with Rel and Atan.

Her first reaction was relief that she'd been able to step through a cleaning frame before facing Atan, who she did not know well. Her impression of Atan was of her exquisite appearance at all times, the innate control of a queen.

But this Atan sat on the edge of the tumbled bed, her simple braid scruffy. She was wrapped in a night robe that had to belong to Rel, judging by the overlong sleeves, her protruding eyes rimmed with tears that gathered and silently fell as Liere began to describe the mage war.

"I should have been there, I should have been there," Atan whispered.

"No," Rel rumbled.

"No," Liere said decisively. "There was nothing you could have done. In the early days there was nothing *I* could do, except take a night watch — until I got the idea of scanning for enemy minds. There, I was truly useful. I did learn some ward protections to rebuild after the Norsundrian mages destroyed them, but anyone could have done that. And it turned out to be unnecessary. Though before we left, Hibern constructed something difficult, just to catch them out. The Tower is thoroughly protected, and the various archives and libraries all have thick wards, and traps that will send the unwary straight to Shendoral."

Liere paused, and rubbed her hands up her arms. "But as I've scanned the mental realm of late, I sense something truly terrible out there. I don't dare try to probe it."

"We know a little about that," Rel said. "Is there more you can tell us about Sartor's state?"

"It's not good." Liere avoided their eyes — she hated the words, but she was not going to lie to them. "So much looting. But one thing I learned while scanning minds, Norsundrians vary. Some are ambivalent, even afraid. For a few it's just a job."

"The mercenary mind," Rel said.

"It could be. Though I studied martial arts, I don't really understand military thinking." Liere was glad to get away from the subject of the mages whose lives had been lost. Though she suspected Atan knew every name, and each of them would extract its meed of grief and regret. "Some of the looters wanted to save what they scavenged—yes, to sell, when people are paying for art again—but the impetus was there to keep the things from mindless destruction."

She sighed. "But the looting is at an end. Bostian is back, and one of the last things I found out is that he's posted orders that all looted artifacts must come to 'his' royal palace."

"Bostian is back?" Atan repeated. "He wasn't there the entire time?"

"No. At first we didn't know he was gone, but in retrospect, that's probably why his occupation warriors ran wild. He might have let them, but his new orders make it clear that looting and rioting is forbidden—unless he grants it. He wants order in his kingdom. I got the impression he was quite angry about all the destruction. Took it personally. Many punishments handed out."

Ren said in a soft voice, "Leander mentioned something about him having been in Marloven Hess." He glanced at Liere. "But we've agreed not to speak about any of it unless Senrid brings it up."

"Senrid?" Liere repeated. "He's here?" Why hadn't she sensed his proximity? Because he had a formidable mind-shield, of course.

Still, guilt harrowed her. She had not tried to dreamwalk to him, the way she had before. Though back then it had been unthinking, even inadvertent, the way they sometimes reached one another in nightmares, it seemed a trespass now that they were adults. Just as she used to run into his bedroom without a second thought, because their private lives were indistinguishable from their public lives. But she knew she had closed that avenue because he now had a private life, with his daughter, and maybe had lovers...

"He's here? Alone?" Shock chilled her. "Or is Crystal Ingrid with the Mearsieans? No, he would never leave her anywhere, unless he was truly desperate—" Her words dried up abruptly when she saw Atan and Rel exchange glances,

No. It couldn't be. Senrid didn't get truly desperate, he'd been preparing to prevent exactly that nearly as long as Liere had known him.

Then Rel said, "This is what Leander told us."

He gave her the briefest summary, as in the other room, Senrid said, "All right, you've smothered six yawns almost in as many breaths. There's no more space in here — this is one of the smallest rooms. But the one across from us is large. Kyale is there, I think alone. I know you get along all right with her. I expect she won't put on a drama about sharing a room with you. Why don't you go in there and sleep?"

Hibern's brain buzzed like a fly bumbling at a window, bumping against the glass without being able to get out. It took all the effort she had left to rise.

Senrid opened the door and pointed across the hall. Yawning yet again, Hibern stepped to Kyale's door, opened it, and slipped inside.

Senrid was about to turn away when a voice halted him, his nerves flashing: "Senrid."

He turned. There was Liere, her form outlined in candle-light. At her back towered Rel and Atan.

Liere approached him, her eyes huge and earnest. "Senrid," she said again. He could hear the genuine sorrow and regret in the way she said his name, and he shut his mind hard. "I'm so sorry about your daughter. I only met her once. I wanted to get to know her."

Instinct prompted a retort that she could have gotten to know her all summer, but he smothered it. A stupid remark. No one had known that they wouldn't have a lifetime to get acquainted.

He was closed off, but she had been studying him intently. "I'll shut up now," she said. "But if you ever want to talk, I'm here." And then, before he could try to force out the mean-ingless phatic thanks that civilization seemed to require, the last door on that side opened, and out stepped Andri Elsarion, straightening the shirt he'd just pulled on as he said, "I thought I heard voices —"

"Andri!" Liere let out a glad cry, and rushed to throw her arms around him. She reached on tiptoe to kiss him.

"Liere," he said, clasping her tight, his laugh bewildered and a little ragged.

Rel said suddenly, "It's still the middle of the night. I suggest unless we want to raise the entire house that everyone get some rest while they can."

Liere looked back, but Senrid was already retreating inside Jilo's room. After all the horrible news, she gave into the delirious joy at seeing Andri so unexpectedly.

The others saw Liere pull Andri back into the room he'd

come out of and that door shut.

Senrid's door shut.

Rel and Atan withdrew to his room. "Shall I put out the light?" he asked.

"No. I can't sleep now." They sat down together on the bed. She reached for the basket of sewing she always carried these days, and began sorting it. "Want to help me here? Which'll it be?"

Rel held out his hand. "That green bundle, if it's straight seams. I'm fast enough with those." He slid from the bed to the floor at her feet and began stitching quickly along the velvet seams of a skirt.

He didn't speak. She said, "You ended that reunion fast."

"Did you see Senrid's face?"

"I didn't. I tend not to look at him because I see the grief he's trying to hide. The grief I feel. Oh, it's all stirred up again." She would remember who died protecting Sartor, oh yes she would. They would be honored—which would not mean anything to them, it was too late for that, but it would to the guild. To their families. The concept of honor was something whose worth she debated internally, except in this situation: grief. "Honor" in this situation was as close as she could get to grace.

She frowned. "I'd hoped that Senrid's grief would lift if Liere showed up. But their reunion wasn't anything like it used to be."

Rel said cautiously, "I don't think there could be a reunion like it used to be."

"I'd forgotten her declaration of love for Andri Elsarion. I guess I assumed it would end as quickly as it began. Is it even love?"

"Who can say?" Rel clipped his thread, and paused to rethread his needle. "She's certainly hot for him."

"And Senrid?" Atan said doubtfully. "I can't imagine him hot for anybody, much less Liere. Though she did go away a troubled child, much like he was at the time, then returned to discover that they had both grown up. Not that he's changed so much outwardly, just gotten taller, but she's changed enough for the both of them. All right, I guess I could see him finding her pretty. She certainly is that. Is that what you saw? Somehow I can't connect tongue-hanging lust with Senrid."

Rel grinned. "You think our tough Marloven is immune to

attraction? I expect he'll probably fall in and out of love a dozen times in the next ten years. And that won't count the tumbles for the fun of it."

"The way you did?" Atan teased.

Rel said simply, "You're my first love. I expect will be my last. But human nature being what it is, I believe I'm the exception, and not the rule."

"I don't suppose there is anything to be said to any of them."

"Most definitely, emphatically not." Rel's needle flashed, and hers a moment later. "They'll sort it out. We're better off pretending not to notice."

Atan paused, eyeing the pattern she was embroidering on the facing of a riding jacket.

Rel wondered if the unknown owner of the jacket would ever find out that the stitching had been done by the Queen of Sartor. He enjoyed the probable reaction—and imagined how, were he to mention his flight of fancy to Atan, she would just shrug it off as irrelevant.

His mind stumbled over the next logical step: that the unknown woman sporting this green over-robe would never know that the putative King of Sartor had finished her seams.

King of Sartor.

He'd assumed a lot of roles in his adventures since his days as the shepherd's ward in Tser Mearsies, roles ranging from tailor to bricklayer to sword master. He'd enjoyed them all, and would willingly do any of them again if circumstances required it, but one role he'd never assumed was king. Before he'd found out that his missing father was a mage, and self-appointed guardian of benighted Chwahirsland, he had never assumed his birth was anything out of the ordinary.

He'd been wrong about that, too. He sustained a pang when he thought of his mother, a runaway Chwahir princess whose last thought before assassination had been of Rel's safety. He wished he could remember her.

He was used to that pain, and turned his thoughts back.

He couldn't really comprehend himself as a king, but Atan had told him before the attack that if she died, she had left an edict with both scribes and heralds inside and outside of Sartor, sealed with the royal seal, declaring that he would be the next king of Sartor.

And that, she had declared, meant that he was now consort

and heir. All that remained was the ceremony.

But! A whole lot had to change (and he had to survive it) before the matter became relevant.

Rel said, "Our problem is going to be forming some kind of plan and dispersing. This idea of meeting here in case of attack seemed good at the time we put it together."

"I know," Atan exclaimed. "Every time I go into your common room, I think about the devastation if Norsunder discovers us here. One strike would be all it takes." Atan crushed the garment in her lap. "I think everyone was waiting for Senrid to show up. Liere and Hibern as well. Why don't we propose a planning session? It might give the restless ones a sense of purpose, and maybe something useful will come out of it."

Rel smiled grimly, and plied his needle again. "I think we're going to start daily training. Right before the sun comes up. And keep them at it until they drop."

Nine

REL HAD NEVER BEEN interested in war or even martial arts, but because he was big and strong, too often as a teenage wanderer he'd been corralled and weapons put into his hands. Out of self-defense he'd learned how to use them.

Then he found himself in a duel with Kessler Sonscarna, as he tried to buy time for the young princess Atan to break the century-old enchantment over Sartor. After he recovered from the wound Kessler gave him, he learned in earnest.

Before Norsunder's invasion, he had wound up as captain of Eidervaen's small city guard, whose primary purpose was maintaining the peace in the city. They held morning drill every day.

In planning this house as a possible retreat, Rel had drawn on all his experiences so far, which included the expected preparations such as laying in army-sized supplies of dried foods such as rice, dried peas and beans, flour, an array of spices, and he'd signed up for magical transfer delivery of fresh fruits and vegetables from the Ghost Islands on the belt of the world, where produce grew year round. He arranged through the Sartoran Mage guild for beginning mages to construct and install cleaning frames in the doorways of all the rooms, earning credit thereby. firesticks as well.

But there were other concerns besides food and bed linens and furnishings not already left behind by the previous owners. *If* Norsunder attacked, and *if* the allies turned up to hide, then it made sense to keep up with training before they dispersed to fight back.

He'd bought the house because of the attic room that ran the length of the building. With Atan's aid he'd brought in carpenters to add roof windows, not unheard of for various types of labor that required the venting of heat. He'd also bought, from places all over the continent, heavy winter bed curtains, the kind that muffled sound. These he had affixed to walls, and hung over the windows, so that any noise in that room would not carry beyond the walls — specifically the clash of steel.

The day after Liere and Hibern arrived, while Senrid and Jilo both slept through the day, Rel let everyone know that from now on, those not actually working would be drilling each morning. If they didn't show up, he would go and fetch them.

"You won't like that," he said, and let his size, and his deep-set dark eyes, help them create a suitable threat in their own minds. Rel had the mildest of tempers, but especially with that thin mustache and the beard that cragged an already craggy face, those who didn't know him decided not to test that.

The next morning, the sun had barely begun to crest the hills beyond the river running alongside Lisdan when Rel made his rounds, gathering all slackers.

He ran the drill himself. Experienced as he was, he could tell by the first round of warmups who had training and approximately how much, but he said nothing.

When they paired up for combinations and sparring, he watched the experts, noting with silent approval that Andri Elsarion, probably the best swordsman there, displayed a habitual patience with the beginners — later, Rel wasn't surprised to learn that Andri had more or less adopted a bunch of war orphans, and taught them to defend themselves.

From the aspect of training, the best was actually Sveneric, who seemed to float through the toughest drill that left most of the rest red-faced and sweating. Once he got a pattern he did it with his eyes closed, an inward focus that did not call attention to itself. One had to be watching to see it.

Dtheldevor was the opposite, loud and flashy but excellent, her chief lieutenants, Ellen and Joey Warren, nearly as good. Dtheldevor, too, had been dealing with youngsters for a long time. Rel put those four in charge so that he could go back to work, which included being seen hobbling about the town getting jobs and dealing with guilds. And, thereby, garnering what news could be gleaned.

Senrid lay staring at the ceiling when he woke just before dawn that morning. Even after sleeping through an entire day and night, it was good not to have to move. He thought over the close calls he'd had of late, and what he considered his weak performance in that fight when he and Kessler took on the patrol. He had been slowing down, mentally and physically, and had not even realized it. That was just stupid.

He decided to start from the fundamentals: he did not want to die. He had promised Stad that he would return to Marloven Hess. Everything else was secondary, a matter of choice; right now, the most demanding task was helping Jilo.

Presently Senrid heard the voices of others moving back and forth down the hall. There was Kyale Marlonen's fluting tones. He had no wish to deal with Kyale. The noise gradually shifted to the floor above. Rhythmic thumping and stamping indicated some kind of practice.

A particularly loud thud caused Jilo to waken with a snort. He sat up, bleary-eyed. "What?"

"It sounds like some kind of drill."

Jilo began to say, "Were we supposed to—"

He was interrupted by a quick rap on the door, which opened before either could respond. To their surprise—and alarm—Mondros stuck his bearded head in, his thick black brows a single line across his forehead. "It's happening."

Jilo surged to his feet. "Where should we—"

Mondros said roughly, "We'll have to fight from my cottage. At least the nails are intact." He tossed down several tokens—Chwahir coins, round with square holes in the center.

"Nails?" Senrid said.

Jilo began to reply, when the door jerked open again, and Hibern entered. "I've got some hot biscuits here." She dropped a couple of biscuits into each of their hands. "Leander, Arthur, and Liere volunteered to help."

"Liere?" Jilo said. "I thought she couldn't learn magic."

"That was before she left Sartorias-deles," Hibern said. "Her knowledge about wards is general, but she learns fast." Hibern considered adding that Liere had been prowling around before and after her turn with the drill, asking after Senrid, but one look at Senrid's shuttered expression kept her silent on that subject.

Jilo and Senrid exchanged glances, neither wanting to say that their light magic skills would be a twig against the sword of that lethal mirror ward in Chwahirsland. In any case, Hibern did not wait for them to answer. She turned abruptly, her long black hair swinging against her blue mage robe, which she still wore proudly, travel-worn and frayed as it was.

Jilo followed her out. Senrid paused long enough to roll both of their quilts up and stash them, then turned toward the door, risking a mental scan to see who he'd be facing downstairs.

But a heartbeat after he tried the scan, he recoiled at a mental poke. It was David.

Senrid shut his eyes, and David's thought came: *Are you going to Mondros's?*

:How did you know I was here? Are you watching us?

:Roy, MV, and I are running the outer perimeter. Senrid, Ilerian is at Chwahirsland. Make sure there's a conduit — don't even try to deal with him yourself.

His mental contact was gone before Senrid could ask what that meant. He considered what to say to the others, then decided he did not want to hear the self-righteous complaints about Detlev's boys that were likely if he brought up the contact. He'd save the question for Mondros.

He left, the frowziness of a day and night of sleep vanishing as he dashed through the cleaning frame. Well done, Rel, he mentally saluted as he ran downstairs. The others had gathered in the hall, Jilo passing out the transfer tokens.

One by one they transferred to Mondros's cottage, the air filling with the warning singed scent which at least the wind took away. Senrid crammed a biscuit into his mouth as Mondros beckoned them in.

Jilo sat down at the table. Senrid dropped down next to him. Hibern hesitated, then took the last space on the bench beside Senrid, so that she could study the scry glass lying on the table.

Liere, Arthur, and Leander, unfamiliar with the cottage, stood behind the other three as Mondros addressed them. "I'll talk quickly. Do you know what a mirror ward is?"

Leander said, "It's a perfect lattice ward."

"Perfect?" Liere repeated, distracted momentarily by Senrid sitting there directly in front of her, one hand drumming on his knee. Her impulse to come on this mission, which she knew she was not trained for, had been solely to talk to him. From the way he'd shut her out the other night she feared that she'd somehow stumbled badly, or perhaps this was how Senrid dealt with grief. She wanted to talk to him—get him to talk—but again, there was the formidable shield, smooth and impenetrable as steel as he listened to Mondros.

Who said, "Mirror has to do with how the lattice is constructed, reflecting power somewhat the way a mirror sconce reflects a candle flame so that you get the effect of two candles, though only one burns."

He paused, looking for comprehension as Hibern watched the surface of the scry glass, which was a round shape with a raised lip. Ah, an old-fashioned inkstone, made of polished slate.

"The mirror is a metaphor, not a result of a physical and reflective surface. It has to do with the way the lattice is constructed. 'Perfect' means lattices of odd numbers bound together in repetitions of another odd number, forming a number only divisible by the first number. Jilo, want to explain more specifically?"

Jilo twisted around. "Wan-Edhe used Norsunder Beyond's outer layer to model his mirror ward. Both are constructed of eleven-strand lattices bound eleven times, the perfect number being one hundred twenty-one."

Hibern glanced up over her shoulder. "Liere, remember we talked about these. The honeycomb wards are kind of the light magic version of dark magic mirror wards. Light magic actually uses light to bind them. How are these bound?"

"Blood," Jilo said. "Living blood, from the inhabitants of the entire city of Narad. Of course against their will. Against their knowledge."

Hibern sucked in a breath. "Is this what that blood mage text was about?"

Leander thought, yes. But he didn't speak up; he'd claimed to have not reached that far in his translation before Kessler Sonscarna took the book away again.

Senrid remembered David's contact. He said to Mondros,

"Do you have a conduit?"

Mondros and Jilo both looked his way. "You understand conduits?" Jilo asked.

"I do," Leander and Hibern said at the same time.

"I think I do," Arthur murmured. "But perhaps light magic conduits are different? I'd welcome specifics here."

"I don't," Liere said. "But if there isn't time — "

Jilo cut in, too stressed for politeness. He swung around on the bench to face her. "You know what spy-eyes are, right? Dark magic artifacts not unlike scry stones." He jerked his thumb back at the scry stone on the table. "Except with a spy-eye there is no exchange between two consenting mages. Spy-eyes enable the user to watch a given space. The wider the space, the more magic it, well, burns. It's hard magic, very wasteful. Norsunder is full of them. Wan-Edhe learned how to make them, so that he could spy on his underlings."

"So far, I'm with you. Is conduit another name for these?" Arthur asked.

"In a way. Conduits enable magic to be applied from far away. Same as a spy-eye. Mondros and I placed a lot of them, in case Wan-Edhe ever returned. We put spy-eyes in, too, because Wan-Edhe would be looking for them. All those are artifacts, like this scry stone here. "

"And they were destroyed, the first year Wan-Edhe returned. As we expected. But our important conduits remained, along with many of our wards and even a few traps," Mondros put in, glancing from his scry stone to the group then back again.

"What are the conduits that Wan-Edhe missed?" Senrid asked, aware of David as a silent listener.

"Nails," Mondros said.

"Nails?" Leander repeated.

David spoke in Senrid mind: *Tiny. But if they were laid right, Detlev says they should be effective.*

: Detlev? Senrid couldn't prevent a jolt, as Jilo said, "Wan-Edhe has never in his life done physical labor. He would never think of testing nails. He looks for constructs similar to his spy-eyes. Artifacts. Books, scrolls. Even rings and crowns."

David's thought came: *Detlev's using Adam and me as conduits, because the entire setup in Chwahirsland is actually a trap for Detlev. And Efael has most likely added our names in.*

: I don't even know what you mean by using a person as conduit.

: *You'll see — just let us ride along.*

And once again, David's voice was gone before Senrid could ask questions. Yet he sensed David's presence at the surface of his thoughts, focus outward. Adam as well, and he did not shut them out.

Mondros said, "Liere, since you know least about mirror wards, but are experienced with Dena Yeresbeth, I entrust guarding this place to you. I mean both physical and mental attack. Can you take that?"

"I'll go outside," she offered, and did, exchanging grim smiles with Hibern: here they were again, at war using magic.

"Leander and Arthur, you two maintain the conduit." Mondros repeated the spell, a complicated one in light magic. "I'll also teach you, oh, there it goes." The scry stone face had turned ink-black. "It's begun."

Leander began the spell, Arthur joining him. The soft murmur of their voices faced into the background as Jilo took the lead; Senrid repeated Jilo's spells.

Then David was in his mind, Adam as well, their magic-wielding so fast that Senrid couldn't follow, but he didn't have to. The path was there, perceivable in the mental realm, provided by Arthur and Leander.

Senrid floundered, then send a thought to David: *How can we protect our minds from invasion?*

: *Detlev is doing that. None of your names are known to Ilerian. He cannot find you — the conduits are all masked, making it seem as if the threat is right there in that castle in Narad.*

Then once again David shut him out. Senrid turned to Jilo, and began repeating everything he said, aware that this new sort of warfare was fast and dangerous. The internal stink of hot metal twanged his nerves. He let Jilo lead, bolstered by David's and Adam's awarenesses. But very soon Senrid got that sickening sense of something slipping farther and farther away. Already they were losing this battle.

Hibern alone held back, sorting through the complexities of perception, Liere's golden aura forming a ring around them. Safety was an illusion, yet it felt safe. Any break would at least give them warning — though Liere would perish in the process.

Leander and Arthur had become green pathways, like ribbons, weaving in and around a structure glowing eerily in the center of thick darkness. This structure was cold and elegant as sculptured ice. No, those patterns were more precise, the refractions too deep for ice: a structure composed of interlocked diamonds. Hibern became aware of herself moving along the ribbon at increasing speed, and then anticipating the loops and angles —

She glimpsed Jilo far below, laboring at the lowest layer of the diamond structure, a bit like tearing a stone from the lowest part of a wall with only one's fingernails.

Here, she tried to yell to him, but she had no mouth, no voice. She jabbed frantically at the right one —

: *You see it.*

The voice was both everywhere and close, right at her elbow. She flung out her awareness, forgetting that this was not visual space. She knew that voice; it had taunted her long, long ago when she thought she knew so very much about Old Sartor, having studied two very questionable books: *Detlev?*

: *Here. Do you want the wider view?*

Of course she wanted the wider view! And there it was: the diamond structure was only a small part, a door, no, a tunnel. No, a portal. If she moved, it changed, the way a stick plunged into a pond bent, depending on where you looked at it. The underlying structure the portal was built upon extended, vast and dark, pulsing with livid crimson. She tried to turn from it, but the side of her vision flung awareness out even farther — and for a single stroke of her heart she perceived thousands and thousands of filaments branching from the vast structure, undulating like live things.

: *Each draws life from an individual.*

Hibern wanted to shut her eyes, to hide away from the horror. But she had learned when small that hiding your eyes doesn't change the cruel things your father does in the name of experiment, even when your mother insists that everything is just as it should be, that it's orders from the Regent. Learn, Hibern commanded herself. Learn. This is what you are fighting.

A sword appeared.

She batted at it, and watched it spin. She reached with her mind, aimed it — and it turned. She tried to strike at the filaments, but the sword moved through them without disturbing them. The sword was too flimsy, or her will was too weak, too ignorant.

: *First the portal.*

She swooped up to the diamond door — portal — and sped

around it, peripherally aware of Jilo working away down lower, and Mondros chipping at it on one side. No, that would not do. She glared at that diamond in the center of the structure, the one slightly turned, slightly cracked. She pushed the sword into it, and pushed, and pushed until sword and diamond shattered into a cloud of tiny shards. Cracks spread – the structure shimmered, shivered – then exploded into spinning shards.

She laughed, then the laughter froze as a sense of cold, icy cold...awareness? Intent? It had been gazing elsewhere, into an unimaginable distance, but now it began to turn.

Instinct screamed that it must not see her.

A blow like a palm striking her forehead knocked her out of the image. She stumbled, falling painfully, and found herself gasping for breath, as if she'd been running. She hauled herself upright. The cottage spun and hitched, spun and hitched. She loathed being dizzy. Fiercely she focused on the scry stone, which had gone blank again, and kept her gaze there until her vision settled, but her head panged still.

The first to speak was Jilo. "You broke it. That was..."

Mondros had thumped down onto the opposite bench, taking up the entire thing as he steadied himself, hands out wide. "Hibern, if I'd known you were that experienced, I would have begged Erai-Yanya on my knees to lend you to me. That was brilliant."

"That wasn't me," she said slowly, as memory sorted the images the way one remembers a dream. "Detlev was there. I couldn't have done anything without that sword he gave me."

"What sword?" Jilo asked. "No, it's all right. I think we see it all differently. When I work I see a mosaic, only three-dimensional, not flat."

"Words," Leander murmured. "Runes and..." He drew in the air.

"That's Chwahir," Jilo exclaimed. "You know my language?"

"No – not really. Only a few characters. I'd like to learn more."

"Let's see if...heh, no, it's definitely gone." Mondros chuckled. He and Jilo bent over the scry stone as images crawled and flickered.

Hibern sank down onto the floor and put her forehead on her knees. Her brain ached, as if compressed to the size of a walnut. There was no sense of Detlev anymore.

Liere came to the doorway. "I followed a little of that. Oh, Hibern, you were wonderful."

"Wasn't." Her tongue was like a sand-filled sock.

"It was you, guiding the light. A great mirror behind you."

"You mean the mirror ward?" Jilo asked, looking up at Liere. "We didn't do any damage to that. I wish we had. But the portal, it's completely gone. You found the weak matrix. Is that what you meant?"

Liere hesitated, then said, "I think we're confusing ourselves. We don't have the vocabulary. Though I suspect they have it in Old Sartoran, all those odd terms I remember struggling over when I thought I had to learn it first. I need to go back and study it again."

She backed out of the cottage and walked to the edge of the cliff, reaction still reverberating through her. They'd done it. They'd actually struck a blow against Norsunder—and won.

"They," not quite. It had largely been Detlev, both guiding and hiding. Oh, yes, there had been a great trap, which, she could see in retrospect, they had avoided solely because that vast burn-ice awareness had been paying no attention to them at all. It was searching for the prey it craved.

She dared the tiniest tendril, no more than a little crab on the bottom of the ocean sticking out a feeler to test the progress of a hurricane on the surface far above. To her surprise, that terrible ice-burn awareness seemed to have moved farther away.

She shivered as she gazed out at Colend below. *How* she wished she had had the sense to learn what Siamis had offered to teach her about Dena Yeresbeth *years* ago. She loathed this feeling, as if she were a toddler trying to walk in an adult's shoes.

The old impulse to tell Senrid, knowing he wouldn't scoff, or lather her with well-meant but sickening praise, caused her to turn to go back into the cottage. She missed their old debates, so very much, and here again a rush of regret and question squeezed her heart; she'd never had to console someone before, and he had shut her out.

She simply had to try again, and express herself better.

She paused in the open door as Mondros poured out mugs of a fruity-smelling drink of some kind. Jilo paged through an old book, bent over it so that his bony shoulder blades poked at the back of his old shirt. Hibern remained on the floor, and Leander sat beside her, looking bemused. Arthur spoke quietly with Mondros.

Senrid was already gone.

Ten

Fortress in Erdrael Danara

SEVERAL DAYS' HARD RIDE directly to the north of Melire, Shontande Lirendi paced by the tiny cell window, back and forth, as he had for uncounted hours day after day. Every hundred lengths he leaped, gripped the bars, pulled himself up and held his face pressed against the rusty iron until his arms trembled, staring up at the sleet-gray clouds. By increments he watched the light change as the sun arced across the northern sky, each day a little lower. Moisture-laden air ruffled across his face, cold, but pure: winter was nigh, here on the heights.

With care, and the desperate patience of unceasing inner control, as he walked he contemplated who his suicide would benefit most: himself or his enemies.

He had no reaction to the loneliness or his grim surroundings. He was used to his own company. Spending time in a cell he could bear. Physical comforts meant little, for his mind could, at will, retreat to a place beyond mortal care. It had served as his escape during the years his father had kept him a virtual prisoner in his effort to keep him from suffering a similar fate, and later as a retreat from excess, after the exquisitely maintained prison suddenly opened. It had afforded him a place to think, to reflect and to repair. To be alone, though that was seldom a need; one might further define it as a place to be alone and to relax.

The decision whether or not to die required consideration, as clear as one could contrive, for of course there was only the one chance. The problem was, he couldn't really evaluate the balance of consequences against either choice. So far he had time for contemplation, but he knew that that would end, summarily, at Norsunder's convenience. Imry Llyenthur might be a liar even in thought, but Shontande, extraordinarily sensitive to subtleties unspoken as well as spoken, had perceived the moment of decision to hand him over to Yeres to be turned into a mindless puppet.

That mental place of retreat might give temporary solace, but he was convinced it was not a solution. His access to magic had been warded, a ward far too strong for him to break, so there was no possibility of physical transfer.

He knew that the masters of Norsunder could take control of his body and animate it as they would. His father had spent years in a similar state, though for some reason Detlev had never commanded him to do anything, as far as Shontande could tell. Maybe it was laxity, or boredom. But his father's blank gaze, his mind open as the sky — vacant of some essential component — had haunted Shontande's dreams ceaselessly.

If he killed himself, he would be beyond Norsunder's reach. Alive, given to the enemy, he would be forced into that death-that-was-no-death that some actually chose. Why? No, that was irrelevant. The true horror was the possibility that his mind would be imprisoned somewhere, cognizant of what his body was forced to do in Norsunder's name.

Yet if he killed himself, there would be Colend left with no heir, no regency council, and a lot of young ambitious aristocrats who all could trace some relation to the crown in their past. Just how long past the end of the Norsunder war would they fight one another, if no one stopped them?

His magic sense flared.

The door-ward? He put a hand out, feeling the strange nerve-brush of heavy magic, and then the furtive sounds of someone manipulating the very old lock.

The door opened, a tall, gray-dressed figure slipped in, and the door almost, but not quite, shut.

Shontande almost didn't recognize Curtas, for he was no

longer the nondescript boy Shontande had last seen years ago, before he found out that Curtas had been a spy—pretending friendship on Detlev's orders. But despite the physical changes, and the weak light from the single tiny window, the changeable light eyes were the same ones, full of humor and question, that had looked at him over the wall that summer day in what seemed another lifetime.

His first reaction was anger.

"Here," Curtas said, holding out a bundle. "Put on this uniform, fast."

Shontande stood where he was. "A question," he said.

Curtas angled his head, listening for steps beyond the door. With his free hand he set the big bundle down at his feet. Then, wedging his foot in the door, he began to pull off the heavy gray battle tunic; beneath it was another uniform, the heavy woolen winter tunic-jacket that Norsundrians wore everywhere but on the battlefield, and over that two sword sheaths, side and back. Riding boots, at the top of which showed worn knife hilts. "Yes?"

Shontande knew very well the unbroken rhythm of patrols past his door, the only sound he'd heard for days and days. "Can your master really prison a mind outside a body?"

In the bleak light Shontande saw Curtas flush.

Curtas said only, "Do you want to be free or not?"

"Why are you here?"

An ironic glance. "Don't you want to get out?"

"If I do. What then?"

"That's up to you." Curtas tossed the battle tunic, which fell to the stones at Shontande's feet.

Curtas stayed at the door, and did not attempt to close the distance between them. He put his hands on his hips. "Isn't anything better than whatever Imry's got planned?"

"You broke the ward on the door," Shontande said, still not moving. "He's surely been alerted."

"Yes, but at this moment he's being yanked away from Ralanor Veleth, which is still holding out, to attend on the Host in Chwahirsland as they try to force a rift to Norsunder Beyond. This is the only chance you'll have."

"Ralanor Veleth?" Shontande repeated doubtfully.

Curtas flushed, as though he'd been accused of lying. "Warrior kingdom on Goerael. Imry shot their king, but someone seems to be just as good at resistance."

True or not, escape was definitely better than waiting around for whatever Imry Llyenthur had planned. In spite of that first, painful betrayal—not so much the assassinations, which Shontande knew Curtas had had no hand in, but that Curtas had not trusted him enough to tell him that he was a spy. Those feelings were tied up with the sense of obligation Shontande had felt ever since he learned that it was Curtas who had tipped the balance when he regained his throne. Shontande hated the turmoil all those old feelings stirred, he hated himself for pettiness, and he hated Curtas for...what?

Not hiding his own self-mockery, Shontande began to unbutton his filthy velvet tunic. But Curtas didn't watch, unlike the others early in his incarceration. He kicked over the heavy bundle, which landed on the stone by Shontande's feet with a muted metallic sound. Then he turned his head, his gaze going diffuse as he listened.

Not yet—but soon. Shontande knew that interval between patrols. It was almost over.

Cold air roughened his flesh as he ripped free of his clammy, sweat-stained linen shirt. The bundle at his feet was chain mail, wrapped up, with something in its center. Curtas hadn't worn it, then; one couldn't keep chain mail quiet. With it was no shirt, only one of the thick cotton-quilt under-vests. No trousers. His silk ones would have to do.

Good enough. He pulled on the quilt vest, and then the mail, which rang and chimed, and last the battle tunic and its belt. Into the back of that he tucked his dirty clothes; to leave them was to announce that he had a disguise.

Lying at his feet was a fine dagger. Shontande thrust it through the stiff blackweave belt.

The last item, a hooded cloak, was in his hands when Curtas's chin lifted.

They looked at one another across the width of the cell.

"Dead end that way," Curtas said, pointing to the left.

Only one way up or down, then—into the oncoming patrol.

"We'd better shut the door," Shontande said. "Wait till they're gone again."

Curtas said ruefully, "We can't. If we shut the door, and it will lock, and as you can see, there is no lock on this side. This key hangs outside. They'll know in an instant if it's gone." Curtas unpocketed the key, still holding the door open by his fingertips; an open door was not going to pass notice either.

"There'll be a fight," Shontande said, still testing. And, because it was his fault they were still here at all, "Want the mail?"

Curtas waved a hand. "We've got the uniforms. They've never seen you. I'll try a bluff. You slide past and go. They don't know who you are."

He drew the blade slung across his back—a heavy cavalry saber. Held it out, and Shontande hastily fastened the cloak and yanked down the hood. Crossed the room, took the hilt, flattened himself against the wall.

"Exit's down, left, left, right. Password at the door today is Aldon."

They fell silent, the only sound the rap of approaching boot heels.

"Who's in there?"

Curtas opened the door wider and stepped out. "We had separate orders," he answered in the language of Norsunder, gesturing into the room. "Straight from HQ."

The eyes followed his hand, and in that moment Shontande slipped behind Curtas and to the side, keeping his hood low as he sided past the guards.

The lead two exchanged looks. The redhead who'd spoken gripped and regripped his sword hilt; the old one with the pale hair next to him licked cracked lips. The two behind looked blank.

Shontande's shoulder blades tightened.

"But our orders were to kill anyone opening that door," came the answer from the redhead in a tight voice. "Or it's our lives."

Shontande couldn't understand the words, but he saw the decision in the faces and bodies.

Curtas slammed the door shut, and all four heads snapped that way.

Run, came his urgent mental voice. Shontande heard Curtas pull his blade.

Shontande ran a few steps, but at each self-hatred rose so strong it tasted bitter in his throat. The whir and clash of steel behind him was desperate, the harsh breathing and scraping of boots of a fight not to disarm and secure, but to kill: whatever the truth about what had happened years ago, he could not leave Curtas to fight four angry guards.

Shontande hefted the saber; he had been trained in rapier.

The thing was heavy, unwieldy. He whirled and ran back. The back two guards were already down. Curtas fought the last two, his back to the wall. One more step. A weak, slow block from Curtas, so slow it surprised Shontande, even against two. Then he was in the fight, blocking the first blade. Backhand strike, feint, feint, strike—and the jolting scrap of steel against splintering collarbone. The blond Norsundrian's head flopped, half severed, spraying blood everywhere.

Curtas whooped, a high, harsh sound like a marsh bird, as he jabbed his knife into the red-haired Norsundrian, and there he left the blade, its hilt slimy with blood.

"Run." His voice was a hoarse whisper.

They ran, Curtas leading the way. His shoulder bumped against walls, but he ran still, one hand clutching his black-smeared side.

They had another fight at a side entrance—though it was hardly a fight, for they took the two sentries by surprise. No question of getting through using the password, not covered with blood.

Shontande had never before killed anyone. Today he did it three times, ugly thrusts that did not kill instantly because he had rarely used this particular weapon in training, only the thin-bladed rapier of rule-circumscribed aristocratic duel. He had to finish each with his knife, action that left his joints feeling like water, his guts shuddering, washes of cold sweat running down under the steel mail, over the bruises forming where he'd taken blows.

He was able to win because Curtas warded the sentries' blows. He was slow, then slower, and finally Shontande realized that the blood splashed down his front did not belong to the dead up in the tower, but it was his, and it was spreading fast. There had been one set of chain mail, and Shontande wore it.

"This way." Curtas's voice was a whisper now.

They made it up the trail perhaps fifty paces, no more than that.

"You have to go," Curtas said, collapsing against the gnarled bole of a tree. "Now. We're at the old Larensar castle. Colend down that way." A weak gesture southeastward.

"Why," Shontande said. His throat was too tight for any further word.

Curtas's brows twitched upward, a faint lingering of the

well-remembered humor. "Promised. Once. Get you out. And." He flicked his gaze sideways, his lips shaping the word, "Go."

Shontande knelt in the snow instead. Cold air whipped at them both, icy drafts from down in the shadowed valley below. In the fading light Shontande saw that Curtas's face had gone pale, drawn with pain. Chuff, chuff, blood dripped onto the trail, hissing. It steamed for a sickening moment, then vanished.

"Patrol won't report in." A slow, bubbling breath. "Search out soon. Run." Blood rimed his lips.

Shontande flung aside his sticky weapon and took hold of Curtas's shoulders. "Why," he said again, in a different voice.

Curtas pressed his arm across his middle. "Oh. How it hurts." A shaky laugh. "Damn." A liquid cough, then he vomited blood, and lay back, for a moment relieved. He blinked, and Shontande felt him fight for consciousness. "Detlev said..." His whisper was so soft, Shontande bent to hear it. "Detlev said. Protect the future."

"Protect the future." The words had no meaning.

"Promise me. Curtas raised a hand black with his own blood. He groped, then his hand dropped. "Promise—" Another of those terrible coughs, from lungs filled with blood.

Shontande dropped his mental barriers, and reached. He saw in Curtas's memory himself as a boy, not from the arrogant superiority of Detlev's trained killer hiding his identity in order to score off the oblivious lighters. Not from the speculative desires of his own Colendi courtiers. Shontande saw none of the reasons for which he had justified his long hatred and self-righteous sense of betrayal. To Curtas it was simple: he'd had once a friend to rescue from the invisible bars of others' ambition—bars that they'd shared in so many ways, though neither had dared talk about them.

Once Curtas had had a friend, and then lost him.

This was the steady, burning light—love—of friendship. Not hot desire, not the scald of expectation. The impulse to rescue the childhood friend, one he believed to be brilliant, transcended all the ideological boundaries, and Shontande sustained a brutal strike at his unexamined moral superiority. He knew that they had traded places, that the hatred he'd harbored all these years had not been returned; in extending Detlev's evil to Curtas he had in his bitterness chosen evil over good, but Curtas, surrounded by evil all his early life had striven for the good. Yet it was Curtas and not he, whose life was now forfeit.

Curtas's mind met his: Promise. *Stay free. Make Colend free.*

"I promise," Shontande said. Then, again, he vowed, "I promise. As long as I live."

But Curtas was beyond hearing. His mind lingered a little longer, his serenity at their reconciliation like splashes of sungold on water in the realm of the spirit, and then that too diffused, leaving the sky-reflecting vastness of a still lake.

Shontande forced himself to act. He straightened Curtas's limp body, even though he heard faint shouts on the rising wind, and the sounds of pursuit being organized. He touched the sweat-stiff hair, and brushed his fingers over the still-warm eyelids, closing them gently.

He rose, looked around, then bent down and with careful hands unbuckled Curtas's sword belt and shoulder sheath. He retrieved the saber, pulled free Curtas's boot knives, and cleaned the weapons on the long autumn grasses tufting from the scattering of rocks around the tree. Shouts rose, carrying on the cold wintry air. But once Shontande was armed, he knelt down once more, caressed Curtas's brow, then spoke the words of Disappearance.

Then he forced himself to his feet, vowing to make recompense for all the years they could have had, and had been denied through his own pettiness.

He slipped up the trail, just as sleeting rain began to fall.

And far away, sitting in the back of a paper-maker's home, Adam stirred the boiling pulp and in the wake of the defeat of Efael's and Ilerian's try at making a portal to Norsunder, he did his usual sweep of the boys in the mental realm. Already one this week one was gone, poor Noser, the lost soul.

The count had diminished once again. Adam ran through their names, then listened more carefully. Listened for the laughing mind, Curtas the seeker, the builder and maker. Listened farther out, and still farther, despite the danger of powerful and prowling minds, until he knew that Curtas's spirit had gone forever beyond the dimly perceived boundaries.

He bowed his head and wept.

Eleven

Border of Ralanor Leleth

IN THE CAVERN HIDEOUT between Lygiera and Ralanor Veleth, jingling, clatters, the overwhelming smells of horse and sharp fear sweat, and a sickening-sweet tang of old blood drifted in with the riders; behind Uncle Jaim walked Markham, and the solid, grandmotherly captain who led the makeshift brigade from Dantherei. They all carried heavy gear slung over their shoulders.

"We're still alive, but we're facing a bad one," Uncle Jaim said.

Uncle Maxl was just behind them. He looked strangely unfamiliar to Viana's eyes, dressed not in fine court raiment but a spare green battle tunic of Uncle Jaim's, his lemon-colored hair tied back like the warriors', a sword at his side.

"Papa! Papa!" Aledra minced forward in court-trained little steps, her cry shrill and false to all the youngsters' ears: she was pretending distress, but really wanted to be the center of attention, petted and cooed over. Even Young Maxl's round face pruned up, then he turned back to play with the two little ones, who didn't even seem to know a war was on. All three were inured to their big sister's behavior.

Uncle Maxl bent and kissed the top of Aledra's head, and Aunt Jewel fondled her daughter's cheek with an indulgent smile as he said to those who still waited. "Norsunder was kind enough to give us a warning." His voice dropped on the word 'kind'.

Garian Herlester sauntered down the tunnel. "We're to surrender, or face annihilation," he drawled. "Is that mere hyperbole of the sort one expects from them, or what?" He, too, was in full battle gear, his tunic violet, the Herlester color. Behind him came some of his personal guard — and Rafael.

Mama had long hated Garian Herlester, and Viana had inherited that hatred, fostered by trouble in the borderland that she heard about from time to time as she got older. She was surprised to discover that he wasn't *totally* horrible. Rafael seemed exactly like his father. He was sarcastic — especially to Lexy — and he could be carelessly mean, but he could also be nice, still in a careless sort of way.

As the adults closed into a group and started talking, Rafael lifted his shoulders in one of his shrugs and sauntered toward Viana. "They'll never listen to us now." He drawled just like his father. "Even if one of us trips and gets impaled on a spike. They have to argue first, but I know what they'll decide."

"What happened?"

"We went out looking for the ones who fired your Lathandra, as we'd planned." He stopped, and was taken by a fierce yawn. "Sorry! We rode all night."

Viana sighed. "I wish they'd let me go too. I'm as good with a sword as you are. I can't help being younger, and I don't see what that has to do with anything!"

"Don't rant at me — they're booting us back with the babies, too." Rafael jerked his thumb toward Viana's small cousins. "We can't even hold the remounts."

Lexan appeared then, already getting tall and beginning to broaden through the chest. He looked like a shadow with his dark hair and dark gray riding clothes. "Someone came by magic," he said. "Spooked the horses. Issued the threat. Vanished."

"Magic," Viana murmured.

"We rode back right away," Rafael said. "It might be threat, but if so, it's an impressive one. Something lies directly to the southeast, beyond our defensive line protecting the Treaty Road. It looks normal, but we saw all the summer birds flying hard northward. Not a sound behind us. Something is going to happen there."

"Did the enemy follow you here?"

"We had ambush parties riding point and rear," Rafael said, with a hint of impatience.

Viana flushed with embarrassment.

"Ambush! Euw!" That was Aledra, nosing in as usual, and planting herself in the middle. "Don't say such horrid things, I might feel faint." There went her hand, up to her head. But she was watching Rafael and Lexan for a reaction.

"Well, then, go away," Jaimas said, drawing attention to himself — a rarity.

Aledra stuck out her tongue — and then looked around worriedly to see if her mother had seen. Viana snickered. She liked Aledra better when she wasn't posing and prissy.

Rafael gave them a sarcastic glance and took Viana's arm. "While the children wrangle, I'll tell you what I think is going to happen."

Aledra flushed with fury.

Rafael pushed past Lexan, or tried to, but Lexan gave way before Rafael could bump into him. Rafael sent one of those same caustic looks at him, but didn't insult him, for once. Instead, he guided Viana away. "Now, here's what we have when we count up the forces..."

Lexan took a step back, and then another, knowing that he was fading from Viana's consciousness at the moment; she was too distracted by Rafael. As his father had warned him would happen.

Anger. Deep breath.

Markham watched the two young ones stroll off down a side tunnel, Rafael's long princely hair gleaming reddish-gold under the torchlight, and Viana's glorious night-black ringlets bouncing on her back. He stepped up next to his son.

"I want to ride with you," Lexan said between gritted teeth.

"No." Markham knew — who better? — what it cost to stand aside, to remain impassive under the studied insults, to seem to serve while one in truth guarded. "Norsunder's orders will be to make certain none of us return. You have to be here for them." He nodded toward the Szinzars.

"You are so certain of our defeat?" It made Lexan sick inside, for his father had never talked that way before.

Markham murmured, "Did you not sense it?"

Lexan tried to articulate what he'd sensed, down below, on the silent fields of early summer. But he failed. The chill along his nerves, the sense of impending doom—he'd never experienced anything like it. He'd tried to put it down to a failure of courage, but instinct insisted it was far, far worse than that. His father's grim expression reinforced the impression.

Markham said, "We will do our best to defend, because that is all we can do. If we lose, you must be here to carry on."

Mountains above Fereladria on Drael Continent

Most of Detlev's boys had already transferred in. They stood in a circle atop a mountain deep in Drael's portion of the Fereledria, the belt of the world. At least half of them were thinking about how much Noser had loathed mountaintops. He'd gone beyond them now.

When it was clear that everyone who was going to come had arrived, Silvanas picked up a ceramic jug and held it in both hands, his head bowed as he shifted from foot to foot.

Everyone acknowledged his right to go first; he had been Noser's companion, guide, and as much of an elder brother as Noser could tolerate. They waited while he got his words together, as a cold wind rippled in sleeves and toyed with hair. "He loved being The Nose, and he hated his given name, so I will forever think of him as The Nose. He went out a hero, trying to steal, to rescue, all the horses Kessler's old company had there in that fortress on Ralanor Veleth's border, they were so beat up. Starved. Even though Norsunder's short of horses in that part of—ah, my point is, The Nose got more than half of them clear, too, before those shits pincushioned him. I think he saw it, before he went out." Silvanas shook his head, took a hefty slug of the distilled drink, and passed the jug to David.

"I'll add to that the fact that they'll have a tougher time facing the Velethi resistance," David said. "I think Noser would be pleased that something he did evened up the odds quite a bit." David paused to reflect. As leader, he'd most often had to step on Noser when he got out of hand. Which was a lot. He could mouth out some general compliments but the words tasted bitter, fake. Especially when they faced one another in a circle like this, there was no lying. So he left it there—Noser would have considered that epitaph fair.

He drank and passed the jug to Leef.

"Noser was broken—we all knew that. He knew it. His way of protecting the world was to hang onto the houseboat days, when we were boys..."

"... he loved jokes. Loved them. No joke was too stupid. Sometimes he could make me laugh just by laughing himself. We could use that now and then, eh?"

"... never had a little brother. I guess he came closest. I know he tried to be, in his way..."

One by one they mumbled, repeated themselves, or let the silence build, feeling awkward, and angry, and sad, Erol bewildered and several of them apprehensive. Sveneric's epitaph was barely audible, a description of small, fumbling kindnesses Noser had done for him—no mention of the years of teasing and testing, and the fact that the others had taken great care to never leave Sveneric alone with Noser until he'd gotten old enough to defend himself. They all knew the ways he'd been broken, far too broken to ever quite heal.

Adam was the last of the boys. "He loved us all. In his way. His purest love was reserved for animals, and they knew it. They loved him back." He choked on a swig, and held out the jug to Detlev as he thumbed his stinging eyes.

Detlev said, "Siamis must remain where he is, but he asked me to share this memory, which will serve for us both."

When Detlev shared memories, there was no distortion. They all saw themselves as small boys, and some smothered laughter at their skinny limbs, their pudgy faces and shrill voices. This was Noser's first horseback lesson. They watched Siamis put him on the back of a horse, his legs so short they barely reached the edge of the saddle. Noser's bright hair lifted in the breeze as his round, freckled face changed from astonishment to sheer joy.

Detlev sipped from the jug, leaving a little at the bottom, and turned to Rolfin, who had volunteered to shoot.

Rolfin lit the oil-wrapped arrow, fitted it to the bow, and gave a jerky nod. Detlev cast the jug high. At the top of its arc, Rolfin shot a fire arrow, which hit the jug straight on, causing a bright fireball; Detlev waved his hand, watched narrowly by David, and the flames brightened, consuming ceramic, wood, and metal.

When the ash had fallen to the snow-patched ground,

Adam picked up the second jug.

The first sips had not numbed anyone's pain, though that had been the intent. Noser had been problematical, but he was one of them. Curtas had been generally loved.

Adam said softly, "Curtas died rescuing a friend, and in that rescue he restored the friendship most important to him. I..."

He shook his head and passed the jug, his suspended voice opening the floodgates of shared emotion and memory. Some spoke a long time, talking about things both small and great that they had all done together. Others couldn't speak at all. A look cast Detlev's way was all it took for him to meet the seeker mind to mind and speak a cherished memory.

When at last the jug came to him, he said, "Curtas designed and built the house in Sartor as his master's project. Every line, every angle of light reminds me of him. He left plans for one more building. Once this war is won, I shall see to it that his plans are carried out."

He hurled the jug into the air, and this time it was David who shot the fire arrow. All the upturned faces reflected the glowing flame, brief as it was.

Detlev said, "David has tokens to return you to wherever you were." A remorselessly vivid image of Curtas's face brought fresh, sharp grief, and he added, "*Be vigilant.*"

He vanished from the mountaintop, and very soon after, he eased into the shadows of an old archway at the foot of another mountain, in what was now called Visegn. It had been a risk, planting the false-memory image of the castle below into the pliant mind of a soulbound flunky. A risk, and an experiment.

He watched Imry Llyenthur stand in the honey-stone courtyard far below, listening to the almost subsonic hum from the mountain tops.

Then Llyenthur lifted his head, shading his eyes against the sun at its midmorning point low in the bleak northern sky.

Detlev calculated that appraisal: the old castle of Larkadhe, the newer wing more of a palace, really, as that renovation would not withstand any kind of real siege. Testament to a couple centuries of peaceful anonymity. Stone in three colors: central the tall, still-smooth tower made of the mysterious white, almost translucent material that was only found and formed with the cooperation of mysterious beings who had existed on this world long -6before humans came; that tower, far older than anything else of human make on the continent, looked the least worn. Its high windows gave spectacular views of mountains to the north and east, bay to the west, forest and farmland south on the gradual slope.

Visegn was a small kingdom, its capital, Larkadhe, known for its beauty. Around the central tower stood shorter towers, this wing in gray granite, the more recent wing built in the warm sand-colored stone common to old Iascan construction. Both wings had since been given ornamental corbels, fine tile roofs, wide windows, and some of south wall had been knocked out to make way for gardens. The outer walls were going up again, stone by stone — forced labor by locals.

Llyenthur's underlings, allies, and enemies had expected him to establish his permanent HQ somewhere more obvious, a place designed for defense, or for intimidation. Some were even so confident about their choices they were busy in those places, laying traps and wards, exactly as Detlev intended to de here. Sierleth in Hael Morvendreon; any of Fhleria's formidable keeps; the capitals of either Damondaen or Toar, over on the Toaran continent; and, far to the north, Twelve Towers in the Land of the Venn. Vadnais in Khanerenth. Even Choreid Dhelerei in Marloven Hess, though the city was a shambles.

Below, Llyenthur gave orders to his aides, his gestures easy enough to interpret. Two perimeters, at least, and sentries with interlocking fields of vision. And then —

A burst behind Detlev's eyes, resolving into a bird in rapid flight, alerted him: tracer triggered. Ilerian was again on the move.

Twelve

Southern Border of Ralanor Veleth

DETLEV WOULD HAVE TO waive laying wards in Larkadhe.

It required a long transfer, not directly to Ralanor Veleth — not with Ilerian in probable proximity — but to the mountains rimming the Goerael's Fereledria at Ralanor Veleth's southern border, where the Host's magic would never prevail against the older, far deeper, indigenous magic. Here the sun barely crested the mountains, the air extraordinarily clear, the wind carrying scents of ripening grass and pollen-drifting blooms. No creatures at all. Even at this relative distance, the threat of imminent magic forming half a day's ride north was potent.

It only took a glance down at the plains to observe the eye-aching coruscation in the early spring light that indicated the coalescing power of a world-threatening intensity. Detlev risked another transfer, orthogonal to the disturbance, knowing his brief spurt of power would be subsumed by the vast flow of magic being drawn in. There was the focus, below the borderland mountains of Drath, where the Treaty Road gave access to Lygiera as well as Drath's north-south road. Detlev used a spyglass to inspect the camps strung between two old Velethi border garrisons.

What would be the best vantage? Detlev raised a hand to transfer, and then hesitated. So much changed from day to day—hour to hour—but amid the torrent of crises superficial and profound there were parallel clue-tracks, evidence so scarce, so ephemeral it was utterly convincing, mad as it seemed. But then the man who might be contemplating such madness was scarcely sane.

Detlev took another risk, activating a very old and subtle ward, knowing that each use might be the last, leaving permanent enmity in place. He used proximity as a Destination, and transferred in.

Prince Kessler Sonscarna turned sharply, poised for fight, and then eased into his usual taut stillness. "I wondered if you'd turn up."

Detlev gestured at the plain below as explanation, for as expected, Kessler had chosen a superlative vantage on this rocky cliff surrounded by tall fir. Implication: that Detlev, too, considered the Norsundrian armies, and Imry Llyenthur, as peripheral. Kessler's focus, then, was the Host. And his goal?

Detlev had to find out. Fast.

"Llyenthur," Kessler said, nodding at the swiftly striking camps below, "erred when he did not investigate here himself. He was here only long enough to take out Jason Szinzar."

Detlev shaded his eyes against the glare of the sun topping the purple, hazy horizon, and easily spotted the big, black-haired figure astride a barrel-chested mount. "It's a common enough mistake when trying to keep ahead of events to confine one's attention to the obvious."

Kessler smiled faintly. "Jason Szinzar was an innovator. But everything he did, or thought, or tried, was discussed first with Markham Glenereth. And no one saw it. I don't even know if his own people did." He waved a hand below.

What was he probing for? With Kessler you got nothing unless you gave. Detlev would relinquish no facts, at least not yet. Far too dangerous. What he'd concede instead would be control of the conversation.

"He sees it, too," Kessler observed. "That the attack is going to be cavalry, not foot."

Force them to war on your terms, and if you do not get terms, at least choose the ground. Jaim Szinzar spoke the words with his customary careless cheer, waving his hand in casual salute as he rode back and forth along the columns forming into attack formation: they were too far for voices to carry, but Detlev listened on the mental plane. The ground was chosen well for advance: the lack of rain had made the plains before them hard, but behind them lay drying spring ponds and streams, marshy, mushy ground on the edge of forest that would benefit neither side's riders. But, if needed, it would afford a good retreat.

"Can you hear Ilerian?" Kessler asked.

His tone was idle, but it was not an idle question.

"No. He would sense my presence first."

Kessler smiled. Ilerian's presence for the duration was inevitable; to release whoever was captured inside one of the spheres from Norsunder Beyond, he had to be physically present at least long enough to trigger the ward binding the sphere. But if he was going to attempt to force the distortion of the sphere to breach the physical boundaries of the world, he would have to remain and perform sustained magic.

A ward border had already been laid; no living thing remained inside that ward. The coruscation began to coalesce into a shimmer. Detlev and Kessler could smell the metallic burn from this distance. Even Ilerian must proceed slowly when releasing a sphere on land, or they would all be consumed by the fire he barely controlled: these spheres were so much less difficult on the sea.

Detlev shifted his attention to the black-haired figure behind the forming defensive lines. While Jaim Szinzar rode back and forth before the assembling heavy infantry, his exhortations visible in his gestures as his two banner-bearers galloped behind him, Markham Glenereth from his unobtrusive vantage watched that shimmer behind the much-diminished Fhlerian force, and Kessler's old company, now forced to be foot warriors, having lost most of their mounts. And even though Markham Glenereth had no experience of magic, his long military experience enabled him to gauge the distance, and the width, suspecting the force that would find this ground most advantageous.

He came to a decision. And when Jaim Szinzar's kingly horse pranced his way again, there followed a swift exchange of words. Then Jaim wheeled the dancing roan and rode off again, calling out commands.

"Wager," Kessler said, looking down. The Landis cast to his Chwahir features caused one of those momentary shifts in perspective wherein people, sometimes places, become palimpsests, past and distant past, present, and probable future glimpsed in half-perceptible layers. "Shall we see Yvandred Montredaun-An and his First Lancers ride out, for the first time in several centuries?"

It was inevitable that Kessler would know that particular piece of Marloven Hess's grim history. Though he pronounced the name Sartoran style, *Yah-vandreth*, instead of the *Ih-vandred* so long unheard in Marloven Hess lest the King who bore the Banner of the Damned hear his name spoken and come riding out again.

"I won't take that wager—that is perfect ground for a charge." It was time to give, starting with the most obvious facts. "Ilerian is trying to break a rift to Norsunder Beyond through releasing a capture sphere."

Kessler sent him a quick look, one of rare, mordant humor, reminding Detlev that those in control of Norsunder had once likened Kessler to that brilliant Marloven mage-king; and that Theronezhe, who dominated Norsunder's military arm, had exerted himself to ensure that Kessler and Ivandred never met.

Kessler's expression was still idle, but there was nothing idle about the magic, the force, or the situation. Detlev wondered if Theronezhe was also somewhere about, fuming over Ilerian's sudden interference, which could burn them all to ash. Theronezhe regarded the Fox Banner First Lancers as the centerpiece of his strike troops.

Below, Jam Szinzar's battalion mixed the remains of the forces of three kingdoms and one principality. Milling warriors resolved into two lines of archers, cavalry short-bows inside, longbows on the wings. In the middle, the Velethi heavy-cavalry riders who had no horses—the greater majority, after the protracted fighting—were busy cutting down their lances.

"Stakes," Kessler predicted.

If it were true, it was an astonishing act of desperation, for the ancient code of war trained humans to spare horses. But the Nelkereth horses were smarter than most of their species.

"Wasn't it you who forced Yvandred Montredaun-An into Norsunder?"

"Yes," Detlev said.

"And left him there."

I don't care where I am interim, Ivandred had said five years ago. *You know what I want.*

On the field to the east, as the sun crowned the distant

mountains, shimmer brightened to a white glare.

"For him, that ride was yesterday," Kessler observed.

"No, not quite. The most effective way to exert control over him was to use time. He knows his own day has passed, though he does not know how long. But it would matter little."

The defending battalion gripped and regripped weapons, shoulders tensed, bodies stilled, faces turned east. The summer wind fretted at hair and cloth, horses' manes and tails, banners.

"He has been camped, then, through an unending twilight against the order to rise and ride? I almost feel sorry for him."

We protect the innocent, Jaim Szinzar shouted from the field below, his voice pitched to carry. Gone was the careless laughter. *They fight to destroy our homes, our loved ones, our lives.*

Not yet, Ivandred, Detlev thought. But Ivandred, being who he was, would take the chance anyway.

The shimmer thinned to a black line. A whisper rustled through the ranks below as though a wind struck from the front, not physically: a soulless, cold wind in the realm of the spirit.

Do not look at that black line. Instead, look about you. See who you are with. Your companions, whether Lygieran, Velethi, from Dantherei or from Drath, will forever remember your heroism today, and will speak of it to your children and your children's children! As you will speak of theirs!

The pearl grew rapidly, coruscating with flashes of lightning. Horns wailed, wild and unmusical, like a cry of triumph from beyond the veil of death. Some of the defenders' horses began to fret, their riders tightening reins, gripping lances and swords.

The pearlescent capture sphere had expanded into a shimmering cloud like silk stretched to the ripping point, beyond which blurred shapes could be described. The shimmer parted with a blast of wind, and here they came, the tight wedge of heavies first, in perfect formation, almost stirrup to stirrup, heels down and locked. At a steady trot, deliberately slow. Those spectacularly beautiful horses from the plains of Nelkereth would not arrive blown and clumsy to battle.

"Did you ever explain your reason for your treachery?" Kessler's amusement was colder than the winds of winter. The slaughter imminent below meant nothing to him.

"My treachery?" Detlev repeated, because Kessler expected it.

The ancient Venn war horn winded again, and there he was, the ill-famed Marloven king, dressed all in black and gold, his bright yellow hair braided below his helm with its long tail of human hair taken from dead enemies, as he led the charge. His warriors shrieked on a high, skull-scouring note, *Yip-yip-yip!*

On the snap of command the heavy cavalry swerved to the right, and rode at full gallop for the Velethi flank. Classic oblique attack—if you had studied this king's methods of warfare.

"You cannot tell me he wanted to ride into Norsunder." A nod at the spreading line of Marloven First Lancers.

"He did not."

"From what I gleaned, for Marloven history appears to be silent on the subject, he was a strong king. And a strong enough commander," Kessler remarked, "to realize that the essence of personal loyalty is to keep coercion implicit. Why did you not permit him to conquer his empire? He could have held it. Or was that your objection?"

More dust. And smoke: someone set fire to the long late-winter grasses on the northern flank, causing the enemy horses to shy and bridle.

"Because coercion was no longer implicit," Detlev said. "Before his famous ride, one of his loyal jarls, to force his hand, killed six jarls in his name."

"That is not what we read in the histories. Enaeraneth. And the annals of northern Halia," Kessler observed. "Which included eyewitness accounts. You say that Ivandred was against invading his neighbors? It's said that he killed them because *they* were against it."

"History," Detlev countered, "is written by the survivors, usually in self-justification. And inconvenient witnesses' words can vanish along with inconvenient witnesses. You know that."

Another soft laugh. "So the ride into Norsunder was...what, an accident?"

"It was a ruse, to keep me out of Darchelde castle long enough for the portal into Norsunder to be destroyed."

Kessler laughed again, a breath. "Then the treachery was aimed at Theronezhe."

"The ruse, yes." Norsunder was going to get them anyway—the risk you take when you have become the best weapon in the world. Someone more powerful was going to want that weapon. But Ivandred's ride (and the subsequent extremely vicious internecine struggle over who would control them) set Norsunder's invasion back for centuries.

Below, Markham Glenereth drew his sword. At the other end of the defending line, Jaim Szinzar turned his head, and his banner-bearers dipped once. Twice. And from behind the right flank, where they'd lain flat on the ground, came ranks of unhorsed heavies, in their armor, their lances shortened to lethal points. They took up position before the mounted defenders.

On another signal they drove them into holes already dug into the ground, making a row of angled spikes, like the teeth of some vast beast, pointed at the approaching riders.

"A good move. But the front rank is too narrow," Kessler said. "They're going to be flanked anyway."

Another signal, and arrows from the long-bow archers arced into the air with a rushing hiss.

Ivandred Montredaun-An raised a mailed fist, darkness scintillated in the air, and the arrows vanished.

"Yi-yi-yi-yi-yi-eeeee!" his men screamed, a high falsetto shriek that caused the watchers' ranks to shiver again.

The enemy had magic. The defenders did not.

"As for treachery, I worked for myself," Detlev said. "You were not very observant if you did not realize that."

Kessler laughed, a short sound, no louder than a puff of breath after running. Then dipped his chin at the thunderous charge. "Break the leader, break the line."

And on the plain below, the front ranks of the Lancers reached the waiting line. Some horses leaped over the spikes, crushing defenders below their hooves, but most of the others turned on a hoof and streamed by as their riders shot with expert aim at the defenders.

As Kessler had predicted, the heavies swarmed round the end ranks, to be met with the Velethi light cavalry, and the sounds of battle rose: shouts, the clash and ring of steel, the hail-tap of arrows hitting armor. The scream of horses. Dust from the animals' feet clouded, obscuring individual battles, but from their vantage, Kessler and Detlev saw the second wave of Lancers ride smooth as a river, then divide into three prongs, each aimed to break that line.

"Yet Ivandred is known as an oath-breaker, and... Wait — what's he — he's signaling them to ...what?" Kessler drew in a breath. "They're riding through the Velethi — is this a break for freedom?"

Detlev shut his eyes and scanned the action on the mental plane. Long practice made it possible for him to wing swiftly from mind to mind, seeing what the combatants saw. The desperate hand-to-hand skirmishing all along the front, cumulatively assessed, showed the defense wavering at each of the three lines. But then in ones and twos, then more, they realized the Marlovens were not attacking, but riding through their lines, leaving behind the detritus of Kessler's old force, which the defenders fell on with renewed vigor.

But as yet the leaders could not see the overall shape of the battle.

Detlev put his hands behind his back.

The maelstrom below resolved into a central duel: hand-to-hand, king against putative king, for Jaim never thought of himself as a king, only as his brother's shield-arm. An error, right now, of mortal proportion, alas, alas.

Thrust, block-and-riposte, another strike, and Jaim fell against his horse's neck, mortally wounded, but before the death-blow could descend there was Markham Glenereth's heavy two-edged infantry blade, wielded from the back of a steed mighty enough to cushion the tremendous blows his rider dealt.

Ivandred's splendidly trained warhorse drifted back from Markham's onslaught, and Ivandred's cold, pale eyes lifted to evaluate this unexpected foe. Choking dust rose, mixing with smoke, rendering Markham as a dark silhouette. Two of the Marloven king's personal guard pressed forward, but he raised a hand: *Get out of our path.*

More dust. "Yip-yip-yip!" Ivandred cried, riding past Markham into the murk, the latter leading away Jaim's mount.

Fall back. Fall back, draw them into the marsh, and then retreat! That was Markham, commanding directly now, repeating the order over and over as he rode in and out of the clouds of dust and smoke. And, as the sun reached its zenith, the marshland filled with twos and threes, mostly wounded, scurrying for their lives. Garian Herlester oversaw the retreat; Maxl Elandersi of Lygiera, though grievously hurt, stayed on the field and marshaled those without weapons to gather the wounded.

Through the drifting smoke and dust rose the smell of blood, and the war-horns sounded again, the triumphant cries high and weird.

But the teeth-vibrating muted thunder that ran through the

ground now was not of their making.

For the third time Kessler laughed. "So he's not fighting for Norsunder."

"He's fighting," Detlev said, "to get home."

But Ilerian had seen the duel that was no duel, and raised his hand. The coruscation that Kessler and Detlev sensed began to coalesce with inexorable rapidity into that pearlescent orb again.

Detlev could feel Ivandred's impotent anger as the Marlovens strove to ride toward the distant mountains, but were forced back and back, horses screaming in terror. Ivandred's army blurred into a mass that swiftly shrank to a glowing ball of white light. Then vanished, leaving the air shimmering with heat, every blade of grass and shrub and tree on fire.

"Ilerian," Kessler whispered with soft, precise hatred, "has failed once again to force a portal to Norsunder Beyond." And he transferred away.

Hot air spiraled up to hit the cold currents above. Thunder crackled, lightning flared, and rain poured down, dousing the fires in boiling smears of smoke.

Detlev stood there until the smoke had drifted lazily to the north, revealing the churned, blood-darkened ground below. He knew without scanning that the survivors were discovering, as so many had discovered over the centuries, that there is no power or glory or triumph in defeat, that war means pain, bewilderment, suffering. Death. But soon enough the fact of survival would bind them together, for that was the human way, and that binding would set them apart from their fellows, and they would find a glimmering of glory after all. It would suffice to send them out yet again, whenever the call came, to rise against Norsunder.

It was the human way. And so Detlev must make it his business to inspire that next rising with purpose. *And then, when there is no Norsunder?*

Later. He spared a thought to whatever Kessler was doing, then dismissed it. Ilerian would not give up, but it was going to be much more difficult to find locales such as this plain, before Theronezhe's howling armies were brought over for the final, decisive strike. He had to find them first

Thirteen

Lisdah - Melire

SENRID TRANSFERRED FROM MONDROS'S back to Jilo's room, and collapsed onto the floor as if his joints had been turned to jelly. One day of sleep had not exactly made up for days of rage-fueled, useless pursuit.

He leaned back on his elbows and sniffed the air coming in under the door. Another sniff: freshly scalded coffee mixed with the aroma of simmering pepper and garlic.

The truth was, Senrid did not want to be here. When he'd promised, he'd thought this would be a last-ditch fallback for himself and Crystal Ingrid—and as always, any image or memory, sometimes a sound, even a touch, brought the grief crashing down on him. Grateful to be alone, he endured, suppressing the nearly overwhelming urge to punch a hole through the wall, or smash the window, imagining Llyenthur's head splitting like a melon.

The paroxysm began, by increments, to ease, and he unclenched his fists, forcing his breathing to slow. He refused to suppress memories of Crystal Ingrid merely because they were agonizing. To do so would be to deny the brief time they had had one another. He longed to remember her without this pain, the guilt, though rationally he knew the fault lay solely with the killer.

Begin with the facts, as always: he was here because he'd promised, even if his reasons for promising no longer had any meaning. He'd also made a promise to Indevan Stad, now hiding somewhere in Marloven Hess; Senrid trusted Stad to stay ahead of pursuit as he began putting together a resistance, one person at a time. But Stad trusted Senrid to return, to lead the fight for freedom, and then to restore order once they won it.

Rel had made it plain that they'd been waiting on Senrid before trying to plan for a situation none of them had faced before. He owed it to them to put in his mite—whatever that might be—then he would consider the promise kept, and he would go home, where every reminder would bring fresh agony.

He pushed himself to his feet and trod downstairs, to find a lot of people hovering around the kitchen door.

"Senrid." Rel loomed over everyone. "Report?"

"We staved off Norsunder creating a portal to the Beyond. Hibern was responsible for most of it. They should be along." As he spoke, he glanced at the window, not surprised to discover that most of the day was gone.

"You're Senrid Montredaun-An?"

Senrid turned, to find the same tall young man Liere had greeted with such enthusiasm the other night. This would be the other half of that ring. "I'm Andri Elsarion. I think we're cousins of a sort, aren't we?"

"Several times over, if many generations back," Senrid said, bracing for questions.

But there weren't any. Andri flashed a rueful grin. "Norsunder. Portals. A year ago I didn't believe magic existed outside of decorations for plays and storefronts. We were too ignorant to know we were ignorant. Ah, when you're ready for it, join us in the mornings up in the attic. We could use another good pair of hands."

"That we can," Dtheldevor declared, elbowing her way through the crowd. "When're them eats comin' out? Belay the jabber if it's holding things up!"

"Not at all," Seshe of the Mearsieans called from inside the kitchen. "We were just waiting on this bread...and it's done."

Joey Warren, on the day's rotation for kitchen duty, pulled

out the bread board, disclosing a long, perfectly browned loaf.

"Excellent timing," Leader said, coming through as he rubbed his hands.

"Where were you?" Kyale demanded. "I was worried!"

"Helping Jilo on a project," Leander said patiently, and Rel forestalled Kyale's demand to know why she wasn't told, or asked for her help, by asking, "Where's Jilo?"

"Stayed back to talk to Mondros." That was Liere, coming with Hibern. Lyren-Sartora, standing in a circle of her own friends, flashed a scowl when she saw Liere stand next to Andri and lace her fingers with his.

"Grab your plates," Seshe called.

There were too many of them now for the dining room adjacent to the kitchen, so they'd thrown open the double doors to the parlor that adjoined the dining room, where three unmatching tables had been dragged in, and along the perimeter a lot of cushions scattered for those who didn't mind eating on their laps.

As late arrivals, Hibern and Liere were among the last to get their food. Liere kept Andri by her side, and once they had plates, remembering her earlier resolution, she tried to tow Andri toward Senrid, with the idea of introducing her new beloved to her oldest friend—trailed by Kyale, who admired Liere more than ever.

But Senrid had retreated to the far corner, sitting on cushions with Leander and Arthur. His back was to the room, his head bent as Leander said, low-voiced, "The more I think about it, the queasier I get."

"They just got done with something big," Andri said to Liere after a considering glance. "Let 'em do their after-action talk."

Liere gave in. At least they were all together at last. She and Andri moved away, and when Liere became aware of Kyale at her elbow, she looked for a table with room for three.

"Same," Arthur said to Leander, oblivious to social currents in the room. "I feel like I did when I was small, and jumped into a pond at Roth Drael, thinking it was shallow, and next thing I knew, the water closed over my head. If it wasn't for Hibern, and Detlev I guess backed her, though I didn't see any sign of him, I wonder if we'd all be here sitting around jawing."

Senrid had always known where Liere was. It had been habit, since they first ran through the forest of Drael together years ago. But now that awareness was a distraction it took effort to shut out. It felt like trespass in a way he had never considered — never had the time, or the interest, to consider.

He made an effort and shut everyone out except Leander and Arthur, who embarked on a blow-by-blow recreation of the attack on the portal, as each perceived it.

Senrid remained silent until the end, then said, "What's taking Jilo? The longer he's gone, the more I wonder what we're missing."

At that moment, as it happened, Jilo was directly overhead, sitting on the floor in their room as he recovered from the transfer. He'd collapsed cross-legged, a thin book held against one knee.

He gazed at it, still a little dazed. He opened it, regarded the small, neat handwriting in Chwahir, then closed it and looked around the nearly empty room. Nowhere to stash it. Would he dare to leave it, even to go downstairs? He would not.

He sighed; when he'd first become one of the allies, he'd had to live with Wan-Edhe's old enemies book carried next to his skin. Back to old habits. He lifted the shirt Terry had given him and tucked the book into the waistband of his pants.

He went downstairs, drawn by enticing smells, and considered the range of voices, Rel's deep voice the bass note, and high above that silver-haired princess, what was her name? Kyale.

In the hall he sorted the vocal tones for the high voices of the underaged, then poked his head into a room. There they were, sitting together; his eyes found the neatly clipped black curls of Prince Kessler's boy. Jilo stood in the doorway wondering what he could say, but before he could speak, Dirk glanced up, quick as a lizard.

Jilo admired lizards for their sleekness and their economy of movement; Dirk reminded him even more of one as he slid off the bench while the others kept talking, and came meet to Jilo. He was short and slight, barely reaching Jilo's shoulder, his eyes the same blue as his father's, but the shape of his face was much different than Prince Kessler's.

"You were with Kessler?" Dirk asked in an undervoice.

How did you know? Jilo wanted to ask, but that could wait — he wasn't ready to draw attention until they understood one another. "May I speak to you?" he asked in Chwahir. "It's work."

The word for 'work' in Chwahir is freighted with meaning that even Wan-Edhe had not been able to strip away. The root word appears in compounds such as *honor* and *merit*, and even *palace*.

"Yes," Dirk said. He couldn't be more than eleven, but he, like the others with Dena Yeresbeth, was self-possessed. Jilo had not even known of his existence until recently, but few had, he'd discovered.

They went up to Jilo's room, their steps quiet, and as soon as the door was shut, Jilo turned to face Dirk. "Do you want Chwahirsland? Please tell me now. I don't want a fight. I just want to destroy that lattice ward. All Wan-Edhe's wards."

Dirk didn't react to the abruptness of this question, or plea, though it was the first real conversation between the two of them.

"I don't," he said. They spoke in Chwahir, which neither used around others. "Not mine anyway. If you go by inheritance, Rel would be next in line for the throne, for his mother was my father's elder."

When Dirk spoke about Kessler to others, he called him Kessler, but when speaking the language of his ancestors, he used the Chwahir term for father, which again had connotations that Sartoran and its many descendants didn't.

Jilo let out a short breath, then looked at the floor. "It's probably stupid to ask now. You might feel differently when you're older."

"I might," Dirk said. "It also might be different if you weren't good for the Chwahir. But you are. This is what I think now: I don't want to be a king."

Jilo's mind flickered with memory images of Dirk and his father: *You will be my sword*; Dirk with fox-faced Darian Selenna and with Sveneric. These memories were not his. As usual he didn't question their origin, just assumed they were his own speculations, or reactions to Dirk's tone, his countenance.

Dirk went on, "He said from my earliest memories that I was born to destroy Wan-Edhe and take his throne. I still want to destroy him. But I really don't want his throne. I have not chosen my work yet, but I have a twi, and they are not Chwahir. I want the freedom that I could not have as a king."

Dirk's steady gaze, the mention of his twi, made it clear he had been thinking about these things, just as Jilo had. Maybe even talking about them to his twi; Jilo, ordinarily not a jealous person, envied him that precious relationship.

Jilo sat down on the floor, and Dirk dropped down to face him. "I would give this to you if you did," Jilo said, pulling out the book.

"What is it — oh, I recognize that. I saw him translating it. The old one smelled mildewy. I think it was writ in blood, wasn't it? Venn runes?"

"We called it the blood mage text," Jilo said. "This isn't all of it. I could not read any of the runes, of course, but that book had been considerably thicker." He set down the new one with both hands. "A little while ago, Prince Kessler came to Mondros's, after we broke the portal the Norsundrians were trying to make to the Beyond."

Dirk flashed an impish grin, utterly unlike any expression Jilo could imagine on Prince Kessler's face. He began to comprehend a little: Prince Kessler might have had one intention when he had a son, but that son had grown past that single-minded purpose. The surprise was that Kessler Sonscarna had allowed that to happen.

"I know about the portal," Dirk said. "I got it from Sveneric." Who was in his twi — of course Dirk had learned from them, and through them, the wisdom of their respective parents. It was one of the fundamentals of the twi: a person not only gets the mutual support of one's twi, but potentially all the wisdom of family and ancestors.

"I don't understand Prince Kessler at all," Jilo admitted. "He doesn't offer to help, but he has helped. I thought for a long time he would kill me. *He's* the next in line for the throne, before Rel and you."

Dirk shook his head. "He won't do it. Either thing. He won't kill you, and he won't take the throne of the Chwahir. He tried conquering once, a plan he still believes had the best merit, but he was betrayed by those he trusted most. He says he doesn't understand people. He wants someone to rule who would do it the way he thinks is good. You're that person. He's said it many times."

Jilo blushed. "Never said that to me."

Dirk flashed that grin again. "As I said. He doesn't understand people."

Jilo let out a long breath. "I was alone at Mondros's — the others had all come back here. We were talking about the next step, and suddenly he was there with us. He put this book down on the table, and vanished. We didn't know if it was a challenge or a reward, or a gift, or a threat."

"All of those, I'd guess," Dirk said. "The threat being to Wan-Edhe. What's in it? I'm not really good at magic, not like Sveneric and others. I like martial arts more."

"This is all the spells for the mirror ward binding Narad," Jilo said in a soft, still-stunned voice, the thin book cradled between his long, sensitive fingers. "I was trying for so long to glean these spells. I know enough now to recognize this magic. It'll take work, hard work, to dismantle that mirror ward. But this book will make a lifetime's task *a lot* shorter."

Dirk whistled softly. "I know I won't get good enough to help with that any time soon. If at all. Look, Jilo. When you want to go up against Wan-Edhe directly, I'll do it with you. But the magic end, you've got to see to that."

Jilo bowed.

Dirk bowed right back.

Dirk grinned once more, a quick flash of mirth as he said, "We've nothing to drink to our agreement with, not even water. Let's go downstairs? I left half my dinner, and I know Seshe saved a plate for you."

Fourteen

THAT NIGHT, JILO TOLD Senrid about the book, then showed it to him. Senrid suggested that they ought to show it to Hibern, which they did the following day — to get stonewalled.

Hibern refused to say anything. She was far too loyal for that.

After Kyale had gone to sleep the previous night, Hibern had made a scry stone in order to report to Erai-Yanya, but that conversation had not been a happy one. Hibern would not tell anyone that Erai-Yanya had been worried, perhaps even appalled, that Hibern had been drawn not just to study dark magic, but into so dangerous a project. She had requested Hibern — with all the moral conviction of an order — to resist the temptation to dabble farther in dark magic, which could only lead down a dark path. She was to return to her proper studies.

Hibern looked down at the book, her lips compressed in a line, then walked out, leaving Jilo and Senrid looking questions at one another.

"What did I do?" Jilo asked.

"You didn't do anything," Senrid said. "I suspect someone else objected. This thing is pretty dangerous, after all. Let's not say anything to anybody. I've known Hibern since we were both fifteen-year-old snots who thought we were smarter than everybody else and that we were the only ones who understood the world. Let her say, and do, whatever she needs to say and do."

Jilo accepted that. It wouldn't occur to him to do anything else.

For a few days they pored over the book, Senrid remembering, with no enthusiasm, that sense of almost grasping a concept, to have it slip out of his mind, into a morass of confusion. Jilo, with more experience with ward magic, had grasped the concept of lattices, but each time he tried to explain what he saw, he, too, fell into a morass of stuttered words that never seemed to come to a point.

With a warning singe of hot metal, reminding them just how very volatile this magic was, even though they had not as yet done the smallest spell. Even reading the spells for comprehension seemed to charge the air with potential lightning. They did not dare to attempt any magic. It would surely draw any prowling Norsundrian mages right to them.

Meanwhile, both became aware that the allies were increasingly restless. Senrid was also restless. He'd recovered his strength after a day or two of rest, good food, and sitting there knocking his head against that book. He wanted, very badly, to go home. But no one seemed to know what to do next.

———

A sleet storm swept across the Sartoran continent, driving everyone inside who had an inside to go to. Sveneric sat in the attic of Rel's house with the other youngsters, watching Falinneh of the Mearsieans and Bren of the Sarendans running about from warm spot to warm spot above the firesticks in the rooms below.

"Are you still missing Curtas?" Lyren-Sartora asked. "You can't be missing that horrible brat Noser."

"Him, too. But what he could have been."

She sighed. "Shrimp, you are weird."

Sveneric had been hearing that ever since his group—what Lilah had fondly called the Bits and Pieces, because they were so small, and what Dirk called their twi—had found one another on the mental plane. He found her teasing oddly comforting; it meant nothing had changed, at least in this regard.

"They're going to be coming up for warmups soon," he said, lifting his voice a little.

Falinneh squawked like a chicken, her bright red braids flapping as she hopped back to where she'd been sleeping. Dhana, like a wisp of vapor, leaped and twirled across the expanse as people folded or rolled their bedding and stashed it against the curtain-covered walls.

Lyren-Sartora dusted her hands. "Now I'd better find some work."

"Stay and spar with me," Sveneric said.

"I hate sparring. You know that."

"You need the practice."

"That means you're going to go hard on me. Oh, no. Uh uh. You keep sparring with Dirk—*he's* nearly as good as you are."

"You know it's better to get variety. And I'll match your skill. Just a little faster. What you need is speed. Strength will come. For us both."

Lyren-Sartora heaved a loud, hissing martyred sigh, aware that he was not wrong. She was also aware that he most likely could beat anyone here, maybe even Rel, even without the strength that would come with growing. You wouldn't know it to look at him, he was so weedy, exactly her height. But he hated drawing attention to himself; drawing attention during the bad old days at Norsunder Base when he was little could have gotten him killed.

He had also gotten into some odd habits during, or because of, those days. For example, the first time they actually met face to face, after several years of talk on the mental plane, he said, "What's it *like*, being a girl?"

"What's it like being a boy?" she'd retorted. "It just *is*."

"Not for everybody."

"Then they go to the healers to either fix their head or their body."

She'd hated any hint, no matter how oblique, that she was not as observant as he—learning being in many ways a competition between them all. Except maybe Carl Delieth of Everon. She was so sensitive, so timid. So easily hurt. She hid behind her twin Jessan the way Sveneric hid in plain sight, only there had never been threats in her life. But to her, even loud, sudden noises hurt. Ugliness hurt. Carl was everybody's little sister—even to Yanli, who was younger.

The stairs creaked. As Sveneric had predicted, everyone

was coming up for practice. Sveneric moved to the back (which was the end of the room away from either Andri or Dtheldevor, who traded off leading the warmups) and waited.

Lyren-Sartora hated getting sweaty, and loathed exercise for the sake of exercise, though she adored tumbling and dancing, even running if there was something fun to run to. She appreciated bodies being graceful, like Dhana over there. Even though Dhana wore human form, you could tell she wasn't human by the way she moved, so effortlessly light and fluid. Like birds riding the currents high above, or the play of a porpoise through water and its burst up into the air for no other reason than the sheer joy of being alive.

Sveneric was nearly that graceful when he did the poopsie warmup. But he never did it when others who didn't know his background could see it. Lyren-Sartora had learned it from Mac, but she usually stopped halfway through, before it got too hard.

Dtheldevor called out the count as they swung their arms and twisted. Sveneric's profile was closed off, but then his thought reached Lyren-Sartora: *I'm glad I refused to cut my hair after we left Norsunder. Then, I just wanted to look as different as I could from how we had to be then. But now, I think when I have to disguise, I'm going to be a girl.*

: Disguise? Is that what we'll be doing?

: I don't know about everybody. Detlev warned me that Efael is probably going to give up hunting him soon, and go after me. He thinks if anyone or anything gives away this group, that will happen immediately.

His tone was noncommittal, but Lyren-Sartora's nerves chilled. She didn't bother asking why Detlev hadn't yanked Sveneric out and stashed him somewhere. Maybe he would, though she knew Sveneric would resist. She didn't understand their relationship at all, and no longer tried.

Still, he was telling her for a reason: *If that happens, do you want me to go with you?*

His laughter sun-splashed through her mind, warm and grateful. Rueful, too: *No — every time our eyes met we'd be laughing. Or awkward, if it is too tense to seem a game. I think I need to learn to mimic someone. That will help me be convincing, and make the experiment more interesting. Adam did it once, living under cover as a girl. He said he learned a lot.*

Lyren-Sartora thought skeptically that they wouldn't learn

much since they weren't girls, and they knew it, any more than putting on the robe of the wheelwrights guild made one a wheelwright. But she shrugged that off. *:Kyale*. Lyren-Sartor's thought was both prompt and definite: *Study Kyale and no one would ever question your disguise.*

: But she never comes up here.

: Exactly. She's too prissy for martial arts, though she'll dance through an entire night if she thinks she has the prettiest clothes in the room. That's just the sort of girl you ought to mimic if you're going to fool those horrible Black Knives.

While Lyren-Sartora resigned herself to what she knew she ought to be doing, Senrid had decided the same, and Jilo followed along. He couldn't remember when he'd done any drill last, though once it had been part of his daily routine, a long time ago.

Senrid left his wrist knives in their room, and the two of them climbed up to the attic, which already smelled of sweat and hot wood.

Jilo was used to group drill all in unison — that was the Chwahir way. Senrid had never had group lessons his early years, having had to learn on the sly for survival. Later, it was easier to have the swordmaster come to him. The only time he'd been able to practice in a group was when he went out with the seniors into the plains for the academy summer games. There, he'd enjoyed himself thoroughly.

This situation was so unlike what he was used to that he was distracted by watching everyone else, so he could follow along. The warmup was just familiar enough for him to make false moves repeatedly, thinking he knew what was coming next. He never caught the rhythm, but at least it felt good to get his blood moving again.

They broke to pair up for sparring with swords. Dtheldevor got people put together, then eyed Senrid, and waved him to Andri. "I've heard about you Marlovens. I don't want me chitlins aired. Jilo! Get over here."

Jilo mooched over to the rack of wooden swords with a resigned air as Senrid chose a sword, and inwardly braced for a pasting, as the academy seniors said.

Within three or four exchanges he knew that Andri Elsarion far outclassed him with the sword. But Senrid was experienced enough to also evaluate through the strength of blows the intent behind, and it was equally clear that Andri had not only got his measure, but had adjusted his approach so that he stayed just ahead of Senrid—like a swordmaster. Either he was so supremely confident he did not need to resort to lambasting his partner the way natural leaders often did, to establish a hierarchy, or it was not in his nature.

Senrid relaxed into the sparring, relishing having to exert himself without the gut-clench of a deathmatch, or the prospect of a beating. He was peripherally aware of Dtheldevor and Jilo a few paces away as she yowled, "Move, Jilo, move! Blast and damn, ye still plant yer feet like them stinkin' Chwahir."

"But I am a Chwahir."

A few snickers met this, but otherwise people awaiting their turn watched Andri and Senrid appreciatively. Those with experience saw Senrid mistake a feint for a lunge half a heartbeat before the blunted point of Elsarion's blade flicked him on the ribs, then he pulled the blade up; if you weren't watching it would look as if they'd ended in a draw.

"Pretty," Ellen Warren said, rubbing her callused hands together.

Senrid turned his hand down flat.

"My guess is, the knife is your weapon," Andri said. "Double knives? Your misses are always a matter of length." Two fingers held up to either side at sword length. "In close, you're fast. And fierce. Bet you're good on horseback, where your distance is determined by the animals."

Senrid said, "I've got the basics. No excuse for not being any better than that."

Dtheldevor said over her shoulder, "Senrid, while we got the time, you need to work on the sword if you're gonna be taking on them Norsundrian chum-suckers."

"Why wouldn't we have the time?" Jilo asked, wringing his hand—he'd just dropped his blade.

Dtheldevor frowned, point down. "All I can say is, we better be up an' doin' in a couple weeks—or I'll be. Gonna go crazy if I don't see some action soon!"

"That's right, time to *kill* them," Deon of Sarendan muttered from the side, to a worried glance from Darian Selenna. "Kill them *dead*."

"And what do you think the rest of us feel like doing, knitting booties all winter?" CJ asked, rounding on Dtheldevor, a mouse before a lynx.

Dtheldevor shrugged. "Don't much care what ye think, if

ye sit around doin' nuthin' about it. I'm goin' out to do something—"

"Where shall we collect the remains?" Andri asked. "Has Norsunder set up scribe services?" His tone was just the right balance between joking and sardonic.

Dtheldevor eyed Andri speculatively, but he lounged against the wall smiling, and she gave a sudden laugh. The tension was gone as Andri turned to Rel. "Want a go?"

Rel was a full head taller, and solid muscle. As he chose among the heavier swords, Andri added, "Let me fetch another sword. Maybe a chair or two."

People laughed, but Arthur said, "You don't really do that, do you? Chairs?"

"Inna real fight? Sure." Dtheldevor snorted. "Chairs, tables, plates, whatever's at hand."

"Whatever gets you out alive. I managed to eel out of an ambush by six that my cousin sent as a present," Andri said reminiscently. "Used a bowl of salt. Another time, dried peas."

Dtheldevor waved her blade at Liere. "Let's see what you learnt over on Nightside."

Liere walked over to the weapons rack, but halted mid-stride, one hand out, as everyone with Dena Yeresbeth stiffened, and then, in unison, swiveled, facing east.

Fifteen

IT WAS AS IF winter had formed intent. Not the clean, bright winter of snow and soughing pines, but a lifeless, dead winter of cracked stone and iron-bleak sky. How does one describe an impression for which there are yet no words? A reek that one senses, not smells, an ice-burning glare one flinches away from, a wail of desolation felt in the marrow rather than heard. The acrid taste of poison though there is no substance.

It was the embodiment of threat, and it was seeking.

"Mind-shields," Liere said softly—though there were no enemy ears in that room.

Most of them had already done so; Falinneh flopped to the floor and stuck her fingers in her ears; though the human-adjacent shape-changers she came from did not have Dena Yeresbeth, instinct clamored with danger.

Liere and Sveneric, the most sensitive there, were able to listen passively outside of their shields enough to be aware that the intent was not seeking persons so much as a locale, and both breathed easier when the intent turned northward and away.

"It's gone," she breathed when she was certain they were safe. Or as safe as could be these days.

"Whew!"

"What was that?"

"It felt like a nightmare but I'm wide awake!"

Senrid, who had been stashing his practice sword while Rel chose one, looked up at Rel. "Want a suggestion?"

Rel said, "If you've got one, let's hear it. I have no idea where to do from here."

"Neither do I," Senrid said, as people began stirring, murmuring. Dtheldevor cursing roundly, and Falinneh snickering. "But whatever we decide, it should be sooner than later. This, here, though admirably put together, is an invitation for disaster with all of us conveniently gathered together."

"I know," Rel said.

The next day icy rain thrummed against the windows of Rel's bedroom, but in the corner a fire burned cozily. Atan and Rel sat near it busy with sewing.

Atan had discovered that ever since the morning drills began the Mearsiean girls, except for Seshe, were at best sporadic with certain kinds of chores. Their promise to help with the sewing had lasted as long as the novelty had. With sewing, that was seldom very long. Seshe was the exception, but her sewing was slow and labored when she wasn't coopted for cooking, at which she excelled.

There was no point in complaining. The conviction that the group was going to break up soon manifested in so many ways besides restlessness. Soon they might all be traveling into danger, and there was an increasing chance that none of them would see the others again. Facing such an uncertain future, it seemed ridiculous to squabble over such matters as being behindhand in sewing. Not that there were that many orders for new things — it was mostly mending of winter clothing, in order to eke another year out of otherwise good fabric, a dreary chore at best.

Atan frowned down at her stitchery, thinking about the recent news, for it had reached her ears through Darian Selenna that two of Detlev's boys had died, both deaths war-related. Curtas had been the only one to find, and rescue, Shontande Lirendi, who had subsequently vanished like smoke. A vision of his face and form painted itself inside her head, bringing back the tingle-fire of allure, so familiar, and just as familiar was the conscious effort to dismiss it.

Until Shontande Lirendi came to Eidervaen, her only experience had been with Rel. She'd been comfortable with that—even complacent about the fact that her intimate life was so easy, so manageable.

Then she met Shontande.

There had been one evening spent entirely alone with him, just the two of them, during which she had retained enough sense to realize through the dazzle of his proximity that to break those vows she had so easily and confidently made with Rel and to tangle with Shontande would bind her in a sensory and emotional knot that might take years to unravel. Her responsibilities precluded that freedom.

Rel's dark eyes narrowed in irony. "Let me guess."

She smiled. Of course she'd told Rel everything. "Aren't you glad to find out that Shon is alive?"

"Very. But I was thinking about Detlev."

"Eh."

"Admit it. You thought if he showed up again he'd have some master plan, some whirlwind idea that would blast Norsunder back across time for ever."

"Uhn." Atan knew that she had indeed unconsciously begun to assume just that—not that she was going to admit it out loud. "He did seem so...so omniscient when he was a villain."

"Except he'd gotten himself nipped and switched in the first place."

"Do you think he was a dolt as a young man, then?" Atan laughed softly at the image.

Rel gave his head a shake. "Wasn't he a dyr-wielder? He had to have known they were coming."

"Not necessarily." Atan dropped her hands, crushing the linen under-robe in her lap. "I'll bet he was one of those mages who never remembers anything practical—like shoes when it's snowing, or meals, or noticing when an enemy is stalking you—and didn't know he was trapped until it was too late."

"Somehow that doesn't seem characteristic. It also doesn't figure Siamis in."

Atan shrugged. "He's easy to forget."

"He was twelve."

"That was long ago. I'm more concerned about now. Apparently Detlev helped Hibern and Jilo and the rest keep Norsunder from making a portal, but how long will he persist, and can he win? Whatever the cause, he did lose all those centuries ago. I do not want to have to depend on him; I suspect he hasn't the faintest idea what to do any more than we have."

"I hope you're wrong. Hope we're both wrong." Rel frowned out the fragmented gray sky through the window panes. "Though I don't see how we can win. Every day that passes the news gets worse."

"Set aside Detlev, then, as he's so obviously done to us. There are two things that disturb me. Well, to be more specific, two people."

Rel thought over the past few days and said, "Which squabbles have you been overhearing?"

She gave him a pained smile. "Nobody takes Kyale seriously."

"She doesn't take herself seriously."

"I'd argue with that."

Rel lifted a shoulder. "I don't consider trying to force a storybook version of life onto the world instead of engaging with it serious. When she gets the courage to do that, things might be different."

"I'll agree with that. I believe she frets about small things because at least those can be fixed. And Hibern doesn't fight."

"Hibern." Rel considered the Marloven mage-student, who usually sat at the back of any gathering, calm, austere, her black eyes observant. "She's not been around much."

"Yes. She's angry about what happened in Marloven Hess—and she's angry because the Mage Guild put her out there to defend Shendoral when she knows more about ward magic than Liere, smart as she is, or even most of the senior mages. And I think there is strain between her and Erai-Yanya."

"And your second worry?"

"Deon of Sarendan—"

Her voice suspended suddenly. She had to confess inwardly that the news that one of Detlev's boys had died—no matter which one, weren't they all pretty much the same?—left her largely unmoved. At least he died doing a very good deed, rescuing one of her friends that no one else had been able to get to. But when she thought of Lilah Selenna, dead by a careless and cruel hand, grief wrenched her heart. Lilah's bright laugh, her vivid face, her sense of fun. Lilah had been Atan's companion when she first freed Sartor. And she had been Peitar Selenna's younger sister.

Peitar. There was another cause for grief, for different reasons.

She pushed that old ache away, and said angrily, "It's obscene, how they can kill someone so easily. Worthless, they considered Lilah, because she knew nothing of war, nothing that could help them. From what young Darian picked up by that mental business, it was Darian Irad who'd earned Norsunder's respect, and that by taking out a dozen of them or so before they brought him down. So much *death*. At least he was able to get his wife and children away, I hear." She stopped and shook her head, then dropped her needle in her lap in order to dash away tears. "Ah, I hate Norsunder, I do, but I am more convinced by day that we'll have to think in some measure the way they do before we can be rid of them."

Rel grunted an acknowledgement.

She looked up, her eyes unhappy. "And that will make of us—what?"

"It won't make us warmongers."

"Are you sure?" Atan's mouth twisted. "Rel, I loved those lessons with Senrid. What's more, I was good at it. I guess that comes of years of having to juggle priorities on the run. Isn't that the essence of command?" She picked up her needle again and jabbed it toward the window before beginning the poke-poke pull, poke-poke pull rhythm of needlework. "I find myself lying awake at night, thinking about how, if I could pull Darian Irad's army over from Sarendan, how we would attack communications and supply first, and Rel, I relish those daydreams. So I can scarcely scowl at any of our group for warlike talk without being an almighty hypocrite."

"Maybe. But you're thinking about defense, not fighting for the sake of fighting. Who was it specifically among our merry band was on your mind? Deon?"

"Yes. You noticed as well?"

Rel gave a reluctant nod.

"She doesn't sing any more. She doesn't laugh, except a hard laugh, at cruel jokes about Norsundrians. And the others are clearly worried about her. And she resents it."

"I've seen it," Rel admitted. "She's the one fostering the worst of the restlessness in those who still retain the Child Spell. Lilah was her best friend, her only civilizing influence, for Derek Diamagan told me years ago she was the bloodthirstiest of their little group during Sarendan's troubles."

Tears burned Atan's eyelids afresh. Loss, regret, memories; she looked up at the window, where a brief, watery sunbeam had broken through.

Rel finished off his seam, folded the garment, and laid it aside. "Weather's lifted. I'd better make my rounds, then roust those not on kitchen rotation or out at another job to get started on the afternoon practice."

Downstairs, he grabbed his coat and cane and walked outside, despite the cold. He leaned for a moment on the hitching post, looking westward down the muddy street. Above, gray-blue clouds stretched out in variegated streamers, promising more weather soon. His breath clouded, froze, fell, vanished.

No one, not even Atan, knew how much impending kingship agonized Rel. Logically he knew that his inadvertent position of leadership over the young allies was not some kind of test. As king, he would have Atan's backing, and centuries of custom and sheer habit behind him. Here, he had no authority over anyone.

And yet, he still felt that if he couldn't haul in the reins on the wild ones—if he couldn't find some direction for the lost ones —how could he expect to do his share of ruling over a vast and demanding land like Sartor? He supposed that many of the old aristocrats would expect him to stand around in an embroidered tunic and be a figurehead consort, but Atan didn't want that, and he knew he couldn't endure such a role.

That didn't mean he was fit for the partnership that she seemed to expect.

He knew what lay beneath Atan's sorrow over Lilah's death. She was wrestling with remorse over her having discovered, too late, that Peitar Selenna had loved her. Rel had seen it long before Atan had had any idea; he'd also suspected why Peitar had deliberately ignored warnings on all sides in his mad pursuit of something that didn't even exist. Sometimes Rel wondered if Peitar had committed suicide by Norsundrian.

Rel still endured late-night fits of remorse, thinking that what he'd reported about vagabond magic had contributed. He'd never stop regretting his and Atan's obliviousness at the emotional pain they'd given Peitar, aside from mysterious magical quests.

He looked down at his hands, now tingling and numb at the fingertips, and shook his head. They were the hands of a man, but inside he still felt like a callow youth.

He pulled his coat tight, and bent into the wind to make his rounds. "Warmongers." In truth, he looked forward to losing himself in a long afternoon of fighting competition. It was better than unrepairable regret.

Sixteen

"WAIT. WAIT." FALINNEH BOUNCED on her toes, her thick, wiry red braids smacking her purple shirt. "Let's go back to stenches. I have at least ten good jokes about stinks, and when it comes to The King of the Chwahir—"

"We've heard 'em," four people said at once.

"Then how about my villain play? It fits any villain. We put Llyenthur's name in when he meets the goat, and the goat barfs at the sight—"

"We did that play when we were in Wnelder Vee chasing poopsies," Dhana said. "Nobody laughed but us."

CJ scowled. "Rel said we should try to cheer people up, and after that creepy attack, people seem to be more tense than ever. If we get too picky, then we'll never get anything done."

"You could ask Troy to play," Seshe suggested. "He's really, really good."

CJ bobbed her head. "True. And Dhana can dance. Even grownups like to watch her."

Dhana just sat there—she didn't care who watched her, or if anyone did. If she heard music, she danced. Even if the music was the wind in the trees, or the chuckle of a brook.

"I can sing a song or two," CJ added. "Real songs, not my made-up ones. I noticed nobody except us laughed at 'Oh My

Dear I Lovest Thee, Thy Teeth are as Green as Green Can Be' villain song, any more than they laughed at Falinneh's play. I may as well save it for people with taste."

"True, true," Falinneh agreed.

"We can go first. Many people feel shy about going first," Seshe suggested. "Once the atmosphere is easier, then ask others if they'd like to do something."

They all agreed to that, and split up.

"Celebration at sundown!" The Mearsieans went around the rest of the day reminding people, whether they wanted to hear it or not. By the time the light began to dim, Rel's house filled with the delicious smells of apples baked in cinnamon, and savory freshwater fish over rice.

The rest of the underage inhabitants helped the Mearsieans by setting up the attic. They ran along the floor pushing towels, and when the floorboards gleamed, they laid out the bedding seam to seam so that everyone could sit comfortably. In supplying the kitchen, Rel had brought in a variety of plates and bowls, and eating utensils from various directions — eating sticks from the north, the tiny-tined forks of the Colendi, which were almost eating sticks, forks, spoons. Many just ate with their knives, scooping food into their mouths from the lip of their bowl.

Troy — Morgeh Troiad of Wnelder Vee, the king who wanted to be a bard — had been staying with Dtheldevor's gang, who were old friends, Dtheldevor's primary hideout being on one of the hundred tiny islands off Wnelder Vee's coast.

As soon as everyone was served, Troy set aside his plate and tuned his tiranthe as his food got cold — not that he noticed. From tuning to strumming, then he played with consummate skill, surprising some, as he usually looked half asleep. His voice was mellow and pleasant, ringing when a song called for it. Then CJ, feeling a sense of responsibility about those who were ambivalent about performing, stood up and sang. To the astonishment of many, she actually had a clear, pretty voice.

She stuck to her conviction, leaving out her own compositions in favor of traditional Mearsiean ballads, in which traces of Sartoran triplets could be heard.

As she sang, Rel circled around and poured a dollop of expensive distilled liquor in all the cups and mugs of those over sixteen. Rel was not much of a drinker, but he and Atan had talked it out, thinking that a bit of whisky in the coffee would give everyone some added warmth, and maybe take the edge off the ever-present stress, at least for an evening.

Senrid didn't notice what Rel was doing until he smelled the heady aroma as the liquor plopped into his coffee. He was about to turn down the whisky, but Rel was already moving on, leaving Senrid staring down at his mug in disgust. He loathed the flavor of anything fermented or distilled, no matter what the ingredient. And he had spent too many years being vigilant to ever want to feel the effects of drinking.

But he also didn't want to insult Rel. Already people were praising whatever it was in the cups. He took a cautious sip, and grimaced. The excellent coffee, which came straight from the Ghost Islands, was ruined by the nasty flavor of the whisky, which burned his throat going down. But then the warmth lingered on his tongue and in his chest, a warmth that was not due to the coffee. The taste was still vile, but he had to admit that the aftereffect was not entirely loathsome.

Then the rowdier of the Sarendan gang joined Falinneh (who could not resist sharing her humor) and the company was subjected to "The Defeat of Imry Llyenthur by a Snail, a Goat, and a Pig" by actors who were their own best audience; halfway through several whispered conversations had begun in the corners of the room, but the performers didn't care. They were all laughing much too hard to notice.

Wondering when that would end, Senrid did not cover his cup when Rel came around with a second helping of the whisky.

When the skit ended amid polite applause and an increase in the conversations, Troy improvised on his tiranthe. His fingers were nimble, the tune a series of glissandos in half-step chords that sounded like falling leaves.

Dhana of the Mearsieans liked that sound. She listened, eyes half-shut, then rose and whirled to the middle of the floor, where she began to dance. Arrestingly graceful, she commanded all the attention once again, some perceiving the charisma of other beings in human form, and one or two pondering, in silence, the ineffable freedom of innocence.

Dhana whirled about the room, leaping, dipping and fluttering her hands evoking autumn leaves, until Troy strummed a last chord. Then she dropped her hands and walked back to sit with her friends, acknowledging with a one-shoulder shrug the storm of applause.

Deon and Falinneh promptly got up and did a parody of Dhana's dance, while murmurs of conversation rose among the older ones.

Senrid had ceased wincing after each sip. The numbing effect of whisky was actually...not so bad. Numbing and warm. Not bad at all.

By then Dtheldevor, the young-old privateer captain, had had plentiful recourse to her own jug. Though she'd never aged past puberty she'd been raised by her privateer (some said pirate) father on fermented drinks and had never seen any reason to stop.

She was therefore quite jolly when she stood up, hefted her jug, then roared, "Play me a sea tune, Troiad, an' I'll make up a verse t'Detlev's nose, see if I don't."

"Ahem!" Falinneh said loudly, catching more attention than Dtheldevor had, and many glances were sidled Sveneric's way.

He looked like he was on the verge of laughter — which escaped him when Dtheldevor clapped a hand to her forehead. "Well, damme hide!" she bellowed. "The ol' soulsucking rumsnugger is on our side, I keep forgettin'!"

The rest of her group tugged her to sit down again.

Liere Fer Eider stood up, and said," How about this one?" She sang a ballad about Peddler Antivad that was popular pretty much over the entire Sartoran continent.

Rel made his rounds again, Senrid's cup was empty of coffee, but he still held it up, and this time got a finger of straight whisky.

When the song ended there was enough applause to inspire Liere to sing a love ballad she'd learned on Geth-deles. It was a plaintive melody, different to the ear then what many were used to; she sang it straight to Andri, and when it was over, Kyale Marlonen cooed, "How I adore romantic songs. That's what we should do, more romance, though I wish I had someone singing to me."

"Ba-a-a-a-r-f," Deon of Sarendan mooed, dragging the word out. She was the smallest person in the entire group, with short, silky dark hair and a diminutive form, but she was the fiercest.

Liere sat down again at Andri's feet, the reflected fire leaping in her golden eyes. Andri's fingers drifted down to brush the curve of Liere's neck, a gesture of appreciation for the intent of her song, and of rueful sympathy at its rude reception, more than a public display of lust, but Deon brayed, "B-a-a-a-rf!" again. "Mush!"

A debate broke out about what sort of song ought to be sung next.

"I ain't sayin' roh-mance is bad," Dtheldevor declared, drowning out everyone else. "What I'm sayin' is, this ain't no time for roh-mance."

"Agreed!"

"Ah, sit down, it's just a song!"

CJ eyed Atan, trying to get up the nerve to offer one of her made-up songs about Norsunder, when everyone jumped.

WHANG-G-G-G!

At the far end of the practice weapons rack hung four swords that Rel had brought just in case.

Two of these swords clashed together, the ring fading into shocked silence.

All gazes snapped to Senrid, silhouetted by the fire, except for the light reflected off his shirt and running up the steel in either hand.

Everyone stilled, except for the snapping fire. Hibern, who also had been enjoying the whisky, knelt down, pulled a stool over, and tapped a galloping drumbeat on it. Troy picked up the beat and enthusiastically drummed on the floorboards as Senrid tossed the swords down in another ringing clang, east-west over north-south—old Iasca over northern Venn—and then began a quick-stepping, whirling dance as dust spiraled into the air, glowing briefly in the fire. His heel-strikes beat a counterpoint to the rumbling drum beat. His hands arced one at a time over head, sometimes both at once, other times fists at his belt. No one could look away.

Some watched open-mouthed, dizzy with admiration, others with narrowed eyes and thoughtful brows. Only Leander suspected he was witnessing at last what he had seen oblique references to in archives, but had no idea why Senrid would choose to perform it outside his kingdom, which had to be an absolute first.

It ended as suddenly as he began, and then Senrid ducked back into the crowd, to be surrounded by Dtheldevor's privateers and the wilder allies, who demanded to be taught that dance at once.

"Now *that* I call purty!" came Dtheldevor's loud voice.

"You gotta teach me that!"

Lisdan to an island on the world Geth-Deles

Later on that evening, Hibern paced back and forth in Atan's room over the tailor shop. "Of course I'll tell you what it was, it was a declaration of war."

"That was obvious." Atan smiled faintly. "But you drummed for him, so I assumed your wholehearted approval."

"As a gesture against Norsunder? Yes. It's more than mere bravado, but so hard to explain. For one thing, Marlovens customarily only do the sword dance for themselves. I'm Marloven enough to support him, though I can't even begin to imagine what Senrid meant by doing it here." Hibern hit her fist against the window sill. "Maybe I drummed for Senrid because of my own private...I don't want to say war. I know I'm strong enough to help, but something keeps the senior mages from taking me seriously. Especially the Sartoran guild mages—and yes, I know, their real trust is reserved for those who went through their training. Except they accept Tsauderei and Erai-Yanya—"

Hibern stopped, face canted upward, her dark eyes unseeing. "I will shut up. In my own mind my grievance is paramount, but each word I speak out loud just sounds like whining."

"It has to be galling, distrust from our own side," Atan said, relieved that Hibern at last was talking.

Hibern's eyes widened. "Yes! Our own side! My question is, is it something in my conduct, some essential insight I'm lacking, that keeps them seeing me as a threat, even though I've explained and explained that I studied dark magic only to know what to fight against? I am far more trained in light magic—Erai-Yanya tells me I know more magic than many of the lower-level masters in both schools, and yet I'm still a journeymage."

"I wish I could answer that."

"I know you can't," Hibern said. "And I thank you for listening to me rant when you've done nothing wrong. Maybe the real answer lies in the fact that I must seek it myself." Her eyes narrowed. "As I shall."

At the other end of the hall, Senrid was already regretting his gesture, as the world revolved faintly and the taste of whisky soured on his tongue.

He'd had to get away from the amazement, the questions, even the gawking admiration. It all made him sick with self-loathing. It had to be the liquor; he would never have done that if Rel hadn't put that damned stuff in the coffee. No, Rel had put it there, but Senrid had poured it down his gullet.

Transfer magic, whished the air around him, and he whirled his back to the corner, fingers going to his wrists—but he'd put his knives in his pack with his coat for the afternoon practice. "Detlev," Senrid said on an exhaled breath.

Detlev said, "Let's talk." He touched Senrid's shoulder and shifted them both.

It was a long transfer, yet somehow it was only slightly disorienting, not the usual wrench. Senrid thought, there's one benefit of being drunk—not feeling transfer malaise.

He did not recognize his surroundings. Here it was day, and the quality of the sunlight reminded him vaguely of Geth, the setting a springtime glade. The ghostly shadow of a three quarters moon sat atop the blue horizon—the ocean. No humans in sight, in earshot, even within reach of mind.

Detlev sat on a convenient stone, his fingers flipping something that gleamed with whitish silver highlights. He said, "Ilerian is trying more and more damaging magic to get armies across."

Information. Senrid was aware of the need to act, settling his emotional turmoil like scorched ground under snow. That was followed by as bleak an insight as he'd ever reached: this sense of purpose, this relief from the agony of loss, was probably one of the prime motivations behind the lure of war.

"And so we have very little time for our own concerns," Detlev said. He looked tired, but alert. Very alert. "And one of mine is you."

Senrid glanced away, and then forced his attention back. That cooling snow—it was too expedient. "Ah. This sense of calm, is it dyranarya trickery? That's a dyr you have there, isn't it?"

For answer Detlev flipped the gleaming thing through the air. Senrid caught it, and looked down at the round disc of not-quite-metal. He hadn't seen one for years—since he'd carried one for Liere, when they first met. When Liere was an earnest ten-year-old bearing the weight of the world on her scrawny shoulders, and Senrid, fifteen and newly king, had rejected the world.

How much they both had had to learn! He banished the memories as he stared down at the dyr. This one was a different size and shape from the one he remembered: it was round like the other, but curved, like a very shallow bowl, fitting into one's palm. It looked a little like winter ice, or like thin-carved marble with strong sunlight behind it. Despite his words, he knew that the peculiar sharpening of sensation—of awareness—that he felt was no trickery, that intense magic was somehow concentrated in material form here.

An impulse to laugh seized him. All those wars over the supposedly dark-warped dyra in the past, all that had to have been a ruse, a feint. Dark magic could never control whatever essence existed here. And Detlev had to have known it—which left one wondering why he had let Norsunder's Host believe he could.

"We are on a Geth-deles island," Detlev said, "because any use of that anywhere on Sartorias-deles would bring the Host running."

"Is it always this coin shape? I don't remember the convexity to the other one."

"The shape can be anything. I find that one convenient, because I never liked wearing jewelry, but my clothing always has pockets."

Laughter trembled in Senrid's gut, this time at the absurdity of practical considerations in the midst of raging battle. Danger. Anguish. And out it came, the question that had always been foremost in mind. "Erdrael. On the cliff above the Pass. Was that you?"

"It was."

"Then it was you, throwing us off-world, and then me, specifically, to Puddlenose and his off-world friend?"

"You needed a lesson in perspective, especially after that reckless magic battle you got into."

Senrid shut his eyes, remembering all the agonizing over that incident, then he was right back on that cliff. "But that Norsundrian battalion. That was not actually yours?"

"No. Your uncle made a deal with an ambitious commander named Baunik, and as you know, the King of Perideth granted them permission to hide within his border.

You know the justifications."

"Hatred," Senrid said. "Which is how I felt about Norsunder. You didn't need to force me to hate them more than I already did. Your lesson in power was a lesson in the reality of war. Yes?"

"It was indeed."

"Because..."

"Because you were too ready to tread down Ivandred's path."

Senrid recoiled, then comprehended Detlev's tone. "Wait, that was you, wasn't it? You were there. You knew him."

"I know him, yes. By the time he began to understand the wider consequences of what I showed you that day, it was too late for him to stop. And Norsunder was watching."

"My uncle's scouts. They all disappeared. Was that you, too?"

"No. Mostly locals. You know how much they were hated, as your uncle used them entirely for spying on his own people. Siamis took out the two assigned to assassinate you. Back to you. At every crisis of your life," Detlev observed, "you've always surprised me. You've always been faster than I expected."

Detlev's dispassionate voice was never effusive, a tone Senrid had distrusted all his life. The effect of the whisky had worn off, the dyr enhancing his sensitivity to sounds, to the scent of the air and its feel on his skin. To awareness—in this case, a sense of truth in what he heard. But the feeble spark of pride did not last longer than a heartbeat. "I'm sure you mean well, but if I'm understanding you right, in your near omniscience you manufactured your own defeats. For whatever reason. You can't possibly understand what it means to lose everything. Every..." He looked away. "Thing," he repeated under his breath.

"Think again, Senrid."

Senrid glanced up—and then remembered that Detlev had, according to all the stories, been there at the Fall of Sartorias-deles nearly 4800 years ago.

"Been there," he repeated, trying to recollect the scarce facts—all of which seemed to contradict the others. "I don't even know what that means. Some records say you betrayed the world and it was lost, others say you were forced into Norsunder and the world was lost."

Detlev said, "Simply stated, I lost everything. And everyone, except one nephew. Though I scarcely knew him, as we were ten years apart, I had to go get him. I began from there."

Begin with the fundamentals, Keriam had taught Senrid from his earliest years. Figure out what you have, what you need to do, and do it. In those days, the goals had been clear: learn to defend himself, and study magic.

Detlev had just repeated his own fundamentals, stripped of emotion—and of detail. But Senrid knew enough of the detail by the outcome: Detlev had rescued Siamis, the cost being himself. Far worse odds than those stacked against Senrid right now.

He turned a questioning gaze to Detlev, who said, "What I have to offer is lessons in Dena Yeresbeth coinherence. You may judge whether or not it's relevant."

Senrid pinched his fingers between his brows. Of course it would be. Detlev's motivations might be obscure, but you couldn't call him frivolous. "All right," he said, aware that the dyr's sense of tranquil detachment, of release from heartache, was all real, but it was also transitory. He wanted to know what to do, so he could do it. But old habit made him flippant about what concerned him closely. "Give it to me. Then tell me how your lessons will make everything right."

"I can't," was the imperturbable answer, and then arrowed straight to what Senrid could not bear to voice. "As well you know. Matters of the heart are seldom logical, nor are they controlled by pretending that there are rules, though various social and cultural forms make the attempt. There is a reason why such things show up most often in the various arts as flame—the two share so many similar qualities."

He paused. Senrid opened his hand, accepting that much as true.

"You've had no family to serve as model, or to answer your questions. Here are some basic truths of which you are probably already aware. Grief is real. Surely you have discovered by now, after your recent experiences chasing Imry Llyenthur, that to dismiss it as mere inconvenience is to force it into another form, usually rage. The only advantage to rage is that it gives more pain than it gets, and one doesn't have to notice that the grief is still there. But it is still there. And retains the power to erupt at unexpected times."

Senrid took a breath, and then another, and then the

question wrung itself out of him, "So what do you do about the pain?"

Detlev began to speak, then his head angled sharply up. Senrid recognized that look: tracer spell.

Kessler appeared. He gave them that strange humorless smile of his. "It is as well you did not ward me," he said. "I owe you a warning, which I will give you now. I have almost finished warding Sartorias-deles."

"The Host have withdrawn to Norsunder?"

"No. They are all out except for the one called Theronezhe, who returned to sulk after the exercise at Ralanor Veleth. When I finish this ward, they will have no access to the Beyond, them to return, or him to get out."

"You know what you're doing?"

"Yes," Kessler said, smiling again. "You have a very short time while I finish the binding." And he vanished.

Seventeen

Lisdan to Colendi Border

ONE THING HIBERN WAS certain of: that miasma, wide-spread and terrifying as it felt, was the magical register of a single person. For two days, Hibern had tried to discuss it with fellow mages, but Arthur and Leander knew nothing beyond the fact that Norsunder was trying something new and terrifying.

After dinner, Atan said much the same. Hibern left her and went in search of Liere. She heard the soft murmur of her voice in the parlor, but she halted a step from the door when Kyale's high, clear voice reached her. Not everything—Kyale seemed to be trying to keep her voice down—but enough words could be made out: Kyale was detailing the loss of Marloven Hess to Liere.

"... and then I tried illusion magic, *my* kind of magic, you know, bringing up water..."

Hibern backed away. Kyale couldn't help but make herself the center of any story—Hibern had known that since they first met, when Senrid was trying to recover his throne from the Regent—but Hibern could not face this reminder that she ought to have been in Marloven Hess. If she had known. Instead of being stuck off protecting Shendoral, which didn't need protection, or showing off in retaliation by adding wards to the already well-warded Tower of Knowledge.

She would not have saved Marloven Hess if she'd gone there instead of where she'd been sent. She knew that already. The magic battle would have worsened. But she could have relieved Senrid enough for him to save his child...

She kept backing away, then prowled restlessly. At least Senrid didn't seem to be around to blunder into that version of what he surely did not want to hear. He'd vanished altogether—no one knew where he was. Hibern wandered around the house, which had seemed so very large compared to the three small rooms at Roth Drael where Hibern had been living for all her apprenticeship. Now somehow it was too small.

She couldn't let the subject go. She'd sensed a familiarity to that miasma, one she'd encountered in the magic-battle over Chwahirsland's capital. Wasn't knowing who your enemy was an important part of figuring out how to defend against them?

Hibern loved research—and she also found irresistible the urge to prove herself. That urge had been behind the ward she'd laid over the Tower of Knowledge in Eidervaen, except that she would not find out if any Norsundrians had been transferred to Shendoral. Nor what the senior mages thought of her excellent and elegant ward, if any had dared to sneak back into the city.

She needed to prove herself some other way, and one thing she was very good at was research and investigation. Why not do a little of that now? She hesitated; nighttime was not optimal for much besides staying indoors, but when she tested wards, she discovered that all the transfer wards were down. Someone, somewhere, was fighting the good fight!

That was practically an invitation to do a little preliminary investigation.

The miasma had come from the east, and from what little she'd gleaned, the speculators agreed that it hadn't been far off. Melire was a midland plain, its border rivers. If Norsunder was looking for a wide-open space for forcing a rift to the Beyond, the land either side of the river would be ideal: Melire on one side, Colend on the other.

Hibern even knew a convenient Destination alongside the river—she could start from Wilderfeld, where the alliance had been born.

She transferred, forcing herself off the open Destination as transfer reaction jolted her. When it faded, she ghosted between dark-windowed buildings to peer into the town square.

There was Wilderfeld Scribes and Messengers, the sign blurred by arrows. Someone had been using it for target practice. The garden was trampled, the plants in the window boxes dead and desiccated. The double doors stood open, golden light streaming out, turning the purple Adrani coats on a pair of warriors to dull gray. One hitched a saddle over his shoulder as he listened to the other, who stood with one booted foot propped on the bench where the family used to sit. She was drinking something out of a fine porcelain cup that Hibern recognized from the days when Thad and Karhin had brought Colendi delicacies upstairs.

Hibern's eyes lifted to Karhin's room; heads bobbed back and forth. A guffaw rang out in the cold air, followed by a crash and tinkle. Not from the warrior at the bench. She set the cup aside, as one who recognized the value of such things, and left it there as she joined the other in walking toward the actual scribe hall part of the building — which, Hibern saw, was now being used as a stable.

For a painful heartbeat she debated running across the square to rescue that cup now sitting on the arm of the bench, but what would she do with it? Karhin was forever gone beyond caring. Thad was somewhere in hiding.

Hibern turned away, disgusted with herself. There was no purpose in coming to this square, except to hurt herself. She ran until she left the little town behind, and she could smell the river.

She made her way down the stone steps toward the riverbank, sorting for traces of that powerful magic. It was these traces she wanted to sift for possible identity, which no one seemed to be able to do. Or they did not dare risk proximity.

And that made sense. There were personal tracers and wards against Tsauderei, Igkai, Erai-Yanya, and every other mage of note. None for her, which was her advantage. Advantage! It was almost an insult, but she may as well use it to explore —

A quiet step caused her to lift her head sharply, hand ready for her transfer. But the hand dropped when she saw a morvende walking in the moonlight, as though enjoying the quiet waters of the river.

He probably didn't even know about the —

"You are interesting," he said in a soft, melodious voice.

Hibern looked up into a beautiful morvende face dominated by light eyes as long, elegant fingers took her shoulder in a merciless grip, and she understood in that moment that she had been lured so subtly she had not been aware.

She tried to wrench free, but the grip tightened excruciatingly as the morvende lifted his head, his long white hair rippling in the wintry breeze. "Kessler Sonscarna is moving. You must wait until I have time for you."

He lifted his other hand, one forefinger pushing her forehead. A pulse of ice-burn, then darkness seized her, hurling her out of the world and time.

Eighteen

Lisdan - Melire

"... HE'S CLOSING OFF THE world. He said it would be soon," Dirk finished, miming a tiny sandglass with thumb and forefinger.

Senrid was back, wondering what to say — but as soon as he joined the group crowded in the parlor and spilling into the hallway, he overheard Dirk. Relieved, he backed against a wall to listen.

"The wards against transfer are gone," Leander said.

"Risking a long-distance transfer might be dangerous," Atan cautioned. "Norsunder's mages know the wards are gone, and they won't be sitting on their hands right now. Surely they are renewing tracers and traps. You could get caught mid-transfer."

Those who knew transfer magic turned to one another, wondering if they dared — but where would they go? Their homes were occupied, if not destroyed altogether.

Leander looked for Arthur to ask his opinion, but couldn't find him, or Hibern. He was about to go to the tailor shop to check when Arthur came downstairs, leading an unfamiliar young woman with wideset gray-blue eyes and dark hair.

Arthur said, "This is Caris-Merian Rhoderan, from Geth-Deles. I've been worried about her since Roth Drael was attacked."

"Thank you," Caris-Merian said, her Geth accent strong. "It was a bad hiding place. I did not know where else to go."

"I'm sorry I couldn't get to you sooner," Arthur said. "And I'm very sorry that our world's troubles put you in danger. Should we try to send you back to Geth-deles?"

"Don't risk it," Atan said from the bottom of the stairs. "Kessler's spell is a world-wide ward, which he is casting now."

"You could be trapped in it," Leander added.

Caris-Merian looked at the floor. Though she professed to be a magic student, and was one, she was here in this world for two reasons. The first, she had failed at: finding out the truth about a younger brother who might have been stolen away; the second she hoped to accomplish, which was to kill her brother's murderer. She would not leave until she had achieved justice for Les.

"I will wait," Caris-Merian said, and Atan offered to give her a tour, after murmuring to Rel's private ear that he probably should circulate and warn people not to transfer just because the wards were briefly down.

Rel began to make his rounds, but discovered shortly that the allies were coming and going so much that he encountered several people three or four times, while not being able to find others.

He finally gave up, suspecting that some were using hoarded transfer tokens to check on, or fetch, friends. He wondered if he would see any of them back.

The first to show up on his own was Puddlenose of the Mearsieans, a tall young man just out of adolescence, having released the Child Spell at last. He was tall and bronzed and fit, as those who wandered tended to be, his expression good-natured in a square face. He wore his thick sun-streaked brown hair neatly tied back instead of shaggy as had been his habit, but the grin quirking his mobile mouth, the humor in his gaze, made it clear that he was in all essentials the breezy person who lived for practical jokes as well as adventure—who managed to make his insult of a name into a thing of pride,

"It worked," was the first thing he said when he dashed in the door. "It finally worked." He held up a transfer token that Clair had given him, using CJ as transfer Destination.

"It won't for long," Leander warned before Rel could speak.

"That's all right—I came to tell CJ and the others that Captain Heraford has the *Tzasilia* right off the coast that way." Puddlenose pointed to the north. "I thought I was going to have to hoof it both ways."

Jilo emerged from behind Rel. "Off the coast of Chwahirsland?"

"No—we're not that crazy, not with them attacking shipping right and left in the strait." Puddlenose grimaced. "Sorry, Jilo. I know it's not your fault. Captain Heraford lies off the coast of Erdrael Danara, his old cruising grounds. There isn't an inlet he doesn't know."

Jilo's head dropped, then he said, "If you go back that way. Could I go with you?"

"Of course!" Puddlenose lifted his voice, looking around at faces familiar and unfamiliar. "I'm also supposed to remind you all that Mearsies Heili is warded from Norsunder. They can't get in. And they've tried."

Atan and Rel looked at one another from opposite sides of the main hallway. "That's what we should consider as a next step? That magic attack has me worried. We know it was located in this region, though not why. If it recurs, it could be they are closing in on us."

"Using Mearsies Heili as a fallback is a good idea, though an arduous journey, Mearsies Heili being on another continent off the far side of this one."

Puddlenose shrugged. "As I just said, you can swing a hammock on the *Tzasilia*. Clair wants the Mearsieans to come home, but you're all welcome."

Dtheldevor elbowed her way to the center of the group. "An' that's what I say, too. Me and my crew, we're gonna get Sharly and Sidres." She named the two centaurs in her crew, who were hiding in the woods a day's travel to the south, centaurs not being native to this continent, though common enough in the wilds of the far north. "It's been good ta see yez all, but it's past time to be fightin' them fart-sniffers on the water, before they take over the seas, too."

Everyone began talking then, striving to be heard.

Senrid ducked, sidestepped, and squeezed his way to Dtheldevor, who looked at him in some surprise, as they seldom had anything to say to the other outside of the practices upstairs. "You gotta teach me that purty dance," she said.

"Never mind that. If you really want to strike at Norsunder, there are some people you could contact. There's a secret rescue ring that is so far confined to land. They could use sea transport, I believe."

"That would be me!" She thumped her chest.

Senrid told her where Remalna lay; not unexpectedly, Dtheldevor was utterly ignorant of land borders, except in a general way, but she was well acquainted with ports and harbors. "I know who to go to first," she exclaimed. "If anyone is a part o' secret rescue runs it's Ma Lenta, the best smuggler I ever met. Though she's in Port o' Jaro. But her sister is down there in Ela. Good idea!" She whacked Senrid on the back, nearly knocking him into the wall, then charged up the stairs three at a time, bellowing for her crew to pack their dunnage.

Senrid ran his hand along the dusty window sill. There you go, Vidanric. A maritime contact. It was the best Senrid could do. He rubbed his temples again, wondering if this pressure in his head was due to the dyr or to the liquor. Maybe both, or maybe there really was some threat building. That miasma again? But it was different this time. More focused; he refused to lift his mind shield to test it, but all his instincts warned him that *something* sought him.

The reason struck without warning midway through that night, when Kyale Marlonen let out a shrill scream. People woke in time to see a diminutive, silver-haired figure flit down the halls in a long white nightgown, shrieking "Senrid! Senrid! Make it stop!"

It wasn't Senrid but Leander who caught hold of her, grabbing her chin to force her head up. As lamps lit, throwing dramatic shadows in angles from doorways, her wide eyes searched sightlessly, then caught Liere's steady gaze as she joined Leander. "Liere, help me!"

Kyale sagged against Liere as the latter reached mentally, warding Kyale in the mental realm from a derisive intent too skilled to reveal identity.

But it now had hers.

Then an attack struck them with the force of a hurricane. Senrid, Liere, and Kyale, squarely in the center of the attack, endured the worst of it: a hurricane in the real world is quiet at the center, but in the mental realm, the eye is the focus.

Liere protected Kyale as time suspended. Maintaining his

shield took all Senrid's concentration, and his strength, until it ended abruptly.

Those with Dena Yeresbeth appeared in various states of undress, Andri with a blanket yanked around him, David of the poopsies appearing out of nowhere in just trousers, Sveneric buttoning his shirt as he soberly listened to all the questions everyone asked and no one listened to long enough to answer.

"They've found us?"

"Who's they?"

"Does it matter? They'll be—"

"Where did you come from?" Rel asked David.

"MV, Roy, and I have been guarding this city's outer perimeter," David said. "Since he has night duty, I was in my bedroll," he added apologetically, indicating his lack of shirt.

Kyale collapsed against Liere, clutching at her and sobbing, "I'm sorry, I'm sorry."

To the sensitive ear, Kyale's sobs were a bit too forced, as though she stood on a stage; beneath the fright she was enjoying being the center of attention as she clung tightly to patient Liere. It was clear that Liere was Kyale's latest crush; Kyale liked men or women, as long as they were beautiful, preferably titled or famous, and nice to her. Liere was all three.

Liere said kindly, "Whoever that was tried names of people." She glanced up in question.

Senrid finished the thought. "People close to me, since he, or she, couldn't get at me." Instinct insisted the mental attacker was a man, but he couldn't be sure. What he could be sure of was that he was done here. "Did they get a location? Where's Hibern? She ought to be able to help."

"I haven't seen her since dinner." Liere shut her eyes, sorting the impressions she'd gained from Kyale's genuine panic. "And no. No location," she said at last. "Kyale's focus was too narrow. All they'll know is that the two of you are together—"

The air around them appeared to freeze, and then to ripple, or shudder. A moment of vertigo seized them all: arms came up to stabilize balance, pupil-wide eyes darted from side to side, mouths opened.

Everyone stilled.

The world stilled.

"What was *that*?" Kyale asked—still clutching Liere.

"I don't know."

Sveneric lifted his chin, and spoke to be heard: "The world is closed off."

Dirk, standing beside him, said, "Norsunder can't get to the Beyond now, and their armies can't get here."

"Who did it?" Leander asked.

"Kessler has been working on that spell for a long time," Dirk said.

Everyone stared consideringly at the two boys of famous — infamous — fathers.

Then they all began talking at once, until Rel waved for silence. "One at a time, if you have something useful to contribute." His deep, booming voice effectively drowned the chatter.

This was it—Senrid could leave with a clear conscience, having kept his promise. "I do," he said. "Maybe. Norsunder might be cut off from the Beyond, but the ones left here are going to come hunting for Kyale and me. Leander as well, most likely; anyone who'd attack Kyale in order to find me would know brother and sister are probably together. That makes me a target. Leander, we need to get out of here."

There was a general movement toward the bedrooms, with many backward looks and pauses for comments and questions as people went to get dressed and pack their things. CJ and Seshe arrived, hand in hand, eyes anxious, having run all the way from the tailor shop. Falinneh told them what had happened as Dhana stood against the wall, eyes mostly shut, face pale — she longed for a body of water to slip into.

Sveneric remained where he was, an island in a sea of movement and muttered wonder and exclamation. Nearby, Deon of Sarendan argued shrilly with Bren and Innon, who were kind of like brothers, or uncles, or cousins, to Darian Selenna, Sveneric's first friend outside Detlev's boys.

"But we're the Sheridan Brothers," Bren was saying, his freckled, skinny arms held tight against his scrawny body, his tilted eyes squinted with misery. "We gotta stay together."

"No, we don't," Deon stated. She was smaller, resembling Bren, her cousin, only in the bony shape of her face. "No. We. Don't. I *always* wanted to join Dtheldevor's gang, for good. You all *know* that. Even before Derek's revolution. Here's my chance."

"But I get sick on ships," Bren said unhappily. "Why don't you come with us? Darian, didn't you say we could visit the morvende in the mountains? Deon, you'd like that."

"I'd like fighting Norsunder on the seas more," Deon said, and added fiercely. "I want to kill Norsundrians. Not fool them. Kill, and kill, and kill, until I get to the one who killed Lilah!"

"Norsunder's recruiting, I'm sure. You're sure to enjoy being on a death squad," Dirk said, looking disgusted.

Small, quiet Darian Selenna took in Deon's stubborn stance, then said in an undervoice to Bren, "I'll talk to her with things are quieter."

They wandered off, tense voices murmuring. Watching them was the person Arthur had just brought. Sveneric's attention flicked to her. To him she appeared to be an older girl, or young woman—he couldn't tell the difference—wide-set gray-blue eyes, black hair, broad forehead that called the Dei family to mind, though her accent was definitely Geth. Rare in Sveneric's life had he seen such concentrated hatred.

Equally rare had he seen someone so effectively wipe it from their demeanor, the moment she was aware of notice. She was too quick to block him for him to discern the intent, except that it was personal.

Sveneric turned away thoughtfully, to find Dirk wanting to talk to him.

A few paces away, Senrid kept trying to get upstairs to retrieve his pack, but people kept stopping him, either to ask questions or to tell him what they thought everyone ought to do. To the former, he mostly said (truthfully) "I don't know," and to the latter, "Why don't you talk to Atan and Rel?"

When, as usual, the response was, "Because everyone else is bending their ears," he sidled away—until Leander caught his arm, and said, 'You'll want to hear who's making death pacts."

"Yes," Senrid said, turning back.

"What are death pacts?" asked Zairna Raadi. He was another off-world mage student who mild, bookish Arthur had risked his life to locate and fetch. Zairna was as pale-skinned as a morvende or a Chwahir, cornsilk hair parted down the middle and sweeping over his ears, nearly hiding the gems he wore in his lobes.

His light eyes flicked to David as he—nearly lost in a shirt borrowed from Rel—said, "Mutual death pacts. In case someone ends up mindripped by Norsunder, and sent back forced to do their bidding."

Arthur said, "Started by a king long ago, another time Norsunder threatened. Made a pact with his queen that if he lost his battle and was possessed by them and sent back to rule his own people for them she'd take a knife to him."

Caris-Merian looked down at her capable hands. "Did it come to pass?"

"Yes."

Leander tipped his head. Ever the scholar, he murmured, "How many of these pacts will actually be honored?"

"Probably few." Senrid gave one shoulder a wry lift. "Which is why I myself have five of 'em going at home. Glad to make them with anyone here. You know I'm good for it, and I'd appreciate the same if they do get to me."

Roy stepped out of the kitchen. "What are you whispering about over here?"

Senrid said, "Death pacts. There are some who disapprove of them. Liere being one."

Lightning flared and Leander glanced toward the curtained window, the light bright in his green eyes. "Weather objecting to all the magic, do you think? Certainly that miasma is still disturbing the air currents."

Thunder rumbled in the distance, gradually getting closer. Even in the dusty attic they could smell snow on the air.

"... need a secret name," CJ insisted, her treble voice rising. "For secret messages!"

"I say, a password is always good idea," Dtheldevor declared, reappearing on the stairs, pack over her shoulder. She elbowed Roy. "You poopsies had 'em, I remember that much. I think the best is Tar-Tares, which—"

Roy smiled. "I know my history." And to the puzzled faces, "Centuries ago. Empire period. Man from the Tar-Tares family taken, or joined Norsunder, depending on the version, then defected from Norsunder, and organized the farmers of an area that the emperor wanted, and conducted a strike-and-hide campaign that was effective against the emperor's forces. Their sign was a pitchfork with a fire over it."

"We could use that," Dtheldevor said. "'specially if we join this rescue run."

"You've got to remember your mind-shields," Liere said.

When Dtheldevor made a face, Senrid and Roy both said at the same time, "Everyone! Mind-shields are your first and best defense."

"Got it, got it, got it," Dtheldevor said. "Mind-shields it is. Senrid! I'm used to runnin' on me own. But I'm willin' to join them rescues. What happens if the enemy sees the code?"

Senrid said, "Add another code. Always keeping it simple. For a run, for example, every contact would have a new name only known to the courier and the one sending the courier. So Melire could be Land of the Venn. Every so often, set aside a place that isn't used, only watched. Manufacture an important meeting there. If the enemy shows up to search, you will know the communication line has been corrupted."

Dtheldevor chortled and slapped her thigh. "I like that!"

Senrid turned again to get upstairs and grab his pack, but Rel's voice boomed out once more.

"Listen! Dirk has a message to relay from Kessler, who is responsible for the ward everyone felt. Norsunder is busy renewing tracers and traps, as we figured they would, but they are also testing what Kessler did. He says they're unlikely to risk transfers at least until morning locally."

"What does that mean?" Kyale asked Liere.

"It means we don't dare use transfer magic, because part of their tests will be to see who gets caught in the new traps and tracers. We're back to where we were yesterday: no magic transfers," Liere said, one hand holding onto her glowering daughter, and the other Andri.

Rel spoke up, "Except for vagabond magic. Waiting for dawn, the best time for vagabond transfers, gives me time to gather some vagabonds. The third benefit of this type of magic — the second being that it doesn't wrench your joints — is that we can send groups without harm. Though only a certain distance. But that's better than having to walk from here."

Some cheers and shouts met this and Rel raised his hand again.

People fell silent.

He said, "The Mearsieans also have a message, which is that Mearsies Heili is completely warded against entry by Norsundrians. No, I don't know for certain, but I'm to say that Erai-Yanya corroborates the fact that it is truly safe from Norsunder. You are all welcome to take refuge there."

Questions burst out from every side.

Senrid turned away, and at last got to the top of the stairs. In the time it took to reach the landing, he'd decided to wait until morning to leave: getting a little sleep in what remained of the night seemed a good idea. He did not relish the idea of walking out into the sleet storm he could hear thudding against the wall. Also, whatever distance they could send him would be a gain over having to walk it.

He stretched out on the bedding, and never remembered falling asleep.

He woke abruptly before dawn, and remembered that he was about to leave. What he craved most was time to himself. He could think. He could plan. A solitary journey was exactly what he needed to deal with the turmoil in his heart.

But when he got downstairs, pack slung over his shoulder, he found the hall once more crowded with chattering people.

Rel waved him over. "There you are. Your group is ready to go."

"My group? I don't have a group."

"Yes you do," David said—having been told by Detlev, *Stick with him.*

And Liere smiled, coming toward him—determined to make up for whatever it was she'd done wrong. She had to recover their old friendship, and would strain every nerve trying. She gestured toward the waiting faces. "We'll all go together."

Part Three

One

THOSE GIVEN TO REFLECTION slept badly. Everyone had known they would have to disperse, but Rel's house had still come to be seen as a safe haven. The illusion of safety was gone. They had to leave *now*. the choice of destination uncertainty (at best) at home, wherever home might be, or a very long journey, nearly halfway around the world, to Mearsies Heili—if it was still safe.

Jilo certainly slept fitfully, then finally got up and tiptoed out, for once not waking Senrid, who seemed to Jilo to be the lightest sleeper on the continent. All Jilo had were the clothes Terry had given him, and the mirror ward book, carried next to his skin.

He peered ahead as he descended the stairs. Ah. There was Dtheldevor, talking earnestly to Julian, who was saying, "You know I'd go with you. But with winter coming on, how good would I be, groaning in my bunk?"

Dtheldevor had to accept that; she recollected that Julian was one of those few who never got over seasickness. She'd been happiest not on board, but in the island hideout, where everyone had liked her.

She clapped Julian on the shoulder and turned away, to find Jilo approaching her. She flashed a grin at him. She liked Jilo, who seemed to be such a woebegone, hapless wight. She couldn't equate this slumping weed with the mighty and formidable mage the others insisted Jilo was—she was sure they were sharing a private joke at her expense. Well, she liked jokes.

Seeing that his attention (two fleeting glances) stayed on her, she greeted him with, "What's buzzing between them ears, Jilo?"

"I wanted to ask," Jilo began in his usual mumble. "Beg you. Don't kill any Chwahir. If you can help it."

"Eh? But..."

"I know they are attacking everyone. I know the world sees them as the enemy. What they did under Wan Edhe was bad, but they are Chwahir, following the orders of their ruler. They have to do it or die. Now, far worse, they are forced to carry out the orders of an enemy." His head came up, his eyes meeting hers briefly, wide and earnest.

Dtheldevor stared back in some perplexity, distracted partly by his gaze, which seldom rose above the floor. You'd expect a Chwahir to have dark eyes—they were all darkhaired. Nearly all black-haired. Yet his eyes were the same shade as Liere's, gold in strong light.

Dtheldevor was so happy to be heading for the sea at last that she didn't hit him with her opinion of the Chwahir, who indeed had been lifetime enemies. She whacked Jilo on his bony back, causing him to stagger, and said, "Self-defense only. Howzat?"

Jilo was surprised to get that much. "Yes. Thank you."

She chortled, turned away, and as he sidled off, she bawled, "Dirk! Try to get past me mind-shield, just try..."

Jilo absently accepted a biscuit stuffed with fried egg and cheese that the day's kitchen rotation brought around. The last day's kitchen rotation.

Wouldn't that draw unwanted attention to the town if they all suddenly vanished? He debated asking, when Arthur addressed Rel, almost in the same words.

Rel said, "I planned ahead for this house being temporary. I've arranged for a renter whose family fled the capital. She needs a larger house to accommodate them all. I've also let gossip spread that since harvest is over and everyone is apprehensive due to the rumors about forced recruitment, most of my laborers are returning home. Since my income is drying up, I'm also returning home—which I've hinted lies in Bermund."

"A kingdom with no military presence," Atan commented.

"Reinforcing my image," Rel added. "In case events require me to return."

"We's ready to lift anchor!" Dtheldevor yelled what she regarded as a subtle hint.

Rel glanced at the window, which had blued considerably. "And here is the sun—another turn of the glass and we'll begin losing the dawn effect on the magic currents. Aronis? Got the vagabonds?"

Aronis Harper had turned up during the night, with a small collection of people experienced with vagabond magic.

"Get in a group. We must encircle you," Aronis said. Even giving terse directions, his was a singer's voice.

Dtheldevor's group clumped together, small Deon standing with her arms crossed and her chin lifted belligerently. She wanted to say farewell to her cousin Bren, and to Darian Selenna and Innon, but she was afraid that if she did, they'd try again to talk her out of joining Dtheldevor's crew. So she remained silent as the privateers shimmered, their edges blurring into luminous colors, then between one blink and another they were gone.

Darian Selenna looked as unhappy as he was. He had failed to keep what remained of his little found family together. Bren, knowing his cousin of old, was apprehensive. He stood hunched, all angles, his head down; Atan squeezed Rel's hand as she joined them. She stood next to Darian, both of them having that rare and precious thing: a welcome to the morvende caves. The morvende had promised to see Atan safely to the farthest border of their reach.

The last thing Rel saw of them was Atan's steady gaze, then they were gone.

By then Senrid had come downstairs. He was surrounded by a group, Hibern not among them, Rel noticed. He was not the only one who tried to find her among the milling, talking people, but the vagabonds were earnest in hurrying them before the magical currents lessened.

Kyale Marlonen stepped to Leander's side, then noticed Senrid in the group. Swinging about so that her skirt and hair flared, she stalked away, expecting Leander to stay with her.

But Leander was busy checking his pack for ink and quills,

and didn't notice. She started, "Wait!" But the group shimmered, and they were gone.

Furious, she marched to Roy's group. The pattern repeated without any of the usual horrible effect of magic transfers until few were left, including the Mearsieans, Dirk, Jilo—and Rel.

But still no Hibern. Rel looked around, puzzled. She must have transferred to Mearsies Heili, where Erai-Yanya was, during the period when transfers were possible.

That meant she was out of reach, so he turned his mind to the next problem. He and Atan had initially settled on traveling together, for both possessed that Sunsider rarity, the gift of morvende sign, which meant not only would they recognize morvende tunnel entrances in mountain heights, they would be welcome at any geliath—a word that meant both cave and community.

But ever since Jilo and the others had gone to Mondros's cottage to fight that magic battle, Rel had observed how Jilo had been a little more mopey, and furtive than his usual manner. His air was much like a pup who has transgressed on the carpet, or rather was about to: this behavior of his threw Rel right back to the days when Jilo was sneaking around with that enemies book of Wan-Edhe's.

In other words, Rel suspected that Jilo was contemplating a plan that he knew everyone would disapprove of.

During the quiet of what had been left of the previous night, Rel and Atan had held each other as they talked it out, finally agreeing—she with some resentment and he with resignation—that he ought to stick to Jilo. As Atan said, winding her fingers through his warm ones, and suppressing the flutter of worry that today might be the last they saw of one another, *It's not that I am indifferent to Jilo's plight. It's just that I've spent a lifetime indifferent at best to the affairs of the Chwahir, individuals as well as a kingdom. But now, I find, I must think differently: it's there in my head, but not my heart.*

Rel responded, *The world has been indifferent to the Chwahir. As I was, until I began meeting individuals, and discovered there is a great wrong here that needs putting right. My discovery of half of my family being Chwahir only reinforces that. It is not the cause.*

"Gather in," Rel said now to the remainder of the Lisdan company. "We're going as far as we can, and dawn is fading to day. For some reason the magic wanes a little with full light. We need all the distance we can win."

"You're...going with us?" Jilo asked, guilt so plain on his face that Rel was hard put not to laugh.

"Yes. What's the matter, don't want me?" Rel asked.

"Captain Heraford will want you," Puddlenose spoke up from the side, where he was propping a wall. "Keeps wishing you'd sail with us again. Especially now — says you're a halyard team all to yourself. We'll need to be nippy with sail trim if we're to avoid notice in the strait. Our one advantage is that the east winds are back and steady."

His easy voice gave Jilo the time he needed to smother his dismay. He liked Rel. He trusted Rel even more. But he knew that Rel would lead the rest in dousing his plan if they figured it out.

Jilo reminded himself that he knew the borderland between Erdrael Danara and Chwahirsland after staying with Terry for so long. Surely he'd find a moment to slip free.

Before their group was sent, Detlev's thought arrowed into David's mind: *Stay with Senrid.*

David did not answer. He knew he couldn't keep an effective mind shield in the midst of noise both aural and in the mental realm. He was not nearly as adept as Adam, or even Sveneric. There were too many inimical minds prowling the realm of the mind.

Looking determined, Liere towed Andri Elsarion toward Senrid, Lyren-Sartora following with a scowl; the vagabonds surrounded a few more people standing in isolation, summarily making them into a group. David slipped among them a heartbeat before the vagabonds performed their magic. He was surprised to discover that vagabond transfer felt a lot like Detlev's "slide" — the form of transfer that only he and Siamis seemed to know.

Only this was different, too. Instead of the universally loathed wrench they all braced for, they felt as light as leaves, and even odder, were aware of wind currents. The sense of leaves driven before a wild wind dissipated, dropping them in a meadow. It felt as if they'd hopped off a short step, but there was no aftereffect. They gazed up at a stone city carved into the side of a towering mountain.

"That's Zranf," David exclaimed involuntarily.

It was a dramatic sight, not only because of the terraced city, but because the mountains comprised a tumble of sheer slabs rising right up to the clouds.

For a short time everyone stood there as a cold wind off the Sea of Mists behind them toyed with their clothes, then one by one they turned to one another. This was no tight unit, as Dtheldevor's privateers were, or even the Selenna company. This was a collection of people who'd happened to be standing near one another, corralled by the vagabond circle into a convenient group.

David, who had been assigned to them, took in the disparate individuals — until his gaze landed on a familiar heart-shaped face dominated by a broad forehead and large, blue-gray, hate-filled eyes, before Caris-Merian Rhoderan turned her back deliberately. In spite of her pretense of ignoring him, David knew she would have joined them for one reason, to find some moment he was not watchful to slip a knife between his ribs.

Sveneric's thought came: *Is that the sister of Les Rhoderan?*

: *Yes.* The bad days on Geth, which David had thought distant in place if not in time, crowded back. There were people who still thought Les Rhoderan a hero, foremost his sister.

Sveneric sent a thought: *Liere is speaking Geth to her. Perhaps she could help there.*

: *Or interfere.* Liere Fer Eider had annoyed David when she was the self-starving, morose Sartora who would grab hold of your shirtfront (in a figurative sense) and moan interminably about how she did not deserve to be Sartora.

Some of his disgust seeped through — no surprise there — and Sveneric responded: *Liere's intent seems to be benign. Not so with this person from Geth. But Detlev thinks it is important to get her to change her mind.*

Detlev wants the impossible, was David's thought, but he didn't share it. He'd simply have to watch his back, but that was nothing new.

He turned his attention outward, assessing the others. On the positive side, Andri displayed all the signs of being good in a fight. Liere's daughter Lyren-Sartora, though spoiled, was competent. Siamis had seen to that.

Bookish Leander Tlennen-Hess was an excellent woodsman, having spent a good part of his boyhood living the outlaw life in Sindan-An Forest while his erstwhile stepmother plotted to kill him. And even better, his step-sister had flounced away unnoticed. She was now Roy's responsibility. David spared a moment to pity him.

The only one David did not know was another of Arthur's mage students, Zairna Raadi—who had gone to get breakfast, and returned to find Arthur's huge group gone. So, with no change in expression, he had joined this one. David knew nothing of him, except that he was an off-worlder, yet he had a formidable mind-shield. Interesting.

"Looks like we're a half a day's walk, maybe less, from Zranf," Leander commented. "I'll scout, if no one else wants to."

David remembered his map, and said, "I wish that magic could have carried us farther south, or father north. And past the mountains."

Senrid jerked a thumb sideways. "Maybe some will want to take a detour south or north." Thus making it clear to anyone who had not already understood from his averted gaze and the tightness of his posture that he had expected, certainly wanted, maybe even needed to be alone.

But, to David's disgust, Liere earnestly plowed right into him, saying, "Senrid, let's all go together. If we're going to leave the continent for Mearsies Heili we have to go west anyway, and we'll be stronger in a group."

Every facet of a diamond reflects a different color; while David saw Liere's motive as annoying and officious, she herself was full of good will. She missed the old, unthinking bond with Senrid, and suspected that she had blundered somehow. It was her self-appointed task to fix things.

What Senrid saw was different from both. He regarded her standing there with one hand tightly clasping Andri Elsarion's, aware of the whipsaw emotions lacerating him when their eyes met. When he heard her voice. It hurt, seeing her so close to Andri. He had never in his life been jealous, but he knew instantly what this was. He refused to let it rule him; people had the right to choose whoever they wanted. He even liked what he'd seen of Andri so far.

So he'd learn to deal with it. Just as he had to deal with waking each day to Crystal Ingrid still being dead, and his kingdom conquered.

He also knew that he would always look out for Liere, and for Lyren-Sartora, too, and for that matter, for Leander. And having David as backup was probably the best part of this collection of people. As for the three teenage girls — two standing next to each other and the gray-eyed one isolated — he wasn't about to tell them to hike off. Leander was talking to the tall fellow with the earrings, what was his name, Zairna something; Zairna dressed like one of the Colendi, but he had a martial artist's stance. He might be good backup as well.

Then there was Detlev's boy, unaccountably with them. Senrid did not know what to make of that, except that he wasn't about to abandon that boy to the wolves.

"Group it is," he said.

David said, "What I know about Zranf is that it sits athwart the best and quickest pass through the mountains. That pass will be guarded, but smugglers and the like have had their own routes through these mountains for centuries."

"Aren't there old morvende caves and tunnels in these mountains?" Leander asked, looking hopeful.

David shrugged. "Only thing I've heard is that what tunnels and so on that the smugglers use have been long abandoned. Centuries ago."

"What land lies beyond the mountains?" Lyren-Sartora asked, thinking that Zranf sounded vaguely familiar. She'd heard it recently, hadn't she?

"Sles Adran," three people said at the same time.

A thoughtful silence fell, as they contemplated crossing the entirety of Sles Adran, which had allied with Norsunder, with winter nigh.

Two

Border Erdrael Danara and Chwahirsland

JILO SLIPPED AWAY THE second night.

Rel and his vagabond circle had taken them to a secluded ravine carved by an ancient waterfall, where he knew King Tereneth of Erdrael Danara—Terry to his many friends—had a retreat, chosen not for its comfort but for its remoteness. Ever since Terry had lost a few fingers, and nearly his life, during the internecine warfare of the generation above his, he'd always needed a bolt hole. In recent years he'd treated the place as more of a retreat from the stresses of his court, to which he brought a few trusted friends, Jilo and Rel numbering among them.

Rel was very certain that this was the place Terry had retreated to when Norsunder attacked.

As Rel expected, after weeks of isolation as the weather steadily worsened, Terry was both anxious and bored. Anxious because he had no way of finding out the news, resulting in the boredom of being essentially locked up in a tiny cottage deep in the ravine, where the sun never penetrated in the winter months.

Terry welcomed them with surprise and relief. "I'm

completely alone," he said, waving them in. "It was just Halad and me." He pointed to the brush just inside the door for ridding shoes and boots of clumps of mud. "After whatever it was that made the world feel like it was ending—did you feel that, too?"

"We can tell you what that was," Rel said easily. "Where's Halad gone to?" Halad was half-Chwahir, something a majority of Erdrael-Danara's court had objected to, but Terry ignored them. The two had become close as boys surviving the civil war, and as they aged up, became companions, much (Rel thought) as he and Atan had.

Terry said, "He was going to sneak into the city. Get some news, and some supplies. I've been looking for him the past day or so."

No one commented on the anxiety underlying his tone.

Shoes cleaned off, they crowded into his tiny hut, where they ate almost all the food he had stocked there, but as he told them, Halad was bringing fresh supplies.

"As soon as Lad gets here, the both of you ought to come to Mearsies Heili," Puddlenose said. "It's safe."

They talked well into the night, Terry listening avidly, though he himself said little. Once or twice Terry gave Jilo questioning glances, which Rel noted. So Terry was suspicious as well.

A storm struck before midnight. They slept elbow to elbow, covering the entire floor of the cottage, which at least generated some warmth; Halad was also intending to forage a firestick, something they hadn't thought about during the summer when they arrived at the run.

Rel was relieved to waken the next morning to find Jilo still there, though the rain had slackened almost to mist. The only one missing was Dhana, but they all knew she would have gone out in the storm to dance in the waterfall in her native form, which would refresh her magic.

Rel considered that as they went about readying and eating pan-fried biscuits. On their arrival, Dhana had muttered to CJ, "It's very like our magic. But air, not water."

In regular magic, that wouldn't matter one way or another, but vagabond magic was different. Rel did not know why or how. He'd been taught by someone who was human part of the time. Indigenous magic and "vagabond" magic seemed to interrelate, and Rel wondered if he and Dhana could effect transfers, drawing on the powerful magic being spent in Wan-Edhe's deadly wards.

The storm moved on midway through the day. By then Seshe had figured out a tasty way to combine most of Terry's remaining stores, as he used a stick to draw a rough map in the mud outside his door, showing the mountain trails that Rel was familiar with, having ridden with Terry's Mountain Guard.

"What happened to them?" Rel asked, mentally seeing faces he knew well.

Terry understood immediately. "It was right after I sent Jilo to Lisdan. An army of Chwahir appeared at the border, led by Norsundrians in gray. They were eight or ten times the number of the Mountain Guard. My last order was to go home, and hide their greens and their weapons. I figure, *somebody* is going to figure out how to fight back. Until then, I don't need a bunch of dead heroes."

"That was a good decision," Rel said, his voice an abyssal growl. "Very good."

"After we were invaded I couldn't stop some of my Mountain Guard from sneaking out and making booby traps. I wouldn't trust any footbridge, for example. They knew I wouldn't land on them for breaking orders." He looked away, his face shadowed by the hair that usually hung over the scar on his face, and the lighting dim except for the single glowglobe. "A few got careless. And Norsunder hunted down a couple of others. They seem to be fond of public executions. Things have been quiet since. As for me, I made sure no one knew where I went, so though there's a huge reward offered for turning me in, nobody can."

Terry and Rel bent over the mud map, both looking Jilo's way from time to time.

Jilo agreed with everything they said. He knew why they wanted his agreement—they wanted to make sure he'd be with them as they made their way down the goat paths to the sea.

But that night, as soon as everyone's breathing deepened to sleep, Jilo picked his way over the bodies, and eased out the door.

One of the spells Kessler had written into the book was the Norsundrian transfer. The last thing he had said was, "I will keep them from warding you, Jilo. The rest is up to you."

Still, Jilo had to test. The first transfer must only be a risk to himself. He set as Destination one of the watch posts on the

Chwahir side of the border.

No one was there. When the transfer wrench, and the frantic beat of his heart, subsided, he ventured out to get water from the stream running alongside the watch post.

The first taste of the water so harsh with underground minerals made him think of the cascades and waterfalls on Terry's side of the mountains. The unnatural mountains, raised by Jilo's own ancestors, and then warded to keep their descendants in—so that all the healing rain fell on the west, creating waterfalls and streams and rivers and lakes, all flowing down and away to the river that marked Colend's border.

Our water, Jilo thought, and sipped bitterness.

He'd known it would hurt to come back with not only Wan-Edhe in control, but Norsunder as well.

Where to next? Anywhere he went, he must prepare himself to see silent resentment in the people's faces—after all, he'd run. He'd argued with himself every day since he'd agreed to go to Lisdan, so that Terry would not have to feel responsible for him when he had been so helpless himself.

Terry had not described how he'd wept at the news of the invasion, nor how he'd pleaded with Jilo to go to safety. Jilo kept silence during Terry's bald recitation, though he'd been very sure Rel could guess at what was not said.

Jilo looked around the mossy walls, as he sat on the narrow plank bench that served as a bed, his emotions veering crazily through anger, anxiety, and relief that he was here, at least. But then came the worry, for he sensed an extra oppression that was not due to his awareness that Wan-Edhe was once again on his throne.

Better to avoid the capital until he knew what he'd find. A report, yes, that was what he needed—and he knew where to go to get that.

He transferred to Uncle Shiam's. The crumbling castle, which had seen the beginnings of cautious repair after years went by and Wan-Edhe had not reappeared, lay quiet, empty-seeming in the dreary, drippy world of gray and mud-brown. Dirty patches of snow lay in the lee of buildings, testifying to slippery ice if one was not cautious.

Jilo knew that the family would be there. It did not do to draw attention to oneself unless it couldn't be avoided, in Wan-Edhe's world. It must be far worse under the iron-shod boot of the Norsundrians, who commanded Wan-Edhe, and who cared nothing for the kingdom except to use its army.

He made his way to the most humble of entrances, readying to face the resentment and disappointment he probably deserved.

But it was Uncle Shiam himself who opened the door, and not the youngest kitchen helper. "You came," Uncle Shiam said simply. "We knew you would come."

Three

Zranf - Halarialgre

LEANDER GLANCED SKYWARD. "I smell snow on the wind," he said. "I'll find a spot to camp while we figure out what to do next, shall I?"

Andri, curious and well-disposed toward Senrid, suggested that the two of them scout the patrol patterns.

"Sure," Senrid said. "If you take the north, I'll look around south of the city."

So much for getting to know Senrid, Andri had reflected ruefully. But there was time.

Liere said, "I'll go farther out. I'm less likely to look interesting to any roaming collaborators than one of you fellows. Anyone want to scout with me?"

Lyren-Sartora, annoyed at her mother for bringing Andri, pretended not to hear. A quiet, accented voice spoke up, "I'll go. It is all the same to me."

Liere turned to discover Caris-Merian there. This was the first time they had ever exchanged a word. Intensely curious, Liere said, "Let's go."

David watched them organize themselves, the four scouts dispersing, and others going with Leander to find a spot to camp. He knew that Senrid wanted to head for home, and David had orders to stick to him. What about the rest of them? Why had they not gone north, to find berth on the ship? Puddlenose had said plainly that everyone was welcome.

West was full of hazards. Beyond Halarialgre, which was a danger in itself, lay the vast, rich kingdom of Sles Adran, whose king had thrown in with Norsunder. Beyond that lay Enaeran. That would explain Andri's being with them, though David had not heard Andri Elsarion say anything about destinations.

West of Enaeran lay Marloven Hess and Vasande Leror. That explained Leander.

Beyond that lay an ocean.

: And Mearsies Heili (came Sveneric's mental contact). *That's where Siamis is. Detlev says that everyone who doesn't have a goal would do well to hide there until they have one.*

David had left the surface of his thoughts open to Sveneric, but still the sudden comment startled him. It was how deft Sveneric was in the mental realm. As imperceptible as Adam. David hadn't thought anyone short of Detlev and Siamis could be that skilled.

: There's a long road between here and there. First we have to survive, David returned wryly. As for Raadi, maybe all directions were the same to him; what puzzled David was why he hadn't shifted to his own world when the warning about Kessler's ward went around. Maybe he couldn't go back. He certainly seemed tightly buttoned for a world traveler merely studying other forms of magic. But Arthur had vouched for him.

"Found a campsite." Leander's voice broke into David's musing. "It seems to be an ancient ruin. There are broken stone blocks here and there. My guess is, the good ones were hauled away over the centuries, probably to build yon city."

He pointed with his chin up at Zranf on the other side of the river, then led them to a clearing well out of sight of the roads. It was sheltered by trees, with a little stream winding eastward to join the waters of the Sea of Mists. Some helped Leander create a rudimentary shelter with brush laid between the mossy stones, so that their camp would be invisible to any roaming patrols.

The low northern sun had dropped beyond the rugged mountains when the four scouts returned.

Andri turned up first, Senrid shortly after. They described

what sounded like a routine single-perimeter round. There had
clearly been no trouble here since Alsaes took the kingdom
over.

Liere and Caris-Merian, who had scouted farther out,
showed up last, before darkness closed in. Liere had tried to
draw out the girl from Geth, finding her extremely diffident,
her answers short and spoken in a soft undervoice difficult to
hear. Not wanting to force her, Liere had given up, and after
their brief foray into the city, they had walked back in total
silence.

Caris-Merian did not speak when they returned, either, so
Liere gave a succinct report, with many glances toward Caris-
Merian as if for corroboration.

What she reported was no surprise. Zranf had been the first
kingdom invaded. By this time, the Norsundrians had forced
everyone to carry identity papers, which were supposedly to be
displayed when demanded. Liere and Caris-Merian had noted
that the gate guards, who looked bored and irritable as the
weather steadily got colder, ignored the stream of former
scribes and others whose livings the invasion had dispossessed.
These folk trod daily into the city to perform whatever menial
labor was going that day. The guards only stopped to demand
papers from people in coaches or carriages, or horse riders who
looked like they might be warriors. They'd ignored the two
girls as if they were invisible.

The next morning was significantly colder under an iron-
gray sky. They all slept—or had tried to sleep—in their clothes,
wrapped in their cloaks. When dawn lifted the darkness they
found frost on the ground, and ice riming the edge of the
stream. The water was so cold it hurt to drink it straight from
the stream.

Liere and Caris-Merian left soon after dawn to join the labor
line at the gate, mimicking the weary and dreary countenances
they saw around them, most bent against the cold. The two
agreed between them that Caris-Merian, whose Geth accent
might draw attention, would scout for food, and Liere would
scout for information.

Again, once the long line snaked to the gates, the sentries
didn't give either of them a second glance.

Shortly after Liere and Caris-Merian left, Senrid walked off
alone.

Within fifty steps he was stopped by Lyren-Sartora, whom

he'd known since she was born. "Are you doing a perimeter run? See, I know what that is," she stated, then muttered, "Liere doesn't know what she's doing, except following that stupid Andri."

Leander caught up as well. "Senrid? Did you hear something suspicious? I thought things were quiet enough not to need a patrol.

Senrid looked from one to the other, and could not make himself say, "I wanted to be alone." Leander, who he'd met the year before he met Liere, would probably understand, but Lyren-Sartora would demand why as if she had the right. At thirteen, maybe she did. From his five-year perspective as a parent, he recognized now that he had in some wise been a parent to her, until Siamis took over. But Senrid had been first.

"Come along," he forced himself to say. "More eyes always good."

Leander—who sensed some of the pain Senrid tried to hide, and attributed it to grief—said, "I know you like honey-figs. I recognized this as a ruin because I spotted what had to be an orchard long, long ago. They seem to have adapted to the colder climate here."

"I saw cranberries," Lyren-Sartora offered. She'd tried to make friends with June, the offworld teenager; she was always curious about other worlds. But her natural gregariousness hit the slammed door of June's sneer, and so Lyren-Sartora turned back. At least June talked to Julian.

Leander turned to her. "If you pick some, I can press them, and mix them with the last of the sweetberries from Rel's place, which were really too withered to eat alone."

Lyren-Sartora scampered off, remembering to stay below the sight line from the city, and Senrid perforce learned how to scavenge the last figs, as Leander talked easily about his forest days, hoping to ease Senrid's grief.

Liere and Caris-Merian returned with the evening flow of laborers who either couldn't afford to live in the city, or preferred sunlight to proximity to work. Caris-Merian lugged a basket to the banked fire. "How did you manage to get that food?" Lyren-Sartora asked.

"A vendor saw my buttons." Caris-Merian pointed to the shanks on the front of her robe, which looked like they had been poured from chocolate and then polished. "These buttons are from a very common wood on my island. It appears to be rare here. But every world, eh, we know how to bargain. I traded for this baked savory pie, and this cheese."

Leander set the pie on a flat stone near the firestick so that it would stay warm as he combined ingredients to make punch of the late cranberries.

Liere sat on a mossy step. "A lot of the daily labor lives behind the river dock," she said. "Patrolled frequently. I think if we all go among the laborers into the city, we have a better chance of going unnoticed."

"In the enemy's midst?" Lyren-Sartora asked, arms crossed in the distinctive manner of the thirteen-year-old who thinks all adults are clueless about the world.

Liere turned to her. "If we're to get through to the pass, we must get to the west gate of the fortress. I walked among people all day, and lifted memories. The sudden searches have subsided. In fact, the garrison is minimal, as there hasn't been any trouble here since Alsaes held a lot of executions. The trouble seems to be all in Fal."

Those who knew about the history of Fal, which was infamous for feuds and duels, laughed a little.

"Also, I think," Liere said with scrupulous care, "I might have found a resistance organization." She hesitated, trying to find the most succinct way to convey what she had gathered from fearful thoughts, some distrusting their own minds lest they betray them. She would have taught them all mind-shields if she could. There might even be a way, if she could successfully make contact with the resistance.

"There is a woman who walks about much as I did, and I think she is seeking those who might be allies. I let her see me twice. I hope she'll get the courage to approach tomorrow. I'll ask her about papers—revealing our own need, which might earn her trust faster. And we could use them, if we do draw attention."

"Going one at a time might help with that," Andri spoke up. "Fade into the crowd. Can we add some illusion, making us skinnier and older? Too decrepit to be bundled off to the slammer, or to their army?" He turned a thumb between himself and David next to him, and tipped his chin in the direction of Leander and Zairna Raadi.

"Decrepit dodderers it is," Leander said, chortling. "I can do the illusions."

And that's what happened the next morning, which was even colder, the stream in places covered with a thin film of ice. No one had slept well in the cold wind. Snow was on the way.

One by one they slipped through a yard full of empty riverboat hulls and parts, joining the crowd treading up the long switchback road into the city. Sveneric and Lyren-Sartora trudged along, Lyren-Sartora carrying Caris-Merian's empty basket. Their youth got them overlooked.

The group joined the mass waiting in a great square for assignment to whatever task was going that day, then wandered off, again one by one, some following other laborers, others alone.

Liere went first. Not long after the last of them reached the upper thoroughfare along the open-air market stalls, she reappeared, bringing with her a grim-faced red-haired woman.

Those years in Geth seemed to have been put to good use, David thought. To which Sveneric replied: *Detlev says she is only beginning to accept that she might have self-worth.*

It was a mild observation, but David grimaced privately against the sting. David found Liere annoying, which caused distorted evaluation. This was every bit as callow, he knew, as Liere constantly pawing Andri in the typical manner of the teenager who has just discovered sex.

Then came Detlev's acerbically dispassionate thought: *She has long thought herself unlovable. Of course she clings.*

: *Lesson received.* David shot the thought back, but Detlev was already gone. Then David forgot the entire matter when he remembered Caris-Merian. He had better not lose sight of her.

She had lingered, going last. As he covertly glanced around to see where she was, she glared at the back of his head. The impulse to catch one of the bored Norsundrian patrollers and point David out had to be resisted. She had been a prisoner of Norsunder long enough to know what would happen, which would begin with her own arrest. She shut her eyes briefly, fighting the nearly overwhelming urge to spit at David's heels. *I will see you dead for what you did to Les. And it is going to take a very long time.*

Then she happened to catch the eye of that odd, still little boy with the hazel eyes. He was too observant, that one. He reminded her of Cath, Dak's brother, whose brilliance had unfortunately drawn Norsunder's attention.

She dropped back a little farther, and forced her attention

to their surroundings, as Sveneric considered what he'd observed. Caris-Merian seemed a hard-working, scrupulous person except when she noticed David. He would simply stay near David, he decided, sadly taking in the abject, closed-in countenances in the people around him. We will fix things, he promised them as he followed the line.

The parts of Zranf that got the least sunlight were of course where workers and servants lived, and those too poor for even such gloomy quarters lurked, preying on the unwary.

"We don't go about alone," the resistance woman said shortly. "Beggars used to go to the guild, but that guild was taken over by the Gray Turds, and there are too many beggars now, people who used to be scribes and stringers and guild counters and the like."

She opened a warped door midway down a narrow alley whose walls were covered by stone lichen. She tapped in a quick pattern and waited.

They stood in the freezing alley, fingers and toes numbing as they watched their breath cloud. It seemed a long time before at last the thuds and metallic clunks indicated a barred and locked door being unbarred and unlocked.

As soon as they got inside the entryway, it became apparent that people had whisked furnishings and food away. The room was bare, but there were scrapes on the stone floor, and the aromas of fresh bread and a pepper soup lingered in the air.

Beyond that room lay some kind of living quarters. A few faces peered from behind curtain-doors as they passed by, then the woman said, "The only space safe enough is in the basement. It's trusting us, and stay there for now, or we'll wish you good traveling."

The first flakes of the coming blizzard were already falling.

Liere glanced back, and saw resignation in enough faces for her to said, "Lead on, and thank you."

They felt their way down a narrow, mossy stair, the flickering candle that their guide carried throwing crazy shadows up the dank walls and causing the stairs before them to seem to shift. More than one person shut eyes against the distracting light and used other senses for guidance until they entered a long, square room in which barrels were stored against one wall. Those who knew fighting noted the barrels, which at last resort could be used to hide behind. Julian and June instantly claimed the farthest corner, June's scowl keeping everyone else at a distance.

"Is this a trap?" Andri murmured, reluctant to try his Dena Yeresbeth, which he did not control very well.

Liere whispered back, "No. She's too bitterly proud of flouting the Norsundrians, who put her husband up against the wall in the first wave of executions. He was the chief scribe."

Not two heartbeats later there was noise on the stairway as a troop of youngsters ranging in age from ten to eighteen or nineteen descended, carrying armloads of worn quilts and a basket of mismatched ceramic and wooden bowls and spoons.

Everyone relaxed a little, and they settled down in clumps of two or three, the divisions between them testament to their total lack of group cohesion.

Liere said, "Her cousin-by-marriage is an expert at forging identity papers. If anyone thought to bring coinage, it might go a ways toward goodwill."

"I've got some," Leander said. "I got paid the day before we left for my work in the carpentry shop. But these are all Lisdan coins. Will that be a problem here?"

"Can't be helped," Andri commented.

Liere accepted the coins, adding, "Rel did say that during his caravan days, coins pass freely, or did, back and forth along this end of the continent."

Presently a burly man came down bearing a cauldron of a watery vegetable soup, and a loaf of bread. These they shared out, the coinage was handed over—earning them a beaming smile, and a cordial invitation, "Them barrels there is barley wine. Help yourselves to the jugs against that wall there" —and though by now at most it was late afternoon, it was generally agreed to bed down, after the sleepless cold of the night previous.

Though there was no light, those who usually woke early were warned by some inner sense. As happens when many people share a small space, the breathings and scrapes and shifts of waking woke the others. Leander brought from his pack a glowglobe he'd brought from Marloven Hess, just in case.

By its light some went about doing what they could in the way of grooming, and folding up the quilts. David sat against the wall, fighting impatience at the total lack of direction. They could have been planning their next step. He couldn't take command—he knew that none of them except Sveneric would listen, and in a sense Sveneric was already under David's orders. At least under his watch.

Impatience was useless and futile. He knew that. Just as he knew that whenever Detlev's orders put you somewhere you did not want to be, it was because he wanted you to learn something.

Presently he ducked past knees and elbows to Senrid. Under cover of the quiet buzz of conversation, he murmured, "You going to get them organized?"

Senrid cut a wary glance his way. "I'm not giving orders, if that's what you mean."

"Why not?"

"Because most of them will argue," Senrid said. "As for experience, seems to me you have more of that than I do, when it comes to covert movement."

"Yes, and how much fun would you get out of listening to me give orders?"

"Go right ahead." Senrid's grin was tight, but it was there. Then his face changed. "The resistance woman is coming back."

Diamond, head of the local resistance, took grim pleasure in flouting the Norsundrians by providing an enormous breakfast, contributed by those who appreciated the donated coins, which apparently were a rarity among the usual run of refugees. She brought hot water, precious Sartoran steep, and freshly scalded coffee along with the fresh-baked tarts, baked eggs, and salted fish. While they ate hungrily, the young people trooped down again, this time bringing armloads of clothing donated by her friends.

"We've not been able to do much against the enemy," Diamond reported. "Except to send refugees on who got onto the enemy capital list. We've made a few rescues from the prison up in the tower, before they put all kinds of magic spells on it that kill you if you step in the wrong doorway. There's a secret relay going on all along the coast here, down through Lamanca to somewhere east. No one knows where they go from there—as it ought to be, in case any of us are caught."

Well done, David thought to Senrid.

There was no response.

The clothing was all castoffs, they discovered shortly after, which had the advantage of subdued colors and general lines in the local styles. Those, with local hairstyles, would render them effectively invisible—and without resorting to illusion magic, which could draw the wrong sort of interest if noticed.

There was a lot of joking about Leander Tlennen-Hess's princely looks; the absent-minded, scholarly Leander seemed genuinely surprised to find himself a target, when Lyren-Sartora twitted him about his handsomeness. "How can we ugly these two up?" Lyren-Sartora asked, indicating Leander, and Zairna's fine features and pale blond locks. "If ever there were too obvious princes, here they are."

Zairna glanced up quickly. Those who noticed wondered what royal house he had run from—and why.

David said, matching her tone, "They can use some fighting practice. I'd be happy to oblige..."

Leander made a terrible face. "I can imagine your style of practice. I'll end up with two black eyes, a cauliflower ear, and checkerboard teeth." He held out both palms. "I'd rather be Betrayed by my Beauty."

Some teasing followed by those who wanted to create an atmosphere of friendliness, even if one did not exist, which ended when Lyren-Sartora commented a little too caustically about Andri's diamond at one ear, while ignoring Zairna's pair.

He could have been justified in sharp retort—she knew quite well that she was being a snot—but he said easily, "I'll tie my hair back over my ears until I can get me a knit hat. No one will see it." He turned to the room. "I'd like to make a suggestion. See what you think."

David bit his lip against responding. Senrid remained silent, knees bent, wrists propped on them.

Liere said, "Go ahead."

"We're stuck here while that blizzard hits. Either we sit tight, which is fine, or we consider doing something."

"Like?" Liere asked, when her daughter rudely turned her back on Andri.

If Andri noticed, he made no sign of it. "Apparently the head Norsundrian is a desk jockey turned commander named Alsaes, yes? During practice I heard a lot about him, most of it from Rel, who seemed to have experience with him."

Leander said, "I heard a lot of it as well. And so?"

"It seems to me that between us we've got some decent shadows—sneaks, I mean. If he's a desk jockey then he's sure to have communications. Maybe even the latest. I'm thinking we could make a raid."

"Not an attack, right? Because fun as that would be, we

might as well wave a flag above our heads and yell, 'Here we are, boys, come and get us!'" Leander responded.

"No attack. Scouting run only," Andri said, hand up in promise. "Might be worth something to the locals, too, even better than coin. Also, I'm not suggesting anything, meaning for others to do the work. I'll go myself."

"I'll go with you," Liere spoke up.

Lyren-Sartora rolled her eyes.

Four

Erdrael Danara to Chwahirsland

HALAD SHOWED UP JUST before dawn, having traveled all night.

His arrival served to wake everyone. They exclaimed over the two baskets and the heavy sack he'd lugged up the mountains — and then someone thought to take count.

"Jilo's gone!"

"What?"

"We shoulda been watching him!"

"Why would he go — maybe he was grabbed!"

Rel held up a hand. "If he'd been grabbed, we wouldn't be sitting here discussing his absence. Laying blame is a waste of time, though if anyone is at fault, that would be me. I thought he might try something like this, but I was afraid that if we set up a guard he'd feel we couldn't trust him."

Dirk looked away. Rel was not the only one who suspected that Dirk knew when Jilo had gone, and had abetted him either covertly or overtly. Dirk is Kessler's son, Rel reminded himself. "I suggest we find him, help him as we can, and go from there."

No one disagreed. Including Dirk, who said slowly, "If he didn't go to the capital. And I don't think he would. Too many bad wards. Even if Kessler removes the personal ones. But there's always his family."

"I was thinking the same," Rel admitted. He turned to Dhana. "I need at least one other person to help shift anyone besides me. Would you be willing to try matching your magic with mine?"

Dhana's shoulders hitched up as if she had been caught in something illegal. She hated notice, especially of her magic. Her light gaze turned to CJ, who nodded slightly, looking troubled.

Dhana said, "All right."

It turned out to be simpler than Rel had allowed himself to hope. Just tedious, as they could only transfer one person at a time. At least there was no transfer wrench.

As the first flurries of snow began to sting their faces, they reached a bare, tumbledown castle beside a river. The group waited until the last of them had transferred in, then Rel led the way into the main courtyard, moving openly.

He stood there and waited impassively.

After a time a tall, grizzled man wearing a faded army uniform came out alone to meet him.

"I hope Jilo is here," Rel said. "We're his allies. He will speak for us if he is here. We want to join him in his work." Rel spoke Chwahir, and he looked mostly Chwahir in spite of his brown skin. A rustle and whisper in the darkened doorway at the north side of the courtyard resolved in Jilo slumping out, his cheeks mottled with embarrassment. "You shouldn't have come," he mumbled.

"Yes, we should," Dirk piped up, with extra meaning.

Jilo reddened even more, then Puddlenose (who had been Wan-Edhe's prisoner long enough to have learnt something of Chwahir custom and hardships) held up Lad's baskets, as Seshe wordlessly offered the sack, and Puddlenose added, "We brought a gift for the house. We hope it's not too small or insignificant."

They were welcomed straightaway.

The Mearsiean girls discovered that the inside was exactly as gloomy as everything else in Land of the Chwahir—except when they got to a small inner chamber, which had a couple of tapestries and a piece of two of carved furniture.

Shiam also had a wife—and a granddaughter!

They knew that Chwahir girls existed. Despite some of The

King's laws about killing "extra" girl babies, younger sisters stayed hidden, or they dressed as boys, sometimes their entire lives.

This girl was actually a young woman, round of face and very small, looking younger than she was. She wore a shapeless gray tube-like garment, a tunic that reached the floor. The Mearsieans could hardly wait to talk to her.

A meal of plain food mixed with some of Halad's offerings was produced—and served out in two separate rooms. The Mearsieans discovered that girls and women ate separately from men.

Which was all right with CJ—she considered this an improvement, in general, though she suppressed a scowl when she noticed that the room for the females was much smaller. But this was Chwahirsland, and Wan-Edhe's attitude toward women was nothing new.

"Please talk to us," CJ said, and when the young woman turned to them, her face solemn, "though you don't have to," CJ added quickly. And reluctantly.

So reluctantly that the young woman smiled.

"I'm CJ," said she. "What's your name?"

"Aran."

"Do you have any brothers or sisters?"

"Three brothers. In the army," Aran added. "You?"

"I kind of have six sisters, most of them back in Mearsies Heili. Not related by blood, but we're adopted into a family of our own." Falinneh, Dhana, and Seshe nodded.

Aran's face brightened. "Almost a twi."

"Twi?"

CJ remembered what little she'd known of the Chwahir. "I remember. The word for a gang." She wanted to ask what it was like being a girl in Chwahirsland, except she knew that was a stupid question—how do you ask someone what their life is like if they haven't known anything else?

But Aran said after a moment of concentration, "Pardon my question if it intrudes. But have I not heard that name, Mearsies Heili, before? Did not the true king come from there? Did not The Hate go there before we were rid of him for the Blessed Time?"

"The Hate?"

She made a spitting motion. "We are only permitted to call him The King. But we all know who the true king is."

"The true king?" They couldn't mean Kessler! Could they? Or maybe Dirk—except he was sitting in the other room, and nobody had done any bowing or your majestying, the usual king talk.

Then meaning hit her. "Oh, you mean *Jilo!*" CJ boggled at the idea of good old Pilo being called *the true king* in that tone. Then she remembered the original question. "Oh yes. We in Mearsies Heili have had plenty of trouble from that stinking, slinking, sliming slobberoo Wan-Edhe!"

Aran's eyes rounded as she whispered, "You name The Hate so easily, as if you do not dread his evil magic hearing."

"Oh, we hate him, too, but he can't hear us say it, or he would have heard a few thousand insults before."

Aran laughed soundlessly. But it was still laughter. And as often happens, laughter opened the way toward real communication.

CJ offered a couple of highly idiomatic and opinionated summaries of the Mearsieans' more spectacular clashes with the hated Wan-Edhe, after which Aran talked about the reforms Jilo had made—how under him the terrible magical barrier had lessened enough that they had begun to have sweet rain in some places, and trees had reportedly bloomed again, and people could travel. Women could have businesses! And make a claim to family names, without having to marry first and provide sons for the army!

Seshe asked, "We walked the streets, and it is so silent. Is music forbidden in Chwahirsland as it was in the Shadow-land?"

Aran looked down, then up, and squared slightly with the manner of one coming to a decision. "It is forbidden." Her voice dropped to a whisper. "But it is not forgotten."

The door opened, and Terry popped his head in. "Time to go. Rel and Jilo both say we might have been noticed, and we don't want to get this family into trouble."

He vanished.

Once they got outside in the darkness, CJ said, "It is so weird. Music, I mean. Maybe even art. All hidden. I always thought the Chwahir were the most boring villains in the world."

"They aren't villains," Dhana said. "They got villained."

"I suspected they had art," Seshe said. "When we discovered that Jilo liked to draw when Kwenz wasn't around.

But now, it's like there's another world here under all the gloom, a secret world."

CJ saw Puddlenose a few steps away, looking back. She hopped to catch up, saying, "What's the plan?"

"Head for the coast." He glanced around, and lowered his voice. "Leastways, Jilo agreed when Rel said let's do it, but I don't know. He's definitely got something on his mind. He's as shifty as a cat in a dog pack."

"Is that why we're walking, and not doing the vagabond magic?"

"Seems like," Puddlenose said.

Jilo had not been able to admit to having the text Kessler had made. He knew Dirk knew, of course, but Dirk was firmly on his side. Nothing would pry it out of him, especially as Dirk knew Jilo intended to go after Wan-Edhe.

But if he told Rel, would Rel take the text away, claiming it was for his own good?

They walked for a time, the air so cold they could see their breath. Jilo didn't dare transfer away, for surely Rel would ask how he was managing transfers when nobody but vagabonds could do it and get away with it — and Rel had proven that he could follow.

Jilo brooded over these things. The road was empty, which was a good thing, as the bleak countryside was barren. Any patrol would easily see them.

When they came across a deserted barn, they decided to camp; fingers and toes were numbing dangerously.

It was late when they settled down — everyone agreeing without speaking to keep Jilo in the middle.

Next morning, they shared out the last loaf of bread, which had been kept back, and walked on, conversations intermittent.

After a while, Jilo slouched up beside CJ.

She side-eyed him. Weird, he didn't quite run, he just kind of shuffled faster. Good ol' Pilo! Clair had said years ago she thought he was smart, and it had turned out she was right. The King had tried his best to squash Jilo's brains with nasty spells. But nothing, it seemed, would change him from being a shambling weed.

"CJ. Got to talk to you."

"Talk away."

"I need your help. You can influence Rel." He raised a hand as CJ began to make scoffing noises. "Influence is maybe the wrong word. At least you might know a way to get him to listen."

He stopped, panting a little as he looked around the dreary landscape They saw no gardens of ornamental plants, only strict rows of vegetables struggling against the faint sunlight behind the nasty, thin smog-layer of heavy ward clouds. Little in their surroundings relieved the sense of drabness. CJ loathed Chwahirsland as the ugliest place in the entire world.

Jilo sent out his breath in a sharp sigh. It froze and fell before he lifted his gaze. CJ was surprised by the purple smudges under his light brown eyes, the marks of exhaustion, as he said, "Kessler gave me the way to do what I want to do more than anything. *Anything.*"

"What's that?" she asked, startled.

"To take down these wards." He glanced at the dirty sky. "Every day the Chwahir suffer under The Hate and the Norsunder invaders is like a stab." He hit his chest. "I want to raise the kingdom against them. The entire kingdom. At once. While I remove the border ward."

"Wow," she breathed, her nerves chilling. They all knew he was antsy about something, but she hadn't thought it would be that big of a deal. "But wait, what about the rest of Norsunder?"

"If we rise at once, we can fight them," Jilo said—less certainly.

CJ rubbed her head, wishing that would stuff more brains into it. Plans that involved kingdoms, Norsunder, and armies made her feel like a bug lost in a rug while waiting for a giant foot to stomp.

CJ grimaced horribly, which Jilo knew meant she was thinking hard. She said, "But Norsunder nosers have to be everywhere, sniffing out plots. The whole country is a lot of people!" She gave her head another fierce rub, her black braids swinging wildly, then said suspiciously, "This sounds like military junk. Have you tried talking to any of the poopsies about this plan? They know a lot about what Norsunder would be capable of, seems to me."

"I can't," Jilo said gloomily. "I tried, a little, but that quiet little one, Sveneric, heard me and said that Detlev's advice is to wait. I don't want to wait. Every day Wan-Edhe restores his rotten magic a little more, and sends Chwahir out to be killed, fighting Norsunder's rotten war."

CJ remembered that evil citadel in Narad, the choking air

that smelled sharp and nasty, the sort of air CJ thought of as stale cigarette breath, though she'd been nowhere near Earth cigarettes for years. It was a poisonous stink, more mental than physical. The evil there had been palpable, seeping through your pores straight into the spirit.

"I sure sympathize. But I think you should wait. If you do it wrong, it won't just be Wan-Edhe squelching you and everybody who tries, it will be a Norsunder squelch. Then you'll never get a chance again. They'll see to that."

Jilo looked up, down, then away. "So you won't help me?"

CJ was torn. She loved being asked to help. She loved big, fast-moving plans, doing things she knew were right, and seeing justice win. But she also felt like Jilo was asking her to jump into a giant rapids full of sharks and rocks. "I'm no good at plans. You know from before, mine pretty much always splat. It's only sheer luck when one works."

The word *luck* came out in English. Jilo had heard it before—but CJ had never been able to explain the concept to anyone's satisfaction.

"So I learned not to break plans when someone else makes one. If I agreed to it. Look, if you're so sure you're right, talk to Rel yourself. If he says it's right, because he sure knows more about war stuff than I do. Anyway, going behind his back feels kinda creepy."

Jilo's jaw jutted, and CJ braced. It had been a long time since Jilo had gotten mad at her. But his shoulders slumped, and he looked down at the ground again, his lank black hair flopping forward, hiding his expression. "All right. Forget I said anything, CJ."

She said in obvious relief, "Great idea."

Jilo loped off, and when next he spoke, it was to Rel as he said, "If we hurry, we can make it to a river town where I know the people. They will give us shelter."

Cold as it was, everyone put their heads down and forced their feet to move faster.

It was nearly dark when they reached the river, which they followed until they spied a worn, warped dock.

Jilo led the way up to a rambling, ramshackle house. This time it was he who stood in the courtyard—but he didn't wait long. People dressed alike in rusty black rushed out to greet him, their voices soft, their manner respectful.

Jilo's companions were accept without question—though

many covert glances were sent Rel's way—until they were settled down with a small, plain potato each, and a bowl of very thin soup with a single ingredient: cabbage.

Jilo sat down, wavering between going off to talk privately with them and eating the food while it was hot. He stared at the small potato, knowing that he'd been given the biggest one, but nothing could hide its wizened shape. Guilt hit him hard for finding this food unappetizing. This was the best the locals had to offer, and he had been eating well outside the border while the Chwahir slowly starved.

But before he could make a decision, Rel rose from the next table over.

"Time to talk," Rel said in Sartoran, sitting across from Jilo.

Rel did not intend to be threatening, but his size and his deep-set dark eyes, and his hard-boned face cut in noble lines, all added to his aura of intimidation.

The weird thing was, Rel seemed completely unaware of it.

Jilo looked down, miserable and disheartened. He had completely failed to keep his plans to himself. In a way, it would be a relief to tell the truth. "I have a plan. To overthrow The King."

"Thought so." Rel gave a nod, and Jilo shot an accusing look CJ's way, but she just shook her head.

Dirk spoke up. "I promised Jilo I'd back him any time he takes on Wan-Edhe." Despite his treble voice, which couldn't be more unlike Kessler's husky, whispery voice, he had his own version of Kessler's mad stare.

"I think you're underestimating Norsunder." Rel's gaze remained steadily on Jilo. "I have no doubt that you could get most of the Chwahir to rise, those not too afraid, or too cynical, or too corrupt. I hate seeing it, too. You know why. But you also know that Norsunder isn't going to stand by and let it happen."

"But Detlev said they are stretched to the limits, on account of Kessler's spell forcing them to live in the world." Jilo indicated Dirk, who just crossed his arms and looked sardonic—increasing the resemblance to his father. "If all Chwahirsland rises at once, I can get control of Narad. And this book will negate so many of the wards!"

"Did Detlev also say that we need to find out more about what Efael is doing and where?"

Dirk looked away.

Jilo sighed. "Yes."

Rel said gently, "It's too soon, Jilo. You've got to wait for the right time. This isn't it."

Jilo swept his papers and the book together with hands that trembled slightly. "No one knows this country and its possibilities, and its limits, like I do. It has to be now. Or there won't be a chance—as always, Chwahirsland will be forgotten while everyone sees to the safety of Colend. Or Sartor. Or any number of other more important kingdoms. You know history as well as I do. So I won't ask for your help—" His voice suspended.

He stared at Dirk, who had suddenly gone very still

Falinneh whispered in Mearsiean, "I knew this soup tasted terrible, but I didn't think anything suspicious was in it." She eyed Dirk. "Hmm, I don't feel the slightest bit frozen, though. Do you, Seshe?"

CJ had already begun to shift her gaze around the plain room of stone walls and plank flooring, the hard planed tables. She'd been forcing down the cabbage soup, saying to herself that at least it was hot. But phew, it could have done with a tiny bit of flavor besides the acidic water.

Then she remembered her nascent Dena Yeresbeth, which was so unreliable—and frequently frightening. "Something's wrong," she said. Her back itched, as if someone stared at her, but they were all alone, and Rel was not the sort to be taken by surprise.

"The only thing wrong is my stomach trying to wiggle up past my other innards to avoid having to receive that soup," Falinneh muttered.

The girls chuckled, and CJ heaved a sigh—the feeling was gone.

Dhana grabbed Falinneh's bowl. "Here. I think it's delicious."

When they were done, they trooped up to the long attic room they'd been given. Pallets lined one wall, directly over the kitchen, so it was less frigid than the outside.

CJ sidled up to Dirk, who said, "Someone else besides The King was trying magical searches. Powerful magic, directed by DY." He added in a flat voice, "Something is going on in the mental realm. Keep your mind-shields tight."

The attack came when they were asleep.

CJ's dreams had turned into a lightless night, her mind running from something terrible down a tunnel away from her body, which made her anxious—she was glad when Dirk's small but callused hand stung her cheek, then relief was followed by terror when her limbs felt heavy, as if she lay underwater.

"Get in a circle," Dirk snapped. Then, "CJ! Give us an image, and everyone concentrate on it if you can't hold a mind-shield."

"Me?" But then CJ understood: she wasn't meant to lead the fight in the mental realm, but to give everyone a mental image so that those who didn't have Dena Yeresbeth could hold onto their minds' integrity.

But where? Not here...CJ imagined them standing in a featureless plain, so that no detail could give away their location. Next—hide identity—on fire—euw—no, pillars of flame! Dirk spread the image around, and each imagined a wall of flame around him or her, doing their best to see the bright, leaping flames, and to feel the warmth.

That lightless night pressed around them, seeking chinks in the flames with icy tendrils as CJ worked hard to keep hers solid yet find and help the girls, and Dirk struggled to hold the ring of fire against the onslaught.

Then the image changed, pulling them all with it: the flames shot skyward in effulgent columns of light.

And the false night vanished.

They got up, making noises of relief. "What was that?" CJ asked Dirk. "You?"

"Jilo." Dirk whooshed out his breath. "I thought you told us you didn't have Dena Yeresbeth."

Jilo mumbled uneasily. "I said I don't know."

"Whatever that was, it ripped us right out of their grip."

"Who is 'they'?"

"Dunno...oh. Oh." Dirk rubbed his eyes. "Sveneric reached me. Fast as lightning. He says, the Host is on the move."

"Let's get back to sleep," Rel said. "Dhana and I will transfer us to the *Tzasilia* in the morning."

Jilo said nothing as he wrapped up in his blanket, which he pulled over his head. His brain hurt. Everything hurt, especially his heart He had failed again. He lay there, teeth clenched lest a sob escape, until exhaustion began to weigh him down, but before he could slip into the threatening nightmares, a thought reached him, quiet and bright as a thread of silver: *Sleep, Jilo. Your time is not yet, but it will come. Before then, you are to build your strength.*

Five

Zranf - Halarialgre

ANDRI AND LIERE LEFT; Liere's voice could be made out from
the top of the stairs telling someone that they were going out to
check on the blizzard, and to do a little scouting if it wasn't too
icy or hard to see.

Senrid remained, fighting the instinct to transfer home to
Marloven Hess. But there was no transferring. He had been
personally warded within moments after that attack on the
mental plane, an attack aimed specifically at him.

He was fairly certain that Imry Llyenthur was behind the
attack, but why? Not knowing anything was almost worse than
grief — about which he could also do absolutely nothing. The
reason that made the most sense was that Marloven Hess,
though conquered, was far from settled. And now that
Norsunder could no longer bring armies over, they had to make
do with what they had. It would make things so much easier if
they could grab Senrid, enchant his brains out, and force him to
mouth out commands to obey the new overlords.

Did Detlev know what was going on? He might. But that
episode at Mondros's cottage, fighting with magic, made it very
clear that there were far more serious matters threatening the

world than the affairs of a single kingdom.

Senrid had begun to suspect that Detlev had sicced David on him, for whatever reason. To guard or to aid? Senrid's futile chase after his daughter's murderer had been singularly useless, other than mostly accidental rescues here and there. David outclassed him in covert movement as well as in martial arts. He also far outclassed Senrid in Dena Yeresbeth, so though David had run up the stairs shortly after Andri and Liere left, Senrid suspected he was in contact with Detlev's son, sitting cross-legged and motionless, the way Liere used to when she was letting her mind wander to the other side of the world.

That meant David was his watchdog. And this particular area was gripped in a blizzard. There was no external escape. What about internal?

When Diamond brought down coffee, he retrieved one of the jugs the brawny man had invited them to sample, and added a generous dollop to his coffee. He had discovered in Lisdan that if you could force down throat-burning, bad-tasting distilled liquor, your senses blunted. You didn't hear on two levels, or see, or imagine, what you did not want to hear and see.

Time to discover if choking down more might smother the torture of thoughts that never ceased.

While he embarked on his experiment, Andri and Liere drifted through the city until they reached the fortress. Here they worked their way along until they found the servants' access, off the kitchens.

"Trying to force through the front is the usual attack, and the worst," Andri murmured. "What we want is the back way. First, let's see what they're wearing. What's going in and out. If there's an alert on, there will be guards all over, and we may as well wait if we intend to do this undiscovered. But a nice, normal morning, right at breakfast time, that's what we want. Rel said the head snake loves luxury, which means he'll be shoveling down a fancy breakfast somewhere in comfort and not in his office..."

Liere provided the illusion of the servants' drab garb, and Andri led the way unerringly in—he'd always believed he had good instincts, without being aware that he'd trained his unreliable Dena Yeresbeth in this sort of focus.

In sometimes heart-stopping zigzags, they made their way to the command floor—and as Andri had predicted, Alsaes was elsewhere, enjoying a leisurely breakfast.

The two worked in silence, Liere scanning the dispatches in the trays. She puzzled out some of the meaning; Norsundrian had adapted Sartoran characters and simplified Sartoran verb forms, but it had its own idioms, and of course it had never been added to the Universal Language Spell. Finally, she murmured, "I think a lot of this is in code. Not much use for us."

"Here's paper. I'm going to copy this map," Andri breathed, pointing to the big table. "Keep watch? I can't do both."

Liere moved to the door, shut her eyes, and monitored the entire floor.

Sveneric had followed them by mind. It was good practice. But now Liere was scanning, her abilities far superior to Andri's. Sveneric let his focus drift, The fortress was somnolent, its conquerors bored with the sameness of the days, knowing that winter still lay ahead—darker and colder.

Sveneric observed Alsaes lingering over his breakfast, moodily staring out at the whirling white beyond the windows and wondering when he would get the promotion he deserved. Halarialgre was a mere flyspeck. He wanted to be king of Colend. Why couldn't he be king?

Sveneric left him and reached for the minds above, all angry, brooding, and suffering from cold and hunger. They were mostly Norsundrians caught breaking orders by hoarding or drunk on patrol duty, except for two thieves caught selling information to both sides. They could be left to their fates.

Sveneric opened his eyes to the basement room, and listened to Lyren-Sartora telling an old Peddler Antivad story, which got Caris-Merian to relate a similar tale about a famous mythic fisher on Geth. Sveneric sympathized with Lyren-Sartora's instinctive attempt to use humor to unite a group that was not going to unite.

He turned his head to take in Senrid sitting alone by the barrels, and withdrew at the intensity of his rage-fueled desolation.

Senrid had built a good wine-fence around his head when Andri and Liere returned, gleefully triumphant. Liere kept bumping up against Andri as they took turns describing what they'd found in Alsaes's office.

Senrid set aside his empty cup and, moving with deliberate care, took his knives from his pack, and began polishing them, as if to prove to the world that he was perfectly in control.

Sveneric rose and began picking up dishes, making sure to retrieve that mug, from which the fumes of liquor rose.

Andri reached inside his outer tunic and unfolded his map. "Alsaes has a pile of paper up there, too much to keep count. I helped myself to a few more sheets, figuring we might be able to use it." He pulled some wrinkled sheets from inside his tunic and stuffed them into his pack.

David had come down behind them from his unnamed errand, brushing snow off himself as he listened. Now he knelt down before the map as Zairna said in his accented voice, "This map, I see what they mark. But I do not understand the markings. Does Norsunder have a standard for such things?"

David said, "No. Each commander will handle such things differently. But we can guess a lot from placement with respect to fronts." He frowned, his gaze snagging on some blotted out notations, with newer notations added. A few of the blots were legible enough for him to say, "Seems they're having some trouble with troop transport. At a guess, Efael is sabotaging Imry's priorities and trying to ram through his own."

Andri drew a finger along several lines. "According to some of the dispatches Liere tried to decipher, these are supply lines." Then he pointed with a callused finger to circled characters, some in what appeared to be remote locations. "I can't figure out these markers. Code of some sort." He looked up inquiringly at David, who shrugged. "If we had more time, we could probably piece it together, but I think we're better off gaining some distance."

"Where is their central HQ?" Zairna wiped his fine, pale blond hair back out of his eyes, and Leander, always distracted by a handsome young man, noted a spiky dragonflower inked up the back of Zairna's neck to curve over one ear. Then his hair covered it again. "Where dwells this Llyenthur?"

Sveneric stashed the dirty dishes by the door, his head averted, as Andri said, "From the indicators, the last place he was listed at was Choreid Dhelerei." Then he caught himself, and winced.

Senrid hated the hesitation in the entire room; he felt the gazes turned his way though he did not look up from polishing his knives.

Leander said, "I doubt he actually *lives* there. It was a mess when we left."

"You'll have to do an unpollution spell once you boot him

out," Lyren-Sartora said to Senrid, hands on hips. "CJ knows lots of spells against villain-cooties."

No one asked what "cooties" were, Sveneric noticed — either they knew CJ and her penchant for throwing about off-world concepts and language, or they equated her with childishness, thus not worth attention.

"And count the silverware," Andri cracked. He too was polishing snow-moisture off his steel. "That's what my cousin always said after my, ah, let's call them visits."

That brought a general laugh, and Sveneric comprehended that humor was the powerful and great leveler only when everyone shared it. It was purest then, when there was no target — or the target was elsewhere. But humor aimed at a present target was just another weapon.

Senrid's grip loosened on the knife and the polishing cloth. He could bear the mention of Choreid Dhelerei; if anyone had brought up Crystal Ingrid, he would have killed them. No, he would have dreamed about killing them, in detail, and then hated himself afterward. So much for numbing these damned emotions —

Footsteps on the stairs brought attention upward. Diamond came down, bearing a tray in order to collect the dishes Sveneric had piled up. "My aunt's knees insist this storm will be gone by tomorrow," she said — then noted the map. "What's that?"

"We made a little visit to Alsaes's office," Andri said, and at Diamond's quick reaction of dismay, added, "No worries. He was not there. And we're pretty good at getting in and out of places without notice."

Diamond drew a slow breath. "We could use such a thing. But none of us dare venture into the fortress. We've tried. It ended badly."

"Here," Andri said. "I thought someone might need it. We'll be moving on soon as we can. Not much use to us."

"Thank you." Diamond gathered the rolled paper to her and made a short bow. Then she said, "I do not know who you are. Nor do I want names. If we are caught, what we do not know cannot be dragged out of us. But...speaking of ending badly, there is one of us being held at the river guard station. We were going to try to rescue him before they bring him up here to the fortress tower, but it must be done before the snow ends."

Andri said, "I'll help."

"I will as well," Liere said.

"Me, too!" Lyren-Sartora declared belligerently.

Sveneric was about to speak up when David grabbed his arm, and murmured in an undervoice, "Let the rest run that rescue. You and I are going to attend to Alsaes."

"Destroy his office?" Sveneric asked, eyes wide.

"No. We're going to use our skill with Norsundrian, and alter all the orders, the map, the reports...we're going to turn their logistics to snot as winter sets in."

Sveneric breathed a soft laugh.

Late that night, he was still occasionally shaking with suppressed hiccoughs when he and David evaded two patrols, eased over a wall in the fortress, and through a window that David had located and unlatched on his earlier scouting foray.

The two made their soundless way down the short hall to Alsaes's empty office about the same time that Senrid discovered he'd actually finished an entire jug of barley wine. All by himself.

He didn't like it, especially as it took continual effort to keep the numbing effect from sliding into headache. But he had *perfect* control, because of Dena Yeresbeth, and to prove it he shut his eyes and listened on the mental plane.

Imry Llyenthur was waiting: *Senrid! Come along, O hero. You know you want to meet me.*

Senrid's head ached with the effort it took to resist answering, especially through the barley wine haze. Which had already betrayed him, or he never would have let his mind-shield slip enough to hear that mocking voice in the mental realm.

Shock jolted him into alertness, but not before an image seared itself onto his mind: a fine drawing room in a tower at some distance, judging by the distant view of the sun setting over mountains that sloped toward the sea. Curule chairs. Carvings of stylized laurel leaves in the door and window frames, the pale blue ceiling.

Central, a mirror image of Llyenthur lounging in one of those cushioned chairs. He appeared to be in his twenties, with long, unkempt light brown hair, wearing a rumpled shirt rolled to the sleeves. Riding boots worn under long trousers. He smiled scornfully into the mirror, his eyes almost as startling a green as Leander's.

Then came his thought: *You should be grateful I gave you enough time to see her off.* With it, the image of Crystal Ingrid with the knife in her chest.

And Senrid was released.

He closed his fingers around the jug and hurled it to smash against the far wall.

At the sudden silence, the startled looks, he dropped his head into his hands, not trusting himself to speak.

Leander motioned to Caris-Merian and Zairna with finger to lips, and for an endless time there was no sound but Senrid's harsh breathing.

Then footsteps and subdued laughter on the stairs as the rescuers returned — followed by David and Sveneric.

As Andri gave a hilarious account of the rescuers lumbering through snow and trying every door but the right one, then leading disgruntled, equally lumbering guards on a half-blind chase through hip-deep snow, David took in the room — the three people sitting almost shoulder to shoulder in a corner, and Senrid on the opposite side, his face averted.

He looked at Leander: *What happened?*

Leander was not very good at contacts; rather than try to frame words without whispering them, he showed the sudden, shocking memory of Senrid apparently asleep, chin sunk on his breast, then he sat upright, and a breath or two later, smashed the barley wine jug.

David met Sveneric's gaze, David with regret. He ought to have stayed instead of giving in to the temptation to have some fun. Something had happened; had the enemy lifted their location? This was not the time to ask.

: *I'll scan*, Sveneric said.

: *No. I'll reach for Adam. That's what he's there for. Nobody is coming immediately, not in this storm.*

Once the triumphant rescue had been retailed, and the hails of congratulation received, Diamond said, "I cannot thank you enough. Nor can we repay you. Our resources are slim, as you know. We have little beside good will. But that we have in abundance: my friends and I agreed to disclose to you the entry way to the Smugglers' Tunnel, our greatest secret. It's a very old tunnel, with some rockfall. Some say the morvende built it then abandoned it a thousand years ago or even more. Don't know. What I do know is, it'll get you through the pass, and well down into Sles Adran on the other side. Where I'm afraid the danger will be higher, but something tells me you folk will know how to navigate. It takes some days to get through. But we'll give you some stores to help you along."

She bowed again, repeated her thanks, and departed.

David said, "Sveneric and I attended to Alsaes's office. All the logistics overseen by Alsaes will be like stung wasps in a day or two." He added, without looking at Senrid, "The storm is already passing; I suggest we make ourselves scarce."

Six

Ela Horbor – Sartoran Sea

THAT LAST NIGHT IN Lisdan, Dtheldevor and her crew had had a lot to talk over, beginning with where the vagabonds ought to set them down.

The first choice would be as close to the Elgar Strait as they could get, which would mean they would have to find a way across the straight to the Port of Jaro in the southeast corner of Imar. From there, they'd have to toil up the coast of Imar and Everon to Wnelder Vee, then to their island where her own ship was hidden. With winter coming on.

Or, they could be set down as close as they could get to the Port of Ela, at the extreme east end of the Sartoran Sea. They'd have to steal a ship, but Dtheldevor shrugged that off. She'd been taking ships with her father and his crew since she was eight years old. There were plenty of enemies to choose from — from the rumors, Norsunder and its allies were the only ones on the sea. Once she and her crew secured a lean, tight, weatherly craft — a pirate ship, in other words — they could hire on some crew and commence action at once.

They argued in circles. The only point in favor of going north, but it was a strong one, was that the *Berdrer* was

Dtheldevor's own ship, familiar all her life. It had all manner of magical enhancements, many given to her by Lilith back in the day when Dtheldevor was defending the coast against repeated Norsundrian attacks.

Dtheldevor longed to get back to the *Berdrer*, which was far more her home than her island hideout. But she also longed to get at the invaders.

The thing was decided by a remark from Peridot Warren, when she said, "But if we steal a ship, we won't have any of the magical aids. We need those."

Down came Dtheldevor's winged eyebrows, meeting in a line over her nose. "Ye think I can't skipper a ship wi'out them tricks? Aye, you're wrong, you are. And I'll just show you. Ela it is."

That decided, the next vexed question was, how to contact the two missing crew. But that didn't last long; Ellen Warren, the most peaceable of the Warrens, pointed out practically, "Sidres always knows where we are, remember."

"It's true," Sarmonwilda declared—the short dawnsinger who had been with Dtheldevor the longest. "He sez he ain't got that mind stuff Liere and them have, but he always knows where we are."

Dtheldevor nodded slowly, "Even better, there's no hidin' centaurs. I'm thinkin' by the time we get us a ship, and steal its provisions and learn its ways, they might just catch up with us. Eh?"

It wasn't really a question. They could tell from her tone of voice that she'd decided.

Ela was at the extreme edge of the vagabonds' reach, but they managed.

Once Dtheldevor and the others were set down in a secluded court in an old caravan inn that Rel knew—now deserted—Dtheldevor said, "First Ellen and me, we'll stroll along. Get a sense o' things. Then go see if Ma Lenta's sister is still at the bakery. Resta yez, stay right here. Joey, they might be grabbing boys your age, still. And they might be suspicious o' groups. Take a look at what's in the harbor.""

Dtheldevor and Ellen left, keeping their heads down. The smell of brine reached the other, sharp and heavy on the cold air. Deon could not suppress excitement. She was truly one of the actual crew, and not merely another wanderer having fun on board, as she had been on all her previous cruises, only one of which had turned out to have any danger. She was almost a pirate, and with the most famous one in the world! She was going to be just as famous — more! And rich, and she would build a home for orphans and call it after Lilah...

None of them had slept the night before. Deon followed Gloriel between a storage building and what smelled like a barn. She discovered they were on a fenced cliff overlooking the harbor, the choppy gray sea filled with a forest of slowly undulating bare masts under a low gray sky. Deon stared, wondering which ship would be theirs. When she'd sailed before, she hadn't had to learn the different types. That had been too much like lessons, and there had always been fun games to play instead.

"Some real old tubs out there," Joey remarked. "They'll be slow as turtles."

The twins began comparing the ships, Peridot mostly criticizing. Deon couldn't see any of the details they either praised or disparaged — most of the terms had to do with how the craft were built, and so were nonsense to her. She dared not ask lest they kick her out for her ignorance. Especially Peridot, whose caustic comments were both pithy and plentiful.

Deon had begun shivering from the knife-sharp cold wind straight off that gray sea when Ellen showed up, long blond braid swinging. "Sign is still good. Found her," she said to her siblings and Sarmonwilda, who was even shorter than Deon. Though she was a teenager. But dawnsingers were shorter than everybody else, she'd learned once.

"You'll never guess who's here," Ellen added low-voiced as they cut across the road and entered a back alley that smelled like fish.

"Detlev and the Host," Peridot cracked.

"Ma Lenta?" Joey asked, scanning the weather-worn row of shops. Sure enough, worked into the decoration around the BAKED GOODS sign was the smugglers' sign, a stylized thumb and its mirror image.

"Right."

They ducked between the buildings, a narrow passage barely wide enough for a wheelbarrow, as Gloriel, last in line, glanced back. She was relieved to note that the patrols all seemed to be below on the quay and the wharf, or rowing to and from the ships. She hadn't seen any at their end of the upper level — which was mostly small shops and old, rambling, much-patched domiciles.

"I had to come down here to me sister's," Ma Lenta was saying to Dtheldevor at that moment, as the two older women sat facing her, mugs of hot punch before each. "Them graybacks has taken Jaro for themselves." She shook her white-streaked head. "Eight hundred years, the Elgar Strait treaty o' freedom of the seas held. Eight centuries, and now them Chwahir broke it." She made a spitting motion to the side. "Helped by the graybacks."

"What else can yez tell us?"

The sisters looked at once another. They had lived on the margins their entire lives, preying on grabby governments, and on pirates riding low, which meant a big haul, and recent—pirates not being known for trade. They stole, they turned their loot into coinage that could be spent, and they lived high until the loot ran out, that was the usual pattern of pirate life. The sisters were raised to an age-old system of barter that skirted customs and guilds, going back to the empire days.

"The enemy is trying to own the seas. Like they said about the Venn in the old days, they got magic, but they don't, as yet, got the ships, except for Chwahir vessels—but those are old, old."

Dtheldevor nodded knowledgeably. "Well-built, but older—they ain't got the wood to build new."

"That's changin'," Ma Lenta said sourly. "No more Wood Guild, so they're cuttin' down trees anywhere near coasts, or upwards of rivers where they can float the logs downstream. But it'll still take time to build weatherly craft."

"Meanwhiles, the Venn up north, some of 'em are fighting up that way. Islanders as well. And off the east coast, the king and queen o' Khanerenth is buildin' a fleet. Need all comers."

Dtheldevor nodded. "That sounds good. We might join 'em till I gets me a new crew worked up good."

The door to the store in the next room banged open, setting the bell over it to jangling. "That'll be them," Dove, Lenta's sister, muttered sourly. "No one else bangs like that, no manners. And like as not no pay. You got papers?"

"Not yet," Dtheldevor said.

"Quick, down the back way to the storeroom, in case they take it into their heads to snout around."

Dtheldevor was gone on the last word, light-footed when she needed to be. She gathered her small crew and they ghosted down to the storeroom—and through the false door to the other storeroom. They crouched down in a circle, surrounded by barrels and boxes of goods. "Now look here. We're gonna do some scoutin', and steal us a likely craft if we can."

"I can scout," Deon exclaimed. "I'm a good scout! I did a lot of scouting in Sarendan in the bad old days, and never got caught."

Dtheldevor looked down at her rough-palmed hands, then up. She said kindly, "But I ain't seen ye doin' it, see? And you don't know what kind o' craft I want, right? When you sailed with us, it was for fun. Nothin' wrong with that. But you never really crewed. Can ye tell the difference betwixt a rake-masted raffee an' a craft rigged for deep oceans, sturdy but slow?"

Deon twitched. "Raffee?"

"Me'n Gloriel can teach Deon about ships," Peridot offered.

Deon hugged her knees to her chest. Weird, how at first she thought the twins looked alike, but now they didn't. It was their expressions—Gloriel seemed always to be lost in a daydream. She kind of reminded Deon of Lilah, a little. But Peridot was so bossy.

"Do that. Get some rest. All o'ya look tired," Dtheldevor said. "Joey'n me will see what's out there. Ellen, you know what you're scoutin'. Make sure you're thievin' from them, not locals."

Ma Lenta gave them a room above the kitchens, tucked into the attic. It contained rag-stuffed mattresses, which was just fine for the gang. The air was warm, being directly over the ovens, so everyone stretched out gratefully and even Deon (who was insisting she wasn't tired, she was used to staying up for days and days) fell asleep almost at once.

Deon slept hard, in spite of a tangle of bad dreams about Norsunder, and Lilah. She woke blearily, troubled by her last glimpse of her cousin Bren and how unhappy he'd looked before they all parted. And the way stolid, blond Innon looked down at the ground. It was much easier to hang onto her sense of affront. Why hadn't they just come along with her? Why should *they* get to decide what the remaining three Sheridan Brothers were going to do?

Noise broke into her thoughts, which she relinquished gladly.

"Come on, rouse up," Peridot said, nudging Deon with a foot. "We're now delivery apprentices, and there's bread ready to be run."

Deon scrambled up, suppressing an unasked-for opinion about getting stuck running boring errands. When were they going to get a ship?

Not for a week, as it happened. Before then, they traded off carrying a piece of paper stating that they were apprentices for Dove's bakery. Being a small establishment, it had no more than four youngsters — two of whom were actual apprentices. Dtheldevor's crew had to trade off going out in the weather to deliver.

When Deon was with Ellen or Gloriel, it was less arduous than usual. Gloriel told stories of their past exploits, and Ellen mostly watched around them — later, she told Deon she was memorizing the guard patrol patterns.

Joey and Peridot made it their business to lecture Deon on types of ships, and then quiz her on them.

Her first two days of lectures ended almost in tears. She could not tell the difference between a trysail and a raffee, especially when no sail had been raised, the ships floating at anchor. Peridot got sarcastic when pointing out the differences in yards and rigging more than twice. The same went for brigantines and three-masted schooners.

But by the end of the week, Deon was beginning to understand the difference between standing and running rigging, what a cut-boom was, the characteristics of handling a square foresail as opposed to the triangle of the fore-and-aft rigged ship.

The day after she successfully named every type in the harbor, and went to sleep triumphant, she seemed to have barely shut her eyes when she was shaken awake.

Faint light from somewhere highlighted Dtheldevor's slanty cheekbones. "We found us our ship, and we gotta get goin' if we want to use the tide."

Seven

DURING THE LONG COUPLE of weeks that they toiled into the mountains, Senrid grimly wrestled with regret.

Sobriety brought conviction that he'd —*just*— retained enough wit not to reveal their location. The contact had lasted no longer than couple of heartbeats, long enough for Llyenthur to loose his poison darts along with the image. Senrid had closed him out before responding.

Regret made him turn down Diamond's offer of more barley wine when the donated stores were handed over. Regret made him endure side-eyed glances from the others, though he offered no explanation.

Finally, regret forced him to answer David's perfectly justified questions, when the two of them walked at the end of the line that first day.

It didn't happen immediately. To Senrid, it appeared that David waited until they had been walking a while, and the others had fallen into conversation, or were engaged in looking around as Leander marched at the front, holding the firestick aloft like a torch.

That was true enough, but he'd also waited until Adam

could listen in on the mental plane: *Adam, remember those long lessons about losing control of dark magic, using the example of bombs and the physics of gunpowder?*

: I remember the lecture on how gunpowder does not work in the worlds around Erhal. Your point?

: My point is, Senrid is like a bomb about to explode. I don't want to ignite it through misunderstanding. Specifically his avoidance of Liere. They don't act like two people after a fight.

David paced beside Senrid for a time, then said conversationally, "You usually don't throw other people's dishware around. I take it you're a mean drunk."

"I wasn't—"

"You," David cut in, not angrily, but firmly, "were drunk."

Senrid looked away sharply, one hand flexing. Then he decided that he deserved it. "My mind-shield slipped long enough for Imry Llyenthur to taunt me about my daughter's murder."

"Ah. Yes, I'd probably throw dishes, too. Maybe knives."

"He didn't get location."

"No," David commented, "or we'd all be guests in his lockup. Or dead. Whichever suited him most." *: Adam, help me out here. Do I ask why?*

: No. Wait.

Senrid's remorse only reached so far. "I turned down Diamond's offer of a jug," he said, his consonants precise. The fire was getting close to the fuse.

: Should I encourage him to take off?

: Don't you see? He can't. He wants to, but he can't abandon Liere. Or Lyren-Sartora, for different reasons, I think.

Crush drama? Senrid? David inwardly shrugged. They could wait it out—those things never lasted, everyone said. Though for unwilling bystanders it could seem to drag on forever. Come-and-go, was the popular expression; it was common at their age, even expected. Senrid's problem couldn't be that simplistic, though it was a shame he got saddle wood and mourning hitting him from two directions—on top of losing his kingdom. But of those three things, surely a crush was the least important.

Then came Sveneric's thought: *Detlev says perhaps it is Adamas Dei's comet.* And he was gone.

David sighed softly at this oblique hint that callowness seemed to be a shared commodity. He'd slogged through

Adamas Dei's few writings years ago, and retained a few scraps of that particular bit: *The cup still warm from our shared wine...the candle end mute evidence of a night of talk...*[something something] branches of a tree, then across the sky flamed the eternal comet on its course...poesy-poesy-poesy.

David shrugged again. If it turned out to be important, he could pester Adam to find that quotation, and then tell him what it meant.

One night they camped early, having reached the middle of a tunnel. Outside a winter storm shrieked down the canyon walls, scouring the rocks and thick-barked trees with icy needles. Inside the air was so frigid that sound bounding from rock to rock struck sharply, almost shattered.

Leander brought out the firestick, and as everybody drew close, looking up the vast, striated rock, their light revealed what they otherwise would not have seen: ancient paintings on the ceiling and walls.

His share of the food forgotten, Leander wandered slowly up and down, staring up at the stylized figures in golden diadems, with tiny chimes hanging down either side of wide-eyed brown faces. The draped clothing hearkened back uncountable centuries.

"Here's your share," Lyren-Sartora said, setting down warmed travel bread and a few segments of orange before Senrid.

He flicked up his hand in a gesture that was both thanks and an end to the conversation.

"I wish there was writing," Leander commented, winding his way through his companions as he kept his gaze on the walls.

Andri took a place at the other end of the cave from Senrid. In their days of travel he'd observed a few things. The worst thing—and the thing he couldn't do anything about—was the realization that the famous Senrid Montredaun-An avoided him. Andri regretted it; in other circumstances, he would have gone first to Senrid, but instead he cut out David, as the others were busy talking and eating. "You've got that?" He tapped his forehead. "Anything we should know?"

David looked up, the fire highlighting the bones of his face, making him look almost familiar at certain angles.

"How much do you want to hear?" David returned.

Andri lifted a shoulder. "Whatever relates to us right now."

"The Host has passed over the strait to Drael. Might be looking for a place to settle."

"Drael?" Andri frowned. "I thought all the big fortresses are here, on the Sartoran continent. No, I forgot the Venn lands way up north."

David snorted. "No fortresses for our fine overlords. The only one who likes stone and dungeons and the aroma of old blood is Efael. But his sister loathes those things, and prefers luxury. Svir and Connanre definitely like refined surroundings."

Andri turned away, and found that Liere had made a space for him. He sat down beside her and she leaned against his arm, and smiled up at him.

He smiled back, wondering where this romance would lead. Here was another famous name, far more famous than Senrid. He was still a little surprised that so famous a person had picked him for her first passion. In his experience, first passions seldom lasted, but he meant to enjoy it while it did — she was smart and beautiful and as kind as the summer sun in the mornings.

Liere relished his proximity as she looked around the cave. His warmth, his masculine scent—a man's scent, but specifically *him*. When he touched her, even so ephemeral a touch as a brush of his fingertips over her cheek, the heat made her shiver, and all the world closed in to that caress and its promise. It was sweet, it was still wonderfully new — and it was such a relief from the old gnawing anxiety that still simmered below the surface, ready to claw her into that old sense of incompetence. Like when she saw Senrid clearly preferring to walk alone, though she'd tried to include him, the way it always used to be. He wasn't angry, or he would have said so. He was just...closed off.

She turned her focus outward and looked around. There were many rocks tumbled about, some ancient, a few fallen from the ceiling, creating gaps in the old paintings. "Someone lived here once," she said, peering at the rocky groupings, some of which formed little walls or cubicles, almost.

"Definitely," Leander called over his shoulder. "But I suppose we've stopped long enough. Time to move on?"

Caris-Merian had set her pack down near Lyren-Sartora's, but silently picked it up again.

Liere got up, sending a glance Senrid's way. He'd already begun walking, Leander loping to catch up, though he sent a last longing glance back, the shadows flickering wildly over the painted figures, making their eyes glitter as if alive.

Liere stared in puzzlement at Senrid's straight back, so familiar, and yet not. It wasn't the square back of Senrid as a boy. It had lengthened and broadened at the top—the man's V, though so different from Andri's long back.

The evaporation of their old friendship, once the center of her life—it must have happened while she was in Geth. And it was natural. People drifted apart. Once she'd seen Hibern often, back when she'd lived in Bereth Ferian. Then, after the alliance lost Karhin, silence. They'd reconnected in Sartor, as peers—that had been the only good thing about that episode. And yet once they got to Lisdan, Hibern had not had ten words to say to her, and had vanished altogether, without a farewell.

These things fretted her over the succeeding days, as they began the gradual downward descent. Thoughts brought up some of the old turmoil, the sense that she simply wasn't good enough, or smart enough, or disciplined enough...and so she clung to Andri the more. She could smother her stupid, *stupid, useless* thoughts in physical proximity.

They reached the end of the tunnels.

The mountains were too vast, as yet, to be patrolled, or even to be warded. Leander, scouting ahead, discovered that the Norsundrians guarded the main roads that led upward into the mountains, which meant the travelers had to turn off the road and pick their way down through ice-white, tumbled pocket-valleys and along blue-ice frozen streams past the amazing lacework of waterfalls stilled by the frosty air.

Leander was invaluable now. He scouted several times a day, returning to tell them when to hide, and when to advance.

Everyone was relieved when he reported signs of civilization at last, a village high up on the mountains at the very farthest reach of Sles Adran, where roads to abandoned mines intersected with the recently closed trade route.

A huge inn—a converted and expanded barn—was the social center of the village and the outlying sheep and yeath farms. Their being so isolated, up where the weather was severe a good part of the year, meant that it was customary to start stocking up for the winter by early summer, so the village had plenty of goods to enhance the delicious suppers the place was famed for among trade caravanners.

Leander ran back and reported his find.

Andri, wearing a rather disreputable, oatmeal-colored knit hat donated by Diamond's resistance gang (Lyren-Sartora commented sourly that not even thieves would want it) pulled down to his eyebrows, ventured out to make inquiries. He discovered that travelers who couldn't, or wouldn't, move on in either direction, had taken up residence at the inn. He reassured the harassed innkeeper family with a lot of boring but comfortable lies—party of prentices—caught by the weather—lost on the road due to snow—making their way home. His accent was close enough to the Adrani speech patterns to not raise questions.

While they waited, a few murmured conversations occurred, smothered by the slow sough of the wind through the cedar trees, and the sudden chuff of slow falling off branches to the drifts below.

Andri returned and reported that he'd managed to secure one room. He'd said he had a party of four, "But the place is so crowded that my guess is, we can get everyone in without a problem, as long as some sleep on the floor."

They started down the rest of the path.

"In books, grief is eased by shared purpose," Sveneric remarked to David as they trooped down through white-coated, soughing pines toward the inn, only visible by its lazily drifting smoke plume.

David cast a glance at Caris-Merian's straight back between Julian and June's shorter forms. "Mmm."

Sveneric looked up, his gaze serious. "I'm trying to learn something about grief."

David looked down at that austere face, the intelligent high brow. Sveneric had been almost frightening, how swiftly he learned and how deeply he thought. Sveneric no doubt had not only read everything Adamas Dei wrote, but recollected it.

However, did he understand it? In so many ways he was still so young—what could he know about grief, much less forms of love and romance? Sveneric missed Curtas, sure. Everybody did who knew him. But Curtas had seldom been around Sveneric after he turned two or three—more often Curtas had been assigned elsewhere, learning to master building. And Noser was problematical—

Ah. He was forgetting Darian Selenna's grief. Useless to say that Sveneric had never met Peitar Selenna. When Peitar had, as MV put it, committed suicide by obsession, Darian had been so small, and utterly devastated. Sveneric had spent days with him in rapport, hours at a time, protected by Adam and Siamis; in those days, the danger of predatory minds had been relatively small.

Yes, he knew grief. Maybe even anticipatory grief? Detlev had been blunt with them as long as David could remember, saying he did not know if he would survive what was to come.

And the "what" was here. Now.

David mentally shelved that subject, and refocused. Sveneric did not need to be worrying about Senrid. Detlev had assigned David that task. "As for Senrid and grief, consider the natural frustration of a Marloven king who can't be home fighting the good fight."

"Oh. Yes." Sveneric slipped in the slush, and thereafter paid attention to his walking.

They mounted the stone steps to the inn, and unloaded their gear in the rented room. Then—immense relief—ducked through the cleaning frame to get rid of weeks of grime, then they put their things through, and spread anything damp to air out.

Senrid stayed in several people's minds. Leander had known Senrid the longest. They didn't interfere in one another's personal lives: if Senrid wanted to talk to him, he knew where Leander was. Zairna saw a prince forced to scuttle to safety instead of defending his home. He sympathized, but silently: there was nothing anyone could say to make the situation easier, certainly not a stranger who was not going to talk about his own home at all, or why he'd left it.

Andri watched Liere as she tracked Senrid setting himself a bedroll at the farthest corner near a window that might leak cold air, but would give egress in danger—and no immediate neighbors.

It was also the opposite side of the room that Liere had chosen.

Senrid left with David to go downstairs.

Andri touched Liere's arm. "Leave him be."

She sighed. "I feel I ought to be doing something. I used to be able to do something. You led your band. You know how important good understanding is for cooperation."

"We don't have a leader," Andri said. "And we're not a

band, we're a collection of people heading in the same direction. Come on, let's get something to eat and enjoy not having our toes frozen."

Liere assented, but she couldn't keep herself from watching where Senrid sat—for he hadn't chosen a place when she and Andri got downstairs, though he'd gone down first. She looked through the haze of smoke and steam, sorting the crowd until she located one straight shoulder, instantly familiar; a shift and there was Senrid's square-cut curly blond hair, grown shaggy in back after six months of neglect. He was over at the counter, buying a bottle of something.

Andri gestured toward a table, where Leander and Caris-Merian had squeezed up to make space for two.

Liere hesitated. Her plan had been to wait until Senrid sat down so she could sit near him. But he dawdled at the counter, apparently chatting to the innkeeper. Question flashed through her, mixed with a little impatience; from all appearances he was talking longer to that grandfather than he had to any of his friends for a week.

She sat down, upset. They hadn't argued. Or disagreed. Nor had Senrid argued or disagreed with Andri. Liere had seen them practicing together several times, and there was never any sign of the shuttered expression Senrid sometimes got when Kyale Marlonen was being especially shrill.

Liere ate mechanically, aware of Senrid drinking again. At least it was slowly. But that was a strange change. He'd always loathed anything distilled or fermented—couldn't even stand the smell, he'd said.

They were among the last to get their food. As people finished and tables emptied, others pushed the tables back to the walls, and someone started up music. The wooden floor thumped and rumbled as pipes and wind instruments screed and tweedled merry tunes. Many of the songs had easy choruses that the entire room joined in on. Lyren-Sartora joined them, dancing and singing happily until her feet, tired from days of walking, protested.

Others paired up, let go, and paired with others, laughing the more breathlessly, aware of their escape, until Andri, sensing Liere's unhappiness, held out his hand. "Let's join 'em."

Her mood changed dragonfly quick and they took their places among the others, faces glowing in the firelight, eyes wide and bright. He held out his hands and she took them, tingling with a rush of honey-fire whenever they touched. The world glowed with her inner flame: the snow framing the windows silvery, the cold sky beyond a pattern of mystery, the plain room a vessel for all-encompassing love.

They danced in a circle, drawing closer and closer together, until fun altered to tenderness, and then to intimacy — intimacy was too intense, too private — she sensed eyes, though she did not see them, and broke away.

Finally, when the room began to feel uncomfortably warm, the air thick with the combined smells of mulled wine, wet wool, fried onions, and too many people, the locals began to leave, easing the crowding.

Zairna drifted upstairs shortly after Leander excused himself and left. He'd been up early scouting. The others had already gone.

"Done?" Andri asked.

"I'll be along," Liere said. "I'm thirsty."

It was not quite a lie, and Andri knew it was not quite a lie. If she wanted to turn to her old friend, it was all right with him; life was sometimes short. Grab love and laughter while you could, he firmly believed.

He ran upstairs, and she watched after for a breath or two. Odd, how empty a room was when he was absent, which had nothing to do with the amount of space his skinny butt took up. She yearned for the comfort of his presence, but not yet.

She turned on the bench — and there was Senrid, easily visible now, alone at the very last little table, his glass empty, but his cheeks were flushed.

"Senrid," she said. "Why are you drinking? And alone?"

Senrid's hands tightened around his wine glass. He said to it, and not to her, "An unsuccessful retreat from stupid questions."

Stupid. He'd actually said the word — to her. Ah, not exactly to her. He was talking to the empty glass. But she was the only listener, for the glass was inert. Instinct clamored to leave him alone — every line and angle of his body was a rebuff — but that very rebuff brought her closer.

"Senrid, we used to talk all the time." And when he didn't respond, she said, "It hurts me to see you like this!"

His chin came up so sharply that she stepped back, but then

his face blanked utterly.

She backed another step, waiting for him to apologize, to stop her. Even to get mad if he needed to—if she'd done something stupid, shouldn't he tell her so she wouldn't do it again? She backed another step, and then retreated, thoroughly upset.

Andri caught her near the top of the stairs. "Liere, he doesn't want to talk. If he changes his mind, we're right in hearing."

"But I want to fix it—I want our old friendship back. If I did something wrong, I need to know. I want to *help*."

"Help is a shared action, can you see it? Remember what you told me when I was trying to get over Yeres's loving attentions?"

"Yes, but—" She realized she was about to say, *But this is about Senrid and me and friendship, not Norsundrian mind-torture*, then she perceived the connection. She was trying to make Senrid responsible for her own pain. It hurt—deeply—but she saw it. "All right."

Later on she did her best to sleep. And the next day, she kept to her side of the room when Senrid appeared, his head wet from a cold dunking in a bucket of cold water, and said to the room in general, "I'm sorry. Llyenthur got into my mind a few nights back. Reacted badly."

Liere willed him to look at her, and talk to her, and rekindle the way they had shared their thoughts, so easy and effortless she'd never considered how valuable it was until it was gone.

"That stinks," Leander said, and others made similar noises. Even June gave him a sober glance, a change from her resting teenage sullen face.

Andri slanted Liere an encouraging smile. Very well, then, she'd leave it to Senrid to speak or not speak. After all, he was a grieving father, but her daughter was alive. Her gaze slid to Lyren-Sartora, who was chatting to Caris-Merian.

Maybe that was it.

Eight

Eastern end of the Sartoran Sea

DEON WAS EAGER TO prove how much she knew about ship types. They scrambled into their shoes and coats, picked up their bags or knapsacks, and followed downstairs in a silent line. At the end, Dtheldevor put a solid gold coin on the main counter next to a waiting row of clean glasses; Dove had insisted she wouldn't take money from Norsunder fighters, but everyone knew how tough things were now, and she was feeding a lot of extra mouths.

The half-moon drifted in and out of clouds, sometimes shedding silvery light. Dtheldevor led them at a rapid pace, Deon almost on her heels, Peridot just behind her.

Gloriel knew her twin was on the watch for a chance to tell Deon what to do. Weird, how over the years she and her twin had gotten farther apart, not closer. Their two younger sibs, Ellen and Joey, were buddies. They even had a kind of secret language, bits remembered of English from when they were still little kids on Earth, that no one else knew. Sometimes Gloriel felt alone in the middle of the gang, though she didn't say anything, because it was disloyal. She'd begun hoping that Deon could be her friend, but already she could tell that Deon was too much like Peridot.

Dtheldevor stopped before one of the many piers that now belonged only to Norsunder. Everyone else had to anchor out in the waters — and wait for the patrol boats to inspect their papers.

Dtheldevor indicated a clean-lined racing yacht, narrow, fore-and-aft rigged, the masts raked for speed. It had been taken by the Norsundrians to use as a patrol boat because it was fast. "That's ours," she breathed as everyone's breath clouds mingling briefly before dissipating. "Right now got only rockheads on board."

Deon had heard so many great terms for Norsundrians she wasn't always sure what somebody meant by them. "Rockheads?" She mouthed at sleepy-eyed Ellen, who just shrugged, but Gloriel mouthed back, "Soul-bound."

Deon's blood sang with ferocious giddiness. At last, at last, she was going to strike back against Lilah's murderers. "Can we kill 'em?"

Dtheldevor turned her way. "Best ya let me tell the plans, then come questions. Sometimes we have to move fast, see." When Deon nodded — after all, this was world-famous Dtheldevor — she went on, "We take the ship fast. Sail out on the tide. Here's how we do it. Up over the side, and each to a station..."

Deon's hand sweated as she gripped her knife and hunched over, following Joey Warren up the side. She knew she was a very good spy — she'd learned to be one during the terrible days when Lilah's uncle Darian Irad had been a villainous king. But there hadn't been any Norsundrians, nor had there been any ocean.

By the time Dtheldevor was halfway through her rapid instructions, Deon was glad she hadn't been sent on the spy mission. She thought she'd learned everything, but she discovered she was still ignorant. There were way too many things she would have missed but the others recognized — like the fact that "rockheads" meant the Norsundrians soul-bound. These were not much good for anything except obediently following orders.

It turned out that Dtheldevor had picked this yacht by the second night, but they'd had to wait, partly for the two centaurs to arrive — which had happened earlier that day — and partly for the ship to be provisioned, and for the rotation to be all soul-bound.

The last of the supplies were on board a little early, and the Norsundrians were waiting for the top of the tide, as instructed. The water splashed over the lower pilings and docks as Dtheldevor's gang slipped along, fast and sure as wharf rats. Sharly and Sidres tripped along behind, blurred by vagabond magic; they were well practiced at running along the dock and leaping over the rail to the deck.

Deon watched the Warrens jump and catch hold of the rail, then copied them, her heat thundering. She held on with all her strength, then got a leg over.

Someone gripped her arm and gave her a yank, then let go—Dtheldevor ran quietly along the deck and vanished.

Peridot came up close in the yellow light of a lantern hanging at the pointy end of the boat. She motioned violently toward the hatch, a dark square in the deck, then gave Deon a boot in the butt. Not hard, but definitely bossy, as one who had the right.

Deon resisted the impulse to protest. She wanted everyone to like her, so she clamped down on her temper as she followed Peridot to the hatch.

Peridot vanished almost like magic. Deon still had to place her foot on each rung of the ladder. She clung hard, trying not to fall when the ship lurched and wiggled, until a hand took her arm, and pulled her somewhat impatiently.

Deon bit back a protest, and let the hand tug—and her feet reached deck at last. It smelled musty wherever they were, like too many people, and old food. Even soul-bound had to eat, because their bodies had to exist, even if the real true self of the person was gone, and only a few memories and habits remained.

Horrible noises reached Deon from aft. Peridot appeared, dots of blood on her clothes, black in the weak moonlight.

Peridot made a meaning gesture: this one is yours.

Deon knew that this fellow was soul-bound, evil, and she really wanted to kill one, but when Peridot pushed her impatiently toward him, she hesitated.

This wasn't some mean-faced, hulking brute. He wasn't much older than Puddlenose of the Mearsieans. His face was just a face, his hair shaggy, like no one bothered to remind him to get it cut any more, but once it had been in the square-over-the-collar cut you saw in most military fellows. He had a lot of scars, some still healing.

He just sat, staring at nothing, one hand on his knees, the other picking at a scab in a mindless way that made her stomach roil.

Deon gripped her knife. If he'd just threaten her, or get mad, or...something. Deon knew that Darian Selenna would hate this. Lilah would have hated this, too. In fact, Deon knew with a sudden, certain conviction that Lilah would have refused to do it. Tie him up, she'd say. Knock him out.

Yeah, and look what happened to her.

An impatient smack on her shoulder made her jump. She whirled around—there was Peridot. "Coward?" Peridot's eyes were black in the weak, flickering light: the candle flame, once straight, had begun to flicker and waver, making the fellow's unblinking gaze seem as if he were looking around.

Deon gritted her teeth. Lunged. Stabbed—and the point of her knife caught on a button of the man's jacket, and her wrist turned. She yelped as he looked up, his right arm coming up in a blocking blow. She reversed her grip and came around with all her strength, striking him behind the ear with the hilt, the way they used to knock out guards.

He slumped over.

"It's good to let 'em go," Peridot whispered. "He's not a real person. His mind's gone."

Deon discovered she was trembling. Somehow trying to stab the knife past that thick jacket into the fellow's heart was just too horrible an idea.

Peridot shoved past her. "Go report that we're done," she said, and Deon left, hands out wide to keep herself from falling.

She wasn't fast enough to get away before hearing the sounds of a throat being slit. She leaned against the ladder, gagging, until roused by Peridot shoving past her, and going up the ladder like magic propelled her.

From the deck came murmurs, then Peridot's sarcastic, "...and I had to croak Deon's, too. Real great help there!"

Deon leaned her forehead against her arm, tears burning her eyes.

"You can't kill, either?" said a soft voice.

She looked upward. Blocking the stars was an odd shape— one of the centaurs, the young one. "If you can't, tell Dtheldevor. Sharly and I can't. She accepts that."

Deon pulled herself up the ladder, clinging with trembling

limbs when the ship lurched, which it seemed to do every time she loosened her hand to attempt another rung. When she reached the deck, Peridot and her siblings were nowhere in sight — Deon heard the rattle and thud from the rigging above, and recognized the sound of sails being set.

Sharly's large eyes reflected pinpoints of starlight. "I can't kill anyone. Neither can Sidres. Even though they are soulbound, and probably need to be freed."

"He wasn't even old," Deon said, her voice squeaking.

"No."

"But he was evil," Deon said, shivering.

"He was bound to evil," Sharly whispered back, her eyes lifted toward the sails. She and Sidres were strong — they could haul a line each by themselves. "We won't know if he was a bully who surrendered his soul, or it was taken. Either way, he had no will or life of his own. But there is always hope, however thin a thread."

Dtheldevor appeared from around one of the masts, "An' that's why I call Sharly my conscience. Heh, keeps me from turnin' pirate!" She laughed, and Sharly smiled. "Maybe now he can ride the waters. Like me dad. Or go on to a new world." She loped aft, gazing up at something in the rigging above.

Peridot whispered to Deon, "She believes in reincarnation." And rolled her eyes.

Deon repeated the word to herself, and whispered back, "You mean you get another life, but you're still you? You don't think that's real?"

Peridot lifted a shoulder. "Do *you* remember any life before this one?"

"No one knows," Gloriel murmured, on Deon's other side. "Dtheldevor likes to believe they get another chance. And who is to say they don't?" She frowned past Deon at her sister. "*I* think there is always a chance. Of something. I dream of it sometimes —"

"Oh, what. Ever," Peridot drawled.

Deon liked Gloriel, but did not want to hear about her dreams. People's dreams were always boring. "Dtheldevor also said, ride the waters like her dad?" She hugged her arms against her skinny ribs. "You mean ghosts?"

"We've seen them once or twice."

"Ghosts!" Deon repeated. Nobody had talked about ghosts during her previous days on Dtheldevor's ship. Now she wondered if she was truly in the inner circle at last, and sighed. "I sure wish Lilah could be a ghost with me. I miss her so much. What makes some people be ghosts?"

"Some think they're just mirages. Like illusion magic on the stage," Peridot muttered. "Only you see what you want to see." She turned her head at the sound of Dtheldevor's step, and shrugged, a sharp movement.

"You talkin' about ghosts again?" Dtheldevor asked. "No use in it, or I'd talk to me dad. They don't talk. But I seen what I seen." She snapped her fingers. "Quiet, now. We're gonna creep out on the tide. Joey's gotta be the only thing anyone sees, there with the soulsucker's jacket." She pointed at the wheel, where Joey stood, wearing a Norsundrian coat.

"Are we attacking more Norsundrians?" Deon whispered.

Dtheldevor gave a snort. "When we ain't drilled? We'd be 'bout as good as a peg-legged snake in a horse race. What we're gonna do is train. Hard. Until your hands know what to do before your brain catches up. One idea is to sail outa the Sartoran Sea, and down south with the winter winds on our beam, until we catch up with the Khanerenth king and his fleet. Another is to stay on this sea. Make it our cruising ground. But first, I promised Senrid I'd see somebody in Remalna. Which is right close by. And maybe betwixt all these we'll be able to get us a real crew—one big enough to fight and sail a real ship—in which case we'll take us a bigger one."

Nine

Sles Adran

THE LAST OF THE mountain gorges and inclines fell away past the tired travelers. They emerged on one of the last rises one sharp, clear morning, so clear the light glared off the snow, which squeaked and cracked under their footsteps. A hilly country stretched below, dark green fir frosted with snow. Their breath froze into powdery motes.

They were barely recognizable; you had to know who wore which coat to tell them apart, because everyone hid as much skin as possible.

David sniffed out dark magic enchantment tracers, which they avoided, and Leander waited for nightfall to find them a place to stay. By now they were accustomed to forming in a tight ring, shoulder to shoulder, around the vagabond fire, in order to stay alive.

"Tomorrow we must spend a night inside," Lyren-Sartora muttered, her face burning, but her back cold.

Leander lifted his head. "Andri, what can you tell us about the king of Sles Adran? Didn't he become a Norsundrian ally before the attack?"

"Yeah," Andri said. "Bartal na Shagal. Long line of kings,

which makes it worse. Or pragmatic, I'm sure he'd say. Until they decide to slit his throat for their own pragmatism."

A few chuckled.

"Capital is Nente, north and somewhat west of here."

"We should avoid it," Lyren-Sartora said reluctantly. "If the king chose Norsunder willingly, won't that make it more dangerous?"

"Contrary," David said. "Because there was no invasion, there's no need for the heavy numbers needed for occupation. And Norsunder is stretched thin. My guess is, this might be one of the easiest cities to get in and out of on the continent. That doesn't mean we shouldn't scout ahead."

"I'm better in woods than in cities," Leander admitted.

David was going to speak when Andri said, "I'm good with city scouting. I can go."

While they were talking, Lyren-Sartora and Sveneric walked hand in hand at his request—with her towing him around objects that might trip him up as he scanned on the mental plane.

He came to an abrupt, swaying halt. "I found it. Her. A place." He passed his mittened hand over his face, and forced his mind back into verbal mode. "A messenger. My age. There is a resistance to Norsunder. Her whole family. She is so proud of being a messenger—I got the password and everything." He sobered. "I think I need to teach her mind-shield. She was like a beacon." He rubbed his face again, then added, "I think her family will take us all. I got echoes from them. Act of resistance."

Sveneric pointed to the southwest.

The journey down the last mountain slope meant floundering through snow. They tried to obliterate their tracks as much as possible, but anyone who decided to hunt them would have an easy time of it. They had to make sure no one would think to search.

David, Lyren-Sartora, and Sveneric walked ahead, one on the watch for physical threat, and Lyren-Sartora again guiding while Sveneric walked sightlessly, his mind shielded as he reached in the realm of the mind.

He led them on a somewhat circuitous route as he listened on the mental plane, thus they avoided houses where people were angry, or frightened, or inclined to curry favor with the enemy by reporting travelers.

They finally descended the last of a sloping valley, bordered by a dark line of forest. The city emerged between forested hills, the lowlands beyond lying obscured by a white haze under low clouds.

By then night was closing in. They drifted single file in the middle of a pathway already marked by foot prints, until they reached a house half-hidden by a sheltering hillock on which sheep probably grazed in summer. The house was long, a single story solidly built then haphazardly added onto. When they knocked, a tall, ruddy-faced man looked out, his face blank.

Sveneric came forward. "The swans fly west," he murmured.

The man's face lifted in a beaming smile; it didn't take Dena Yeresbeth to feel his delight. "It works," he murmured, as the patter of footsteps announced the arrival of a girl of eleven or twelve, who peeked around her father at them. Her gaze settled on Sveneric and Lyren-Sartora, people her age.

"Ah, how many?" the man asked, seeing more silhouettes in the dark.

"If they have no gray jackets, they can all come in, come in," called a woman from beyond.

They trooped into a mud room, where they shed coats, cloaks, scarves, and muddy shoes and boots. From there they were ushered into a long kitchen, crowding up to a huge fireplace that took up one wall, and the next with all the pots and pans. Against a third had been set a great preparation table at which the family obviously ate in winter.

"Where did you come from? Who sent you—" the girl began eagerly, until her father raised a hand.

"That is rude, to interrogate allies who have yet to sit down," he said mildly. "And secondly, remember, no names. No places. The less we know, the less the enemy can find out."

The daughter turned her intense brown gaze to Sveneric, her own age. Then she smiled. David was the only one who noticed the flickering look that passed between the two youngsters.

The adults of the household flew about the kitchen, finding ways to expand their evening meal: A fast stirring of batter and a frying of pan biscuits; the careful unwrapping of a dense date and plum cake studded with nuts that had been stored against New Year's, now drenched with wine; extra handfuls of carrots and beans chopped fine and thrown into the soup that had been simmering all day, and was brought to boil (with a couple of cups of white wine added, pepper, and garlic); a more generous hand with the cheese wheel, and the thing was done.

By hauling a work table from another room, and an end table, everyone got a seat. Not quite everyone had a plate; the family made do with mixing bowls and saucers, as they'd run out of dishware, but they insisted proudly that this was no hardship — it was little enough they could do for the Cause.

As the travelers thawed out, hunger, which most had been ignoring for the last half day, replaced cold most insistently. For a time there was little conversation and much passing and scooping

Presently the father (who had once been the village scribe) sat up a little, rubbed his jowl, and said with an assumption of off-handedness, "Might I ask if you are traveling or on the run? I ask only to determine advice about the best road from here."

He was talking to Raadi, who smiled politely, but did not speak.

Sveneric said innocently, "No one is chasing us this moment, sir."

"Good," the man said, fists on either side of his plate. "Our oldest is off helping the Resistance. She wants to go." A tip of the head toward the girl sitting beside Sveneric. "We said maybe next spring."

The girl wriggled with impatience mixed with pride.

"We keep on the move," David said in his mildest voice.

More eating, then the man said heavily, "We're trying to get organized up in the capital. No right direction since —"

His wife dug her elbow into his side, and he buried his face in his mug. "Right. No names."

The wife got up and moved to the cauldron, which had been swung near the fire to mull wine, from the smell; she looked back to calculate her spices, then put them in a cloth to dip into the liquid, which had just begun to steam.

Little conversation followed, as people finished their meal. Then Caris-Merian, Leander, and Liere rose to help the middle-aged aunt, or servant (or combination of the two) who had begun stacking plates.

The four formed a line and in no time the dishware had been dipped, wiped, and restored to shelves and cupboards.

The father lifted the cauldron to the table, and his wife served out hot mulled wine in cups, glasses, goblets, and finally in small bowls. Again, everyone got one.

The father raised his glass, but the way he looked around, it was clear he was expecting something. Of course, a toast!

Liere said politely, "To our hosts and their generosity with food, drink, and the warmth of their hearth."

Father smiled, Mother beamed, everyone raised their glasses then began to sip—and the daughter leaped to her feet. "Down with the traitor Bartal n'Shagal and long live Andri Malcolin Elsarion, and may he rescue us soon!"

Andri choked, spewing wine into his lap. Eyes snapped his way as he gasped, eyes watering. Lyren-Sartora pounded him with unnecessary vigor on the back.

The daughter scowled at him in reproach.

"Please excuse," Andri gasped. "Swallowed wrong."

The daughter took in the hidden laughs in some, and the strictly averted gazes in others. "He can, you know!"

The mother said with a slightly questioning air, "If anyone can. Did in Enaeran almost single-handed, even if he was betrayed when they came back."

Now the entire family looked wary. The father said, "You did not know? And yet you have the secret password."

Andri raised his palms in protest. "We've been traveling from over the mountain."

Liere said in a calm, soothing voice, "We are fighting against Norsunder, and our connection is the resistance in Halarialgre. They did not know of that particular goal."

"Oh-h-h," the family exclaimed on a long note.

"We've got connections all the way there?" the mother asked, smiling. "That's good, that's very good news."

Andri added uncertainly, "Ah, does everyone in the Adrani resistance, um, share the same sentiment?"

"Of course! Don't you know the Elsarion swan? Well, it's *very old*," the girl stated with pride.

Lyren-Sartora leaned forward, chin on her hands. "And where is Andri Malcolin Elsarion now? Heading your movement? Making daring raids, and stirring speeches?"

The mother said, "Some say he went to Sartor to borrow their army. But news came that Sartor fell. We believe he is back in Enaeran, which is historically part of *us*. If he is organizing there, surely he will come here to help us." She added, "Norsunder put it about he was cravenly hiding in another land, but we do not give their rumors much credence."

That assured comment effectively doused a lot of the hidden humor, and Senrid knew without asking what Andri was thinking: such comments would be even more rife at home.

What is the king doing for us?

Nothing.

Andri kept his mouth shut until they were far down the road the next day, walking two by two in the marks already made by local carts and hooves and feet.

Sveneric was the first to speak. "I taught Feila how to make a mind-shield. She did not even know she was somewhat sensitive on the mental plane. She thought she had better hearing and a better sense of smell than others. I also told her some things about being watchful."

David said, "That family is good-hearted, but they wouldn't last a day in any real action. As well they live so isolated. That ought to be their best protection unless Feila learns fast."

Chuff, chuff, chuff, no sound but footsteps. Some side-eyed Andri.

Finally, after turning around twice as he glared at all bushes, trees, and the rolling landscape under its layers of snow, he said, "You know that wasn't my fault. And you don't have to worry that I'm going to do anything about this misbegotten aim of theirs."

"It might be a setup," David said.

Andri's head snapped up, and his eyes widened, then narrowed consideringly. "You mean, Norsunder spreads the rumor around themselves? Why, to lure me out?"

"Variation on a well-known gambit. Watch a group coalesce around the leader, then take out the leader." David dusted his gloved hands. "Watch 'em fall apart."

Andri was silent, then at last looked up. "What we might do," he said slowly, "is go through Nente, since we're here, stock up on provisions, as it will be a long run across the lowlands, and see what we can learn."

This idea met general approval.

Ten

Sartoran Sea

THE FIRST CRUISE OF the renamed *Tar-Tares* was a short one.

Remalna lay tucked against Gil al Mardgar on the south-eastern side, its western border curving northward against even smaller ink blot countries. But what looks small on a map can mean days of toiling about purposelessly if one has to duck the occasional patrol of the purple-coated Adranis, and if locals take one look at those golden earrings, the crimson sash with a knife hilt protruding by one hip, the billowing pantaloons stuffed into boots, and think, *pirate*. And clam up.

Dtheldevor wasted four endless days trying to find this King Vidanric. She'd prowled the estuary of the river that bordered Shevraeth, and even ventured up into the city she'd glimpsed one crisp, clear morning. It seemed to be a prosperous city (her definition of prosperous pretty much defined by houses having glass pane windows instead of shutters) but the well-kept streets were eerily deserted, though she could sense eyes peering at her from behind curtains and doors. The few people who had to be out did not want to talk, and scurried away, head bent, or tugged at their animals if driving a cart. At first no one in the city spoke to her, and she had to dodge roaming Adranis swaggering about.

She finally got a teenage girl out wanding horse droppings to listen; the girl blinked rapidly when Dtheldevor mentioned Vidanric, then said, "I don't know anything. I'll tell my ..." Dtheldevor didn't hear the last word as the girl tucked her wand under her arm and bolted away.

An old codger with a fishing boat was the only one who let her speak her piece. He had to be a local, Dtheldevor thought, and (missing her old friend Carsen) told herself that codgers of either sex were always more knowledgeable than anyone younger ever allowed.

He listened — grunted — and he turned back to stashing his pole and bucket in the boat.

She turned away, sighing.

She returned at the end of the fourth day, when the *Tar-Tares* lay off an estuary at the top of the flood tide. Her small crew had been working hard each day, first scrubbing the ship to Sharly the centaur's exacting standards, and then learning the yacht's peculiarities as they cruised about in freezing weather, trimming sail. Deon had thought she had plenty of experience, having occasionally come to help pull on a halyard whenever she wished, during her happy sailing days on the *Berdrer*. She was discovering the difference between fun cruises and actual crewing.

Dtheldevor peered out, casting an expert eye over the set of the sails before hauling her rowboat out from the shrubbery where she'd hidden it. She was dragging it toward the surf when a voice hailed from the top of the beach.

She pulled her knives and waited. No gray uniform. But that didn't mean she could relax; it had been a smiling aristocrat dressed in rose-colored silk who had treacherously killed her father.

"Are you the one looking for Vidanric Renselaeus?" a man called as he dismounted from a horse.

He was tall and fair-haired. Dtheldevor eyed him, arms crossed, knife in reach of her right hand. In her world, adults under eighty, outside of a chosen few, were potential enemies until they proved themselves.

"Senrid sent me," she said. And if this pretty looking fellow in the fine riding clothes tried to ask where Senrid was, or anything that remotely sounded suspicious, out she'd go. And if he tried a run on her, he'd get a knife for his effort.

"Senrid," the man repeated on another note, a lighter one. "Is he all right?"

"Was when I saw'm last. A long ways away," she added quickly.

Vidanric understood then that she might be what she said she was, but she didn't trust him. He remained standing on the little bluff, empty hands out, and asked what the message was. It took some back-and-forth before Dtheldevor finally came out with her offer to be a sea courier for the rescue effort.

Then he smiled, and said, "We could use an extra method of transport." Vidanric had decided early on that they would only trust people they knew—but he was willing to try, if Senrid really had sent her. If she was really the famed Dtheldevor, they'd find out soon enough. Maybe he'd begin with a tough volunteer who'd pretend to be a rescue...

"Good," she said, flashing a grin. "Let's set us up a message drop. And a code. Oh, and we've a chart, that is, a *map*, and we can code all the countries by swapping names."

"That's a clever idea," Vidanric said. "Might keep an enemy busy. However, we already have a number system in place, and we are now so spread out it would be difficult to alter it without risk of confusion—which can be dangerous. "

"I can see that," Dtheldevor admitted, thinking that she'd make up a map code anyway. She'd always loved secret codes.

Vidanric said, "We can also set up a drop if needed, but we usually have to act fast, so if one of you—or a number of you in rotation—don't mind taking up a menial position in the city to wait for the summons—"

Dtheldevor's grin disappeared. "Wait?"

And that is when two roads diverged. Vidanric needed someone ready to take a hot target straight to sea, if it didn't seem safe to take the person into the colorwoods; Dtheldevor's idea of helping was to stop by every so often, when the real action lulled, and see if there was something going; the Remalnans could keep their targets in some hiding place until she contacted them, couldn't they? Or why have a drop?

They did set up a drop, and he thanked her gravely, but as she rowed back to the *Tar-Tares*, she frowned as she reviewed that conversation.

When she climbed aboard, she said shortly, "Found 'em. They want us to sit tight, waiting, while they git all the action."

"What?"

"No way!" That was Peridot.

"Then we'd be sitting around, just like in Lisdan, except worse. Because we don't know anybody," Gloriel pointed out. "At least there, it was fun."

Dtheldevor brought her chin down sharply. "We's settin' sail. If there's no action in this sea, we'll go to Khanerenth." Then it occurred to her that in Khanerenth there would be yet another king, who might try to be commodore of the fleet. But she captained her own ship. Maybe it was best to wait and see what the wind brought.

And late that night, Vidanric sat with Meliara, telling her about the conversation. "It was very strange. At first she would not tell me her name—I was not yet certain that she was a she. When I heard 'Dtheldevor——"

"Dtheldevor! I remember stories about her! Pirate—privateer—enemy of Norsunder."

Vidanric nodded soberly. "I heard those stories, too. She looks no more than fifteen, but when she let me close enough, she seemed both young and old in a way I cannot explain. She finally trusted me enough for me to use my spyglass as she pointed out the ship she apparently took from Norsunder—which I am very sure they will be seeking—and I saw no one over her age on board. Though with centaurs, it is difficult to estimate age."

"Centaurs?" Meliara repeated in wonder.

"Two. Both the size of deer—the smaller one in particular. Even if she had been cooperative, I don't feel at all certain about a little ship full of teens and younger."

"But...aren't they old? I mean, in spite of that spell that keeps them children, or is it even possible to stay one age?"

"Our ancestors before the Fall were said to control the aging process from within. I don't know how true that is; in any case, I doubt anyone stays exactly the same, even if they never reach adolescence."

"So she wasn't cooperative after all?" Meliara asked.

He perceived her unspoken question and said, "It was an interesting but odd conversation. It was clear she had vast experience. More than I, especially in maritime matters. Yet in some ways she sounded no older than fifteen. I don't want to say emotionally stunted. It was more like her perception of, ah, interactions was perpendicular to mine, rather than parallel? No, that doesn't help. The important thing is, I got the impression that she doesn't take orders. She wasn't belligerent about it. I suspect it's more that she has never taken orders, and has no idea how to begin: she wanted our relay to go a certain way, operating when she had time for it. And that was it. No compromise."

Meliara rubbed her hands up and down her outer arms. "It sounds as if she meant well, but would she be reliable?"

"Oh, I've no doubt that under certain circumstances, she's very reliable. But those circumstances are entirely of her own choosing. I wonder if she *can* compromise."

He peered out at the softly falling snow, which at least had held off until he reached the hideout. "At least we know Senrid is still alive."

Eleven

Nente – Sles Adran

ANDRI WAS USED TO hearing his name thrown about, though it had usually been insults. Blame for actions he had never committed. Most of those rumors had been diligently fostered by his distant cousin Adon Marsael, who Norsunder had put right back on the throne mere weeks after Andri had won it.

But that had been in Enaeran. It made him a little queasy to hear his name invoked here in Sles Adran as the group made their way into Nente, Sles Adran's capital. Twice they stopped, the first due to weather. Again, Sveneric scouted a resistance family with an ease that was worrisome. Time to teach mind-shields, those with Dena Yeresbeth agreed.

This family passed them to friends in the city center, who welcomed the travelers loudly as long lost relatives, as if that would look convincing. David and Sveneric silently kept watch for suspicious observers; as they had guessed, Bartal na Shagal's willing alliance with Norsunder had bred complacence in his guard — which was stretched fairly thin these days, as his Norsundrian allies had handed him orders in the form of a suggestion that he volunteer his army for patrol duty from the Ghildraith mountains between Sles Adran and

Marloven Hess all the way east through Colend.

At the last house, they were once again invited to a meal. Leander was wondering how to bring up the possibility of obtaining provisions, though they had run through all their coins, when once again it was time for the inevitable toast.

They lifted glasses, and their host brayed, "Till the return!"

"Whose return?" Lyren-Sartora asked, before Liere could elbow her.

"Andri Elsarion," their host said reproachfully.

"Oh! Right, right, right," Lyren-Sartora said, shooting a mirthful glance Andri's way. She could not get enough of how discomfited he was.

And when everyone rose to go into the next room, Caris-Merian drifted up on Andri's side. "Someone sure has it in for you," she murmured.

Andri sent a puzzled look after her. Leander said softly, "Her brother was a hero on the other world. Arthur heard that he began to believe all the gassing about his greatness, and it got him killed. Almost got her killed, too."

Andri watched Caris-Merian's long, glossy black braid as she retreated along the wall—as usual keeping to the other side of the room from David—and wondered if he had half the story, or only a quarter.

He was going to ask, but when they began to settle in the family's parlor, as a couple of young people brought out musical instruments, a newcomer whose clothes were dotted with snow entered from another door and pulled their host out.

When she returned, she looked unsettled.

Everyone quieted. She twisted her hands as though wondering what to say—if she ought to speak—then in a low voice, "You are allies, so. I think you ought to hear. It seems someone important was seen brought into the lower fortress."

"You mean the prison?" a son piped up. "Who? Anybody we know?"

The host shook her head. "According to your uncle, it's someone hauled all the way from over the border."

"Which border?" Andri asked.

The host pointed west, toward Enaeran.

A little later, Andri said to the rest of the travelers, "Just a scouting run. And I'll do it. If it's anyone I know, I can't just leave them there. If there's any hint of trouble, run for it. I can look out for myself."

The teens of the household loved being consulted about the best way to broach the royal castle.

The next day, the two elder siblings smuggled in a pile of clothing—two lavender and gray liveries and a kitchen helper's robe, the eldest daughter saying, "My cousin is assistant to the state floor steward. She picked one item of clothing from each shelf. In the men's storeroom. There was a crowd sitting about gossiping in the women's. That kitchen thing is her sister's old one."

Thus began a series of changes as those who were willing to snoop about the royal castle tried the clothes to see who they fit best. Liere took the shapeless gray kitchen robe, which would have an apron over it.

David was too tall for either set of trousers, and his arms too long. Andri fit the one tunic, which had been made for someone long-waisted, and the longer pair of trousers was just a little too short. Leander was too tall for the other tunic, which fit Senrid all right, though he complained that the trousers, though the right length, had been made for someone with chicken legs. At least the tunic hid how tight they were at thigh and calf. The gray-dyed leddas-woven shoes fit most feet, as they were fastened by ties.

The plain caps the servants wore hid both the length of Andri's long straw-colored hanks and Senrid's shaggy waves, which at least had begun to look less like a military haircut the longer he neglected it.

There were tunnels leading into the palace—secret ones, they were told, but those were more dangerous than the service ones, as the "secrecy" was an old Shagal back exit. The king used them for sending out assassins and spies. They stuck to the service tunnels, relying on the livery and covered baskets to render them effectively invisible.

The royal castle was every bit as large as Brydon in Shiovhan, if not even larger. The assistant steward took them through the storage areas, where Andri and Senrid picked up dust cloths and Liere a tray. Their guide pointed out the way to the fortress's dungeons cut into the mountain; the military side turned out to be a warren of dim tunnels giving onto heavy iron-reinforced iron doors. Senrid and Andri tried three different routes to the prison section, to get turned away by curt guards; Liere vanished in another direction.

When the pair finally figured out the right corridor, the guards were on alert. They had no excuse to be there — they had seen no liveried servants in that wing, only guards, and there was certainly nothing to dust or polish. They apologized and retreated, to be promptly annexed by a harassed steward from another wing, and added to a train of servants ferrying in dishes for a banquet.

After they deposited their load, Andri said, "Let's try that hall. Looks promising."

Senrid shrugged, aware that he wouldn't really mind a fight, and he was carrying four knives on him.

Andri's guess that the more elaborate the decorations, the closer to power, was correct. They ended up in the hall outside Bartal's vast state suite. They heard men's voices within one chamber, and began sedulously dusting and polishing in the vicinity as Andri tried to listen. There was plenty to polish and dust — two decorated statues of much-beautified Shagal ancestors were set either side of a fantastic carved door opposite a historical battlefield treaty tapestry, the royal figures gilt with thin gold wire. Gold-framed pictures of Shagals in old-fashioned clothing lined the walls.

Senrid was on his third round of the statue-polishing, thinking that if he had to look at that insipid face any longer he'd kick the thing over. He could tell by Andri's frustrated expression that he couldn't hear but a word here and there. He was about to suggest they call it a day when the royal interview room doors sprang open and two footmen came through to hold the doors, dressed exactly like Senrid and Andri, who exchanged looks — what do we do now? — and froze in place, gazing into the distance as if made of wood.

Four exquisitely dressed men and two huge armed guards stepped onto the thick, patterned carpet that softened impact of the cold marble floor. The foremost was a slim, dark-haired man of medium height, a purple baldric across his brocade tunic-jacket, diamonds white and blue-purple set into the arms blazoned on his sword sheath. His hair was long, and he affected a thin mustache. Physically he was dominated by the tall, dark, powerfully built man walking next to him, but the latter's deferential manner, and the former's load of diamonds, made it plain which was Sles Adran's king.

Senrid flicked a glance at Andri — was he going to take them all on?

Andri had already decided that even if he succeeded in killing Bartal, Norsunder would make the entire kingdom pay by putting in someone worse. He bowed low, copied a moment later by Senrid, and Bartal na Shagal passed with no more than a slack-lidded glance at the tops of their caps.

When Bartal and his train disappeared in the direction of the banquet, Andri murmured in an undervoice to one of the footmen, "What's going toward?"

"*Him* giving orders again." The "him" got a roll-eyed glance to the west.

Adon Marsael?

The footmen took up stations at either side of the door, so Senrid and Andri gave the statues and picture frames a last wipe and retreated.

At the bottom of the service stairway, they met Liere. She had ditched her tray. "We have to run," she whispered.

"You found something?" Andri asked.

"Sh. Tell you later."

The three speed-walked the rest of the way downstairs, slowing when they heard footsteps. Occasional servants appeared, running this way or that. No one gave them a second look.

They'd reached the courtyard beyond the kitchen when Andri gave in to smothered laughter. "Bartal walked right past us."

"You saw him?" Liere asked.

"We did, eh, Senrid?"

"If that was the one flashing enough diamonds to start a shop," Senrid said.

They reached the outer door, bending into an icy wind that cut through the livery as though it were gauze.

"He looked right at us," Andri said, walking fast to warm up—not that it was the least successful. "It took everything I had not to howl with laughter—here he was, checking the depths of our bows by scowling at our caps without knowing that under those were a pair of kings who'd net him an extra kingdom or two, no doubt, if he laid us by the heels."

"I wonder," Liere began, breathing in to bring up her core warmth, though it would leave her very hungry later. "If he's even heard those rumors about you."

"Hope not. I mean, I wish that would stop." Andri cast a sideways glance at her. "As for that," he mused in a provocative tone, "there must be any number of people strongly wishing that Sartora would come again."

Liere peered ahead at the empty street, light from windows reflecting on the slushy snow. Almost there. "I didn't think of that." Then she braced her shoulders, and looked up, and smiled, raising a hand to her forehead. "It's such a trial, being alive in one's own time."

Andri snorted, and Senrid said, "You legends are all alike. Never as many mysterious powers in person as in the stories."

"I guess I'll tone down the next bunch of rumors I spread about myself," Liere said, giddy with hilarity — not at the stupid exchange, but at the fact that Senrid was joking, like the old days. "Otherwise they'll be saying in twenty years that I never existed."

"They'll —" Andri began, then abandoned words when they spotted a clump of people crowding through the door of their host's house. Though they were just silhouettes in the moonlight, their manner was too furtive for a guard raid.

Andri and Senrid crossed the street, and were recognized by their host, who was about to close the door. She yanked it wide again, whispering, "Hurry! Get inside!"

The door was shut and locked, and the two followed the wet footprints into the kitchen, where a circle of people stood about, looking at the table, on which lay a filthy, bloodstained young man with long dark hair.

"*Marten?*" Andri exclaimed, his wits completely flown.

Martande Eldias groaned.

Liere said, "Adon Marsael sent him to be interrogated by Bartal's specialists. His entire family was also arrested, on Adon Marsael's insistence, but Bartal released them a few hours ago."

Andri said numbly, "His family is mainly Adrani. The county of Eldias is old." Inwardly he was thinking, Marten. The kindest and gentlest of his followers, by the looks of him at death's door.

The sudden silence brought his attention back to the present — and the surprised stares of the local resistance. "You know him?" the host asked. "He's part of a noble family."

"Ah..."

Need overcame curiosity. The host whispered urgently, "You've got to take him away. He can't be here by the time the searches come through."

Senrid said, "Why aren't they coming now?"

Liere smiled, but another of the teens said, "It was the neatest thing. See, we have two of us among the guard. With them, and her." She pointed at Liere. "They set it up so that it looks like the keys were left by Kinarde. That's the Norsunder spy the king made commander of the guard. Everybody hates him. Including the king. No one will believe him when he says he didn't do it. He lies all the time, they say."

"We should have until the morning watch change," Liere added, bringing them back to the point.

"Then we'd better leave tonight," Andri murmured. "Any chance of a wagon?"

The resistance people looked at each other, then one said, "My da won't like it, but we've three barrel wagons. We could have one stolen."

"Let's get it now," the eldest boy said, and the two hurried out.

"We can heap straw on him, for warmth, and to hide him," the host suggested, eager to get the evidence out of her house. Her mind filled with the horrifying vision of the sun coming up on squads of purples searching every house, and demanding identity papers of everything that moved, right down to stray cats and dogs.

Marten stirred again. Silence once again gripped the room. His eyes opened — he stared up at Andri, too bewildered and hurt to question why Andri was suddenly here. He murmured, "Adon Marsael has Gared." And passed out again.

Everyone began talking at once — and that was when a ripple in the magic currents, as if the air had briefly congealed and then loosened again, staggered those with the slightest sensitivity to magic.

"What was that?"

"I felt something horrible —"

Many stared at one another in total incomprehension.

"The Universal Language Spell. It's warded," Liere said.

At that moment, Caris-Merian slipped free the knife she had been carrying, and slid along the wall toward David. Whose head turned, and for an endless moment their eyes locked.

Twelve

EVERYONE LIVES WITH THE consequences of their actions. Most of them seldom realize it. They will never need to. That will not be true for any of you, Detlev had said once.

David remembered that as his gaze met the hate-filled glare of Caris-Merian Rhoderan. In that moment her unshielded mind blasted his with the acidic burn of distorted memory. He barely recognized his own face as he stabbed her brother Leskander, how Les's face slowly changed from laughter to pain, and the sound of his own shrill, mocking, gloating laughter as he twisted the knife. He did not remember laughing.

But that was what she remembered. She wrenched her gaze away, the knife clutched in her white-knuckled fingers: he had grown in the years between then and now. She knew she would win no duel. It was her purpose to take him by stealth.

She ran back to where they had slept the previous night, leaving David to recollect his own, vastly different memory of that incident: the effort to strike true with the enchanted knife going awry. The sudden realization in Les's eyes—the recognition that not only did David know who the brother was that Les denied, he had also seen through Les's pose to his real intent. Les, so much bigger, fought back, to kill. To silence David—he could hear the intent on the mental plane, raw and almost overwhelming.

David had found himself fighting for his life, driven by anger at being duped by Leskander Rhoderan, the popular, funny, friendly leader, who was one by one building a potential army loyal only to him. How everyone slandered Norsunder, but Les was doing exactly what Norsunder does, and getting nothing but praise for it, because no one actually knew his real goal: to keep the vagabond magic a secret just so he could build enough power on Geth to return to Sartorias-deles to claim what he considered his family's right to a throne.

But Caris-Merian did not know any of that. She had not known Les's true intent. And he could not be the one to tell her. *You will have cause to regret every decision, every action, every light word, every utterance of laughter. Welcome to the world of ethics,* Detlev had said when they first left Norsunder.

David let Caris-Merian go, though he knew she would try again, and probably keep trying, because Les was still dead.

He forced his attention away—and there was Senrid. David's mind reverted instantly to the urgency that had been forefront before he sensed Cari-Merian making her move.

"Sveneric took off," David murmured in Marloven. "Efael is on his trail. It was probably he who blocked the Universal Language Spell."

"Why would Sveneric leave?"

"To spare us from Efael."

"Efael?" Senrid repeated. "Can't the bunch of us handle him, even if he is a turd?"

"He won't come alone. The Black Knives will kill everyone in sight and make a game of it." David passed his hand over his face, then dropped it. "Sveneric's no doubt gone to ground. Detlev taught him himself, these past couple of years. I'm not going to try hunting him down. I think I'm better employed laying a false trail to win him time."

"Is he that good?" Senrid asked.

David had turned away, but then he turned back, one brow up, his mouth a slant. "Seems to me," he said, "you don't know anything about Efael, or you wouldn't ask that." And then, without warning, he thrust a memory at Senrid, hiding nothing.

The psychic impact caused Senrid to recoil. He stared back shocked speechless.

"I think I'd better add," David finished, teeth showing. "He likes children."

He let that sink in for a painful heartbeat or two, then turned abruptly. He was gone in a few steps, leaving Senrid leaning against the wall in intense internal turmoil; Julian, peeking around the opposite corner, backed away fast. She did not understand Marloven, but the looks on both their faces, before David vanished, made it clear that something very, very bad had either happened, or was about to happen.

She turned to June. Julian had always been drawn to the outsiders, the isolated. She glanced down the hall into the kitchen, where everyone was talking at once, Andri's yellow hair central.

She had enjoyed traveling with Andri at the outset of the invasion. She liked him. She also liked Liere. But the two together effectively cancelled out that liking; she had no use for romance, finding all the touching and cooing annoying. Repulsive, even; she had utterly no inclinations that way, and as those two seemed to be together all the time, she'd fallen into the habit of walking with June, who avoided everybody.

June had at least picked up a smattering of Sartoran before she chanced across the Universal Language Spell.

"I think it's time to run for it," Julian said to June.

June jerked a shoulder, hiding how intimidating it was to suddenly not understand anyone. "Where?"

"There's a mage. South of here. A hermit. He might know a way around the transfer spells."

June shrugged again. "Your world. Your rules."

"My rules," said Julian, "would have Norsunder dropping dead."

June snickered. The two retrieved their things, and vanished into the night.

Everyone else was trying to figure out what to do—as the locals made it clear by increasingly urgent hints that they wanted the travelers gone.

Lyren-Sartora scowled at Liere, who jabbered away with Andri in Enaeran's language; Lyren-Sartora had never bothered to learn the language of a place she had no intention of living in, or even visiting again. She sensed Liere's worry about Marten, and fought ambivalence, hugging her own sense of hurt close. Marten was one of the kindest, and most interesting, of the Enaeraneth. But he was an adult. And Liere seemed more preoccupied with him than with her own daughter. As usual, everything of Andri Elsarion's came first.

Leander and Zairna were trying to find mutual languages in one corner, as Caris-Merian looked about in bewilderment at the edge of the room, her fingers gripping her carryall tightly, with the knife hidden inside. Her chance to kill David had slipped away while she was retrieving her things. He was definitely gone. That left her nowhere to go, and unable to speak to anyone.

It was about time, Lyren-Sartora thought, to show the world that she could take care of herself. If she went straight north, all the way to the strait, maybe she could reach the Mearsieans by Dena Yeresbeth, and get on that ship. So *there*, Liere.

She snatched up her carryall, turned — and nearly knocked Caris-Merian down. She paused. Caris-Merian paused. The two had chatted from time to time, Lyren-Sartora because she was naturally friendly, and Caris-Merian seemed so very alone.

Caris-Merian found her typical of her age, except when she wasn't. For example, in those caves back in the mountains, with the ancient paintings. Some of the others had ignored them, or had focused on the barely discernable script. Others had tried to see a battle in the fading figures, until Lyren-Sartora had said, "It's a dance. I think it's a sun dance. Look how everything is turned upwards."

Lyren-Sartora would always pick traveling with someone over the tedium of being alone. Caris-Merian was alone, and clearly didn't understand a thing.

Lyren-Sartora gestured, smiling...and the two were soon gone, without a backward glance.

Liere and Andri hastily bandaged Marten, then carried him out to where the cart was waiting. Anxious to see them on their way, the locals stuffed straw around him, donated a very old quilt that would not be missed, and tucked some bread, cheese, and a couple of jars of preserves into the wagon.

While working, Liere kept an oblique eye out for her daughter, who was studiously ignoring her. On the other side of the room, Senrid also observed Lyren-Sartora out of old habit. Both Senrid and Liere saw Lyren-Sartora select Caris-Merian Rhoderan as a traveling companion; Liere had already observed that Caris-Merian was quite competent, whatever else was going on with her. Lyren-Sartora, trained by Siamis, would be as safe with her as she would be with Liere...probably safer, considering poor Marten. And Liere could monitor her by night, if the predators in the realm of the mind were busy elsewhere.

Senrid came to the same conclusion, consciously reminding himself that he had to learn to disengage. The Fer Eiders were moving on in their lives, and he had no right to interfere.

And so, Andri pulling and Liere pushing, they got the cart bumping over the snowy street—as it happened, just behind Leander and Senrid.

Leander knew that expression of Senrid's by now. Something had disturbed him, but he wasn't going to talk about it. Leander chatted easily about pushing on straight west till they reached the Ghildraith Mountains, in which— somewhere—there was reputed to be a morvende geliath. He would give anything to actually see one...

Imry Llyenthur's HQ - Larkadhe

Marshig the Murderer, commander of the Brotherhood of Blood eight centuries previous, and at that time the terror of the seas, did not last a day past his re-entry into the world.

He had been warned by scar-faced Ramis on his capture into Nightland that once he emerged into the world again, he would be at the command of Norsunder. Nonetheless, Marshig, used to giving commands and killing anyone who dared to offer a *but*, took one look at these fancily dressed prancers called Fhlerians, and spat at the feet of the one who tried to tell him, in a very weird form of Venn, to shift his dunnage from the command cabin.

He then discovered, moments before he died, that fancy dress didn't have to interfere with the range of a superlative fighter who had survived close to half a year of occasional toe-to-toe slaughter with Venn berserkers.

But other forces annexed, commandeered, conquered, or bought off by Norsunder were not always as successful as this battalion of Fhlerians.

In Imry Llyenthur's command center at the top of a tower in Larkadhe, two aides, phlegmatic Duin and tall, rangy Colleron, stood before the big map and tried to see things as being better than they were.

Didn't work.

"That's two more ships brought out of the capture spheres,

and two down," Colleron said, scratching absently at his wild thatch of wheat-colored hair. They're *all* pirates?"

Duin grunted. "That's what I hear."

Colleron crossed his arms, a sure sign that he was about to benefit the staffers with an opinion, whether they wanted to hear it or not. "I can see grabbing the toughest pirates on the sea. Telling them they would be fighting the world's toughest when they came out again. But, being an idiot, Detlev never considered that pirates are going to be *pirates*. Am I right?" He looked around for corroboration.

Bergan, over at the supplies desk, sneered then went back to comparing lists.

Duin grunted again—always safest not to trust actual words.

Colleron took this as encouragement. "'nother words, he ought to have thought ahead a little, that pirates would be just as likely to fight *us*. There's no way around it. Two shipfuls of Adranis, their throats slit or dumped into the drink, either way, we'll never see 'em again, while these shits go on to attack anyone they want to. Which, these days, is us. *He's* not going to like it, oh, no. And it's not our blunder, but guess who'll catch it hot—"

"Wouldn't you like a little heat in this weather?" Llyenthur entered at his usual quick pace. Of course he'd heard it all, but he expected a certain amount of grousing—and unlike Efael, his main rival for command, he took little pleasure in stepping on otherwise functional underlings just because he could. Until the Host could figure out a way to cancel Kessler Sonscarna's spell pinning them in the world, functional underlings might become a rare commodity.

Seeing his staff standing around looking stuffed, he glanced over the map, noting the pattern before Colleron could try to finesse it. "Two companies of Adranis lost to pirates. We'll have to deal with that. A transport ship lost off Khanerenth? Another, I should say?"

"Last report was, hot fighting aboard two," Duin said, pointing to the dispatch tray. "One fought clear, but took damage."

"Jehan Merindar again, no doubt. We shall have to do something about that, too. What about these two couriers down here in the Sartoran Sea?"

Colleron shrugged. "Just couriers—might be weather."

"Or Efael," Llyenthur said. "He's out in the field. Did you know that?"

No one did. They were supposed to report any movement by Efael or his Black Knives, but few ever saw them. Except of course for the informer among them—whom Llyenthur had pegged at the outset, and cherished, dropping the occasional bits of misinformation.

Llyenthur did not inform his staff that he'd removed Efael's mirror wards from the dispatch tray yet again, also from the transfer magic. These had been nearly daily occurrences of late, until Efael distracted himself by some other pursuit. It was because of these constant attempts at sabotage that Llyenthur had put the couriers into the sea, and runner relays on land, for extra lines of communication. Slow as they were.

But maybe Efael had found the couriers. Llyenthur frowned at the markers; if any more couriers vanished, he would have to investigate himself. Somehow. Between all the other demands.

Eh, that was the game. As long as he remained half a step ahead of Efael (and Aldon)—and kept Svir and Ilerian amused—the game was worth the play.

In the meantime, while Efael was running around in the midlands, he would be able to do some hunting of his own. Come, now, Senrid Montredaun-An, he thought. Where are you?

Thirteen

Sartoran Sea

WHILE SLEET AND HAIL drummed the deck of the yacht
Dtheldevor's gang had renamed *Tar-Tares*, everybody except
the miserable two stuck on deck (Gloriel as lookout and Sharly
at the helm) sat in the tiny wardroom. It was really just an oddly
shaped space between the galley at the bow end, with a tiny
cabin beyond, bunks along the hull, and the captain's small
cabin aft, which Dtheldevor shared with Sarmonwilda when
quarters were tight.

In the center of the wardroom a table had been bolted to the
deck, which they ate at, and used for navigation and planning.

"Grub's on," Joey said, bringing out their dinner—this
being his turn in the galley a few steps away.

They descended on the food like wild things, and it was
gone in no time. Then Joey reminded Peridot that she had dish-
dunking duty. For answer she picked up Dtheldevor's fork and
threw it at him. He caught it neatly and tucked it into the
silverware tray, as Dtheldevor had neglected to use it.

Joey then threw his wrist knife across the table, not at
Peridot, who he knew would catch it, but at Deon.

But Deon had been expecting that, after days of drill. Not

that she trusted herself to catch a knife spinning through the air yet, the way the Warrens and Dtheldevor did. But she swept up the empty chafing dish that had held their biscuits, and captured it between lid and dish, which made a satisfying loud clank.

She lifted the lid. "Anyone want seconds?" She offered the dish around.

Ellen chuckled. Deon laughed proudly as Peridot rolled her eyes; she despised clowning, especially showing off. She thought it was pointless, not funny, and her brother an idiot for kidding around so much.

Deon ignored her, reveling in the laughter. She had practiced hard, almost always thinking with angry regret of Lilah. If the other Sheridan Brothers had been diligent with their fighting practice, would Lilah still be alive?

She watched, and learned, and practiced on her own. Her immediate goal was to get better than Peridot, who was really annoying—as annoying as her twin was easy-going, if a little dreamy and sometimes slow. Deon liked Gloriel, except at things that required pairing up. Gloriel was forever staring off into space, or at the water, trying to see mer people, or thinking about old stories, stupid things like that instead of paying attention.

Even so, Deon had never worked so hard in her life.

"No, here, you paint up under the strake," Gloriel said a few days later. "See, from a distance, it's gonna look like these nice tight strakes are all a-foo—about to come apart. Then you do this."

Gloriel paused expertly as a wave heaved the yacht up, then out, swinging the girls out away from the side, then swinging them back. Gloriel widened her feet and braced them from smashing against the hull, then she slapped paint on a strake. No feathering, no neatness.

Bren would be appalled, Deon knew. When he painted, he talked about light and shadow, making things three dimensional in look. She'd tried that, but Gloriel said it wouldn't show up when seen through a glass at a distance.

"Big and sloppy," she said, giving the ugly colors another stir so they mixed into a nasty mess. "From a distance they won't see a nice tight hull, they'll see an ugly old floater, especially when Sharly and Sidres put the finishing touches on those sails. They'll look a hundred years old, and not in a good way."

They had seen that so far, at least, Norsunder wasn't bothering with fishing boats. Though they sometimes stopped them and took their catch.

A head appeared over the rail, mirror image to Gloriel's. "Not done yet?" Peridot called.

"Sure we are," Gloriel called back cheerily, paying no attention to the nasty tone of that 'yet'. "We just like being splashed by ice water."

Deon and Gloriel redoubled their efforts, though by now Deon was thoroughly sick of painting. This was the fourth time they had painted the yacht.

Ever since Dtheldevor had talked about ghosts, Deon had begun talking to Lilah in her home language. Just in case Lilah was around. "I never thought pirating was painting and sail-sewing," she muttered. "Let's see, that's two actual battles, if you count going on board the soul-bound ones, and other than that? Six chases, but we lost 'em 'cause they were sailing close in a fleet, or they had the wind."

No answer, as usual.

They finished up, to discover that Peridot and Ellen had already done the other side. The light was fast disappearing behind the clouds, which meant no more stuff on the outside of the yacht, Deon thought, gloating.

Inside the wardroom, everything was warm.

Deon sat down next to Gloriel. "Did you really see Dtheldevor's father as a ghost?" she asked. "I mean, to see and speak to?"

"Oh yes," Gloriel said, surprised. "Dtheldevor didn't make that up, you know." Her expression changed. "She might exaggerate some, but she never lies."

"I know, I know," Deon said quickly. "It's just that...ghosts. You'd think, if Lilah comes back, she'd come and find us."

"Well, maybe she's not back. Maybe she's with her brother. Somewhere. Or maybe my sister is right, and you just snuff out, like a candle. But I don't believe that. Though maybe it happens to some, if they want it. Getting off the wheel, my friend Tran said once, when I was back on Earth. She was a Buddhist."

"A what?" But Deon didn't care about the answer. She turned to Sharly. "Do you think, if we kill the Norsundrians that killed Lilah, her ghost will come to us?"

The centaur swung around to regard Deon. Her expression in the changing light of the swinging lamps was mild surprise.

"No," she said.

"No?"

"I never saw sign yet that the world works that way."

"Ah that's cuz you got all that weird junk in yer blood." Sarmonwilda dismissed the subject with a flippant shrug.

Sharly laughed. "And you don't, dawnsinger girl?"

Sarmonwilda grinned. "You know I been with the gang so long I don't even remember ta bring down the sun anymore."

"Much less wake up to raise it," Sidres commented. "Lazy!"

Deon said to Sharly, 'How old *are* you?"

"I turned my century. We tend to be long-lived." Sharly smiled. "Sidres is considered a babe where I was born. They don't take your thoughts seriously until you've been in the world at least fifty years."

"Well, I've been me, in the Child Spell, for, oh, is it really twenty-five years?" Deon chortled, still feeling as if she'd gotten away with something

"You are?" Sharly seemed surprised.

Deon grinned, thinking of the years that had slid by, and she never had to do boring adult things. She'd spent two years in Delfina Valley, just so she could become one of the fastest flyers among the youngsters—but then they started going past her in age and interest, so she'd returned home again.

Oh, it was good to think about all the fun she'd had...except when she'd bump up against things like Peitar and Derek being killed. Not that she'd thought much of Peitar one way or another. Truth? He was really boring. But Lilah had grieved so hard, for so long. She'd drifted around that palace like a wraith, and it had been ages before she'd smile.

And now she was gone—and once again, by Norsunder.

Deon's expression hardened, and Sharly, who'd been watching her, picked up where she'd left off. "You could kill this man—if you even know which it was—but then he is dead. You feel justice, but his mates won't. His mother wouldn't, if she still lives."

Deon smacked a fist into her palm. "You think it's wrong to kill him?"

"I think it wrong to take a life. Any life. Which is why Sidres and I do not even eat chicken or fish. We eat what the ground and trees give."

"But Norsundrians," Deon exclaimed, appalled. "They're nothing but killers!"

"I understand if you kill this man, you keep him from killing others. But then if you go on killing Norsundrians, and they kill your side in turn, where does the killing stop?"

"But they are evil! They are wrong! They—they—"

"Peace, Deon. This is an old argument with us. I fight against evil. Sidres and I handle our ship when the rest of you carry out attacks. On land, I bop Norsundrians behind the ear if they attack me, and leave them to deal with the consequences. Dtheldevor doesn't leave a trail of corpses because of me, you must have seen by now. We are just as effective throwing them overboard, to swim as they can."

"No, I'll continue it," Dtheldevor said, swinging down the hatch and into the tiny wardroom, shedding snow in all directions as she brandished a bottle of wine. "Hey! He's in the pit, right, see? Battling them poison-snake monsters, and all, right? So with a mighty belch o' fire, he leaps from the pit—"

Joey had thrown himself onto one of the bunks bolted to the bulkhead, booted feet stretched out. With his red bandana round his brow, long hair straggling down, his wide embroidered sash and his many weapons, he looked very piratical.

He lifted his chin and uttered a long, loud, and artistic belch.

"That's stench, not fire." Sarmonwilda cackled, a startling sound from such a delicate-featured face. She flung back her golden hair, grabbed Dtheldevor's bottle, and took a swig. Then handed it back before she said, "Sounds like the story's mowr—mull—mor-r-r-al." She hiccoughed.

Dtheldevor shook her head, then winced. Then slammed the bottle down, so wine slopped on the table. "Don't like moral tales. Don't lissen to 'em. Don't never bore someone's ears off ta tell 'em."

"Odd," Ellen said sleepily. "Even if there were no snakes...but then I am not telling the story."

"No. I am," Dtheldevor said. "Oh, soul-sucking farts! Lost me place."

She got up just as the ship gave a lurch, and she promptly took a header. That made her laugh so hard she rolled over—and Sarmonwilda poured out the bottle onto her, causing her to gasp and curse.

She yanked Sarmonwilda's ankle. The dawnsinger fell, and the girls rolled around, wrestling and yelling, each trying to get the drop on the other.

Two days later, Deon was sound asleep in the afternoon, after having done a night watch.

"Wake up!" Dtheldevor smacked her on the shoulder. "We're finally ready to make a try on a shark, now that you've seen success with a coupla minnows." She turned to Sidres. "Make us invisible."

Sidres had given up years ago trying to convince Dtheldevor that illusion magic did not, in any way, make anything invisible. At its best, it tricked the eye. Admittedly that was easiest in wintry weather, when the sun arced far north, and sea and sky were pretty much solid gray.

Dtheldevor jerked her thumb over her shoulder. "Those not on watch can get some rest, because I figger, 'round midnight if the wind holds, we'll be nigh our target." She turned to Sharly. "Splain?"

Sharly leaned over the chart she had taken off the last courier, the fringes on the vest she wore on her human half brushing the paper as she brushed dainty fingers over the coast off Mardgar. "This last courier was to swap written reports with a transport coming off Mardgar, with reinforcements heading for Halia."

"We need to stop them." Dtheldevor looked up at them all. "Now, I knows some of yez don't hold with killin' if ye can avoid it. Even them chum-suckers. This will be a tougher fight if we're caught at it, as we'll be outnumbered."

She paused, then grimaced as the lamp swung to the left and then to the right of her face, shifting the shadows. Odd, how at one angle the planes sharpened and she looked old — maybe as old as she really was. But then the shadows smoothed out again, and she was, as always, around fifteen. Then the lamp swung, and she was old again.

Her head dropped, her eyelashes hiding her black eyes, and she said, "So, quiet is our best weapon. Take out anyone on watch. Set the fires."

"Fires?" Deon said. "We'll burn them?"

"Not them. The ship around them." Dtheldevor laughed heartily.

"But that's..."

"Cheating?" Peridot sneered. "Oh, goodness gracious!"

"Norsunder cheats," Dtheldevor stated.

"Everywhere and everyhow they can," Joey put in breezily.

"Whereja get yer idee o' being fair to Norsunder, Deon? Not from me!" Dtheldevor proclaimed in such horror that the Warrens laughed. Dtheldevor raised her voice above theirs. "It's me compromise with Sharly. I don't care what happens to 'em, but they can leave the ship alive, jump into the sea and maybe they make it to shore, and maybe the mers take 'em. I don't know what happens after that. Nobody does. But they ain't deaders, see? And—the reason we are doin' this—they aren't goin' off to kick people around, probably in Senrid's country. I don't imagine anyone else on Halia is givin' any trouble."

Deon nodded. That sounded perfectly fine. Even Lilah wouldn't argue with that. Or, even Darian Selenna, who had gotten mighty pushy soon as he turned ten, though he was still a pipsqueak. Maybe it was being a prince. Derek would think so.

Dtheldevor jerked a thumb toward Ellen. "You try the binnacle. Maybe messages to go out is there. More likely the wardroom or the captain's cabin."

"I'll check," Ellen said.

The courier's chart was correct, as expected. They spotted what had to be the Norsunder vessel hull down on the horizon late the next day. Sidres refreshed the illusion spell, and they kept pace with the transport on the lee side, lessening their chances of creating an anomaly for the lookouts in the tops to spot.

They waited till midway through the night.

Then came the scary part. Deon's heart hammered as she followed Sarmonwilda over the side. Then each spread to do their assigned job.

Sarmonwilda and Joey ran soundlessly fore and aft to take out the deck watch. Dtheldevor nocked arrows, and shot the lookout, who tumbled into the sea.

Deon's hands shook as she ran along the deck, flinging oil over everything. It was cold and slimy on her hands. She had made it most of the way around the deck when the sharp scent of burning wood reached her. Through wreathing smoke she spotted the rest heading for the side.

She was right after Peridot, who turned to help her down. Deon then turned to see if Sarmonwilda needed help—but she leaped lightly past and landed perfectly on the bow at the top of a swell. The boat only shivered slightly.

Then Joey and Ellen rowed their hardest, skimming them over the choppy waves to the *Tar-Tares*; behind them flames shot up the masts, throwing a beating ruddy glow over the water.

Eyes glittered, reflecting the flames, as they hauled themselves aboard the yacht, and then Sharly threw the helm over, Sidres sheeted the mainsail home, and they began to pick up speed with every pitch of a wave.

They hadn't gone far, though, before the wind brought across the water the yells and screams from the burning ship.

Fourteen

Sles Adran to Enaeran

WINTER PASTURE WAS YOUR hidden ally, if you had been taught how to find such places — and how to lure the horses.

Andri's oldest friend, Gared Inmael, was the son of the former king's Master of Horse. When Andri was disinherited by his father, the Master of Horse had taught both boys everything there was to know about horses.

Liere had learned in early childhood how to differentiate types of minds. She scanned for horses, and when she found a herd, Andri caught them. That meant foraging for three horses as well as three people. Again Liere was crucially important, for she was able to use farsense to find sympathetic hosts. The reward was not only shared food but good clover hay, and salt licks, which kept the animals healthy and ready, even eager, to run.

As soon as Marten could sit a horse, they left the cart behind an inn where there were already more than a dozen wheeled vehicles, and thus would not draw undue attention. That sped them up considerably.

In excellent weather, it's possible to ride between Nente, Sles Adran's capital, and Shiovhan, the capital of Enaeran in ten days to two weeks. In winter, three was considered a very good pace, especially changing horses, which Andri insisted on; he didn't want the borrowed animals to have too far to go when trotting back home; the problem was finding water that was not iced over.

They made up for lost time with speed. Liere was peerless scouting not only for danger, but for possible aid on the mental plane, but it was Andri who rose early to scout the territory. As a result he fell into his old habit of shorting sleep — and so, two weeks into their journey, as icy winds swept the plains, he began snuffling and sneezing, and then coughing. But when asked if he was all right, he invariably said, "I'm fine."

Deeply concerned, Liere asked Marten if they should insist on hiding up until Andri recovered.

Marten shook his head. "I don't remember a winter when he didn't get colds. The better years, he'd get over it in a week or so. The bad years, it would drag on for a month or longer. But he straight-arms any hint that he might slow down."

After a summer reunited with her almost-thirteen-year-old daughter, Liere was hyper-sensitive to anything that might seem to be nagging; as they traveled, she checked each night on Lyren-Sartora within the mental realm, but otherwise waited for Lyren-Sartora to communicate when she was ready. And she said nothing about these matters. She knew Andri was driven by his own worry that he would arrive too late to rescue Gared.

"There is one thing I can do," Liere said to Marten when Andri departed right before dawn yet again. "Your Dena Yeresbeth. You've learned naturally how to make a mind-shield. It's time to train your farsense."

"Farsense?"

"Hearing other minds." She tapped her head and swept a hand out. "I sense that you've been doing it, but in a peculiar way."

Peculiar as in trying to determine whether those he saw were ghosts or real, he could have said, but a lifetime of habit kept him silent. "I would like to learn."

"Great! We can practice as we ride."

Three weeks into their hasty retreat from Nente, they spotted the roof of Enaeran's royal palace on its bluff. By then Marten had brought Andri up to date on Adon Marsael's exertions in establishing a tight control over the capital, and thereby the kingdom. No more pretending he was everyone's friend. Adon Marsael was a lot blunter about what he expected the nobles to furnish.

After a short conversation, Marten and Andri decided the best way to enter Shiovhan was down the river, which rarely froze, due to the fluctuations of the hot springs beneath the city that fed into it.

The core of Andri's old gang had always believed that their king would be back. Imagine the joy the night a voiceless Andri, whose red nose and flushed cheeks made it plain he was laboring in the throes of a colossal cold, sauntered into a low storeroom where they were gathered, Liere and Marten at his either side.

He greeted them cheerfully, croaking, "Where's Gared being kept, and what's the patrol schedule?"

Bassl, one of his oldest allies, said, "You know he's holding Gared to lure you."

"Of course. And he can make his try. But first he'll get so much trouble he won't have time to enjoy it," Andri wheezed.

The barking cough was nothing new to them: they were so happy to see him again, and he was so happy to be home again, that he seemed somehow larger than life as he strode along the narrow alleys of his city, ducking through secret doors in seemingly solid walls, and clattering down into dank basements that led up into charming houses, thence to beautifully paved streets. He laughed, he listened, he bound his scattered, frightened people together again in enthusiasm and ferocious fellowship that was all the more pleasurable, and intense, after the betrayal of the Enaeraneth Royal Guard that had brought Marsael back at the front of a battalion of Adranis.

By the second morning after his arrival, Andri's plan was set. All he had to do was disperse them to the jobs they fit best. By then Marten had recovered enough to act as scout on the mental plane. He and Liere went with each group to scan each target for hidden danger, so that the enemy was always taken completely by surprise.

By the end of that week, Andri had turned the city into a frantic ants' nest, leaving Adon Marsael furious but impotent in his palace. Watch houses burned to the ground. Horses stampeded. Supplies looted.

Since the invasion, Marsael had insisted that Andri was lurking about, ordering frequent searches. But with this sudden change, he realized that he'd been wrong. Andri had been gone. But was now back again, though more slippery than ever, for Andri and his gang knew every bolt hole in the city, whereas the Adranis Bartal had given him were foreigners. And, Adon Marsael had long suspected, Bartal had sent the worst slackers and idiots in his entire army, a battalion of total incompetents.

That was going to change.

Llyenthur's HQ to Shiovan, Capital of Enaeran

That night, light glowed in the tower windows in Larkadhe, signaling that the commander, Imry Llyenthur, was back from Marloven Hess.

"... raid on Lathandra, fourteen dead, and half a corral of horses taken —"

"Damn." Who *was* that in Ralanor Veleth, commanding those coverts? "I'll have to go myself. Next."

"... and an urgent request for magical backup from Marsael of Enaeran," Duin said, chuckling the paper onto the pile of dispatches that he'd already read aloud.

Llyenthur, tipping his chair back on two legs as he stared at the ceiling, said, "Enaeran. No magic there. These idiots always want the impossible. Next." Then the first part of the request registered. "Wait."

Duin froze, the next dispatch in hand, mouth open.

"Read that last one again."

A rustle of paper, then Duin's slightly nasal drone, "Request, marked urgent, from Adon King of Enaeran —"

Llyenthur sighed. "Him. Yes. Skip over all the usual complaining about Bartal na Shagal and Kinarde — no doubt the next one will be from one or both of them, complaining about Marsael. And each other." Llyenthur smiled as he said this. It suited him very well to have those three wasting time eyeing one another and snarling, like three rats over a single cheese.

"... and though I've had no cooperation from these incompetents, and I realize that I had claimed that Andri Elsarion was at large here, the recent depredations make it clear that —"

"Andri Elsarion," Llyenthur repeated, the chair creaking as it tipped farther back. The silent staffers registered the creak, ever hoping to see the commander go ass over head amid toothpicks of broken chair. What they didn't know was that he'd had this habit since he was small — copied less successfully by those he'd lived among — and he knew to a nicety how much tension the wood could take.

His eyes closed as he searched his memory once more. He'd only gained a heartbeat of connection with Senrid Montredaun-An the previous month, after intermittent attempts. And no location. He disliked sinking into that memory, ephemeral as it was, as with it came the smeary emotional contortions of drunkenness. He had to be grateful for that, or Senrid's control would not have slipped at all. That much had become apparent after many repeated tries.

Senrid had shut him out after that one moment, but within it, Llyenthur had descried Senrid's awareness of others, mostly by Senrid's liquor-infused concentration on shutting them out. The easiest one to identify was Liere Fer Eider. But behind that, or connected to that, was the briefest image of a tall, blond figure: identity, Andri Elsarion.

And now — supposedly — Elsarion was in Enaeran. Was it possible these others were as well, all traveling together? Enaeran was one range of mountains away from Marloven Hess. Llyenthur recognized wishful thinking in the idea that Senrid was trotting home like a lamb to mama sheep. He so needed a puppet in the disaster that was Marloven Hess — he'd already had to rid himself of two commanders — and Senrid would be perfect, once he was properly controlled.

But they had to catch him first.

Crash! The chair came down on all four legs, and Llyenthur hid his spurt of amusement at the not quite smothered disappointment of his wooden-faced staff. He got up and scowled at the map, his internal marker for Efael moving west toward Zranf. Still busy on whatever nasty pursuit his nasty little brain, or his sister's equally nasty brain, had concocted.

Ralanor Veleth was going to take time. But this fool in Enaeran — no doubt he could deal with it within a turn of the glass.

Llyenthur concentrated on Adon Marsael as a Destination, and transferred. He found himself in a dark room. The dim blue starlight in the tall windows outlined forms burrowed in a bed. "Marsael!" he said sharply.

One head shot upwards, and a second lump let out a snort

and burrowed deeper. "I protest this rude intrusion—"

"You wanted my attention. You've got it. For the next five breaths..." Llyenthur considered ordering him to throw out whoever it was in the bed, but decided that would take too long—from the looks of the room, with bits of clothing everywhere, and the lour of sweat, stale wine, and sex in the air, the occupants of the bed were coming down off a drunken orgy of spectacular proportion, and it might take them half a watch to figure out what belonged to whom. "Four," he said, walking to the nearest door. "Three." He slammed it behind him, relieved to discover he hadn't just shut himself into a wardrobe.

Behind, he heard muffled voices, one high and female, two low and male: not one but two bedfellows. Make that more than half a watch to sort of what belonged to whom. His breath clouding on a laugh, Llyenthur called out, "Two!"

The door opened, and Marsael lunged out, pulling a robe around him, hair straggling down in hanks. His bare feet encountered the marble floor, and his toes crimped.

"Report," Llyenthur said. "If you haven't seen Andri Elsarion, what makes you think he's here, since you've been wrong for the past several months?"

For a man who had just been yanked from hungover sleep, Adon Marsael made a valiant effort to marshal his thoughts. The more he spoke, the more he woke. When he got to the damage done to the local occupiers over the last day, he was quite coherent, as well as indignant.

"... and so I beg of you, do some magic and take him out!"

"'Take him out.'" Llyenthur sighed. "If magic worked that way, I would not be answering stupid dispatches two hours from dawn, would I? Stop whining, and blaming Bartal. Tell me why Andri Elsarion would suddenly show up after having been away all this time."

"I don't know," Adon Marsael said, and then in a different voice, "I'd thought he was here when we managed to nab two of his lackeys. I even had them paraded out and beaten publicly. No sign of Andri. I had to send Eldias to Bartal, because there were so many protests from nobles in both countries—you must understand that these are the cooperative nobles—"

"Back to Martande Eldias. When did you send him to Bartal?"

"It was three and a half, almost four weeks ago. I used one of the transfer tokens you gave me, as I didn't think —"

"Three, four weeks." Llyenthur looks around for a map, but of course there was no map in that hallway. He shut his eyes, mentally measuring the distances. Three weeks, a possible ride — if Andri Elsarion and Martande Eldias were together. Efael heading for Zranf, on the other side of the mountains from Nente. Had a pack of his capital list targets been slithering westward?

There was as yet no proof, but circumstances were pointing to the possibility that Efael was on the trail of one of Llyenthur's own targets. Of course he was. And that was why Llyenthur had no information on his movements. Shit.

Adon Marsael was still talking, calling up an exact timeline. Llyenthur cut through it. "You said that his two followers are in your custody, but the one is gone from Bartal's custody. You have the other one, right?"

"Gared Inmael —"

"Whatever. And the random burnings are where, in reference to where you are holding this Gared? Because it seems pretty obvious from your own report that the attacks are bleeding off your forces in one direction so they can hit in another."

Adon Marsael was shifting his weight from foot to foot, but he was alert now. "Right. That did occur to me. But these incompetent Adranis —"

"Never mind that. I'll...no I won't. I don't have time. There's something else I need to run down first. I'm going to send one of the mages to help bait your trap. But you'll listen to him, Marsael. You don't know anything about magic."

Marsael grinned. Even barefoot in his night robe, he was far too elegant to slaver and rub his hands. But it was there in his voice as he said, "Tell me what to do."

Fifteen

THE PLAN TO RESCUE Gared had begun.

Marten had discovered that farsense was so much easier if he didn't try Liere's "tendril." He could visualize a little ivy creeper, or a blackberry strand, but it just stayed there. However, if he imagined himself a ghost, passing invisibly through territory he knew, suddenly what had seemed impossible was as easy as breathing.

In fact, it occurred to him as he sat in a warm attic room, eyes closed as his ghost floated up the zigzag road from the lower city to the nobles' ridge, he might actually have been doing this all his life. Only in dreams.

Liere had put together the elements for him, step by step, so that he was now aware of what he was doing, and controlled it consciously. Reveling in its ease, he sped through Brydon castle, then out through the gardens, and back to the old ruin that had once housed recalcitrant princes, now a very dreary prison. He knew he was invisible to other minds. That was the equivalent of Liere's little tendril, or to get rid of the images: he shielded his mind except for this wisp of awareness that drifted along, far less likely to be noticed by the looming, distorted figures he now knew were powerful minds on the prowl. He would not be visible to the vast ones that seemed to cover the sky, but Liere had been quite blunt about those: if he sensed or saw one, he was to withdraw at once. Distance was absolutely relative, and he'd be invisible only because they were seeking someone else.

His ghost halted when he perceived blood-red glows around the door, the lower windows, and even in the old oak that had been allowed to grow next to the building, its branches brushing one wall.

Instinct caused him to retreat from those glows. He opened his eyes, breath held against the pulse of vertigo as his mind settled back into his body, awakening his senses and locking sight into his skull.

He was supposed to be scanning for persons lurking about. He hadn't found any, but Liere had taught him that on the mental plane, that could be deceptive: he wouldn't sense anyone with a strong mind-shield. Just as he was hiding from them.

But those glows? What were those?

He looked around for his shoes and coat. Could he even catch up with Andri and Liere in time? Then he remembered he could reach for Liere by mind—contact, she had called it. The only way he understood it was that she somehow thinned her mind-shield so that she was aware of proximity outside it, but it had to be someone she knew...

: Liere?

Liere, drifting through the shrubbery toward the huge oak tree before the prison, caught that call, and the image: *I see the transfer traps.* And she shut Marten out.

But that was all it took for the watcher on the mental plane, quiescent until Liere caught a flash of intent. She had already shut her mind, and forced her attention outward as someone shouted a word, and then light from a dozen glow globes blazed, revealing her standing there. The cleverly placed glow globes had been entirely inert, so she hadn't seen or sensed them.

Then a familiar voice exclaimed, "That's Liere Feriadar! Ah, Fer Eider! What's—never mind. She's another of Andri's string of women. They'll be together."

Adon Marsael himself. And Liere had tripped the trap too soon. Time to recover. She turned her head and screamed in the direction of the river, "Andri! Go back!"

Then she began to run.

She and Andri and had calculated how far off the guards would have to be to remain unseen on her approach. Bassl and Andri had both gone over the terrain with her as best as they could, with drawings and words. She zigzagged through the tangle of the overgrown garden, which hampered her but it hampered the larger, weapon-laden guards that little bit more, evening out the speed of the chase.

"Andri," she yelled again, when she neared the ridge. "Help me!"

She risked a quick check: they'd believed her! The guards were all in pursuit, spreading in a line-of-sight half circle with her at center. Dart, sidestep, run, run, run...and there it was, nearly invisible in the darkness: what looked like a foxhole. She dove in, ignoring a thousand tiny scratches, and then scrambled down the path that paralleled a waterfall. Her pursuit slowly converged on that fall. At a violent stream of orders from Marsael, a patrol at either side began picking their way down from slippery, icy rock to slippery rock, convinced she'd taken the dive, as others began an intensive search through tangles of blackberry brambles and overgrown roses.

By then, Andri had navigated the tunnel underneath the building, neglected since his sister Alismira had locked him in it when he was five or six. Ah, Alismira, he thought as he vaulted up the steps and worked the ancient latch. He had found out only she and her family had taken to the sea when the invasion first came; he hoped they were safe.

Up the steps to what was once the kitchen's cold room, which was currently being used as a cell. Andri slid open the bar from the outside, and ventured in, grimacing against the stink of dried blood and sickness sweat.

Gared hated waking up.

Why wake up when there was nothing but pain? It made his vision blurry, dark red around the edges. But in the faint light of a flickering candle he recognized drifting yellow hair. Eye socket. The extravagant curve of cheekbone. "Andri..."

"Yep, I'm here. You're going to have to help me just a little. We'll be going down some very mossy stairs. I can't carry you and watch them."

Gared had an objection. Took a moment for him to remember it—the fog was worsening. "...You go..."

"I am. With you."

"I think...I'm going to die..."

"Horseshit."

"But I want to..." Gared lifted his free hand and pawed at Andri's chest, his grip too weak to catch hold.

Andri uttered a harking laugh, or maybe it was a cough. He tried to hide how very worried he was. "You said much the same thing, I recall, the last time I thumped you, when we were fourteen and thought that would make us tougher. But you lived—and you jumped me the next week. Remember those days?"

"But that was nothing..."

"Want to make Adon happy?" Andri croaked.

Gared tried to think this over. His eyes blurred over so much he shut them. "The pain..."

"Few more steps, There, that's right. Now we're in a tunnel. Whew this is dusty. Help me count my paces. I don't want to miss the turnoff..."

Talking rapidly, mostly a nonsensical mix of old jokes and encouragement, he took most of Gared's weight.

Gared sighed. If Andri would only be serious, then he could give up. He wanted so much to give up. It hurt so much just to breathe. But Andri didn't understand. He tried to work out an explanation, and passed out in the middle of it.

He woke up again when a sharp pain shot up his leg, then branched through his body. He moaned.

"Sorry, Gared." Andri sounded breathless, and his voice was nearly gone. "We'll be done soon. We're under Brydon now. These tunnels. Not the smoothest stairs in the world."

Tunnel. Brydon. Gared knew those tunnels. Somehow that was important. Familiar was important. He relaxed, and opened his eyes. He could see Andri's chin above him. At his feet was Bassl—oh. He lay on a litter. Ahead, someone carried a torch. The flickering light hurt his eyes, so he shut them.

When he woke up again, Andri's face was half-revealed by candlelight from the side, which made the planes sharper than ever. "Gared," Andri said.

"Mm..."

"I'm back. But I can't stay long. I'm depending on you, see? I've got a plan."

"Plan?"

"As soon as you get better, I'm off to a place called Mearsies Heili, because I'm told Detlev will be there. He's the only one who can command us in retaking the world from Norsunder, and I mean to be there to make damned certain that Enaeran is not forgotten when he hands out magic, or orders, or armies, whatever he's got. So. When I come back, I expect to find a resistance ready to implement said plan. Or at least ready to fight back. Are you with me?"

"Andri. I...my leg...I don't think I'm going to make it."

"Gared, you've got to. I'm counting on you. You're my steward, the king in my place. Promise?" Andri was fumbling with Gared's hand, and shoved his royal signet ring past Gared's larger knuckles onto his ring finger—the one Liere had handed him moments ago, whispering, *I think this might help.*

"Promise..." Gared whispered, a flush blotching his thin cheeks. Andri's Dena Yeresbeth was as wild and untrustworthy as the wind, but he sensed as well as saw the little signs of change in Gared: the 'promise' was Gared's first attempt at a rally.

"Good. Soon's I see you sitting up again, I'm off, and you're in charge. Your first order of business is to recover."

Gared shut his eyes, but he was clutching the ring in a way that enabled Andri to back away, fighting the sting of angry tears. He understood messing someone up in a fight. He'd done it. He'd endured it. But this viciously deliberate cruelty to someone helpless—the sheer rage made him want to rip straight back to the royal palace and gut Adon Marsael. No, to hurl him from the highest window, and let him see how good it felt to lie there with broken bones.

He heaved a hard breath, but that set off the damn coughing. Black spots swam before his eyes until he was able to catch his breath. He braced himself against the wall until the trembling ceased, while Gared slipped into sleep.

The pressure of urgency got Andri moving again. He rejoined the others in the narrow kitchen.

Liere was there with Devea and Banisa, the tailor couple who had been staunch supporters of Andri since the beginning. Adon Marsael did not know about them—his intent had always been to weed out any support among nobles. He could never see commoners as anything but entities to control and to tax.

Andri appeared, looking unspeakably weary. Liere observed him with unspoken concern; one of the first things she'd learned about him was how impatient he was with what he thought of as his own weakness. He said, "You were right. He took the ring—though he never saw me wear it, ever, it still seemed to have meaning. How does that even work?"

Liere let out a breath of relief. She had not liked giving his ring back, but Gared's wretched state had shocked her, especially the defeat she had sensed in him. That leg, so long unset; it was possible he would never walk again, a grim prospect for someone so active.

When Andri's followers turned their eyes to her in question, she said, "The signet ring is a symbol of kingship among nobles and royalty. Gared would know that, wouldn't he? He grew up around nobles. I hoped that your putting him in your place, even symbolically, would give him a reason to live."

Devea gave a short nod. "That's right. And he'll need it. From the looks of him, he'll be laid up all winter. That soul-sucking shit Marsael," she added. "But Banisa's cousin's aunt is a famous healer. One of the best. I know she'll be on her way soon's Banisa sends word."

Everyone in the room firmly agreed, as Andri crossed to Liere. "He's safe. But you're not. I never expected magical lights revealing your identity like that. Or I never would have agreed to that plan."

Liere shook her head. "It was better that it wasn't one of your local people, who would be forced to run away, and where would they go? It's not the same for me."

"But Marsael will be frantic to catch either of us, now. And if he gets you, it'll be Gared all over again." A paroxysm of coughing wracked Andri's ribs. He leaned against the wall, fighting it off, then said hoarsely, "Can't bear to even think about it. Which is why we need to get you on the road right now."

Banisa nodded firmly. "Speaking of searches, I'd better get going right now to fetch then healer. You two, you have to fix up Gared's trunk before the house-to-house searches get to our street. Bury him in so much fabric they'll never find him." She and the two she'd pointed to whisked themselves away.

"Let's go," Andri whispered. "Get you outside the city walls while it's still snowing. Cover your tracks."

Devea came forward and hugged Liere hard. "Come back soon."

Liere smiled, her heart filling with affection for Andri's staunch friends, who each hugged her, or gripped her hand, and wished her a safe journey. Bright eyes, some with the glimmer of tears, looked back at her with a mixture of exhaustion and worry and hope and, yes, she could acknowledge the admiration she saw there. There was no expectation of the impossible, the way people had regarded Sartora, the Girl Who Saved the World. Liere had earned their regard, and all the more cherished their freely given friendship.

This could be home, right here, she understood with a heady sense of wonder as she picked up her carryall — which was now significantly heavier. From the warmth, someone had silently been stuffing it with food.

But everything had become so fragile, so desperately fragile. They had won a small triumph in freeing Gared, but the enemy still held the kingdom. The world.

She and Andri stepped out into the cold. At the wet slap of soggy snow on her face, she could not prevent herself from saying, "Go back inside, Andri. I can find my way out of the city."

"Not likely," he said. "The entire battalion is searching, Skinner said. And I can't rest until I see you on the road."

Hand in mittened hand, she sped with Andri along alleyways and they narrow passages between buildings; she sensed search parties everywhere.

As they crossed the city, stopping to hide and listen every so often, she didn't even try to learn the labyrinthine trail. That could come one day. More important, she decided, before they parted, she would have one firm thing to hold onto.

His thoughts were running not quite parallel, but close.

"You were right," Andri murmured presently, as they halted behind a fence to wait for a party of Adranis to ride by. "You were right. I never would have thought of using that ring, but you were right. I could feel the difference. He needed a reason to live. What would I do without you?"

"You don't have to do without me." They began to run again. She shivered, but not from the cold; she was adept at raising her inner warmth. The shiver was from the intensity of her awareness that she was taking a step into a new world.

They reached the outskirts of the city. "No farther," she forced herself to say. "Beyond this is road and countryside. I'll go from here. Go back before the snow gets worse."

"It'll get worse for you, too."

But as yet neither of them had let go of the other.

"And I'll hole up. I know how to go to ground." She peered up at him. There was his chin just above her head and the curtain of his yellow hair. Her gaze shifted past the angular line of his jaw to the sword-ripped gap in his coat sleeve. "But first. Promise me," she whispered fiercely.

Promise. Andri heard the echo of his own voice to Gared, lying asleep in that room, and tightened his arms around her. He'd spent half his life fighting to stay alive, then fighting to unite his kingdom. Now fighting against Norsunder. He trusted his wits and his right arm, but he knew that magic, especially the brain-scouring horrors propagated by Norsunder, left him without much defense.

But Liere always knew what to do. And a promise was a log to hold onto in the running current of life. "This is only for a short time," he said, bitterly regretting the necessity of parting. But he had to get her out of the city, and he had to stay by Gared until he was sure that Gared would recover — it felt like a betrayal, his not even knowing Gared was a prisoner. "I'll catch up with you at one of our three stops."

Liere repeated, 'Ruin beside the river. Arbanion. And the Selenseh Redian in the north."

He still did not really understand what Selenseh Redians were, but she'd insisted that Norsunder could not get into these mysterious caves, that there was one at the northeast of Halia, and that he'd find it by Dena Yeresbeth. In any case, he meant to catch up with her long before that. "Keep to the north road," he said.

She shut her eyes, leaning into Andri's solidity. His strength. And there was the nerve flare of love, all the more precious now — for this moment, because they were about to part once more, and no one could predict the outcome.

But she could try.

"Promise," she whispered. "When we see one another again, whether it's two days from now, or a month. We'll marry. And I will make Enaeran, and you, my home."

Marriage! He'd never meant to marry. But that was before he lost everything yet again. Marriage sounded right and true, maybe the one permanent thing he could have in life. Andri looked down into her face. How did she manage to be beautiful even when grimy and tired? Liere was strong, and sure. She knew magic as well as the sword. Side by side they could restore Enaeran...

"I promise," he whispered into her hair. "Go. I need to see you on your road."

She kissed him, hard. Then backed a step, and another step. The snow fell softly all around them both, blurring their outlines. A few more steps, and she was gone.

He turned away, leaning against a tree as coughing shook his entire body. His strength was all but gone. Yes, he needed to see Gared on his road to recovery, but the dismal truth was: he knew he wouldn't last a day on the road. He needed rest.

He lifted his head, gazing into the stippled white curtain. Simple enough: cross the city. Get back inside. That warm kitchen, where a dollop of whisky in coffee would feel so good on his throat. So, so good. Maybe numb this fire in his chest...

Darkness was already falling, making it difficult to see. Good. That meant he would be hard to see.

A soft bed. Warmth — as soon as the searches were over. But he could lie up on a roof over a kitchen, where there would be some warmth. He might even sleep a little, if it was warm enough.

Then he'd check on Gared. Make sure he was still breathing. Gared. He burned with fury. That was another account to settle with Cousin Adon. Gared had babbled during the long tunnel journey. Marsael had been there not only watching, but laying wagers on how soon the howls would begin under different tortures...

Andri's head jerked up at the sound of horse hooves.

Falling into musing had been a mistake: there were two riders, and they'd seen him. Damnation! Coughs shook him. He fought them back, but then came a piercing whistle from behind: six more, a patrol.

Adranis appeared on the path, one saying, "Do you know there's an edict against tra—"

"Save it," one of the horsemen called — he wore Marsael's tabard. One of Marsael's liveried men. "That's Andri Elsarion."

Andri's hand dropped to his side. No sword. All he had was his knife.

As Andri fought to get control of his breath, the two parties held a short conference, on the surface polite, as they each claimed the prisoner for their own master. But the conclusion was foregone as there were six Adranis and Adon Marsael's liegemen numbered two. With studied politesse, the Adranis insisted that Bartal would be more grateful than Adon Marsael, who, as one put it, acted all friendly but rarely kept his promises. Bartal, the biggest man insisted, had more pull with the Norsundrian rankers in any case.

It remained only to take Andri alive.

The Adrani horsemen dismounted and pulled their swords as the six ranged in a half-circle. Two came at Andri, one sword high, the other low, as the third said, "I've got rope."

Andri charged, knife high. They meant to take him alive. He had no such restriction. He blocked, slashed, whirled around a restive horse, and tripped up Rope Man. Andri took his sword, and now he had two weapons.

He fought off two horsemen, dropped one — then four came at him, making sure not to foul each other's reach. He backed a step, trying to breathe past the pain in his ribs as he planned the sequence of his attack — and was tackled from behind.

Someone brained Andri with the hilt of his sword. They flung Andri's body over the back of a horse and rode east for Sles Adran.

Sixteen

Sles Adran's midlands

THE WOMAN'S VOICE WAS so strident it could easily be heard outside the shop door. "This is revolting! It's really revolting. This is the last time — the *last* time you will see us. Jhermina, take that rag off and let's go." The expostulations which had formed a background to the tirade ceased abruptly. There was silence, colder than the air outside, till Strident Voice said, "Come, Jhermina. Our friends will hear of this, you can be sure!" and out swept a tall woman with a scowling face. An equally scowly daughter stalked behind her, and almost collided with a boy who was just then entering the tailor's shop. She frowned at the boy, who quickly ducked aside, and climbed into the coach waiting outside the door.

The shopkeeper and the boy watched the retreating coach. A swath of peach-colored hem had been caught in its door.

The shopkeeper sighed and bent to pick up articles flung down on the floor, casting an appraising glance at her new customer. The boy contrasted with the two who'd just left just by his quietness. With those two, every motion had to be a bustle and a noise, to draw the most attention. This boy moved quietly as he studied the ready-made shawls and cloaks and hats hanging on hooks around the shop. Here and there on clothes trees hung robes with long sleeves, robes with tube sleeves, tunic and floor length.

As he looked at the clothes, the shopkeeper studied her only customer. He was around the same age as Jhermina, twelve or thirteen, slender, square of face with bones beginning to emerge from little-boy roundness, brown hair neatly tied clubbed at his nape. The corner of his mouth curled as he watched the coach bowl away.

"They were mighty rude," he said, on seeing the shopkeeper turned his way.

"Eh! If she carries out her threat she will find how very few people have any regard for her. Especially now, things being as they are. Her husband is the richest man in town, yet she insists on coming here for fittings to cut my fee. And then, half the time—" She realized she was complaining about a customer to another customer, and a young one at that. Foolish, foolish.

She forced a smile. "What may I do to help you?"

"I'm not sure how to go about this—" The boy smiled apologetically and a little shyly. The proprietress smiled back, lowering her estimation of his age by two years, and how had she missed his crooked nose? "I have a sister. Her Name Day is tomorrow. She's going to be twelve. I want to get her a fine winter robe. She likes clothes, but Seselin, that is, the house tailor up in Nente, makes all hers. I want to buy one I picked out myself. Something in the new fashion."

The shopkeeper smiled with anticipation. He really was an ugly little urchin, the more she looked at him, but at least he'd been taught manners. "I don't really have ready-made clothes—those models you see are just models—" Her voice faltered as her eye caught on the folds of heavy green cotton-linen piled into the box on the counter. "How large is your sister?"

"My height. She's small for her age."

"It would be long. You said something about Nente?"

"My uncle is a captain under the new commander, so we all live in the capital, but sometimes come south to visit Grandmother."

The shopkeeper scarcely heard these words. She was thinking that here was a chance to get rid of what had been a very fine robe, plenty of work put into it...If, that is, the urchin had someone who could pay. It was probably too much to expect that he had any money.

Still, she pulled the heavy green robe from the box. Diagonal sleeves whose ends reached knee length, hem to the floor on Jhermina, but if the unknown sister was much of a size...The line was ruined by the heavy lace at the collar and sleeves, which would be suitable for a woman of years, but had looked ridiculous on Jhermina. And so they'd been warned, but no, Jhermina, who had inherited her mother's temper had insisted on lace—and pink rosettes down the front.

"Ugh," the boy said firmly.

"That's Jhermina's taste." The shopkeeper laughed as she pulled scissors from her pocket, and began cutting the rosettes. "Rumor has it the Count Orlanda wore rosettes to the duchas's last ball. Jhermina loves pink. There. Look. Now the robe is faultless."

"Well..." the boy said, sensing the woman's immediate thoughts. "Isn't lace for mothers and aunts?"

"Easily fixed," the shopkeeper said, glad that she had only tacked the lace on: knowing Jhermina's mother of old, she had decided not to sew anything to the robe until money was in hand. "I'll give you the bonnet to match—just let me remove the rosettes."

"I'll take it." The boy smiled, revealing gaps in his front teeth.

And then, oh joy of joys, he opened his hand and disclosed coinage.

The dress was folded neatly. Since he had not brought a basket or bag to carry it in, she slipped it into the cheap scrap-bags she had her prentices stitch together for the rare customers who were unprepared to carry their purchases away. She slid the little bonnet now so fashionable on top.

The boy handed over what she asked, and departed with his Name Day present, leaving the shopkeeper humming as she tossed rosettes into a carved box—someone would surely want them, preferably for a spring shawl, and meanwhile she'd gotten rid of that robe, though in former days she might have regretted overcharging a gap-toothed nine-year-old, these days a body did what she must...

The ugly little boy, meanwhile, had taken on the air of a sneak, and proceeded through the town. In another shop he appeared to be a storky blond with a rash across his nose who needed under-robes for his cousin. At a shop at the edge of town, he was short and dark as he bought stockings, then slipped quietly through a side door in a small inn up the street.

Three days later, he and his bulging sack leaped onto the back of a coach rolling northward again; by the time it was stopped on the outskirts of a village by perimeter riders, he'd wormed his way onto the ribbed roof, where he lay flat, unseen by the unsuspecting driver, who had all the proper papers.

He swung himself into the tree they passed under when the coach turned off the road toward some estate. The twinkling lights below, in a gentle valley, indicated a sizable market town built alongside a great river.

His father had given him a single warning by farsense: Efael is on your trail. No magic.

For that first week, he had taken great care to move without being seen by anyone. But one cannot long emulate a ghost without becoming one. Especially when, as he drifted behind an inn in hopes of scraps, scanning the surface thoughts of customers above, he overheard chatter that gave him a possible plan. It was daring. It was dangerous. It might even be called far too risky, but he knew he was going to risk it: what he heard he had never thought to have.

The difference between running not to be caught and running because one has a plan was, to him, the difference between fear and challenge. First, he to set up a false trail, leading somewhere that would make sense to Efael. Like, southward to Al Caba, and the sea. Then he had to vanish, get tracelessly to his target town back up north again and westward, and finally, to become someone else.

Like a girl.

One night Adam appeared in a dream, as he did occasionally. Sveneric told Adam his idea. Adam's dream-person promptly took on girl form, showing Sveneric what he would need.

And so began the shopping expedition, using money he'd lifted from two different watch stations and a garrison along the way.

The town was not walled. Under a low gray sky full of threat, he trudged along a winding, reed-banked canal to the outskirts of the town, where he sought a barn. There, among the quiet munching oxen, he dressed carefully, then surveyed himself critically. The darkness of the green robe flattened his skin tones to a pale brown. His shoulders vanished into the rich folds of the sleeves that trailed down to his knees. The under robe was undyed, signaling a thrifty household.

He tied his coat and shirt around his hips by the sleeves, to help alter the line of his body. Then he parted his hair in the middle, braided it away from his face on both sides, and pulled the bonnet over it. It had a band made with something hard that fitted closely to the face just in front of the ears. There was a raised part that made a frame for the face, tapering down at the sides. The hood's fabric hung down in back to his waist. Perfect for keeping ears and neck warm. He could also tuck the braids up into it if they got annoying; he had grown out his hair as an utter rejection of his Norsunder life, but he hated having it down as it always caught under his elbows, or in his buttons.

He moved around the animals' water trough until he was able to get the light just right to cast a reflection. The dress brought out the green in his hazel eyes. The rest of him looked all right—except the hood seemed to emphasize the emerging bones of his chin. He had to make his face appear rounder—different.

How? Ah. Inside a cubby off the barn door he spotted a small table with a chained book of farm accounts, a quill pen, and an inkwell. He stuck his forefinger into the inkwell and cautiously dyed his long, light brown eyelashes. It left his lashes stiff and sticky, and made a black haze across his vision, but when he looked at his reflection in the animals' water trough, the effect was startling.

Now to the problem of the long hem. Jhermina had been taller than he was by half a hand. He had to walk on his toes so as not to drag the hem along the slushy ground, but that was good—it changed his walk.

He slipped outside and started down the street, which opened onto a square framed by buildings of stone and whitewashed wood, decorated with orange-brown brick. It had been added to over the years, breaking the ground floor uniformity with corbels, jutting terraces and cupolas, and a few rooms built over arches spanning narrower streets. Here and there, particularly on obviously added second and third stories, were arched windows and stone relief colonnades. Only the materials matched. The windows, especially on the ground floor in the buildings, were made with slightly tinted glass in diamond shaped panes. All signs of prosperity.

Snow began to drift gently down. Time to make a decision.

Oh, he knew he was going to try it.

It was easy to find his target. In the square a small crowd had gathered around a corner shop. Its windows were large, one on the square and another on the street.

His heart pounded. Had he miscalculated the date—was it too late? A cluster of apprentice-aged youths lounged around a door. A sign was posted on it, written in a beautiful hand, stating that Master Cribess Orthal would be interviewing for apprentices to fill the three places he had open.

Two days to go.

"Young honor?"

Sveneric was startled by a hand on his shoulder; he almost went for his knife, but killed the impulse before his voluminous sleeve could betray the movement.

An old man smiled down at him.

"Yes sir?" he said a trifle breathlessly, then remembered he was supposed to mimic Kyale Marlonen.

"Did you wish to be interviewed?"

"Oh, yes!" Sveneric said, copying Kyale's hair toss.

"Then come this way."

The interview was to begin with a test, apparently.

He was led to a room with a dais with a scene set up on it in the center, and several large tables around it. Three youngsters his age sat at the tables, engrossed in drawing. He passed directly behind a gangling girl around twelve. She was totally wrapped up in a graceful sketch of three girls dancing hand in hand in a rocky glade. Their hair and skirts were flying, and their bodies caught in an instant of motion. The forest behind faded away into uneven shadow, with shafts of light coming in now and then. He would use her skill as a safe measure for his own.

"Here," the old man said, putting a large white piece of paper down before him and a grayish pencil, a piece of charcoal and a gum eraser. "Do on one side the arrangement, and on the other anything you like."

"Thank you," Sveneric said, trying for Kyale's coo.

The man went away and Sveneric looked at the "arrangement." A pretty, round girl around sixteen posed in an ornately carved chair. She wore a blue robe embroidered with poppies, her hands resting on the wicker basket filled with dried flowers and weeds in her lap. She wore a hat with plumes. On a table beside her sat a pile of books, a stringed tiranthe, and a piece of rough sacking.

Sveneric swiftly gave shape to the whole, the way he'd been taught. But this was no recon report. He took pleasure in the folds in the robe, soft and complicated, the faint ridges in her hands, the sharpness of the weeds and the woven basket, the delicate feathers in the plume, and the roughness of the hempen sack. All these textures required different pencil strokes and ways of shading.

When he was done he was satisfied that he'd done an accurate representation. But what for the other side? He dragged his sleeves into his lap impatiently. They were so heavy it was hard to draw in them. His temper was beginning to wear thin—if only he wasn't so tired!

He dismissed the idea of doing the view from the window. That was just another type of model. Detlev's house? No! He made one up instead, using architectural elements from the local area. It looked almost real when he was done.

When he stood up a teenaged boy lounging near the door jerked his thumb toward another door across the hall. "In there."

As Sveneric entered a man stalked out, face angry, leading a bored-looking boy who grinned at Sveneric as he passed, and whispered, "He's only got one left, so yer probably safe!"

The old man sat behind a fine mahogany desk. It as well as the matching furniture with its graceful legs and stylized wheat edging, and the red silk wallpaper evidenced a successful gallery as well as a school for artists.

"Have a seat, young honor," he said as Sveneric handed him his drawing. The old man's gaze went to Sveneric's stiff black eyelashes, and Sveneric sensed a pulse of humor, and the master's assumption that this little girl had made a valiant attempt to seem older.

Sveneric glanced at the handiwork of the last candidate. The scrawls on the paper were barely recognizable as the girl on the dais. Sharp worry tense Sveneric—now he was afraid he'd stand out.

"What's your name? And age?"

Sveneric twitched, hating his own stupidity. No, it was exhaustion: he should have thought all this out. He rejected the urge to style himself Grasael Thellen. Half the people who would recognize the name—Lilith, whose true name having been Grasael Thellen, having pulled off one of her most famous escapes from Norsunder while disguised as a boy — were those he was trying to escape from

"Serena," he said, using a name he'd heard in Nente. "I'm fourteen." He aged himself a couple years, hoping that he looked like a fourteen-year-old girl

"Last name?"

"I'm an orphan."

"War orphan? From Enaeran?"

His surface thoughts made it clear there were a lot of these, corroborating bits of conversation that Sveneric had overheard from Andri as he chatted with Liere. Sveneric had listened so that he could learn the rhythms of the local language.

He nodded in agreement.

The old man pursed his lips. "You seem to have landed in a generous home, judging by your fine clothes."

"I did," Sveneric said hoping he sounded like Kyale.

The man's attention had already gone to his drawing. He looked at both sides, then up at Sveneric. "You've been well trained," he said expectantly — uneasiness, not yet suspicion, in the narrow gaze. "*Very* well trained."

Sveneric picked up a dismaying thought: the man was afraid that he was a runaway apprentice. Sveneric hunched his shoulders and muttered, "I'm not an orphan. My father's an artist, too, over in Enaeran. I was studying under him till he — when the Norsundrians came he — volunteered. My brother and I ran away. I came here, as everyone knows how famous you are —" Those were the exact words Sveneric had heard that day in the Nente alley behind the inn, *Everyone knows how famous Master Orthal is. It's a shame he won't come to the capital, but insists on staying there with his school.*

"A collaborator. I understand." The suspicion was replaced by pity; Master Orthal said, "Life is rough enough for the scribes, thrown out of their life's work. Of course they will do whatever they can to survive."

He looked at Sveneric, decision firming his lips into a line before he said, "Let us keep that between us, shall we not? There is already so much dread, and anger. The others will be curious. Shall we tell them only that you are an orphan, sent by distant relations in the capital?"

Sveneric hid his surge of relief. "I will."

"Good. Events being what they are, we must lay aside the formalities anyway. I am Master Orthal. Ordinarily we would of course go to the guild with your parents, but the office has closed, the scribes dispersed, along with all the rest of guild scribes. We keep our own records."

Sveneric uttered thanks, then Master Orthal cleared his throat. "Welcome among us, Serena. In spite of events, we still endeavor to live peacefully, and to carry on good work, the making of art." He moved to the door. "Lemeth!" he said, and a young man disappearing down the hall turned and came back.

"Yes sir?" Lemeth was tall and loose-limbed, long-faced with jug-handle ears, a friendly grin, and beautiful hands.

"This is Serena, the third of our new apprentices. Would you show her around, then turn her over to Baran?"

"Come with me, Serena," Lemeth said, as Master Orthal closed the door to the office and went off to tell the remaining hopefuls that the last place had been filled. "The house has three stories, all of which belong to Master Orthal. The top story is really an attic, which is where you'll be staying..."

Lemeth talked in a stream as they whirled through all the rooms downstairs—mixing rooms, drying rooms, various types of room whose purpose escaped Sveneric, leaving the sharp pang of many slamming doors.

Sveneric had to concentrate despite hunger to take in the jumbled account of how Master Orthal came first to town, rented one room for a studio, and ended up with the place. Lemeth rapidly gave a rundown on the household, from the Master, and Master Gilian (who was recently promoted to craftsman status but who was staying with the Master till the war was over and she could open a place of her own), down to the older apprentices. In between were journey-artists in various stages of their careers. There were also three servants, though the apprentices would not receive benefit of these except for having their food cooked and served them, and their clothes kept in repair. They were expected to keep themselves, their clothes, and the attic clean, as well as do any tasks set them by the masters and journey-artists.

After the rules (and a vague hand waved toward the stairs), Lemeth turned Sveneric over to Baran, a newly appointed journeyman—the lowest of the authorities.

As they finished the tour, Sveneric observed that Baran was popular with everyone in the household. He related humorously how he'd been apprenticed at age seven because his father had died unexpectedly, and as Master Orthal had then been his nearest living relative, he'd been dumped on him. And had been put to work.

"I've grown up loving art. And I've worked hard. But I'm only good enough for backgrounds on portraits or murals. Here we are," he said, as they reached the top of the stairs. He threw open the door with a grand gesture.

Sveneric stepped in first. The room was spacious with a steeply slanting ceiling, as could be expected. One end offered three or four decrepit chairs, an overstuffed bookcase, and a couple old, rump-sprung couches. The other end was divided up by partitions, making six little sleeping compartments.

"Go ahead and take your pick of any of the empty ones," said Baran. "The ones on this side have windows. I know Nacolas has one of them but I don't think the two new apprentices picked a spot yet. Both went home to get clothes and say goodbye to their families," Baran remarked with ill-concealed curiosity.

"Being an orphan, I won't need to do that," Sveneric said, stepping into the farthest cubicle down. There was a curtained window—a secondary exit, if needed—a bed and a trunk. "Guess I'll take this one." And, hiding a tremor of worry, "If the other girls won't mind?"

Baran looked around, scratching his head through his thick dark hair. "Dunno where the other girls are right now." He lifted his shoulders. "You're free till dinner, which is at lily-pattern, and I've got to return..."

Sveneric understood that Baran needed to get to his work. "Thank you. I think I'll take a nap. I hardly slept last night at all, for excitement," he added with the ring of truth.

"Sure." Baran grinned, and left.

Sveneric retired into his cubicle and pulled off his hood. *Lily-pattern has to be a ring chime, probably sunset.*

He peered tiredly into the tiny mirror on the wall opposite the bed, worried that real girls would take one look at him and point, shouting, *Fake! Imposter! Send for the guards!*

His eyelashes were a mess, but that didn't worry him. He suspected that everyone would assume what Master Orthal had: that he'd tried, ineptly, to look older. Otherwise his face was just a face.

Or was it? What did he look like to others? He shared the color of his eyes with his father, but it was such a common color.

A common face, he'd always thought. The braids helped define him as girl, but he could not rely solely on them to stay free of the Black Knives.

What he had to do was change his manner—he had to become prissy, fluttery, finicky Kyale. That meant he'd have to think about every movement. He'd have to think about how he sat and stood. It was going to be irksome.

Which was all right, because he had just achieved his heart's desire, despite the war, and the lies he'd just spun to kindly Master Orthal, and missing everyone he knew: he was going to steep his days in the world of art.

Seventeen

Sartoran Sea to Remalna

WHAT FOR ONE IS a successful plan to be smoothed and reused — why mess with success? — for another is a pattern.

Imry Llyenthur looked at the dispatches from the Sartoran Sea, and then at the reports from his best trackers drifting through the middle of the continent. These burned ships were not characteristic of the Black Knives. But it may as well have been Efael behind them. The badly-needed reinforcements for Marloven Hess would have to cajoled from Efael, as everyone in the south was stretched thin.

New orders went out to all vessels in the Sartoran sea.

A storm had blown all shipping eastward, enemy and ally alike, carried on the slowly whirlpooling current that made the tides along those shores somewhat tricky.

On the *Tar-Tares*, two days outside Mardgar, Peridot swung down from above. "Three-master, hull down on the horizon. And we've got the wind," she reported.

"Same plan as we been doin'," Dtheldevor bawled. "Sidres! Are we invisible?"

"As much as we ever are, O Captain," he called from his place at the helm. He then shut his eyes, scanned on the mental plane, and after a time, murmured, "These are Adrani navy, with a few Norsundrians from the Base." He had long ago given up explaining to Dtheldevor the jumble of images, reactions, and intent that he picked up. Dtheldevor hated Dena Yeresbeth—it had forever changed a world she'd thought she understood.

Rather than explain the murky soup of impressions, he said, "The clearest I can get is that they smuggled barrels of hard cider aboard."

"They'll be drinkin'," Dtheldevor said, and laughed with anticipation. "But don't let that make yez lazy!"

As the sky dropped the occasional snowflake, the *Tar-Tares* crew executed the plan with precision: the boat went over the side with scarcely a splash, and as Sidres moved to the mast, lines in reach, and Sharly took the wheel, the boat began skimming toward the enemy ship, which was lit up, lanterns at every masthead, and the cabin's windows a row of golden rectangles.

Illusion magic, so flimsy, only works if you aren't looking at the object diffused by tricks of light. Sharly and Sidres watched the boat reach the enemy. It was Gloriel's turn to keep it steady as the others boarded from the stern, swarmed over the rail, and dispersed, each their assigned station; as one they uncorked their jugs and began splashing the oil about.

But as soon as the smell wafted to the masthead, a hoarse cry rose, "Boarders! Boarders! Boarders!"

And armed marines raced out to the attack.

Dtheldevor bulled her way into the cabin, her sword a flicker of steel. It was guarded by a single sentry, now lying sprawled on the deck. She had just stuffed random papers into her shirt for Sharly to sort later when Joey pounded up, his face blanched. "You better come now," he panted.

The captain had been playing cards in the wardroom, as no one had expected to be attacked. But he reached the deck to find himself nose to nose with Sarmonwilda. A marine tossed him a sword, and now it was six against one.

"Mine, mine," the captain roared, furious that some undersized urchin had the arrogance to attack his ship.

Dtheldevor bolted down the gangway in a red rage.

The captain waved off the marines, who had already landed several cuts on Sarmonwilda. They stood around watching the fun. She was quick, though bleeding freely. It was clear how this was going to end. The betting was fast: head, heart, neck?

When she slipped in her own blood, hands flung high and head thrown back, the captain slit her throat.

He did not get long to enjoy it. Dtheldevor's body fought with the skill of many years' experience, but her mind insisted on seeing, over and over how Sarmonwilda leaped, gold hair flying, her laughter changing to a gull-like cry as the captain's blade slit her throat and she fell, slowly, slowly, her blue eyes startled.

The twins smashed their oil jugs to the deck then tossed down lanterns, sending marine defenders skidding back. As flames whooshed up, both vaulted over the side into the boat; Joey stabbed the captain from behind. Dtheldevor kneecapped him with her steel. And then the two leaped, swung over the defenders' heads, and vanished, a hail of arrows following.

They seemed to be swallowed by the darkness as Ellen and Joey rowed fast for the *Tar-Tares*.

"I couldn't get her. I couldn't get her," Dtheldevor said tightly.

"They'll Disappear her," Ellen murmured.

Dtheldevor turned on her. "They'll throw her over the side."

That silenced them; Peridot prudently bit back an observation that Sarmonwilda was beyond knowing. Because maybe she wasn't. Dtheldevor, whom she had followed for years, didn't believe so.

By the time they reached the *Tar-Tares*, Dtheldevor had decided what to do. "I won't leave her. They won't expect us to try twice. We're going back. And we're gonna burn the whole ship to send her off proper." She was shivering with rage by the time they clambered aboard the *Tar-Tares*. "Shadow them."

A day, a night, and another day passed. Dtheldevor only came out of the tiny cabin to survey the ship hull up in the distance, the mastheads full of lookouts. Everyone in sight was armed with steel as well as strung bows.

The weather cleared, and the *Tar-Tares* dropped farther back.

Under the winter sun the air was almost warm as Sharly took the helm, watch after watch, as Dtheldevor had yet to come forth. Late that day, as the slanting rays of the sun glowed in the whitecaps, Gloriel looked into Sharly's calm face, and her dark eyes. "You're sad," she observed.

Sharly lifted her head, scanning the sky and sniffing the wind. "Strange," she said. "How memory of a place, or weather, can be poignant, but not painful. However, memories of people can hurt so very much. Is it merely that places, and weather, endure, but the person is gone?"

"Sarmonwilda," Gloriel breathed. "Except I keep expecting to see her. Sometimes I think I do, out of the corner of my eye."

Peridot said tightly, "She died the way she wanted to. In action."

Sharly looked out to sea. "And yet, she is still dead. And there is no one from her kin to know, to sing her to the dance of the stars."

Gloriel sent her twin an anxious look, but Peridot was not going to say anything. She knew that clan and kin was important to the centaurs. She also knew that, annoying as she often found her three sibs, she did have family about her, and nobody else did. Except, of course, family that they made of each other.

Dtheldevor stayed locked in her cabin for two more days until thy woke to what Gloriel and Peridot privately called "that refrigerator smell," meaning snow on the air. A heavy storm coming.

Dtheldevor came out at last. "We'll hit them tonight, under cover of the weather."

And though they moved as drilled, making no noise, as snow fell softly all around them, the new captain had not been drinking cider. As the first thump of Joey's feet hitting the deck, a bow creaked, and the hiss of arrows filled the air. The illusion spell on each boarder kept them blurry enough to enable them to retreat in haste, but as soon as they dropped into the boat, the sound of the thumps caused another alarm to go up: the new captain understood magic, and had the lookouts peering in the direction of the sound until they spotted the yacht.

"Shoot!"

Dtheldevor stood in the boat, feet braced wide, Joey at the back. The two wielded their swords, knocking arrows aside as the boat skimmed over the choppy waves, arrows following them. The arrows continued to zip and hiss through the air; Sidres, seeing their hasty approach, loosened the *Tar-Tares*'s mainsail, readying to sheet it home the moment the last of them was on board.

Arrows sank into the side, punctured the sail, and clattered over the deck, shot from the topgallants.

The last aboard was Dtheldevor, hooking the boat to the stern — they'd raise it later. Sidres, stronger than two or three humans, tightened the wind-drummed sail and knotted it securely. The yacht came alive, surging away from the ship, which had begun to come about for chase, sail after sail billowing.

It was only when the *Tar-Tares* gained distance from the arrows that first Ellen, then Deon realized that Sharly was not leaning in the spokes of the wheel as they all did when the helm barely needed tending. She slumped, head down, her auburn hair sweeping the snowy deck.

She — while holding the yacht steady — had been shot. One arrow in her flank, the second in her back, just inside her shoulder blade.

"Those blood-sucking shits," Dtheldevor cried.

"What do we do? What do we do?" Ellen whispered. "We can't put her in a bunk..."

More gently than even her closest friends thought possible, Dtheldevor disengaged Sharly's arms from the spokes, and held her, careful not to jar the deadlier of the two arrows. Joey slid in, keeping the yacht tight with the wind on the beam as they sped away.

"One step, another," Dtheldevor murmured. "There. Now —"

Unhearing, Sharly moaned, then said sluggishly. "Steel... Steel."

"Steel's bad for her," Sidres cried at the same time Dtheldevor said, "Them arrowheads is poison."

Sharly, no fighter, had never been shot before.

"We have to get them out," Sidres demanded. But even he was afraid to touch that one in her back.

"I'll do it. Hold her for me," Dtheldevor said between her teeth. Ellen braced herself on one side and Sidres on the other, supporting Sharly as best they could as Dtheldevor eased the arrow from Sharly's flank. The centaur grunted and slumped against Sidres as bright blood dribbled down her back, soaking her vest.

"She's fainted," Dtheldevor said. "I'll yank this one out while she can't feel it."

And did.

Sharly stiffened, head thrown back, and gave a high, faint

scream and then completely collapsed, her legs giving way beneath her.

"She's dying," Sidres sobbed, then began to coax and plead with Sharly in a language none of them understood.

"What do we do?" Ellen turned to Dtheldevor, whose eyes burned with tears she would not let fall.

Sidres turned toward them, his pupils wide and black with terror. "I can hear her thoughts. She needs the woods. Her secondary heart, it's..." He shook his head. "She'll die. On the water. Our magic is empty here. She needs the woods."

Dtheldevor gazed tightlipped from Sharly to Sidres to the little boat still attached to the stern by a line. "Sidres. You can sail the boat single. Take her to that place with the Colorwoods. Remalna. It's maybe a day's sail off Mardgar."

"I can take her," Ellen said. "We need Sidres's magic."

Dtheldevor turned on her. "You think I lean on that magic?"

"No—I—"

"Let's get her boomed over the side. Sidres, you, too."

The crack of Dtheldevor's voice made everyone flinch. She didn't speak again until the two centaurs were in the boat. Sharly was settled under the little shelter, not quite a cabin, her legs folded beneath her. Ellen and Peridot settled several blankets around her, though it didn't seem to help. Her face had gone slack, her lips bluish.

Sidres looked up, his face pale. He knew it was futile, but still he called, "Remember your mind-shields! This is a different kind of war."

"Get movin'," Dtheldevor called, not unkindly, and under her breath, "I think we've proved that war is still war. And those bloodsuckers are going to *burn* for this."

They all watched as Sidres stepped the mast and set the sail; very soon the snow hid them as they skimmed away, the wind taking the little boat faster than the yacht.

For Sidres, there began what at the time felt like endless misery. There was no one to sail and tend to Sharly. The distance was not long, but measured as it was, drip by drip, in Sharly's heart's blood, it extended unbearably, extended by the sun's slow wheel, and the capricious tides.

He had memorized the chart, and knew what features to watch for on the headlands of Remalna. He did not have much time: the driving wind sent them flying over the gray waters, and it seemed that no sooner had he recognized the peaks that defined the principality of Renselaeus, then he was heading for the estuary of a river that defined the border of Shevraeth. Then he endured the worst terror of a terrible journey as he tried to tend both the boat and to keep Sharly from being jarred overboard.

But for once the wind had its own mercy: it drove him straight into the mushy ice, and stuck fast. Trembling with reaction, and with hunger, he shakily left the boat to scout for someone besides enemies.

But his flying approach had not gone unseen.

He stepped out onto the ice, uncertain on his hooves for a moment or two. Centaurs had lived in the cold north for uncounted centuries, and he had learned since he could walk how to angle the back edge of his hooves to chip into ice enough for purchase. But he'd lived most of his life at Dthel Rendm, Dtheldevor's island hideout, which was near the warm belt of the world. The island seldom got colder than the occasion frost.

He had to recollect ice-walking, but habit is strong. Soon he trotted over the treacherous ice to the reed-dotted snowy shore, where a figure stumped over a hillock toward him. His head throbbed. He gathered his strength to scan as an old, cracked voice cried, "Hail, traveler! What brings you here? Are you being chased?"

The person was old, and surely that would not be the first question from Norsundrians. Would they not be demanding identity papers, and his purpose in illegal travel?

He said, in Sartoran, "She's hurt."

The old person eyed him, squinted at the boat, then back at him. "She?" Her form of Sartoran was barely comprehensible. "Another like you?"

"Yes."

"You bein' chased?" she asked.

What more could he lose by telling the truth? "I don't think so. But I might be."

A grunt. "Tell you what. Let's get something into ye — if you can eat aught but clover and hay — and I'll send a message. Then let's see what we can do for your friend."

Sidres hesitated, then admitted in a low voice, "She's my mother."

The face softened at this admission, which neither he nor Sharly had disclosed aboard the *Berdrer*. A loyal and tight-woven family of sorts they were, but the prejudice against adults ran too deep in Dtheldevor: she would never willingly permit an adult to sail on crew, with only one exception, and Carsen had died a few years before.

"Bide," the woman said, squinting skyward. "Won't be long."

Nor was it, despite Sidres's anxiety.

Vidanric's coastal watchers were all old people, so easily overlooked. Especially fisher folk in ragged clothing, whose little boats reeked of fish guts. The candle change rang across the snowy expanse as the old widow's replacement paddled up, and the buckets of nasty-smelling stuff were handed off.

The widow hefted her day's catch to take back to her family, and trudged alongside a frozen creek to where her replacement had left a pony cart. She drove that along back ways, and through the royal palace grounds to Remalna-city, where she handed off the cart to be readied for the next watch.

A short time later, she stood with Meliara, who walked back and forth, one hand under her belly as she listened. She groaned inwardly; the one time Vidanric was away, and something happens, after weeks and weeks of quiet.

Another turn or two—and no, it was not pacing, but walking, she told herself. The midwife had said to walk, and walk she did. Even if it was more of a waddle these days.

An earnest kick from the one within coincided with a pang of horror: a mother! Not that any person deserved to be lying out in the snow with a hole in their heart. (Or one of their hearts.) It was just that, right now, she felt an especial affinity for mothers.

What to do? She had made the weekly visit to town with Oria, ostensibly to visit the midwife. Which she had done, though under a false name and home: her papers stated that she was Nana Tidic of Lumm, a bath attendant.

Meliara wished Oria had come with her. Nee was wonderful, especially when it came to matters of babies and birth, but Oria was a planner. If Mel couldn't have Vidanric, who was somewhere to the northeast, along the Colendi border, Oria was just as good.

What would Oria do?

Oria would say, "Combine your errands!" She would quote her mother about making time work for you, instead of you working for time, and she would...

She looked up. "Centaur, you said?"

The old widow, and Nee, both nodded.

"We wanted to go home anyway, but..." They had stayed because of the prediction of another storm coming in. But that might actually be one of Julen's time savers...

"Yes."

"Yes?" Nee asked.

"We've still got the sled, right?"

"Yes." That was the widow. "His majesty insisted on it."

"Of course he did," Meliara said briskly, hiding the eddy of emotions: worry, apprehension, exhilaration, and always, always, how very much she adored Vidanric. "Because he's married to me, and knows that if there is ever a chance of terrible timing, I'm sure to find it." She turned a mock frown on the widow. "I'm afraid I'm going to need *all* your fish guts."

Before the next candle-change, an old, patched sled full of hay proceeded brisky up the Lios River, approaching the border between Shevraeth and Gharivar. In the heavy snow, it seemed as if a shaggy old donkey pulled the sled, which left a reek in its wake.

"Two things to remember," Meliara said, holding the reins loosely so as not to jar Sidres, who ran as fast as he could. It was the fact that the river had iced over that made the impossible possible: instead of slogging through snow, Sidres ran with swift speed. But getting to the woods in time was only a part of their problem.

"You know I'm not much of a mage," Meliara said.

"You're a wonderful mage," Nee retorted loyally—because of course she would. She meant it, too.

"Compared to people who don't know any magic, maybe," Mel said. "But real mages don't take me seriously because my knowledge is so patchy. It's not that I don't try, it's that I have so many responsibilities that magic often has to come last—and if I wait too long to crack the books again, everything I studied falls right out of my head."

"I still think you're wonderful. And Bran does, too."

Mel laughed inwardly at the idea of her brother thinking any such thing, but she said nothing. For one thing, they might come across the Adranis at any time. Certainly before they reached the regional border, which got patrolled regularly. She had to explain, yet not scare Nee. "But even a bad mage can be good with illusion," she said. "Life! Take stage mages. They are not actually mages. They only make the pretties on stage, and if the players are not careful they walk right through them, right?"

Nee admitted the truth of this.

"It's the same here. I'm pretty good at illusion."

"You are! Sidres there looks just like a donkey. If you don't look too closely. Then you see a centaur bending over, and where his human part and his horse part come together."

"That is so," Mel said. "But we don't want the enemy looking closely, do we?"

"No!"

"One thing I picked up while listening to some of Vidanric's war planning sessions with the Queen of Sartor and the others is that a successful war campaign has to have, um, certain elements, to be successful. Like, terrain, and logistics—it's a fancy name for supplies—and a good commander, la la la."

Nee nodded vigorously, her expression one of anxious hope.

"This here is a bit of a war, between us and these Adranis. We need to keep their attention on us. Not on the sled or the 'donkey' pulling it. That means our terrain is the stench of those buckets back there."

"Is that good terrain or bad terrain?"

"It's good-bad terrain," Mel said, wishing Nee would stick with the subject—was that riders up ahead? Yes it was! She lowered her voice, saying in a fierce whisper, "And the supplies are us. Our voices. We have to screech and yowl like a couple of mad cats, so they can't look away from us. We want them to get rid of us as fast as they can. Then we win the war. See?"

"I do," Nee breathed. "I see!"

"We don't want them escorting us to Lumm, which is off to the left at the fork. We want them to wave us on, so we can bear right, and get home as quick as we can."

Nee bobbed her head, and as the cavalcade approached, splitting so that five riders closed in on one side and five on the other, Mel raised her voice, "*Now* look what you did!"

Nee's eyes widened, then she uttered a shrill, "Why are you blaming me?" Her voice trembled with fear, which Mel hoped sounded like ire to the Adranis.

"If we'd left when I *said* we should, we shoulda been ahead of this storm, and the stops would be behind us—"

"Papers," bawled the leader, and in a lower voice, "What is that stench?"

"It's fish. For my cats," Mel shrieked. "Do you know how much twenty-seven cats eat? I'll tell you how much—"

As she went on blabbering about cats and fish, she and Nee held out the papers that Vidanric had given them weeks ago.

The Adranis made a motion toward the straw-covered hay, and Mel broke off her tirade, shouting, "Don't spill my chum! Do you know how long it took to collect it? They actually charge for it, those dockside robbers! You'd think they'd thank me to—"

In front, Sidres, trembling, bent forward, head hanging. He could see nothing, but most of his attention was on Sharly, whose mind was slowly sinking deeper and deeper.

Nee shrilled, "If you didn't *argue* so much, they would give it to you for free, but ohhhhhh no, you had to pick, pick, pick, *just* like your mother—"

The Adrani with the sword poked at the edges of the straw, and encountered one of the buckets, which sloshed with a glutinously disgusting sound, freshening the smell.

The woman with the sword gagged. The man next to her choked. They turned strained faces toward their leader, as Mel and Nee began to squabble about whose blanket was warmer.

A gloved hand dropped the papers in Nee's lap and waved them on, the other hand pinching the leader's nose.

They kept up the arguing until they were sure that the Adrani patrol was out of sight, and then Nee heaved a trembling sigh. "It's hard to think of things to argue about when you don't actually want to argue."

Mel kept to herself how very easy it was for her to argue, and called encouragement to Sidres, adding, "That should be all of them."

The sun had vanished by the time they reached Carad-on-Whitewater. Though they were very nearly under the view of the old military fortress Vesingrui, which the Adranis had taken over, Meliara directed Sidres, who was very tired by now, through narrow winding streets in the town until they reached one of Vidanric's secret outposts.

From here, things progressed far more rapidly, once their contacts understood the emergency. With faces full of wonder—for no one had ever seen a centaur, much less two—Sharly was carried by numerous gentle, willing hands to a snow sled, and four fast horses were hooked up to haul it up into the mountains.

It was very late when at last Meliara knew by the sense of expansion in her heart, and by a quality to the air that she could not name, that the forest had given way to the Colorwoods. Somewhere the Hill Folk were nearby.

"Stop here," she said.

No one questioned.

The horses were unhitched, and Sidres and all the humans except Meliara withdrew respectfully. Mel now had to try to get the Hill Folk's attention. She raised her tired voice to explain her mission—but she didn't get far when a rustling, whispering sound soughed around her.

Sidres's drooping head jerked up, and he gave a sob, but it was not one of grief or terror. He looked around, his expression impossible for Mel to discern in the wintry darkness. But she felt his bewilderment, and wonder.

Then he was at her side. "We have to get her into the pool," he said in Sartoran. "They say, quick."

Meliara did not question how he knew. Things were always odd with the Hill Folk. She winced. Getting into water in winter was a serious proposition. But she couldn't let the mama centaur die.

Her belly tightened, as if in resistance, as she and Sidres moved to Sharly's side. Sidres coaxed Sharly to rise. She tried he best to stand, her legs trembling so much that Mel's heart squeezed, and she forgot her own worries. She slid her shoulder under Sharly's good shoulder, and Sidres bent to support Sharly's front legs as they guided her the few steps to a pool that Meliara hadn't even known was there.

The three stepped into it, and found the water warm. The strangest sensation shimmered over Mel through her wet clothes, as if a thousand hummingbirds winged over her skin. Then all the aches in her joints, especially her hips after that long ride, eased as they stepped deeper. Sharly let out a long breath, and another, leaning her head back so that her hair floated in the water, her face upturned toward the stars.

Mel stood silently, waiting for she knew not what. She became aware of the babe within her kicking and turning about, as if swimming in its own pond.

Sidres said, "They say she shall be blessed."

Mel looked over, startled. "Blessed"—what did that mean in non-human terms? When humans blessed a person or place, they called upon family, friends, and any listening spirits of the place to unite in protection and to dwell in harmony. But what did that mean here?

Also, she? Sharly?

Afterward, she could never say for certain how long she stood in that pond at the end of a very strange day. Only that at last the three of them emerged from the pond, and here was the cold again, making her shiver in her sodden clothes.

Sharly turned to her. "I must go to recover," she said. "I thank you for your aid."

"You're part of those privateers, are you not?" Meliara asked. She remembered what Vidanric had seen when he met Dtheldevor. Might not the others come along to fetch them? "Do you want me to pass on a message?"

Sharly looked up, and away, for a long moment, as Mel squished from foot to foot in her ruined shoes. Then Sharly said, low and full of an emotion Mel could not name, "Be at peace."

Mel wanted to ask, who? Me? Your privateer friends? Is that what I'm to say? But Sharly and Sidres were swallowed in the deep shadows, the Hill Folk rustling around them. And then her own friends swarmed about her, Nee twittering with worry, "You're wet! That can't be good for the baby! Here's a blanket, and some hot pear-cider..."

Eighteen

Sartoran Sea

ONCE THEY LOST SIGHT of the little boat containing the centaurs, Dtheldevor whirled and stamped into the cabin.

Everyone else stayed on deck, looking at one another, Ellen sighed. "I'll go talk to her."

The rest who were not tending sail or helm busied themselves removing the enemy arrows from the hull and the masts, laying them aside to be reused.

The sun had begun to rise when Ellen and Dtheldevor emerged from the cabin, Ellen smiling, and Dtheldevor glaring over the water. "Ellen thinks our sticking to one plan was a mistake. She may be right. Let's change it up." One side of her mouth curved up in a terrible smile. "They'll be expecting us in Mardgar. Our mistake was to hang off the coast, attacking anyone leaving. We got predictable. My mistake. Won't make that again."

She grinned fiercely. "Set sail for Al Caba. We are going to torch the harbor."

Joey let out a whoop of angry joy, and threw the helm over. Peridot shrieked laughter as she ran to the sails, but Gloriel said, "Isn't that all Adranis?"

Dtheldevor whirled around to glare at her. "D'you think you're gonna replace Sharly an' start in with oooh, we don't kill?" Her voice rose high and mocking.

"They're Norsundrians," Peridot drawled. "Allies of Norsunder, you'll say, but what's the difference? Those were Adranis shooting at us, or have you forgotten?"

Gloriel wanted to say, *But we fired their ship.* She struggled to define what it was that she objected to. However the time — late — the shock of loss, the war, made it difficult to separate out those who volunteered to be killers, such as Norsunder Base's warriors, and Adranis who had joined the navy, and were carrying out orders. Especially as she knew the others saw no difference. All were enemies.

She shrugged, and went to tend the sail with her twin, her throat aching, though she could not define why even to herself.

Dtheldevor called after her, "Gloriel, you'll just be tossing oil. As usual. Not slitting throats."

Gloriel let that reassure her, and the matter dropped as the yacht tacked, the ship slanting in the driving wind.

"Are we going to lose our invisibility?" Deon whispered to Gloriel two days later, when the first bumps of land appeared on the horizon. They had to round the peninsula of Valian before cutting up into Al Caba, chief harbor of Sles Adran, but Dtheldevor kept at a prudent distance, no more than the highest mountain tops visible.

"I think it lasts a while," Gloriel said. "Sidres always laid on extra spells, though I don't know if that's like pouring more water into a bucket that just spills over, wasting the magic, or if it's like painting extra layers, which helps to brighten the colors."

"As long as they can't see us," Deon muttered — to herself.

Everything so far had been exactly what she had wanted. She was a part of Dtheldevor's crew. They had singlehandedly destroyed a bunch of Norsunder ships.

She had seen death before. Plenty of it, during Sarendan's revolution, years ago. Derek Diamagan had cheered on the revolutionaries, saying that that was what the noble oppressors deserved. It had been easier to look away, especially when she didn't know any of the dead.

But laughing, vitally bright Sarmonwilda, and gentle, kindly Sharly, who never hurt anyone — it was so *unfair*. The Warrens thought so, too. The wardroom talk at meals was all about hitting Norsunder and its allies hard. Make it hurt.

"They'll pay," Dtheldevor said, swigging from a bottle. "And pay again. We'll see to that."

Deon held onto that thought: they were getting justice, which was never wrong. Derek had said so, all those years ago.

She worked willingly all afternoon as Dtheldevor drilled them, making them repeat their specific job over and over, not just by acting it out on board, but by tracing their fingers along the rudimentary sketch she'd made of Al Caba's harbor. Taking on a whole harbor at night, especially one they had only once visited years before, would be tough, but they could do it if everyone remembered to orient on the harbormaster's tower—and carried out their designated job.

On a ship half a day's sailing away, Imry Llyenthur stood at the prow, eyes closed as he slowly turned and scanned on the mental plane. He had to suppress his impatience. There were far too many demands for his time, but this was the only way he could scan for a specific vessel on an ocean: the mystery ship's location would be water, which meant lifting visuals from unsuspecting minds would be useless. He needed to be in the same ocean so that he could locate them in reference to him.

He was peripherally aware of human life forms behind him, watching. He had to scan and to sort the distrust and derision of the watchers for intent. There were also life forms far below the ship, unimaginably alien, and some human-like ones closer to the surface—all those he could dismiss as irrelevant.

He ignored the comments of the crew—*what does he think he's doing—he thinks we're impressed—he has no idea how stupid he looks staring at nothing, just like a soul-bound.*

Then one of Bostian's bruisers could not resist what, he muttered to his cronies, would be a little fun. He took a step toward Llyenthur's back. Another. Hefted his sword, just to goose him, see him jump, and—

Llyenthur sighed inwardly, and in one fast movement pulled a knife from his wrist sheath, pivoted and nailed the brute in the heart. The thud froze the rest in shock as he turned back to scanning.

So predictable. But predictable was good. Ah!

There: a cluster of minds, completely unshielded, *You'll take the eastmost pier at Al Caba. I'll deal with the lookouts...*Llyenthur braced against the rail as he located them in reference to himself. Impossible to judge distance, but he knew their intent.

And he had a vector.

But if he sent a team, that meant taking the time to make transfer tokens.

He stood there debating furiously as the entire crew waited in perfect silence behind him. Efael's search across Sles Adran was for a boy of twelve, brown hair, hazel eyes: Detlev's son, no less, according to reports; Llyenthur hadn't known Detlev had spawned again until a couple of years ago. If Efael nabbed that little shit, he'd be halfway to nabbing Detlev, and then he could name his price as far as the Host was concerned.

Llyenthur had to find out how close he was — but there was this asinine band of fire-happy idiots keeping his badly needed reinforcements from...

Time pressure warred with expedience, and expedience won.

Without a backward glance he transferred, fixed on the last mind he'd skimmed, and appeared on the *Tar-Tares*. There was only one of them on deck, at the helm. In two fast moves, he killed her, and set fire to the ship, trade for trade.

The singe of burning wood reached the wardroom, right then in the middle of their meal. They smelled it at the same time, and looked question at one another. Why hadn't Peridot, who was at the wheel on watch, taken care of it?

Dtheldevor stampeded first up through the hatch, yelling, "Peridot, are you aslee — get out of my *mind!*"

"So you're Dtheldevor," Llyenthur said. "I thought you were all bluster and no brains. Seems I was right."

Gloriel, the night's cook, took a moment to douse the firestick then followed, startled by the sounds of fighting. She surged to the deck and swayed, stunned by the sight of her twin lying on the deck, unmoved by flames licking the wood near one foot, her eyes staring into infinity.

Gloriel raised her gaze to the man fighting with two knives against Dtheldevor and Joey. Should she help? But he moved so fast, far faster than the others, getting inside their defenses, and Dtheldevor fell.

She couldn't fall! She was the strongest, the best, the fastest!

As Joey dropped, blood spraying, Deon shrieked, a noise cut off with one fast stroke of a knife. She recoiled, both hands fumbling at her neck, dead before she hit the deck.

Ellen flew to the attack. Gloriel could not bear to watch — she knew what was coming next, and she, the worst fighter of them all, was helpless to stop it. She turned away, tears blurring the sea and the sky as her old, old fears burst forth in gasping sobs.

When she heard her sister fall to the burning deck behind her, she could not bear to look, but gave in to old instinct: she vaulted to the rail, and dove into the sea.

Nineteen

Along the river in Sles Adran

LIFE AT MASTER ORTHAL'S art school and studio was
strictly regulated, particularly for those on the bottom of the
hierarchy. It was a small world, complete in itself.

Sveneric loved it. Even having to be Serena/Kyale could not
disturb the purity of his happiness. It wasn't as if having to
consider every move, every word, was new. Living at
Norsunder Base had been like that. Memory of those days
served as a reminder not to relax his vigilance even for a
moment, no matter how irksome he found braiding his hair
every day, and tying ribbons to it, or moving fussily when
everyone else stood and sat and walked without thinking about
it.

But once he sat to his easel and sank into the daily
assignment, the euphoria of art-making washed away any
residue of impatience or irritation.

Two days passed, as he learned names and rules, those spoken and unspoken. He had already decided he must not stand
out. As it happened, the other girl in their trio of apprentices
was quite talented, so Sveneric had only to make certain his
skill never surpassed hers, which he decided to regard as a

challenge. Someday he would be able to do his best to make art. At least right now, he was getting training, and he was surrounded by art. He could pretend the war was very far away.

Until the day it wasn't.

A week had passed when he woke abruptly to the sound of sweetly chiming bells mixed with horse hooves in the square outside, swept of snow every day. Before he opened his eyes, he was aware of a pounding headache, a sign that something had tried to batter at his mind-shield during the night, and his body had not been able to rest, but had had to fight against either magical or mental attack.

From the square rose cursing in Norsundrian. He was up and peering through a crack in the curtains at once, his heart ramming his ribs in time to the hammer of the headache against the backs of his eyes.

A troop of Black Knives had arrived, one slipping on the icy flagstones. They halted, as their leader rode up.

Efael did not wear the Norsunder jacket. Light slithered in an unfamiliar, almost oily pattern over the heel-length coat of black man-leather that fell from his shoulders across the horse's back and down to the dully gleaming black-weave riding boots. The early morning light threw into relief his sharp features and sneering mouth.

For one sick moment Sveneric thought Master Orthal had betrayed him. No. Efael lifted a gloved finger from the pommel of his saddle, and the Black Knives spread out, and began kicking down doors that did not open immediately. People poured out of houses, some half-dressed, looking bewildered, frightened. Angry.

"Who do you think you are," an older woman demanded of a Black Knife passing by. "You're not one of —"

His hand moved almost too fast to see; she fell dead, her head half severed. After that, no one protested. Most returned to their houses. Those who lingered stood in clumps as far from the Black Knives as possible.

Sveneric knew that he was nothing more than bait to lure Detlev, who was of course completely silent. Even before they caught their bait, traps and tracers and lethal wards lay in wait for Detlev. And yet Sveneric sensed Detlev out there somewhere, the way one senses the position of the sun long before dawn. Gratitude welled up in Sveneric: he could have been yanked. Siamis could have shown up at any time. Adam, too. David could have been sent back to watch over him, but instead he was on some other far more urgent task. Adam was also there, a moon to the sun, and Siamis as well. All of them trusting him to use all the skills they had given him since he was small, to stay out of reach of the enemy.

Out in the square, a Black Knife emerged from a house, dragging a terrified boy of ten or eleven. The assassin stopped before the horse Efael still sat on, and jerked the boy's face up by his hair. Efael waved a careless hand, and the Black Knife flung the boy away. He scrambled barefoot over the icy flagstones, and back to safety, trembling hard.

Boys.

That meant whatever trace Sveneric had left had not been Jhermina's robe, or the other girl clothes that he had taken care to buy one item at a time, each visit wearing a different face under illusion. That meant this was a systematic search of the region. That was one slim hope. Another, the fact that he and Efael had only met face to face once, when Sveneric was about six. It would be too much to expect that Efael wouldn't recognize Detlev's bone structure in his face, and the similar eye color. Sveneric had to make sure that he was not dragged out to that square.

From another direction, a couple Norsundrians manhandled another boy, this one again younger than Sveneric, though his coloring was much the same. Sveneric didn't see the outcome; he turned when Baran called up the stairwell, "Serena! Time for breakfast!"

"Coming," Sveneric called, and willed his fingers not to shake as he braided his hair and ribboned it. Then he dressed by feel, making sure to smooth the old clothes he tied over his hips so they hinted at what was beginning to be a pear-shaped form. Then he peered into his tiny glass. What else could he do? Brown hair was at least common, but there was nothing to be done about his eyes. And he did not dare to use illusion magic — Efael would recognize it at once.

A glance out the window: another boy, this one nine or ten. Efael was relying on memory, then. Did he know how much time had passed since they'd seen one another at Norsunder Base? It was difficult to say how Efael viewed time. But instinct was certain: Efael must not see him. To the sorting Black Knives, Sveneric needed not only to look girlish, but older.

What had Siamis said once...ah.

Sveneric closed his lips, and opened his teeth behind them. No, not that far — that looked weird. Just that much...yes. It was subtle, but it emphasized his cheekbones, pulling the skin of his cheeks down, and lengthening his face a little. Then he pulled in his jaw slightly, so it looked as if his chin receded a bit. Yes. That altered the shape of his face.

He started out of the cubicle, then remembered Kyale. He must not stand out, though — and everything Kyale had done was to gain as much attention as possible. It had become habit with her. He wished he hadn't chosen Kyale to mimic. Be Lyren-Sartora, then, he told himself as he followed the other two apprentices down the stairs.

Baran waited on the first landing. Sveneric stopped halfway down, then consciously mimed one of Lyren-Sartora's gestures when she mimicked courtiers. "Oh! I forgot my hood!"

Baran looked tense. "You might have noticed that we're not exactly formal around here, Serena. Leave it be till you go outside."

"Oh, thank you." Sveneric descended the rest of the way, then looked up at Baran from under his lashes, another Lyren-Sartora gesture from when she was trying to wheedle extra pastries.

Baran's smile was perfunctory, his thoughts on those people outside. Who were they? The king had sent no outriders or heralds to announce a search.

They started down the second set of stairs, reaching halfway when the door crashed open and in clattered a pair of Black Knives. These separated, poking cursorily into the downstairs rooms as Baran and the three apprentices stood frozen on the stairs. Sveneric turned a shoulder the way Lyren-Sartora did, and kept his teeth consciously parted behind his closed lips.

The two Black Knives emerged at the same time, and started up the stairs. Sveneric clutched at Baran's arm in a nervous gesture as two cold, hard gazes raked down from his ribboned braids to his robe...and passed on.

Their gazes fell on the third apprentice, then one muttered in Norsundrian, "Too pale."

They shoved by and ran up the stairs, where thumps and clatters were soon heard as they searched every room.

Sveneric, the apprentices, and Baran reached the dining room. There was one long table, everyone in rank order. Master

Orthal sat in a large throne-like chair at the head of the table, Master Gilian at his right, a woman of imposing size and formidable mien. The apprentices took their places at the bottom.

A loud thud from above caused everyone to look up. One of the older journeymen winced. "My wardrobe, I'm certain," he muttered. "Why can't they just push it aside?"

"Who's the desperate criminal?" Baran asked.

"A boy of ten." Master Gilian enunciated. "If they're to be believed it's that accursed Detlev's son, but I think they only say that to make people want to turn him in."

The Norsundrians clattered downstairs, slammed out, and Master Orthal said quietly, "We shall go on as though nothing happened." He helped himself to boiled oats and jam.

"Hey Baran!" Ion, one of the older journey-artists said in a determinedly cheery voice. "You'd never guess who I saw last night at the Shield — Old Massl!"

Most of the table burst out laughing, as outside, a Black Knife said to Efael, *This is the last town of size. The river is the border. Are we to cross?*

Baran grimaced, then shrugged. "I don't see why you have to turn up your nose at Massl. If there weren't book copiers, 'twould be a pretty dull world."

"But giving up art to scribble other people's words? The most he can do is fiddly flowers and the like in the margins! Think of the tedium." Ion shuddered elaborately. "Sure we need books, but leave making them to the wood-handed!"

Baran snorted as he poured a cup of hot spice-milk. "A fine hand that all can read is an art, as you know very well, Ion. Just as margin drawings are art."

No, said Efael, from horseback. *Turn back. Ride for Al Caba — and search every village. I'll transfer ahead.*

"So claims our margin-master," Ion retorted, which brought some smiles from Ion's friends.

Baran shrugged and smiled good-naturedly. "That's right, give a good example for the new apprentices. Just think, you three. If you're bad enough for long enough, you'll be advanced up the table till you occupy the spot of the chief buffoon, right in the center of the table." He pointed to Ion.

Sveneric did his best to simper. Everyone laughed far more than the weak joke warranted as they tried to shed tension, and grasp at a semblance of normal life.

Twenty

Valian Peninsula

THE SHORELINE OF THE tiny principality of Valian is rocky and ugly, but if one picks one's way along its flat beach at low tide one can find all sorts of things cast up from the sea to lie bleaching in the sun.

Late the next afternoon a cold wind swooped low and harsh off the water, but old Mathen Erdaya bent his head and pushed on in hopes of filling a copious sack with driftwood before returning to his home. There would be no firestick, not for the likes of him, this year: the Adranis and their Norsundrian conquerors were locked in a mostly-silent duel with the nobles and guilds of Valian for control of the principality, and as always in war, the common people suffered most.

Mathen's progress was slow because he had to watch the sink holes half-hidden by sea wrack as well as scan for chunks of driftwood small enough to carry. He veered toward the water's edge for a likely-looking piece, then caught up short.

That was no stick. A blunt, badly burned hand trailed in the rilling tide, moving with each gentle ripple. As Mathen hesitated, the hand twitched and grabbed blindly at a rock before subsiding.

A wave of compassion prompted Mathen to cast down his sack and untangle the boy from the piece of mast he was draped across. How to pick the boy up? Mathen hesitated. Ever since ships belonging to the conquerors had been burned and sunk in the sea, the conquerors had promised harsh penalties too anyone aiding any foreigners whatsoever. Mathen hesitated. He and his wife were old, living so carefully and frugally.

Apparently aroused by the touch of hands, the boy opened his eyes briefly and muttered; Mathen bent to hear. He caught three words, and the start of a chant, "Lee Han Anaer."

Mathen gasped, his neck chilling. *Lee Han Anaer*: Sartoran for "Ship Without Sails," the ancient lament for sailors dying lost at sea, taught and sung by sailors over Sartorias-deles since time out of mind.

Mathen had been a sailor for fifty years before the rickety bones of old age forced him to settle in a house by the sea.

He tied the corners of his sack around his neck then knelt, braced himself, lifted the unconscious boy and draped him across his shoulders. Then he slumped across the rocky shore toward home, chanting in his tuneless, cracked voice as he lamented the destruction of a ship he'd never seen. That's what sailors did for one another.

He arrived at his seaside hut breathless from his exertion, and kicked the door open. "Ylein."

His wife gasped as she whisked the arm pillows off the settle. "Mathen Erdaya! Whoever is *that*?"

"Sailor boy...Found him...on the shore..." Mathen wheezed as he lowered the boy onto the settle cushions.

"*Why* did you — oh..." The old woman ran her hands across her forehead perplexedly. "These new orders are a *shame*, but if we are caught — "

Mathen cut her short. "Who will know? No one saw me. Besides, he asked for the Lee Han Anaer. Can't leave him to die out there on the water alone."

He turned his gaze to the carvings set on shelves built into the adjacent wall, mostly ships, but also trees, dancing figures, and here and there a unicorn, glimpsed once far, far in the north, where the skies caught fire every summer. The statues glowed richly in the firelight, the red in the driftwood burnished almost to gold. The carvings testified to his years of gathering driftwood, carving and fitting together tiny pieces, and slow and careful polishing and oiling. It took him so long to finish one, so many days of relived memories went into each piece, he found it hard to sell one until they were next to starving. Then he'd trudge to Perth, where he knew another old sailor who gave him enough coin to see them through to the next. This winter so far had caused three empty spaces on the shelves.

Ylein turned to the pot on the fireplace. "I wish you hadn't done it, but I can't ask you to put him out now. Perhaps some broth. First, cover him, Mathen."

Mathen shook out the neatly folded quilt, then paused. "Has a bad wound." He spread his fingers in instinctive protection, not quite touching the boy's matted hair. "Skull's cracked. And his side! Cold saltwater must've stopped the bleeding, but now it's starting again."

Ylein grabbed at a pile of clean rags she'd been working into another quilt. She twitched one into a pad and pressed it over the deep gash in the boy's ribs. "He's so burned I daren't wrap a bandage round him." She gazed sadly at bruised eyelids, the burns on the side of the boy's face. He only had wisps of hair left; in one ear a misshapen earring. The one in the left ear was still round. "Poor thing…I don't think he will last the night anyway."

"Then we shall make his last night comfortable," Mathen said firmly.

Ylein made no demur.

It was sometime later, while Mathen was sorting the day's driftwood, carefully considering each piece as Ylein polished a fragment that he had taken a week to carve, that the boy stirred, and groaned.

Both white heads lifted.

The boy's dark, tilted eyes opened. He stared blearily upwards. He said a couple words they didn't understand, then again, "Lee Han Anaer."

Mathen and his wife had sat down at their tiny table. He crossed to the settle so the boy could see him. "Lee Han Anaer, yes, I sang it for you. Maybe you'll know it if I repeat the words again, Lee Han Anaer, and nod, so."

Ylein appeared at his side with a cup of broth. Together they lifted the boy, and she held the cup to his lips. He gulped once then gasped from pain. One hand clutched at his side, and he muttered, gesturing with his free hand as if writing.

"Pen and paper!" Mathen said.

"Oh!" Ylein fetched both from a box: although Mathen could barely write his name, Ylein had learned reading and writing as a child and handled any written communication the Erdayas needed to make.

Mathen continued holding the boy up as Ylein set a board in his lap. His lips were bluing. His breathing rasped, but he gripped the pen determinedly.

"Julian. Julian Landis," he said two or three times as he wrote. Halfway through one page he gasped as another spasm shook him. His hand jerked, and the pen blotted the page. Muttering what could only be a curse he turned the paper over. This time he got farther, painfully spelling each word, until he coughed, blood and ink splattering hid page.

He swept the paper to the floor and started another. He was interrupted by pains twice more, and each time he lifted the pen free. When he had finished he shut his eyes and pushed at the paper. "Julian Landis," he breathed, collapsing back.

"A name. Must be," Mathen said, taking board and paper.

"Landis. Is that not the name of the ruling family across the water to the south?" Ylein asked.

Mathen grunted assent. He waved the paper in the air so the ink would dry, watching as the boy's breathing harshened. One hand groped, as if reaching, and Ylein moved to his side to take his hand. The difficult breathing stopped in one long sigh, and the boy's face slackened.

"He can't—couldn't have been more than fifteen," Ylein said softly, letting go the hand. She indicated the paper as her husband folded it. "What do we do with that?"

He shrugged. "Wait till the war's over, then find someone who can read that language. Might give a clue to Julian Landis' whereabouts. We could start with Sartor, I suppose, if the scribes ever come back."

His wife looked at the scrawled message, then sighed. "Never seen such letters before. I may as well Disappear our poor young sailor."

"I think—" Mathen was interrupted by a sudden step outside their door. He rose and went toward it just as the door was pulled open and a tall young man stepped in. His gaze searched the room swiftly, then lit on the boy. "I thought I still heard that voice." He tapped his head. "Looks like you took care of the matter for me," he said to Ylein, smiling.

"Oh!" She smiled back. "Then you know him! Well—you

can perhaps help us, and we may be able to ease your loss by showing you this—" She took the folded paper from her husband and handed it to the young man.

"I hadn't known Dtheldevor was literate. I see now I wasn't far from wrong. So she regrets not dying on her ship—but leaves her treasure to Julian Landis in case Sidres doesn't win free." He cast the letter into the fire.

Then he turned on the old couple. "So now we come to the question: why did you break the rules concerning the harboring of strangers?" His voice was pleasantly interested and his face anything but sinister, but just the same, Mathen's eyes fell before the young man's interested green gaze, and Ylein paled. "Can it be our communication is faulty, and you did not hear the word? Indeed, it took me rather longer than I'd wished to spend to trace her (she was a girl, you know) to this spot."

The stranger didn't look like any Norsundrian Mathen had ever seen—his quick gestures, ordinary clothes instead of the infamous gray, smiling face—but he had to be one. A nasty one, too. Mathen's jaw tightened. "We heard," he said.

Ylein spoke up suddenly. "Twas I made him do it—the poor b—girl so young—"

"Hush, Ylein," Mathen said softly, taking his wife's hand. He turned a stony face on the enemy. "I brought him—her—because she spoke some words only us sailors know, and I couldn't let him be, not and finishing the Lament for him."

"Ah. Compassion is an expensive luxury, you see. My orders must be obeyed, or it's a waste of time for me to make them." He smiled slightly, then went on in a meditative voice. "I was the sloppy one; she was supposed to burn with her ship. Death smacks distastefully of heroism—" His gaze traveled the room, and stopped on the shelves of carvings. "Ah."

Mathen shut his eyes as white/blue fire flashed where the young man pointed, and within seconds every carving was reduced to ash. He nodded at them both and transferred by magic.

The old couple was left with the dead sailor. Ylein straightened her limbs, then they did the spell of Disappearance. Then Mathen sighed deeply and took a rag from his wife's pile. He began carefully to scrape the piles of ash onto the cloth. Ylein turned her shocked gazed to the small room, as if she could find evidence of the carvings elsewhere. Nothing.

Yet there was something. Not Mathen's work, but under the

settle lay the piece of paper Dtheldevor had first discarded.

"Look," she said, retrieving it. "What shall I do with this?"

Mathen scowled down at the paper in her hand. It was a long time before he answered, but she waited till eventually he did.

"Write across the top the name Julian Landis, and hide it away. When the war is over we will find this person and see that the letter is given into their hands. Meantime," he said grimly on an exhaling breath, "I start over."

And, humming the Sailors' Lament, he reached for a piece of driftwood.

About the Author

Sherwood Smith writes fantasy, science fiction, and historical fiction. Her full bibliography can be found on her website at https://www.sherwoodsmith.net

About Book View Cafe

Book View Café is an author-owned cooperative of professional writers, publishing in a variety of genres including fantasy, science fiction, romance, mystery, and more.

Its authors include New York Times and USA Today best-sellers as well as winners and nominees of many prestigious awards such as the Agatha Award, Hugo Award, Lambda Literary Award, Locus Award, Nebula Award, RITA Award, Philip K. Dick Award, World Fantasy Award, and many others.

Since its debut in 2008, Book View Café has gained a reputation for producing high quality books in both print and electronic form. BVC's e-books are DRM-free and distributed around the world.

Book View Café's monthly newsletter includes new releases, specials, author news, and event announcements. To sign up, visit https://www.bookviewcafe.com/bookstore/newsletter/

www.ingramcontent.com/pod-product-compliance
Lightning Source LLC
Chambersburg PA
CBHW060300100726
47907CB00002B/220